Praise for *The Midnight Rambler*

"With his debut novel, *The Midnight Rambler*, Don Carr delivers a story that's not only a joyride of a thriller but is also wrapped around an important environmental message. Set in Italy and full of lush location details, *The Midnight Rambler* is an utterly masterful interweave of compelling characters, relentless action, and swift, unpredictable plot twists. I thoroughly enjoyed this novel from the first page to the last. Mark my words, Don Carr has everything it takes to become our next Robert Ludlum."

—William Kent Kreuger, *New York Times* Best-Selling Author and Award-Winning Author of *This Tender Land*, *Ordinary Grace*, and the Cork O'Connor Mystery Series

"If you like a good, crazy-terrifying eco-thriller, grab Don Carr's first novel, *The Midnight Rambler*. Carr, a professional environmental science expert, knows his way around a poison pit. He dispatches his fictional hero, Sophie, an environmental investigator with a strong stomach and even tougher nerves, on an excruciating expedition into toxic waste dumps created by organized crime for profit. While Sophie and her cohort are fictional, the crime they're fighting is all too true, and it's swollen into a worldwide crisis that we have ignored at our peril. Bonus points for Carr's depiction of his eco-sleuth's tradecraft—it's full-on bonkers, in a good way, especially the Q-worthy tech gear."

—Elaine Shannon, Best-Selling Author of *Hunting LeRoux*, *Desperados*, *The Spy Next Door*, and *No Heroes: Inside the FBI's Secret Counter-Terror Force*

"Crackerjack plotting, amazing characters, a truly original environmental theme, and a relentless pace. It's Erin Brockovich crashing into Jason Bourne. Like all the best roller coasters, *The Midnight Rambler*'s ride leads to an incredible climax."

—Bob Mayer, Best-Selling Author of over Eighty Books, Including *The Green Berets*, *Area 51*, and *Atlantis*

"Don Carr's *The Midnight Rambler* is a fast-paced, page-turner that will leave you breathless and wanting more. Carr gives environmental crimes their due attention in engaging, exciting prose with a stunning story arch and vibrant characters. This is a must-read book for anyone who cares about the future of the planet."

—Heather White, Best-Selling Author of *One Green Thing*, Environmental Activist

"As a former special agent with EPA's Criminal Investigation Division, it was great to dive into *The Midnight Rambler* and be entertained by the adventures of Agent Grant. Well done, Don Carr!"

—Doug Parker, Former Director of Criminal Investigations, Environmental Protection Agency

The
MIDNIGHT RAMBLER

The Midnight Rambler

by Don Carr

© Copyright 2023 Don Carr

ISBN 979-8-88824-179-0

All rights reserved. No part of this publication may be reproduced, stored in a retrieval system, or transmitted in any form or by any means—electronic, mechanical, photocopy, recording, or any other—except for brief quotations in printed reviews, without the prior written permission of the author.

This is a work of fiction. All the characters in this book are fictitious, and any resemblance to actual persons, living or dead, is purely coincidental. The names, incidents, dialogue, and opinions expressed are products of the author's imagination and are not to be construed as real.

Published by

köehlerbooks™

3705 Shore Drive
Virginia Beach, VA 23455
800-435-4811
www.koehlerbooks.com

The

MIDNIGHT RAMBLER

Don Carr

VIRGINIA BEACH
CAPE CHARLES

CHAPTER 1

Sophie stood at one end of the swimming pool, toes curled on the edge, about to dive headfirst into a sea of dead bodies.

Cadavers, technically.

The University of Colorado's Medical School had been built on top of an old athletic center. In a cost-cutting move, school administrators approved a plan to repurpose the competition swimming pool as storage for anatomy class corpses. Inevitably, Boulder students in the late '90s egged each other on in a campus hijinks known as Night of the Swimming Dead. A race fifty meters from one end to the other of the cadaver pool. It was mostly a joke, a dare made after seven beers at The Sink. No one followed through, at least not at first. You would have to break into a school building at night, risking arrest and expulsion.

Sophie had heard of it happening only twice. Both times there was no declared winner. Contestants got so spooked they made it no more than ten meters, reportedly shrieking in terror as they clawed their way out of the liquid preserving the cadavers.

But there she was. Just after midnight on a Tuesday. Ready to take the plunge into Corpse Ocean and race to the end against Gary the Trustifarian. Gary whose dad owned clusters of Texaco oil bulk plants across the Front Range. Gary who drove around Boulder in a mint Land Rover Defender and declared his life was dedicated to fighting for the environment. Gary who called his skateboard "the ball and chain."

Sophie's crime was correcting Gary in front of their chemistry class over the number of hydroxyphenyl groups in Bisphenol A. Chastened, on his heels, a sputtering Gary had no other choice but to challenge Sophie to Night of the Swimming Dead.

Poor Gary. He got so freaked out pushing aside bloated corpses carpeted with stitched wounds from student surgeries, that he puked in the mixture of water and preservation fluid. That prompted a full flush of the pool. Turned out Gary being a wealthy, connected shit paid off for Sophie. They both received probation, not expulsion. She didn't come out of it unharmed, though. For a week, she endured a raspy cough from the chemicals. Months afterward, Sophie dreamed of cadaver eyes popping open during her swim.

"SAC Grant? The Marines? They're getting restless."

Special Agent in Charge. That never got old. Sophie keyed her radio mic. "On my way, Agent Jones."

She hadn't thought of the Night of the Swimming Dead for years. But tonight, staring up at the iconic humpback silhouette of Mount Vesuvius, the villainous Italian volcano best known for dumping lethal ash and lava on twenty thousand unlucky citizens of Pompeii all the way back in 79 AD, Sophie wanted extra motivation.

After two long years in goon-chasing purgatory, her return to a command position needed to go smoothly. No more hunting fugitives from the EPA's Most Wanted List in in every corner of the country. No more living out of hotel rooms with stale bagels at the breakfast bar. Sophie had yearned for a return to the type of investigations that had lured her to the US Environmental Protection Agency fifteen years ago. Cases that took two or three years to develop, that sprawled across multiple jurisdictions from tax law to forgery to customs regulations and unfolded like an epic novel.

Medium height with olive skin and long brown hair pulled into a ponytail, Sophie walked a short distance down the volcano to face thirty anxious armed US Marines. They all wore an EPA issued, Level B self-contained breathing apparatus—helmet, sealed faceplate, and oxygen tank—paired with hazardous chemical resistant gloves and boots. Sophie and her escorts were about to enter a sprawling toxic waste crime scene with an unknown number of Camorra gunmen lurking about. Properly preparing her security team for what they may encounter on Vesuvius was key to tonight's success.

"First, the Camorra are *everywhere*."

"SAC Grant," Tommy Jones said.

Her partner, EPA Special Agent Tommy Jones, was standing off to the side. He pointed at his helmet christened by a Green Bay Packers logo. "Check your coms. Still on our private channel."

Sophie reached to her hip, switched her radio to the predetermined channel for everyone's use, and repeated her opening statement.

"Second, they never call themselves *Camorra*. No. To them, it's *the System*."

Sophie regurgitated memorized details from her US State Department issued briefing files to the assembled Marines. She went on about how the centuries-old crime syndicate's power didn't come from top-down, monarch-style management systems, but more a network of quasi-independent gangs with tentacles in every fissure of the southern Italian boot. Of the nine clans operating in Southern Italy, the Pecora System was in State's estimation the most formidable.

"SAC Grant . . . we get it," said the Marine's commanding officer, master sergeant Tipton. The man was the size of a double mattress. "We know all about the Camorra. There's that movie? The Netflix show? Off base you can get anything from drugs to fake fashion brands. Wife bought a knockoff Prada bag last week. Piece of shit fell apart the next day."

She took a deep breath. There was always another *Gary*. As a veteran of detecting thinly veiled contempt from male counterparts in the field, this, Sophie could handle. She raised her gloved left hand. Strapped to her forearm was a flexible LED screen. It showed a detailed map of their side of Vesuvius. With her other hand, Sophie traced a brown line from a black rectangle marking their current position at the base of the volcano, up to clusters of multi-colored circles. The colored spots were about halfway between the base and Vesuvius's caldera.

"See these spots? One of the Pecora System's biggest moneymakers is the dumping of hazardous, sometimes radioactive waste, right there on the side of Vesuvius. The more toxic the better. Then they set it on fire."

Sophie couldn't argue that the modern world wasn't a technological marvel. The entirety of human knowledge was at her fingertips, and a friend on the opposite side of the globe accessible with the push of a button. But everything had a cost. Budget flat screen TV manufacturers operated on tight margins, and it often made more economic sense to have the Camorra dispose of excess banned chemicals than get crosswise with EU regulators. They had a friend in the Pecora System. For a steep price.

"Good thing we have these masks, then," the bulky sergeant said.

"More of a precaution," Sophie said. "What you really want to do is watch where you're walking. These red spots on the map? That's dumped cadmium sulfide. If you step in a fresh pool, linger for even a second, you're not leaving alive. Be ready for a horrible death drowning in blood as you liquefy."

Sophie jabbed a finger at a cluster of lime-colored ovals on her map. "Now see these green spots. That's tardum, an early weaponized nerve agent. Favorite of the Iraqis during the war with Iran. You'll be able to recognize it from a gray vapor. If you smell garlic that means the mask is malfunctioning. Run like hell."

"Garlic?" Sergeant Tipton said. "It's Italy. Everything smells like garlic."

"Rotten cabbage if that helps. Never had the pleasure, and don't intend to."

Sophie was suddenly aware of everyone's eyes on her, including Tommy's. For this particular *Gary*, Sophie figured the best defense was a good offense.

"Can I ask you a personal question? Married? Children?"

"Yes, and yes. Boy and a girl," the sergeant said, shifting from foot to foot.

"And do they live on base?"

"They do."

Sophie gestured at the color cluster on the map. "After they burn it, whatever's dumped up there still seeps down into the water table." Pointing at a spot a foot off the bottom of the map, Sophie said, "Remember the little girl that was hanging around our villa? Where we staged? In Malodini?"

The sergeant nodded. "Cute kid."

Sophie jerked her head up toward Vesuvius. "It's a small town. Five hundred residents total and they draw well water from the contaminated aquifer running straight under the mountain. At the turn of the century, Malodini had maybe one case of childhood cancer every decade. Today? Nine brain tumors and over a dozen blood cancers in the past year. Been worse on the adults."

"How so?"

"Well for starters, Maria is an orphan."

"Jesus Christ." Tipton looked stunned that a sweet child would have to endure the death of her parents in such a manner. *He'll never get over it,* Sophie thought, *once he gets home and hugs his own children.* It was like what every industry has done through the entirety of human history—shift the cost of production onto someone else. It was always somebody poorer, forced to live with the pollution, with no means to fight back. Like Maria's family.

"Farther downstream, samples we took from the Apulia aquifer show traces of hexchrome and heavy metals. They are at safe levels. For now. But the ten thousand US Navy personal operating fifty different commands at the Naples Naval Support Base—*and their families*—get their water from Apulia. If we don't' stop it—"

The master sergeant's posture slackened as it sunk in that his family was in danger. Now he had skin in the game. He needed Sophie. A gust of wind blew a white cloud of unknown provenance over them.

The prospect of traipsing through a toxic hellscape sent the Marines to check the tightness of the breathing masks strapped to their helmets, while others fidgeted with the screens lashed to their forearms.

"It's nothing," Sophie said. "Gas venting. Level B protection is more than enough for what you're going to encounter. I'm more worried about what the Camorra's going to do when they find us messing with their cash machine."

"Doesn't Interpol have its own environmental crime division?" Tipton said, his tone softer than before. The sign of another vanquished *Gary*.

"They do. The gold standard. But Vesuvius is too remote. Too inhospitable for a sustained presence. They came. Last year. The detection equipment they installed to monitor illegal dumping was destroyed the next day by the Camorra. They left." Sophie pointed at two shapes cloaked in darkness behind the Marines. "But tonight, we have a surprise for the Camorra that Interpol didn't have."

The sergeant turned to his men. "Let's make sure the lady does her job."

Tommy came forward, a smile behind his plastic shield. Full of muscle and a head and a half taller than Sophie, Tommy was clad in identical black fatigues as Sophie, an assault rifle slung across his back. Even behind his breathing mask, Tommy had one of those open pie faces that always made him look like the most sympathetic person in a crowd. More than once, Italians on vacation from the north had stopped and asked him for directions. The fact her partner was also ex-Army had proved useful in forging a quick relationship with their Marine escort.

"Good work. Getting a Jarhead's respect ain't easy," he said.

Sophie thought back to that horrifying night in college, her body clad in neoprene, exposed skin slathered in Vaseline for protection from the preservation fluids, arms outstretched over the amber-hued water brimming with corpses. She felt her body entering the viscous sludge in a perfect dive, cadavers bumping off her arms while

Gary thrashed wildly. The satisfaction from making it to the end of fifty-meter pool with a single breath had not waned in the years that passed.

"It's not their respect I'm worried about."

CHAPTER 2

The SPAGO climbed Vesuvius's southern slope, dual sets of treads churning through fist-sized rocks and hunks of pumice. Behind the machine's controls was Sophie's partner, Tommy. A squad of fifteen Marines were spread in front of the research vehicle. With their weapons out, marching up the near treeless moonscape, the soldiers looked alien in their breathing masks and air tanks against a hazy orange tint infecting the air from an occasional flare of volcanic gas.

While Vesuvius vented and oozed hot magma on occasion, there hadn't been a major eruption since 1944. The seismologist Sophie consulted a month earlier on their arrival to Italy believed another eruption was inevitable. "It is a ticking time bomb," a professor from the University of Naples had told her. The metropolis of Naples carpeted the opposite side of the famous volcano in an ocean of twinkling lights. A new eruption could kill over a million people according to the professor. Yet Neapolitans merrily went about their days, counting on their patron saint San Gennaro to protect them.

The LED screen on her wrist showed Sophie's oxygen level at fifty-three minutes. She needed to better regulate her breathing. During their morning runs, Sophie and Tommy had each worn breathing masks and tanks to simulate the rigors of oxygenated work on Vesuvius. Most days, Tommy hardly broke a sweat while Sophie's lungs ached. And she prided herself on running five, eight-minute miles every day.

Sophie keyed the radio mic from her SPAGO. "Jones. Air?"

"Pure Sheboygan."

Sophie thought she knew what Tommy meant, having heard him lovingly refer to the sausages made in his beloved hometown of Sheboygan, Wisconsin, whenever he was served the Italian version.

"Translation?"

"Flush with air. Sixty-five minutes left, SAC Grant." Tommy said.

"And your SPAGO?"

"Climbing well. Pitch is four degrees off."

The Self Propelled All Terrain Geoprobe model 840, or SPAGO, was a dependable field tool for the EPA back in the States. Engineers took a metal cabin the size of a shipping container and mounted it on dual sets of carbon tipped tank treads. In the front cabin were seats for the driver and a passenger, and a wide bubble windshield. The two vehicles they brought over were festooned on the outside with industrial-scale instruments, drills, and probes. Crammed inside behind the cabin were more tools, computers, and a compact lab for on-site testing.

Sophie had spent a week before departure modifying both of their SPAGOs. The pair of tracked research vehicles were flown to Italy in the cargo hold of a C-47 for a specific task—to drill deep through the hard-volcanic rock of Mount Vesuvius. The sensors Sophie designed and built would be shot deep into the mountain by powerful pneumatic augers mounted on each SPAGO's bumper.

"Whoa," Tommy said. "Pitch at five degrees. Six! Fuck! Curds!"

Sophie held her breath. Two weeks earlier while learning to drive the tank-like vehicle, Tommy knocked down a crumbling section of rock wall by the house they rented in the small town of Malodini at Vesuvius's base. The accident bent the SPAGO's auger chute. Now he was in danger of tipping over. But Tommy had learned from the accident. He slowed down enough to plane his vehicle and continue up the mountain's flank.

While gunning her SPAGO's diesel engine to supply maximum charge to the instrument battery, Sophie tapped a screen to the left of the steering wheel and confirmed that power levels for the hydraulic stabilizers were at a hundred percent. Designed to be lightweight, yet powerful, the SPAGO could achieve a top speed of forty-five miles per hour and left only seven psi of ground pressure so as not to disturb sensitive environmental crime scenes back in the States.

Pushing the accelerator levers forward on her front two treads, Sophie advanced until her GPS chirped. She braked to a stop, flipped the hydraulic stabilizer switch, and four outriggers mounted on her SPAGO's corners extended and augured themselves to the ground. Next, she activated the seismic hammer. The device reported back a four-hundred-foot-deep snapshot of layers of volcanic rock. Sure enough, as Sophie guessed, there was a shale fissure fifty feet down, well within her bore drill's range. That meant she could place a sensor shallow enough to be effective, but deep enough to be out of reach for the Camorra.

After Sophie finished deploying the full suite of thirty-five sensors needed to cover the entire southern slope where the bulk of the toxic dumping took place, authorities would know in seconds from data wirelessly transmitted, not only when and where an illegal substance was dumped, but the type of pollutant. The reading was admissible in Italian court. Tonight, was a test-run. They planned to deploy the first four sensors and head home.

Through her windshield, Sophie watched as the master sergeant dropped to one knee, clenched fist in the air. His men all stopped and crouched, rifles aimed upslope.

"What is it, sergeant?" Sophie said into her radio mic, heart thumping in her chest. From a higher vantage point, a Camorra sniper could pick them off at will. Seated in her SPAGO with lights blazing, Sophie was an easy target.

"Movement up ahead."

Sophie powered down her LED spots. After thirty breathless seconds waiting in the dark, Sergeant Tipton stood. "All clear," he said over the radio.

After powering up the lights, Sophie switched her screen from detect to drill mode. Satisfied she was aimed at the right spot, Sophie set the bit depth at fifty meters and pushed a red button on the dash. With twenty tons of downforce, the rotary bit chewed into the hard rock. Her SPAGO barely twitched as the drill punctured the volcano, the hydraulic stabilizers doing their jobs. After five minutes, an electronic chirp in the cab alerted Sophie that the drill had found the shale fissure at forty-two meters. She pulled the drill up and shut it down. A camera mounted above the drill showed a perfect ten centimeter in diameter symmetrical hole.

Next, Sophie used a rubber joystick mounted to the right of the tread levers to maneuver the sensor chute over the fresh hole in the ground. With the push of another button, a hard but flexible two-inch auger tube leapt from the chute, plunging into the hole. After it reached the bottom, Sophie pressed a green button and the tube retracted, leaving the sensor at the bottom. With the reverse flip of a switch, she retracted the hydraulic stabilizers.

"Agent Jones? Do you copy? First sensor deployed."

"One down, one to go for us, too." Tommy was annoyingly calm and composed, even a little giddy. "Sheboygan."

To Sophie's surprise, Tommy's first year on the job did little to dampen his enthusiasm. When he wasn't extolling the virtues of his native Wisconsin to anyone that would listen. Tommy started calling he and Sophie the "Power Behind the Flower" to fellow agents in a nod to the tulip in the EPA logo. What made his passion more confounding was that Italy was his first real case as an agent. He'd spent his rookie year chasing with Sophie fugitives on the EPA's Most Wanted List. Yet after long hours apprehending another polluting bail-jumper on the run, Tommy headed straight to the Agency library to study old cases. He was even taking night classes in chemistry and biology.

Like Tommy, they all came to the EPA eager to save the world, to hand scrub spilled crude from sea otters and put the greedy oil company CEO responsible behind bars. But for most of them, their enthusiasm evaporated in the face of callous gas tycoons and agrichemical conglomerates whose ownership of Members of Congress rendered most environmental laws toothless. Watching case after case end with a corporate lawyer negotiating a violation down to a fine—the amount registering as a rounding error in their client's yearly profit statement—eventually turned even the most gung-ho newbies into a jaded bureaucratic cog.

The trick, Sophie had found, was to embrace, even chase, cases that combined with other agencies. Unlike say an IRS agent, if Sophie's investigation started with an environmental violation, she had the unique authority to pursue any subsequent federal crime, anything from drug trafficking to counterfeiting. Most federal agents were deathly allergic to sharing credit, but it took way less effort to put a polluter behind bars if they'd defrauded investors or cheated on their taxes.

It was also much easier to get information from people as a woman because they were less intimidated. It didn't fit their vision of a cop from TV. There was an arrogance in EPA criminals most agents didn't see with other crimes. Before being demoted to fugitive hunting purgatory, Sophie relished targets that had PhDs. Without fail they believed they were the smartest people in the room. Men, mostly, who were convinced they could get away with any crime. When confronted by a woman from the EPA, the perp didn't think to call a lawyer. They just talked and talked until she slapped the cuffs on them.

"Tardum! Tardum at ten o'clock. SAC Grant, advise." Peering through her windshield and the smokey haze, Sophie spied the master sergeant waving his arm to signal her.

Leaving the engine running but the caterpillar treads locked, Sophie opened her door and stepped onto the ground. She trotted to Tipton's side. He and four of his men were keeping their distance from a black pond of liquid the size of a backyard swimming pool.

"Close, but that's cadmium sulfide."

Sophie pointed a gloved finger at the display on her wrist. Making sure the sergeant could see and follow along, she traced with her forefinger on a set of crimson splashes on the map. Sophie pointed at the thin mustache of fog over the pool brimming with toxic waste. "Yup. This tracks as cadmium sulfide. See the gray vapor right there, wafting off?"

"I do," the sergeant said.

Sophie saw a different pool, fifty yards farther uphill, the telltale shimmer of another dangerous dumped substance. She held the map up so her escorts could see it and pointed at the pool upslope.

"These green spots, now *that's* tardum." Sophie said. "You won't see tardum, unlike cadmium sulfide, unless it's been recently dumped then it shakes like Jell-O." She pointed at the pool of discarded nerve agent above them.

"That's fresh. They had to dump it . . . three days ago, max. Tell your men to set up a defensive perimeter. I'll use the SPAGO to deploy the next sensor between these two dump sites." Sophie nodded upslope. "Right by that clump of cypress."

"Affirmative."

Tipton's eyes darted back and forth. She asked him if anything was wrong. He relayed that one of his Marines had come across two old shepherds and a flock of a couple dozen sheep.

"Shit!" Sophie could feel her anxiety boil. The sergeant had read the same briefing book she had. In the section listed WARNINGS were two paragraphs about how the Camorra used shepherds as lookouts on the mountain. Now as they moved to the next drill site, Sophie, driving the SPAGO with Marines on either flank, realized every foot they moved forward put them deeper into Camorra territory.

As one of two hundred agents in the EPA's Criminal Investigation Division, Sophie Grant had boarded tankers at sea and conducted investigations in seven countries. All but one of her cases ended in a conviction, racking up millions in fines. She even had sent a few polluters with the bad luck of hiring terrible lawyers to jail.

Yet despite her experience, no matter what Sophie tried, tonight she couldn't slow her labored breathing. She was draining her air tank just sitting in her SPAGO's cab. Her back was soaked with sweat. Around every rock they passed she worried a Camorra assassin lay, waiting to open fire on Sophie and the Marines fanned out on either side of her. Sophie glanced down at her wrist display. Thirty-nine minutes of air left. Her heavy breathing echoed in the confines of the breathing mask.

A chirp from the display inside her mask told Sophie they were at the next drill site, information confirmed by a strand of aged cypress trees before them. Sophie marveled for a moment at the trees, able to survive in the harsh volcanic climate. To withstand intense heat, wind, fire and now the chemical vagaries of human consumption.

Sergeant Tipton and two other Marines marched into the short, thick-bushed trees, weapons at the ready. Sophie put the SPAGO in park and activated the hydraulic stabilizers. An alarm and red blinking light alerted her that one of the arms had not fully extended. Likely, a pebble from the churning treads landed in one of the arm joints. Sophie opened the door to the cab and jumped to the ground.

Out in the darkness in front of her a rock tumbled. Sophie looked up. She saw a flare. Nothing came out of her mouth despite every synapse screaming for her to warn her team. Frozen in place, Sophie's eyes fixed on a lit match set to the cloth dangling from a Molotov cocktail. Sophie stared, transfixed by the flaming bottle hurtling toward her.

"Incoming!" the sergeant yelled as it sailed end over end in an arc toward them, little droplets of flame falling in its wake. Jolted by Tipton's warning, Sophie dove to her left as the Molotov cocktail exploded on the SPAGO's cab. Rolling painfully over rocks, jagged points digging into her back, Sophie avoided being burned as the cab was engulfed by an orange ball of fire. Intense heat and pressure from the blast washed over her as she tumbled into a shallow, pumice rock-filled depression.

Drawing her pistol, she got on one knee and scanned the darkness in front of her. Sophie couldn't see well, her mask fogged by her heavy breathing. Two more flaming bottles soared toward their position. The Marines returned fire into the dark, guns crackling, muzzle flashes the only visible light until the homemade bombs landed and exploded. One fell short, but another landed next to a Marine, setting his arm afire. He screamed and beat at the fire until a fellow Marine tackled him to the ground, smothering out the fire with his body.

"Grant!"

Sophie turned at the sound of the Marine sergeant's voice. He was pointing in front of her.

"Twelve o'clock!"

Backlit by glowing volcanic fissure, a man ran toward Sophie, pistol aimed at her from an outstretched hand. About to die, she could only think how absurd it was the man had wrapped a scarf around his face in a failed attempt to stem any toxic fumes wafting across Vesuvius's flank. Sophie figured he would contract thyroid cancer in a month, two tops, if the air was as contaminated as they feared.

A long burst from the sergeant's rifle stitched bullets diagonally across the man's chest. He crumpled to the ground, air rushing from his lungs. Another armed figure appeared before her. This time Tipton was turned away from her, his attention on more attackers rushing their position from the left, firing short bursts to suppress their fire.

Sophie rolled to the right on the ground as the second attacker opened fire with a pump shotgun. His first shot missed sending pellets into the dirt. That was all the time she needed. Sophie scrambled to her feet, sprinting for an outcropping of rock between two old trees. The Camorra foot soldier lost her in the dark, but he was close. Sophie could hear his heavy breathing. Again, her mind went somewhere else, thinking there had to be millions of N17 masks floating around post-pandemic Italy, yet these fools kept using scarves. A loud metallic sound rang out. The attacker had pumped another round into his shotgun's chamber.

She looked down at her pistol and thumbed the safety off. There was a deep gurgling sound to Sophie's left. With fear swelling in her chest, she peered around the white, gnarled bark of a tree to spy a large hole filled with clear, bubbling liquid—a massive lake of the deadly nerve agent, tardum.

The counter on Sophie's wrist showed twenty-seven minutes of air left. Picking up a stick from the ground, Sophie tossed it to her right. The attacker sprinted forward, firing at the sound. She spun around the rock outcropping, hearing him racking another round, and blindly fired her weapon five times.

One round found the man, striking him in the shoulder. He yelped as the bullet spun him around and his finger reflexively pulled the trigger on his shotgun. There was a loud bang and flash of orange. Sophie heard pellets whistling by her head even as she felt a white-hot sting in her ear.

The attacker looked at his feet. He was knee deep in the pool of toxic tardum. The man began wheezing.

"*Aiutami, aiutami, per favore,*" he croaked, lurching toward Sophie, gobs of blackish mucus erupted from his nostrils, a thin rivulet of blood ran down from his left eye.

"*Aituami.*" Two rounds fired from over Sophie's left shoulder struck the man in the head. He dropped into the muck like his skeleton had been removed and disappeared under the toxic liquid.

Sophie turned to face her partner, Tommy Jones, his pistol out, a curl of smoke escaping the barrel.

"What does *aituami* mean?" Tommy said.

"Help me."

"Oh God!"

"Believe me, you did," Sophie said.

"Check your ear," Tommy said.

Sophie put her hand to the side of her head. It came away wet and sticky. When she looked at her hand it was covered in blood. Some of the man's shotgun pellets had found their mark just under her helmet's rim. Another six inches to the right and she would've taken the brunt in her face mask. Tommy pulled out a small flashlight and looked at her head. "Nothing serious. Couple new earring holes. Mask integrity intact."

Sophie keyed her radio. "Sergeant Tipton. Anymore out there we need to worry about?"

"Nope, SAC Grant, looks like they turned tail and ran."

"Let's get back and I'll stitch you up," Tommy said.

Sophie put her hand back up to her ear and then looked down at her red-smeared palm. Acrid black smoke from burning diesel fuel drifted over them. After wiping the blood on her pant leg, Sophie stuck her open hand out to Tommy.

"I have one sensor left to deploy. Your SPAGO keys. Hand them over, Sheboygan."

CHAPTER 3

Hodges cleared his throat in Carter's earpiece, something he did over a hundred times a day. Each time, Carter had learned, the sound communicated something specific. During the nine years working together, Carter was able to assemble a rudimentary esophageal-venting dictionary of his boss. A Rosetta Stone of phlegm.

The most common, the SCUD, was a blatant "fuck off" characterized by a guttural hawk that sounded like a lawnmower on a gravel road. Hodges had just blasted a SCUD into Carter's earpiece. Issued in response to Carter's quest to convince Hodges to quit using US State Department cover identities.

"It's not a matter of if, Bill, but when."

"Boyd, when you're station chief, it's your decision. Do whatever you want. Make everyone wear flip flops for all I care. But until then, you're Carter Boyd, State Department attaché."

It was true; once Hodges retired and Carter oversaw the US Central Intelligence Agency's Italian operations, he had a laundry list of changes. Not that his boss ran a bad operation. Quite the opposite. Bill Hodges was a bona fide legend. Getting his start young in the clandestine services as a Navy SEAL in Vietnam, Hodges's fingerprints were on many of the Agency's most consequential operations of the past thirty years, including a mythic, CIA-wide rumor that in the late nineties, the man intercepted a suitcase nuke smuggled out of the crumbling Soviet Union. Apparently, that success landed him in the plum Italian station chief job, and he never left.

But Hodges had grown too old. Overconfident, at least in Carter's estimation.

Under covert presidential orders, CIA agents in each posting were authorized to use the US State Department as a cover identity. For decades it worked well. But after Chinese hackers identified intelligence operatives by comparing salaries, most senior CIA operatives like Carter questioned the practice. Few stations still employed them. Diplomatic immunity shielded the old guard. But it did little in the modern world to stop bad actors from putting a bullet in your head or sprinkling poisonous radioactive isotopes in your morning coffee.

Carter was perched in a café midway up the stunningly beautiful, swanky seaside Italian cliff town of Positano. Tucked into a ravine, the village's four thousand residents relied on tourism for their income. Positano's cantilevered, tight-clustered vertiginous hotels and villas spilled from the Lattari Mountains down to the glittering Tyrrhenian Sea in a cascade of sun-bleached pastels and terracotta. Located just below the knee of the Italian boot, with Naples an hour's drive to the north, Positano was the rare Campania town unscathed by the Second World War.

Below him, Positano's Marina Grande beach was crowded with sunbathers and swimmers. Carter turned his back to the water. From the beach extended a bay jammed with boats ranging from fishing skiffs to mega yachts. Positano was booming.

After ensuring his earpiece was not showing, Carter held his phone up this face and took several photos, making sure the three islands of Lil Galli, home of the sirens from Homer's Odyseus, were in the background. Farther out to sea was the hazy shape of the Isle of Capri.

"Time to post a selfie to State's Instagram."

Hodges cleared his throat. "You're joking. Now?"

"New regs, boss. Gotta geotag to keep the State cover believable."

"I'm in no fucking mood, Boyd."

It may sound counterintuitive to Cold Warhorses like Hodges that had operated for decades in the shadows, but the Agency had started to embrace social media. The more an intelligence officer posted from their fake identities, the more credible the cover. Carter would have to abandon his cover when he ascending to station chief, but for now he'd keep posting as a Statie if for no other reason than to needle Hodges. Carter turned back to face the ocean and took one last selfie on the café's veranda, with Positano behind him.

Because of its beautiful, dramatic location, Positano was a favorite setting for filmmakers. The vertical, sunbaked town also did double duty as a real estate haven for wealthy Russians looking to park ill-gotten gains. Some was money made from drug trafficking, but more importantly to Carter's current work as a senior CIA counter-terrorism officer, much of it came from illegal international weapons sales. Carter had viewed bank records showing at least a third of property transactions on the Amalfi Coast originated in Russia, including a dozen multi-million-dollar villas perched above Carter's café.

Carter sat back in his chair. With customers nested on either side on the noisy veranda, he sipped his coffee, enjoying the deep fruitiness of his espresso. From under a saucer, he removed a napkin and dabbed the sweat forming on his brow. Hodges had been making noises about retiring since the first day Carter arrived in Italy. But here they were, about to button up his final op. They were taking aim at Luca Pecora, the head of the Pecora System, the region's dominant Camorra crime syndicate clan. The man may be epochs old and tough as the pizza crust they sold to tourists in the Naples airport, but Bill Hodges was going to be a hard act for Carter to follow.

It'd be a perfect day if it wasn't so goddamn hot, Carter thought, looking down at his light blue, short-sleeved collared shirt spotting from his sweat. If it got any steamier, meat would fall off the bone. All things being equal, Carter had been much hotter at his last posting, a black site in Syria. Compared to the body armor he wore while working at that brutal desert gulag, being overdressed while sipping coffee on a southern Italian veranda was a dream.

A waiter appeared with a plate of *frito misto* for Carter. He ate a piece of fried calamari that exploded with intense lemon flavor.

Carter beckoned the waiter back to his table. In Italian, he asked what was different about the Amalfi Coast staple. While he could speak conversational in the popular War on Terror languages of Farsi and Arabic, it was Carter's fluency in Russian and Italian that caught Hodges's attention.

The waiter told Carter the chef had dehydrated hundreds of the legendary Amalfi lemons and ground them into powder to infuse his batter for the fried shellfish appetizer. "*Genio*," Carter said.

"Any sign of the Nicchi kids?" Hodges said in his ear.

Chris and Madeline Nicchi were in their mid-thirties, but from Hodges's aged perch everyone was a kid. After slowly moving his head back and forth to make certain no one was watching, Carter looked down at the live video feed on his phone. A surveillance drone orbited Positano's bay at ten thousand feet. It fed him constant high-resolution video of one boat in Positano's bay, a sleek medium-sized luxury yacht called the *Esperanza,* flying an American flag. Bugs planted in the yacht provided clear audio.

"Out having a drink a few minutes ago."

Carter pictured Bill Hodges standing before a bank of monitors at their Naples's facility, barking orders at drone techs seated at their workstations, snorting like a wild boar, left shirt sleeve pinned to his shoulder where his missing arm should be.

"*Pecora?*" Carter said to Hodges. "How close?"

"Black Audi, tab three-three-nine."

Carter punched the code into his phone. He was rewarded with live drone footage of a black sedan speeding down the unmistakable curves of the *Strada Statale Amalfitana*, a forty-mile stretch of highway carved into the steep coastal cliffs, toward Positano. Cater once read that ancient Romans killed over a million horses building the vertigo-inducing, serpentine road.

Three cars had left the Camorra chief's compound an hour ago. The vehicles immediately veered in three separate directions. Carter wasn't surprised considering Luca Pecora was a careful man.

Helped by sophisticated communications that included his own telecom, phones built in-house on closed networks, and IT experts that created impenetrable thickets of encrypted comms, Pecora had eluded Italian authorities for over a decade. It was rumored that the Pecora System leader's latest innovation was a dark web marketplace for every piece of contraband that moved through Naples, the world's third largest port.

Hodges was confident his own techs had identified the two decoy cars and the one with Pecora. Soon his quarry would arrive at Positano's bay. A dingy dispatched from the *Esperanza* would ferry the Camorra leader to the yacht. Once on board, Pecora aimed to purchase a shipment of high-tech, stolen US military weapons from Chris Nicchi, the son of a Kansas City crime boss, in the same deal Pecora made for years with Chris's father. Except this time, Chris and his wife worked for the CIA.

Fish in a barrel.

Carter popped another piece of the lemon infused *frito misto* into his mouth. He marveled at how the simple technique transformed the dish, like a similar meal he ate on a culinary tour of Central America. A Guatemalan chef spotted several coati gorging on allspice berries over several weeks, hunted them, and then spit-roasted the jungle rodents pre-seasoned. Inspired, Carter opened his phone and found a document marked *MTape*. He started typing fast with his thumbs.

Hodges issued another throat clearing SCUD. "What kind of pen name is J.T. Crete, anyway?"

Carter froze, his thumbs hovering over his phone's screen. The sweat on his forehead turned into an ocean.

"Come again?"

"*My Food Mixtape* by J.T. Crete. Submitted to fourteen publishers last year by the fictitious literary agent Sara Stockton. All rejected. Please tell me you're not having the CIA go through all the trouble to build a front biz, just so you can vanity publish Grandma Boyd's tater tot casserole recipe?"

How does the old bastard know? Carter shook his head. Of course, he knew. *Probably had my apartment bugged.* "It's not like that, Bill, I—"

"So, after I retire and fuck off to Florida, you still hot on this, this . . . you're going to actually have the machines? To print? Am I getting this right? To print your own cookbooks?"

"Yes. New American cookbooks. Translated into Italian. To start." It really was a perfect new strawman entity for the CIA's Italian operations, Carter reasoned. One that didn't rely on flimsy State Department covers. His operatives could travel the country, the entire European Union for that matter under the guise of publishing house representatives.

"Don't worry. Just fucking with you. Secret's safe with me. We all have our things, kid."

A florescent blue ball bounced off Carter's ankle. He looked away from his phone to see a boy no older than seven standing a few feet away. The boy's parents were seated two tables over. A pained expression was on the father's face while the mother cradled an infant to her chest.

"Sorry, I mean . . . *scusa*. Byron didn't mean to, did you Byron?" said the dad.

Carter muted his earpiece. "It's fine, I mean, *va bene*," Carter said. "Beautiful boy."

"Oh, thanks," said the dad.

"Where are you from?" the mom said.

"Philly," Carter said despite being born on the Air Force base in Minot, North Dakota. "You?"

"Oh. We're neighbors. From Baltimore," said the mom. "I love Philadelphia."

Carter picked up the ball and handed it to Byron. "It's Italian law that every young boy must eat gelato at least once a day. Look it up." Carter squinted at Byron. "Have you broken the law?"

"Nope. I just had some chocolate."

"Good boy."

Carter's phone buzzed. He unmuted his earpiece to the sound of Bill Hodges shouting several decibel levels above a howler monkey.

"Jesus Christ, Boyd are you there? Did you see that?"

"See what?" Carter sat forward and peered at the screen.

"Movement off the bow. A splash."

Carter's screen went white. He looked up as the sound of the explosion reached him. Where the *Esperanza* once floated in a sea of glittering blue was a mushrooming cloud of fire and smoke. Then the wave of heat from the blast washed over the café's veranda.

Screams erupted from the family to his right as the father dove on top of his wife and children, shielding them from bits of flaming yacht debris raining down around them. Carter spied the boy wiping blood from his chin, likely caused from his dad tackling them to the ground. Grabbing a napkin from his table, he rushed to his side, and pressed it to the boy's mouth.

"It's going to be alright," Carter said.

He tossed more than enough euros to cover his bill and ran down the stairs from the veranda to the plaza below. There was only one path from the steep cliffs to the beach, a narrow run of thousands of steps that wove in between clothing stores, bars, cafés, and markets. It funneled dense foot traffic back and forth from the water to Positano's higher environs.

"Boyd! Where are you? On the beach?" Hodges said in his ear.

"Almost there," Carter dodged between panicked beachgoers fleeing the blast zone. Twice he was forced from the narrow stairs into a shop doorway to keep from getting trampled by the throng of tourists desperate to escape the beach. Bodies slammed into him on either side, one knocking the glasses from his face. Carter was luckily able to scoop them from the brick lined path before they were crushed underfoot by the stampeding mob.

"Good grief, Boyd. Pick up the pace."

Sweat poured down his face. He thundered down steps three at time when a gap in the frightened crowds allowed. After he made it to the beach, Carter was greeted with a surreal vision. The luxury yachts crammed into the bay had fled, leaving a floating pile of burning wreckage and nothing else. Same with the beach, which ten minutes ago was filled with bathers and tourists. Now empty.

Carter wiped the perspiration off his forehead and thought about Chris and Madeline Nicchi. His stomach lurched. Just hours ago, he was on the *Esperanza*, coaching the beautiful young couple for their meeting with Pecora. They were nervous, but also bright and happy. Buoyed by the prospect of new identities and new lives outside their crime family. Madeline playfully bullied Carter into eating some of her grilled prawns, while Chris showed off a new pair of white loafers with gold trim purchased in Positano. Now they were probably dead.

He found a secluded spot under a palm tree next to a deserted pizza café. The alarming yet melodic sound of approaching Italian police sirens filled his ears. *Quick response,* Carter thought. Faster than a small tourist town was accustomed to.

"Above you, to the left," Hodges said in his ear. "Stay put. They should go right past."

Just as Hodges said, several police cars stopped above him. Carter used one of the pizza restaurant's massive plastic-coated menus to shield his face. Italian police and white-coated emergency workers stampeded down the stone stairs over his left shoulder, spilled out on the beach and rushed toward the water. Carter peeked over the menu. At least five patrol boats appeared in the bay, circling the floating gasoline blaze from the obliterated *Esperanza*.

"Medics are treating what looks like three people on the beach. Hard to tell on the feed how bad the injuries are," Hodges said in his ear. Carter heard Hodges take a deep breath. "Oh shit. What's *she* doing here?"

"Who?"

"Get the hell out of there. Go. Now."

Fleeing wasn't in Carter's plans. He was going to stay put until bodies were pulled out of the water that he could positively ID. He needed to see with his own eyes, not from the drone feed after-action report, what happened to the Nicchi kids under his protection.

"Not leaving. I have to see them, Bill."

"It's Fattore."

Time to go. Madeline and Chris Nicchi would have to wait. Captain Adele Fattore had arrived. She was the commanding officer for the Polizia Speciale Campania, a detachment of elite, highly trained local police tasked with fighting the Camorra crime syndicate in Southern Italy. Carter and Fattore had met several times. Maybe it was her height, or a storied career reputation that rivaled Hodges's, but Carter found the woman to be more than intimidating.

And she would be pissed off to find a CIA officer on site without first alerting her to their presence. They had an intelligence sharing agreement that stipulated in the strongest of terms Fattore be notified of an Agency operation in her region. It was crafted in the aftermath of a rendition scandal. CIA agents had illegally held high-ranking Islamic State fighters swept up from the Iraq battlespace in covert Italian safehouses for interrogation without clearing it with the PSC. The fallout resulted in five agents being kicked out of the country. The Italians had even issued arrest warrants for all those involved. Carter often wondered what dirt Hodges had on superiors to escape the blunder without any splatter.

"Get me out of here," Carter said to Hodges.

"Walk up that small path to your right, there's a set of wrought iron stairs leading to the promenade."

"Is that Carter Boyd? From the US Central Intelligence Agency?"

Carter's face flushed. He felt like his sweat-soaked clothes had just been ripped off his body. Carter let the menu drop from his face. Before him stood the tall, dark, raptor-like Captain Fattore.

"I think you meant the US State Department, captain."

"Ah yes," Fattore said. She pointed at her ear. "Tell Bill Hodges he is getting lazy in his old age What's next? A red carnation?"

Hodges detonated a cluster of SCUDS so loud it forced Carter to remove his earpiece. He held the device out to Fattore.

"Be my guest."

CHAPTER 4

Candied watermelon rind. Unexpected. Delightful.

After Carter typed the words into his cookbook notes, he took another *taralli* from a silver bowl, dipped the cracker into a creamy ball of burrata cheese and ate it. Combined with maple vinegar lingering on his palate, the watermelon infused in the cheese elevated the classic Italian appetizer to a place worthy of plagiarism.

He was grateful for the culinary distraction. Hodges had sent Carter video from the drone feed. It showed a thin black figure diving from the bow of the *Esperanza*, seconds before the Nicchi's yacht exploded. He played the video repeatedly while seated at a beachfront café. Chris and Madeline had been Carter's responsibility. The station chief wasn't going to let him forget that. Until Carter's Agency mentor stepped down, every move, every word, every request was part of the audition for the top job. Like the ancient fucker loved to say, "I may be too old to cut the mustard, but I can still lick the jar."

A loud whistle snapped Carter's head up from his phone screen. He spied the tall, bent figure of Captain Fattore standing like the Reaper's scythe, with two fingers in her mouth. She beckoned Carter back to the beach with a nod. The area was still cordoned off with police tape. Yellow strands fluttered in a light sea breeze. Carter met Fattore at the water's edge. Four PSC officers were stationed a dozen feet further down the beach.

"They found a body," Hodges said in his ear. "Hopefully Fattore's nimrods aren't destroying all the evidence. If Uncle Sam wasn't underwriting her operation, they'd be hunting Camorra with muskets and spears and whatever other dusty shit they could pull out of a museum."

Hodges had told Carter he could go home, that the drone would keep circling. Carter declined. It was another obvious test. But more than the eternal game of proving himself to Hodges, Carter wanted to see Chris Nicchi and his wife when they were pulled out of the sea. He owed them that.

Two officers were knee deep in the water, holding on to a pink and black burnt body floating face down twenty feet from shore. One foot was bare, the other clad in an unmistakable white and gold trimmed loafer belonging to Chris Nicchi. Fattore waved at one of the patrol boats, which slowly motored toward the corpse.

"Carter Boyd of the US State Department?" Fattore said. Her lip curled in a knowing smile. "Do you know this person?"

Fattore was rightly suspicious about the appearance of a high-level CIA officer just as a luxury yacht exploded in Positano's bay. Carter would've been.

"I don't know what to say," Carter said. Except that he was sorry. But the audience for that apology was gone forever.

"Why not? Your Italian is . . . *perfetto*."

"Time to go, Boyd. She's going to pick your pocket," Hodges said.

Sure, Fattore was intimidating in a lioness with a sniper rifle sort of way, but he was Carter Boyd. A veteran counter-terrorism officer soon to be station chief. Madeline Nicchi's body was still out there. He wasn't giving up.

"Need any assistance with the scene? I can arrange helicopters. Dive teams. We have resources at our disposal that you can use."

Fattore stared through Carter, her brown eyes showing no warmth, boring deep into his soul. Fattore pointed up into the sky.

"Footage from the drone flying overhead would be helpful."

"Request fucking denied," Hodges said in Carter's ear.

"What drone?"

"Until next time, Carter Boyd from the US State Department."

She lifted a black gloved hand in a dismissive goodbye.

Getting the message, Carter turned and walked back through the sand back to the café. After finding a secluded booth in the back, he ordered a lemonade from a nervous looking waiter. When the waiter disappeared from earshot, Carter keyed his mic.

"It was him. Chris. It was Chis Nicchi. They got them. He's dead."

"You sure? Body looked flame-broiled from up here," Hodges said.

"Yeah, I'm sure."

"And Madeline?"

"No sign," Carter said. *"Pecora?"*

"I had Fattore's cops pull the Audi over. He wasn't in it. My bet is the bald fuck never left Scampia. Whole thing was a set up."

The waiter approached with Carter's lemonade and the check. He reached into his pocket for his wallet and handed a Euro to the server. After he left, Carter put the wallet back, but paused when he felt a foreign object. Carefully, he pulled a *cornicello* from his pocket. The two-inch long, horn-shaped charm was a common Campania talisman. Used to ward off an evil-eye curse, *cornicellos* took many forms and colors. Sold in the trinket stores lining Positano's main artery, some were gold, others silver. The *cornicello* placed in Carter's pocket was blood-red like a fresh Thai chili and crowned with a silver skull. Carter turned the souvenir over in his hands. Two words were etched in Latin on the object's surface.

Memento mori.

Carter froze. From ground shaking mortar attacks in Syria to terrorist guns fired in his direction outside Rome, dangerous situations were not foreign to him. But the words chiseled into the talisman were cold ice in his veins. He now knew exactly who wrote it and who killed Chris and Madeline Nicchi. Carter stumbled out of the café and whipped his head around taking in a three-hundred-and-sixty-degree view of Positano's harbor. The man that had placed the engraved red *cornicello* in his pocket needed to be close. But there was no one around. Then it hit Carter. In his hurried dash down to the beach, bouncing off dozens of bodies racing to flee the yacht, one of them had been the killer. And the assassin knew exactly who Carter was.

"Bill. I know who planted the bomb."

"Until a forensics team—"

"Bill."

"Fine. Who?"

Carter held the red *cornicello* out in his outstretched palm. "Zoom down. On my hand. I found this in my pocket *after I got to the beach*." He waited a few moments for Hodges to yell at one of the techs to order the drone's camera to focus on the talisman in his open hand.

"*Il Ramingo.*"

CHAPTER 5

"I'm hungry."

The eleven-year-old Italian girl tugged at Sophie's belt, her brown saucer-sized eyes staring up. She noticed the girl was wearing a dirt-stained, white-lace dress.

"Maria. *Mi apologia. Un momento.* I have to say goodbye to the nice master sergeant." Sophie brushed the girl's cheek.

"We can finish our match?"

Maria loved games. Especially card games. Her new obsession was Rack-O. They were in the middle of a seven-game match, currently set at 3-1 for Maria.

"After I check some things. Head back into the house. *Sfogliatellas.* Find the white paper bag the kitchen. Tommy's inside, ask him to help if you can't find them." Maria punched the sky in joy at the promise of the traditional Italian lobster-tail-shaped breakfast pastry. She ran through the early morning sunshine, opened the red wooden front door, and darted inside.

The day after Sophie and Tommy arrived in Malodini, Maria appeared on the doorstep of their crumbling rented villa. Word had spread fast in the community that the Americans had come to finally put a stop to the bad guys from dumping bad stuff. Maria heard the chatter at her orphanage. But she was unconvinced.

"The police came. The System still dumps what they want to, again and again," she had said in impressive English to the EPA agents.

"This is different," Tommy had said to the girl. He pointed at Sophie. "She's the best."

"Don't tell her that," Sophie remembered scolding her partner. In her hard-earned experience chasing eco-crooks in the US, poor rural towns like Malodini didn't matter in the bigger picture of wealthy interests getting richer. It wasn't until Uncle Sam's strategic military assets at the Naval Support Activity Naples base were threatened in the region that the EPA was called in. Couldn't have the home of both the US Navy's Europe forces and the US Sixth Fleet ingesting carcinogens in their drinking water.

"How'd she learn English without her—?" Sergeant Tipton said.

"Orphanage between here and Caserta. Nuns taught her. But she stays with me and Jones most nights." Sophie shook her head. Of course, after admonishing Tommy for overpromising the girl, they took her in anyway. She was smart. It didn't matter the game once they played three or four hands she started winning. Kind, too. Always asked how Sophie was feeling. But there was also a toughness about her stemming from losing her parents to cancer. Sophie heard from the nuns the previous week that Maria had knocked out two teeth of a local boy just for pushing her out of line at mealtime.

Sophie understood Maria's simmering anger. Her own mother had been ripped away in a similar fashion. She could draw a straight line from her mom's final breath to her mission in Italy. That's why in her spare time, Sophie had been trying to find someone to adopt Maria in Campania, or at least find the poor girl a spot in the Italian equivalent of foster care. She had failed so far.

Sophie stuck her hand out to the sergeant. "Thanks for saving my bacon out there."

"Least I could do," he said shaking her hand, Sophie's fingers disappeared inside his dinner plate-sized appendage.

Two of their Marine escorts were injured in the skirmish with the Camorra on Vesuvius; one burn victim and a gunshot wound to the leg of another. Both caught a ride on their remaining SPAGO back down the mountain to Malodini with the squad medic. Tipton counted five dead Camorra on Vesuvius before they left. The Marines were preparing to travel back to the US Navy base near Naples in a convoy of Humvees parked next to Sophie's villa. She still needed to brief the EPA's Transnational Desk on the night's mission. But Sophie wanted to check the data first. Best to arm herself with what she hoped was good news.

The master sergeant pointed at Sophie's villa. "You're staying?"

Sophie nodded. How could she leave now? If the sensors worked, and she was certain they would, they could track the Camorra in seconds after they dumped toxic waste. With her tech they could then identify the chemical composition with enough granular detail to link it back to the criminal clan.

"You know that was a warning, back there?" said Tipton, genuine concern etched on the sergeant's face. "They'll kill you if they can."

She nodded. "Good thing I've got the Marines as back up."

Tipton smiled and gave her a casual salute, spun, and jogged to a black van holding the rest of his squad. After he closed the back door behind his massive frame, the van sped away.

Sophie walked into the villa dog-tired. Maria was happily devouring a pastry while listening to Tommy talk about his favorite topic, Wisconsin.

"Did you know Harry Houdini was from there?" he said as he plugged a long, braided strand of multi-colored wires that ran from the small uplink dish on their roof into a converter that would feed the military encrypted data.

"Who?" Maria looked pleased just to be in the mix.

"Oprah? Oprah Winfrey ring any bells? Harrison Ford? Han Solo . . . *Star Wars*?" Tommy made finger guns.

"No."

"What about *Titanic*? Did you see it?"

Maria nodded, her eyes bright. "I'm the King of the World."

Beaming, Tommy bent down and mused her hair. "Jack Dawson was from Chippewa Falls."

"Fictional characters don't count," Sophie said.

Adrenaline leaving her body and being awake for twenty-four hours had left Sophie drained. With the three Advil she took to calm the throbbing pain in her shotgun pellet perforated ear, all Sophie wanted to do was pass out on the ratty green sofa in the corner. But the sensor data beckoned her like a treasure map.

"Maria believes."

"Show her your tattoo."

While Sophie plugged her laptop into the converter, Tommy pulled his shirt up to reveal CHEESEHEAD tattooed in large letters across his chest. Maria wrinkled her nose. Sophie shook her head and opened the mapping and tracking program a software specialist in the EPA's Criminal Investigation Division wrote for her.

"I shouldn't be showing you this. It's highly classified. Can I trust you?"

Maria nodded, smiling broadly at the notion of learning secrets.

"See that, right there?" Sophie said to Maria. Even though her machine was pumped up performance-wise, the processor cooling fans whirred processing the terabytes of information.

Morning sun streaked through the windows of their rented Malodini villa as Sophie and Maria stared at the screen together. She was eager to show the young orphan her work, work that someday would make Maria's town livable again so that the next generation of young girls wouldn't have to grow up alone.

"Those orange and red dots?"

"Yes." Sophie said. "When they dump. We see. We can stop them. We're in control now."

"And are you seeing what I'm seeing?" Tommy said. "Picking up tardum deposits, beryllium, tetrachloride and even traces of toluene." She peeked over her laptop and met his eyes. "You did it."

"*We* did it, Agent Jones."

And that was just with four sensors deployed. The data coming in was undeniable. Sophie's plan worked. Still, she mused, that didn't mean the broader problem would be solved. Shut down one site and polluters would find another. There was always money to be made scouring the EU for waste to dump in Italy, always another town to poison.

In Italy, a whole middle class of independent brokers called *stakes*, drove the country's toxic pollution disposal business. Stakes were usually well educated and impeccably dressed. Appearance was everything to a stake. After studying environmental policy in the States or the UK, they returned home to Italy to act as middlemen in the giant illicit money-making enterprise.

"I have a better way," the stake would say as an entree to a chemical plant owner or electronics manufacturer about the high cost of complying with EU environmental regulations. "Cheaper in the long run," was the sales pitch. Then the stake contracts with the Camorra to dump and burn. Everyone makes money. Their independence and lack of involvement in the crime syndicate's other businesses, like drugs, kidnapping and guns, made them much harder to track by law enforcement. By design.

As far as Sophie knew, if Italian-like stakes did operate in America, they hadn't popped up on the EPA's radar. No need for them. Polluters had a different system back home. They cut fat checks to politicians right out in the open when they needed the kind of help stakes trafficked in Italy. But what was dumped on Vesuvius was conducted by no ordinary stake. There was an elite broker operating on the mountain. One who could coordinate the disposal of the type of highly dangerous materials that got you a first-class ticket to the Hague. No one had yet identified the person, but Sophie had been briefed that the PSC had a few suspects under surveillance.

"Time to give my biggest fan the good news."

"What did you ever do to that guy?" Tommy said.

"Long story." Sophie squeezed Maria. "Be back in a second. Then I'll take you to the orphanage."

"But I want to stay here tonight. Tommy promised to teach me cribbage."

"You know the rules. The sisters are very strict. No more than four nights a week here."

"I hate it there." Maria started crying. It made Sophie's heart ache. Which, of course, was the point. She kissed Maria on the head. "Fine, I'll ask if you can stay the night once I get done with my call. No promises."

Sophie left Maria and walked into her bedroom. From a safe in her closet Sophie retrieved the phone assigned to her. Like their satellite uplink, it utilized military intelligence encryption. Her in-country supervisor warned Sophie to use it judiciously. The Camorra employed Russian intelligence trained hackers and experts in cyber-intrusion as part of their counter-surveillance capabilities.

Special Agent in Charge Owen Davies answered. Davies ran EPA's Transnational Desk for its Office of International Affairs. He coordinated Sophie's current operation with Interpol and the Italian government from his desk in Brussels. When working in the States, she reported to the Agency's Criminal Investigation Division regional director. But on foreign operations, Agent Davies was her de facto supervisor.

"Agent Grant," he said, not trying to hide his disgust.

"*Special Agent in Charge*, Grant."

"I'm aware." There was a clicking sound. Davies was biting his nails over the phone. "You should know I'm on the record opposing giving you a command position."

"I'm aware."

"I'd always assumed HQ knew what a fuck up you could be, but apparently someone *waaaay* up in the rafters likes you."

Sophie didn't know how many times she'd tried to explain her motives. Davies knew the whole story but chose not to care. As for who in upper management had decided Sophie was ready to lead her own case again, she couldn't say.

"You saw the after-action report?" Sophie said, anxious to change the subject. She had dashed off her initial accounting of events in an email to Davies while they were still fresh.

"I did. Two Marines injured and five Camorra KIA? Were you able to insult the pope, too?"

Sophie reached to her aching, bandaged ear, and decided not to mention it to Davies. Speaking in fast chunks of information, Sophie detailed the night's operation, from the destruction of her SPAGO to the rolling gun battle. After Sophie forwarded Davies a batch of the recent data, he grudgingly authorized Sophie and Tommy to keep plowing ahead with the sensor and mapping tests. Two replacement SPAGO's would be fast-tracked and flown into Italy by the following week. Davies told Sophie in no uncertain terms that he was assigning another squad of Marines to a twenty-four-hour protection detail. They would be arriving in Malodini within a day. He just needed the orders to clear. Until then they should be on high alert and always armed.

"My life may be easier with you gone, but the paperwork would be murder," he said, then hung up without saying goodbye.

"Sheboygan." She heard Tommy say from the other room. She walked into the space. Tommy was pointing at his computer screen. "Remember the air quality samples you asked me to take while we were up there? On Vesuvius?"

"Yes?"

"I wouldn't recommend an overnight stay, but the particulate counts are much lower than we thought. Might not even have to wear masks next time."

"Better safe than—"

There were three rapid knocks on their front door. With her phone, Sophie accessed the video from a security cam they had mounted over the front door. A tall dark man with a thin beard stood outside the door. Behind him, a silver BMW sedan was parked on the road in front of their villa.

Sophie waved Maria into her bedroom. She and Tommy both drew their sidearms and spread out on either side of the door.

"*Chiela*? Who's there?"

"Carter Boyd. I'm with the US State Department. I'm looking for EPA Special Agent in Charge Sophie Grant."

"ID."

The man held up a laminated badge with his picture identifying him as a US State Department senior foreign service officer to the camera. Sophie and Tommy holstered their pistols. She opened the door.

"I'm Grant," Sophie said. "Is this about last night? Because we coordinated everything through Interpol and—"

"No, it's not about last night, it's about your sister," Carter said, shaking his head.

"I don't have a sister."

"Sorry. Half-sister. Madeline Nicchi?"

Sophie's vision blurred so fast she thought she was having a stroke. "What about Madeline?"

"She's dead."

CHAPTER 6

Luca Pecora had been on his own since he was fifteen. He felt just as isolated and alone today, except a sprawling criminal empire counted on his leadership to survive.

The same 1980 earthquake that devastated Naples and dropped an apartment building on his parents, also gave rise to the modern System. Two thirds of the government relief was siphoned off by the crime syndicate, supercharging the organization's growth. At the same time, with no help to rebuild, destroyed neighborhoods became slums. Breeding grounds for illicit trades. An infinite well of street soldiers.

The System took in Luca. Taught him how to sell drugs. Taught him how to kill. Taught Pecora how to trust others in an untrustworthy business, and how to be ruthless when that trust was violated.

"Luca. They are ready for you."

He sat in the second story office of a warehouse in the Port of Naples. An empty Singapore-based container ship could be seen moored through a window to his left. To his right, another window through which rows of barrels disappeared into the warehouse's bowels.

Chiara Opizzi held out a tablet computer to her boss. Tall and thin, she wore a blue pantsuit and an American style baseball cap with a dark ponytail coming out the back. The hat was the white and blue colors of SSC Naples Soccer Club with the number *10* outlined in gold glitter. What was the point? Poor Chiara was living in the past. *Once Maradona left, it was over,* Pecora thought. Napoli would never see greatness again. He took the tablet.

A live video feed played on the device. It showed a Nigerian man, naked to the waist, bathed in sweat, his face red and swollen. His hands were both tied palms down to a wooden table with thick wire so tight, blood seeped from his wrists.

"Please, please don't..." the man said in hard to decipher Italian. "I promise..."

"We had an agreement. Sell all the heroin you want in Castel Volturno. But here you are. Dealing drugs. In Naples."

From behind the Nigerian one of Pecora's men appeared. With two practiced chops with a razor-sharp hatchet, he severed all the fingers on the Nigerian's right hand. Before the man could scream, two more chops, five more orphaned digits. Pecora handed the tablet back to Chiara.

"Tell them to collect all ten. Take them to the house."

Chiara, the daughter of Pecora's predecessor and an experienced killer in her own right, looked like she was going to be sick.

"Forgive me, Luca, but is that necessary?"

"I admit it's unpleasant. Extreme. But when the Americans arrive, I need them to pay attention."

"I understand."

"On to the next unpleasantness."

Pecora stood and walked to the interior door next to the window. Fit and in his mid-fifties, Pecora strode with the air of a bird of prey. He wore a tight fitting black T-shirt with a tanned, shaved head, his face dominated by a great halberd nose and framed by a long, dark beard. Before opening the door, he turned to Chiara.

"How mad is he?"

"Mad?" Chiara looked down for a moment, then back up at Pecora. "Mr. Sokolov is... concerned."

Chiara was being diplomatic. Andre Sokolov rarely left his fortified enclave above Positano. For him to come in person to the warehouse was a signal that their Russian partner was very displeased with what was happening on Vesuvius.

"We're all concerned, Chiara."

The warehouse, one of dozens along the waterfront of the world's third busiest port, was owned by the Pecora System. It operated with a false front section filled to the ceiling with canned San Marzano tomatoes. Should a cop not on their payroll poke around the Pecora property, he would find nothing nefarious about the building.

As a force of habit, Pecora touched a panel next to the door. A separate exit, designed to meld unnoticed into the wall sprung open. Beyond it was a fire escape down to the parking lot. *Always have more than one exit plan*, he thought. It had saved him before. Every warehouse the Pecora System owned had the same escape route installed. Pecora closed the secret door.

With Chiara following, they went through the office door and descended a steel staircase to a narrow hallway. The hallway was lined with a dozen doors on either side. The air was hot and damp. An old woman with a deep-lined face and sweat-stained scarf popped out of a door, expelling a cloud of steam into the hallway. When she spied Pecora and Chiara approaching, the woman squeaked and pulled her head back inside, slamming the door shut behind her.

Much of Chiara's time was spent managing their counterfeit fashion enterprise. The Pecora System rented out individual sew and tailor spaces to Naples residents engaged in a sharecropper-like business with the syndicate. Pecora's people acquired new designs from the elite brand fashion houses in Milan. For a hefty sum they handed the designs to workers trained in the exacting age-old seamstress culture of Naples. And for higher fees they rented workspaces and sold the knockoffs for them.

Pecora was also aware that Chiara chaffed at the job. He had no children, no family to groom for his position when he was gone. Chiara was it. One day she would takeover the Naples System and needed to know every facet of the organization, whether she cared for one revenue stream over another. They all mattered. Good thing the woman was clever and ambitious, and most important, cold-blooded when needed. Traits inherited from her father.

At the end of the hallway was a locked door. Chiara punched a code on a pad next to the door and it swung open. Inside were rows of yellow-and-blue-stripped barrels.

"*Che cazzo! Fanculo!*" Pecora said to Chiara. "Why didn't I listen?"

What happened up on Mount Vesuvius last night was his mistake and his alone. Chiara had warned him. Several times. They employed a cadre of ex-intelligence Agency experts and operatives for their System's counter-intelligence efforts. She told Pecora the day the American woman from the EPA landed in Italy they needed to kill her.

But Pecora hesitated. Waived Chiara off. Murdering a US federal officer brought attention. Attention they didn't need. Her father, who ran the System in Naples before Pecora, discovered that fact in a hail of early morning bullets. A fusillade delivered by an international DEA strike team after he had two of their agents killed. Plus, Pecora was fighting a turf war with the Nigerians. The West Africans were intent on encroaching on their drug-dealing territory. How many different fronts could he battle on and survive?

Now, because of his poor decision, Pecora had a huge problem—a warehouse stuffed with hundreds of fifty-gallon drums of tardum, forty squat barrels of cadmium sulfide and three dozen containers of concentrated toxic residue from the fire-fighting foam PFOA. Plus, two new pallets stacked with dangerous dioxin cans. The weedkiller was banned in most countries since the American's employed it as the defoliant Agent Orange in Vietnam. The dioxin shipment had arrived from Bulgaria four days earlier by cargo ship around the same time eighty thousand euros landed in Pecora's account as payment.

While guns and drugs were both important revenue streams, hazardous materials, the deadlier the better, paid the bills. Bills that would start to go unpaid after last night's fiasco on Vesuvius. The Americans killed five of his men while installing monitoring sensors Chiara said they still had no clue how to disable. The devices were buried too deep in the heart of the ancient volcano.

But Pecora's most pressing problem was with his stake. The

short, broad-shouldered man with a tight black-and-gray beard stood by the rows of barrels. Barrels brokered by Sokolov.

"Why are you here, Andre?" Pecora walked to Sokolov and gripped his hand. "We've worked hard over the years to keep you and your involvement secret."

"First. The phone." Sokolov held his hand out, palm up.

Pecora reached into his pocket and produced a silver and red phone custom made by a private Israeli security firm for Sokolov. The device employed 256-bit AES encryption and was used by defense forces worldwide for secure communications among each other. It was the only way for Pecora to reach him and vice a versa. Sokolov pocketed the device and from the opposite side of his body produced a silver and blue phone of near identical size.

"They finally solved the biometrics issue," he said in refined Italian that still carried a whiff of his native Russian accent. Sokolov handed the phone to Pecora. As Luca understood it, while fingerprint scanners for modern smartphones were ubiquitous, they kept several copies in their memory. Not ideal for anyone helming a criminal enterprise on Interpol's turf. Pecora had spent a lot of money and resources to keep his biometric data secret.

"I'm here because the Americans have you in their sights. I'm here because the CIA almost trapped you on that yacht. I'm here because Pico is in their custody and singing like bird. I'm here because of what's on that mountain is too valuable." Sokolov took off his pair of round Windsor glasses and held the lens up to the light. "You kill the EPA woman. Tonight."

"No," Pecora said. "Too risky. They still don't know what's up there. It will tip our hand if we send more men." He held his hands out in mock surrender. "She has US Marines protecting her."

Pecora had faced down armed men wanting him dead. Exchanged gunfire with the police. Watched friends brutally die in those early days on the streets pushing cocaine and heroin. He ran a vaunted Mafia clan, could muster one hundred foot soldiers with one call, and lorded over billions in business conducted through the Port of Naples.

But telling Sokolov no? That took real courage.

Unlike the other stakes making deals with Camorra families, Sokolov only had one customer—Pecora. The man's connections spanned from Boko Haram in Africa to the highest levels of the Federal Security Service of the Russian Federation—what used to be the KGB. Sokolov's network enabled the Pecora System to sell the weapons they got from America to a worldwide black market willing to pay top dollar, while also finding the perfect customers desperate to offload toxic waste no one else would take. For which Sokolov took a healthy cut of the profits.

But the business was changing. After embedding themselves in Italy, Chinese stakes from Hong Kong imported the practices they learned to their highly industrialized homeland and took it to a whole new level. Giant manmade lakes in the Chinese interior were created just to dump waste. Now Sokolov was competing with Chinese stakes for EU waste. A global war over pollution disposal was brewing. He'd taken an American protégée under his wing, planning for the day when Sokolov expanded to the New World.

"I have a better idea," Pecora said. "*Il Ramingo.*"

A look of blissful relief on Sokolov's face was quickly displaced with apprehension. "Will he do it? Remember the deal we struck. His code?"

Pecora nodded. "After he completes another errand for me."

CHAPTER 7

Sophie Grant found catching up on her sleep impossible during the ninety-minute drive from Malodini to Positano. Due to the stomach-lurching hairpin turns on the forty-mile stretch of the coastal *Strada Statale Amalfitana*, all she could do was grip the armrest and try not to vomit.

"It's still hard to believe."

"What is?" Carter said.

"That I needed to leave my work to ID Madeline's body," Sophie said.

"Nothing we can do. Italian law. You're next of kin," Carter said as he turned off the *Amalfitina* and into Positano proper.

The State Department attaché explained that her half-sister died in a boat explosion. Carter seemed affected by Madeline's death. Sad, even. So, even though Sophie was exhausted from a night filled with Molotov cocktails and Camorra goons, she got into Carter's BMW. She blamed sleep deprivation for allowing him to talk her into accompanying him to Positano. Tommy came along as moral support. Maria seemed to understand something important had happened. She didn't complain when they dropped her off at the orphanage. Sophie promised they'd be back to pick her up as soon as they finished. She could stay in touch via text.

"Did you two talk while you were here?" Carter said, somehow driving down a claustrophobic Positano street buzzing with scooter and tourists without killing anyone.

"Nope. Like I said. Hadn't seen Madeline in twelve, maybe thirteen years."

"Quite the coincidence," Tommy said.

"What is?" Sophie said.

"That you and your sister where in Italy at the same time," Tommy said.

Sophie shrugged. "I guess."

She felt a pang of sadness. Sophie had hated that Madeline replaced her for as long as she could remember. But she never actually wanted anything bad to happen to her sister. It wasn't Madeline's fault their father was an asshole. You don't get to choose family.

The car stopped. Carter had parked next to a corner market. After descending five hundred narrow, calf-cramping steps that wound between shops and restaurants, she was on a beach.

"Normally it's packed with people," Carter said over his shoulder. Sophie followed Carter through the sand. On the left side of the beach were hundreds of umbrellas and chairs; on the right a stone dock. And in the center, the public beach, cordoned off with yellow police tape. Behind the tape, parked near the water, was a large black van.

Tommy trailed a few steps behind them, craning his neck up at the dramatic calcareous rock cliffs jam packed with pastel-colored homes. "Sheboygan, I heard it was beautiful, but—"

Approaching the spot where Madeline died, Sophie was hit by a strange sense of obligation. This was her blood. Her family. If she needed to ID the body, it was the least she could do.

A tall woman was standing next to the van as they approached.

"What the hell is she still doing here?" Sophie heard Carter say under his breath.

"Who?"

Carter stopped walking. "Captain Adele Fattore, *Polizia Speciale Campania*."

"I know the PSC," Sophie said. "Liasoned with them for last night's operation."

"Well, she's the major *domo* around here. Twice the System's made attempts on Fattore's life and twice the tough old bird survived,"

Carter said. "Best to let me do the talking."

As they approached, Fattore turned to face them. She smiled but didn't look happy.

"Carter Boyd. What do I owe for another visit from the American State Department to my crime scene? No embassy parties?"

"Crime scene?" Sophie said. She turned to Carter. "I thought it was an accident."

"Pardone," Captain Fattore said. "My English suffers. We still do not know what happened. And you are?"

"Special Agent Sophie Grant, US Environmental Protection Agency."

"Environ—?" Fattore struggled with the pronunciation, but then squinted at Sophie's bandaged ear. "The Americans up on Vesuvius. Helping us with our Camorra problem. I heard something about your incident. Tell me more."

For five minutes Sophie described the gun battle and the deployment of her sensors. Fattore looked particularly concerned by the part of her story when her SPAGO was hit by a Molotov cocktail. "Was it destroyed? Are you hurt?"

Sophie touched her injured ear. "It was. I'm fine, and my agency is sending over a replacement vehicle."

"Good. Good to hear," Fattore said. "But why are you here at the beach?"

Sophie pointed out at the water. "My, um, my sister, *mi sorrella* was on that boat."

"Really?" Fattore stiffened. She looked at Carter for help.

"Yes, half-sister. We got word you needed someone to identify the body?"

"Si, but not the girl, Madeline. The husband." Fattore motioned at the van. Sophie could hear a faint whir of an engine running. "We need you to identify the husband." Fattore took out a notebook and opened it. "Christopher Nicchi. We haven't found your sister's body yet, but we are still looking. The explosion was big. Very big. So, you know, she could be anywhere."

Fattore walked to the van, opened the rear doors. Cold air from the refrigerated compartment hit Sophie in the face. Fattore pulled a stretcher out with a zipped body bag. Fattore unzipped the bag to show her the badly burnt body of what Sophie presumed was her brother-in-law, Chris Nicchi.

"Can you identify him?" Fattore said.

"Never met Chris." Sophie said shrugging. "Only know him from pictures." Sophie started feeling anxious to get back to Malodini. The data from the new sensors was pouring in. And leaving Maria with the nuns for too long increased the odds the girl would get into trouble. There was also the lurking dread she felt talking about her father's family. She'd been careful to the point of insubordination keeping those details from her EPA superiors.

"I must ask. Why are you back here on the beach? Surely the PSC captain has more pressing matters?" Carter said.

Fattore zipped up the bag, pushed the stretcher into the refrigerated van, and closed the doors. She turned back and fixed Carter with a dead-eye stare. To Sophie it looked like Fattore was debating between answering his question or digging her teeth into his neck.

"My family's home is still here. Decided to stay the night." She squinted up at the white stone cliffs and sighed. "When I was growing up in Positano it was just a sleepy little town. Now you have so many tourists, and the Russians. The Russians with their piles of money." she said.

"Are we done here? Can you call me when you find Madeline?"

Fattore shook her head. "Unfortunately, no. Italian law. If a family member is present, you must accompany the body to the morgue. The System. They make everything so hard. They steal corpses and dump them in the ocean if families don't pay a ransom."

"What are you saying?"

"You need to come with me and the body of your brother-in-law to Naples."

CHAPTER 8

Huge gasps of air, in and out, in and out, filled his lungs, blasted oxygen back into his blood and ordered his aching leg muscles to keep pushing. During his hurried decent of three vertical miles from the Attali Mountains back to the blazing cobalt of the Tyrrhenian Sea, the phone in his chest pocket buzzed over and over like a nest of angry hornets. DeSalvo was calling. Always DeSalvo. Concerned he was taking too long to check in. DeSalvo who saved him. DeSalvo who made everything happen.

All he had to do was show up and kill.

Hidden between piles of rotting garbage and walls of dense, lush green foliage, he stood at the mouth of a long-discarded, above-ground sewer system. A century before, the culverts shot waste from the mountain town of Revello down to the Tyrrhenian Sea. The ancient, stone-lined Amalfi aqueduct system built by the Romans, and improved upon by Italian engineers over the centuries, crisscrossed the cliffs of Campania. Before modern plumbing and sewage, the aqueducts brought fresh water to villages and shipped waste to valley lagoons. Today, they were overgrown with weeds and plagued by gaping sinkholes.

For him, since he was a young boy, the aqueducts acted as a covert highway system. Italy was full of such hidden passages. Tunnels and crypts below cities, honeycombed throughout the country, available for clandestine journeys to those few who knew they existed and brave enough to endure the legions of rodents that called them home.

The phone buzzed again. DeSalvo would have to wait.

His tight-fitting black pants and black long-sleeved shirt were soaked with sweat. He removed a pair of matte black, military grade tactical goggles and sat them on a rock. Next, he pulled off a drenched black head sock. Running both his hands over a hairless, scar-laced scalp, he wiped the sweat away.

After unbuckling a small pack strapped around his waist, he removed a cloth, and then touched his right pinky finger to a sensor on his palm. A nine-inch, double-edged Szell knife sprung from a spring-loaded sheath strapped to his forearm. He used the cloth to wipe fresh blood off the blade. After the long knife was clean, he pushed it back in its slot and repeated the action with the Szell strapped to his left forearm.

His front pocket vibrated, again. Removing the flat black phone, he answered.

"Ciao, DeSalvo."

"Il Ramingo."

The name. The name DeSalvo gave him. A name chosen to evoke death and chaos. A name stolen from a devil's hymn that had haunted him his entire life. A name designed to strike fear.

"What took you so long? I was getting worried."

"You know."

DeSalvo chuckled, the sound devolving into a series of electronic hisses. They used voice decoders with new, single-use phones. Years ago, when they worked with Pecora System foot soldiers as spotters, DeSalvo detected eavesdroppers on his phone while Il Ramingo assassinated a magistrate leaving his courthouse in Pompeii. Since then, they employed very strict communications protocols.

"You sound out of breath," DeSalvo said.

"It was harder than we thought."

"Too hard?"

"No."

"But you didn't collect the *pieatara*?"

"I'm about to."

"And the American?"

"Done."

"Are you sure?"

"It was easy." Il Ramingo's chest tightened at the challenge from DeSalvo. "After the explosion, there was panic. He was surrounded by people trying to escape. The only one going to the beach while everyone else ran away. It was easy." He swallowed. "Did you talk to Pecora?"

"Of course. He's pleased you solved the problem for him."

"And you'll tell him? Tell him about violating the code? About how there wasn't supposed to be a woman on the boat?"

"I passed along your concerns." DeSalvo said. There was a click as the line went silent.

Il Ramingo stared at the phone for a full minute before removing the SIM card. He ground the chip into silicon dust under the heel of his boot. Next, he wiped the phone down and then tossed it as far out into the sea as he could throw. From the pack on the ground Il Ramingo retrieved a compact pair of binoculars and scanned the shoreline along Positano's main beach.

Standing among the police officers and emergency personal was a woman he recognized. The raptor-like Captain Adele Fattore ran the *Polizia Speciale Campania* and was very familiar to Il Ramingo. He swung the binoculars to the right down the shoreline, and seeing nothing out of place, back to the left. A tall, dark-skinned man in a blue suit was walking across the sand. He was followed by a shorter woman and a younger man who walked with a purpose he recognized. The man was a soldier.

The first man, the one posing as a US State Department attaché, worked for the CIA. They knew he went by the name Carter Boyd. At least that was the name he used with Madeline and Chris Nicchi. And on his Instagram account. Il Ramingo had recorded their conversations on the yacht. Deeply incriminating conversations about luring Luca Pecora into trap. Probing questions about terrorists buying weapons. Conversations DeSalvo passed on to Pecora. Conversations that lead to death in Positano's bay at Il Ramingo's hands.

Il Ramingo zoomed in on the new woman's face as she was introduced to Fattore. She looked Italian. But her skin was lighter than those from Campania, likely a northerner from Turin or Venice. He wished he could hear what they were discussing. There was a lot of gesturing out into the water.

Fattore opened the doors to the refrigerated van. Showed the woman the body. The new woman shrugged. After a few moments of discussion, the unknown female, Boyd, and the younger man followed Fattore off the beach.

Then came the moment Il Ramingo was waiting for. The van departed and Il Ramingo gathered his belongings. From his pack he removed a reliable disguise. In a flash he went from head-to-toe black tactical gear, to looking like any other vagrant surviving off the wealthy Positano detritus—stained pants, tattered shoes, and a loose and dirty long-sleeved shirt. A floppy sunhat covered his scar-carpeted scalp. He strapped the pack around his waist and left.

While scurrying up the trash-strewn aqueduct, he was stopped by a faint mewing. Peering into a dark hole in between two loose stones, he spied a dirty black kitten entangled in an old extension cord. He pulled it out of the hole, removed the cable from around its legs, and held the feral cat at eye level. The walls of the aqueduct were covered over and over with the same phrase, spray painted on the old stone bricks years ago.

Memento mori.

Il Ramingo carefully set the cat on the ground. It padded away in search of its next meal. After scuttling up the viaduct, he mimicked the lurching and intoxicated gate of one of Positano's homeless. Il Ramingo dodged a shower of garbage dumped from an overheard porch. The viaducts were lined with low-income housing units to keep the lesser advantaged away from the glitz of downtown Positano.

"*Bastrardo,*" he heard a voice from above mutter. Was the man mad he didn't hit him with his trash? One Szell knife extended, and the flick of his wrist, and the fat litterbug would be gurgling his last insult through a severed carotid artery.

Il Ramingo arrived at a junction of the viaduct and a long flight of cement stairs that lead up to the plaza above. Satisfied no one was looking, he shed the homeless disguise while climbing the steps. Once at street level he peered around a corner and spied the black van from the beach carrying Chris Nicchi's body. There was a man in a dark uniform standing next to the van.

It was time for Il Ramingo to claim his prize. A prize secured from all his previous kills but prevented until now by the day's extraordinary events.

Vespas, cars, and pedestrians jostled for room on the tight Positano street. No one witnessed Il Ramingo change back into the black uniform from the pack strapped around his waist. With only a few storefronts between him and the driver it was five quick steps in the crowded street.

"*Excusa?*" Il Ramingo said to the driver.

CHAPTER 9

Texting left-handed, vision hampered by thick sheets of rain glancing off the windshield, David Granttano almost drove his vintage red Mustang GT off the Highway 9 interchange where it crossed Kansas City's 16th Avenue. A thirty-foot drop loomed. To compound the lack of visibility, every other streetlight seemed to be burned out on the North KC Highway. He let the phone drop into his lap to concentrate on driving. David took the exit for Armor Road. Turning right, he drove for two blocks, passing by car washes, check cashing joints and liquor stores. Back in the nineties, the Nicchi would've been earning protection money from every business on this stretch of road.

At the end of the two blocks, David wheeled his Mustang into a dingy used car lot. KC Classic Cars, sandwiched between a shuttered Sears department store and a tattoo parlor, used to be the Nicchi's fence for a thriving car theft operation. Now it just cleaned dirty money.

Not just dirty, but blood-soaked money, David thought.

Littering the lot were vehicles for sale one could charitably refer to as classic. There was a dented Nova SS and a red Volkswagen Karmann Ghia showing clear Bondo patch marks. The cars were priced for poverty-stricken customers desperate for four working wheels, and cool with acrophobic interest rates. He used to have the pick of the lot back when their crew was boosting high dollar rides. David would never drive one of their current junkers. Now he preferred to do his car shopping at the monthly auto show down on Kemper.

David stepped out of his Mustang opening an umbrella. He wore a blue silk shirt and a dark brown blazer and brown pants. Holding the umbrella tight with his right hand to ward off the pounding rain, David used his left to adjust his pants around a swollen belly. Balding, sixty-two, and feeling every minute of it, David lit a cigarette while gazing around the lot.

Squinting into the front glass of the dark dealership's single-story sales office, David could see a light on in the rear of the building. After a couple of drags, he tossed his cigarette, landing with a hiss in a puddle. David shuffled to the front door. It was unlocked. Walking past a desk with computer monitor toward an office in the back with the light on, David gently pushed the door open.

His older brother sat in a chair at his desk, holding in trembling hands a framed picture of his daughter, Madeleine.

"Raymond."

A startled Ray Granttano leapt from his seat, wiping the tears from his creased cheeks.

"Jesus Christ, Davey, what are you doing here?"

Two years older and the fucking guy still looks south of fifty, David thought. Full head of dark hair streaked with gray. Trim and athletic with a square jaw, whereas David's jowls protruded from his face like slab bacon. There used to be a picture on their mother's mantle of their great grandfather and uncle. Both men were young, just out of their teens, leaning on the railing of a migrant steamer departing Palermo, Italy for New York City. David clearly adopted Uncle Giuseppe's pear-shaped body and early pattern baldness, while Ray took to Grandpa Lorenzo's movie star looks.

"Checking in on you."

"You driving that Mustang? Is that a mint sixty-five?"

"Sixty-four and a half."

"What happened to the Charger?"

"Still got it. Parked at the hanger. How you doing?"

Ray slumped into his black office swivel chair clutching the picture of his daughter to his chest. "You shouldn't be here." He pointed at his ear. "You never know who's listening."

"My big brother, always the cop."

"I haven't been a cop for thirty years."

David waved his hand like swatting a fly. "BTO swept everyone yesterday. You included. Clean bills of health all around. And they don't need wires no more, didn't you hear? They just point one of those sonic guns at you from a car or a drone, hit record and off to the clink you go. Feel better?"

"Yeah. I feel fucking fantastic."

In the three years Ray managed the dealership, not one member of the Nicchi crew had stepped foot inside. The organization was small and extremely careful. After surviving a Mafia war, the last thing anyone wanted was twenty years in a federal prison. Ray wasn't a numbers guy. Their boss, Ken Nicchi, had an excellent bookkeeper that did the actual laundering. Ray was the guy they brought in to manage the front business. Implicitly trusted. And as a former police detective, he had a unique ability to identify cops sniffing around their operations. There'd been a succession of laundries before the dealership, like the Subway franchise in Independence, and a print shop downtown by the river. David's favorite was a blues club in Westport that once booked Elvin Bishop. Ray had run them all.

David sat in a chair across from his brother. He pulled a folded white handkerchief from his pocket and handed it to Ray. "I'm really sorry. I don't know what to say. Madeline." David exhaled a deep breath. "She was an angel." He'd buried a lot of friends over the years, but this hurt. David was determined not to wallow in their pain. His boss Ken and his brother Ray had both lost a child. They were brokenhearted. They needed him to remain strong.

Ray took the handkerchief, held it for a moment, his brother realizing he was contemplating whether to throw it back in David's face, then decided to keep it and used the cloth to wipe his eyes. "How's Ken?"

"Like you, I guess. Well, not exactly like you. Watched him take a baseball bat to that vintage Wurlitzer in his office. The one he won from the mayor in a charity poker game?"

"I remember it."

"Ken didn't stop until every forty-five was destroyed. Dust." What David didn't tell his brother was how the Nicchi family boss slumped to the floor, crying, begging God to bring his son back to him. David pulled his chair closer to his brother. From inside his coat pocket a silver flask appeared. After unscrewing the cap, he took a long pull. "Stoli?" He said holding the flask out to Ray. "A toast to the Paris of the Plains and better days?"

Ray shook his head. "None for me. You drunk?"

"Sober as a bird." He took another pull from the flask then put it back in his coat. "How's Gwen taking it?"

"Not great, Davey, not great."

Ray told his brother in a voice laced with feral pain how he gave his wife two Percocet and put her to bed, a sobbing, grief-stricken mess. He figured coming into work would take his mind off Madeline's death. Then, after walking into his office, he spied her picture on his desk.

"I should've told you no."

Ray gestured around the dealership with his hands. "Haven't we taken care of you?" He swallowed. "If you said no to me, to Ken, back in ninety-two? I'd be dead." David made his hand into a gun a pointed at his head. "Bang! Bang! Probably dissolved in a vat of acid so the cops wouldn't find my body. Is that what you want?"

Ray dropped his head. "No."

The two brothers sat in silence while the humming fluorescent lights overhead occasionally flickered. After a while Ray composed himself enough to ask David, "What were they doing over there in the first place? Madeline said it was a vacation."

David paused for a long moment before answering. "It was. I know you don't like to know much. Let's just say while they were there, Chris was negotiating some new business with our international partners."

"And Ken. He say anything about what happened? He talk to anyone over there? An international *partner*?"

David nodded. "He did. Kinda the other reason why I'm here." He removed a thick manila folder, folded in half, from inside his jacket and handed it to his brother.

Ray took the folder and turned it over and over in his hands, stopped, and held it out to David. "Not interested."

David snatched the folder from Ray's hand so hard his brother flinched. After tearing the top off the sealed folder, David shook the contents of the folder out on his brother's desk. A passport tumbled out and landed open next to Madeline's portrait.

"Wheels up nine am. Ken thought you'd want to come along. You know, for Madeline and Chris, to bring 'em back home."

Ray picked up the passport. It was his picture. "Greg Clayton from Council Bluffs? What else are you doing over there, Davey?"

"We've been summoned," David sipped from his flask, "for a meeting."

"Isn't the whole idea behind international partners is that you never have to meet face to face?" Ray fixed his cornflower blue eyes on his brother's. "Unless—"

"Unless what?"

"It wasn't an accident, was it Davey?"

CHAPTER 10

Once again, Sophie Grant was traveling the twisting Amalfi Highway, having left Positano for Naples. Tommy sat in the front passenger seat while Sophie rode in the back. Fattore and one of her men were in a police car in front of them, the coroner's van carrying Chris's body trailing. Bouncing around the backseat as they wove between tight turns and stomach sloshing elevation changes, she prayed the official business with her brother-in-law would be brief. Sophie needed to get back to Malodini.

"The coroner's van. He's really up on my bumper," Carter said from behind the wheel.

Sophie turned and peered through the rear window at the vehicle filling the entire field of vision.

"We're on the Strata Amalfi. Maybe he's just trying to keep up?" Tommy said.

Her phone chirped with a message from Maria, saying the other kids were hassling her at the orphanage, asking when Sophie would return to Malodini. She'd call once they stopped. It's not like Sophie was enjoying the journey to Naples. Sophie could feel the stress inside her building. She was tired and more than anxious to process the data streaming in from Mount Vesuvius. And her injured ear throbbed.

"What a cool place," Tommy said, twisting his neck to marvel at the steep walls of rock on one side and the ocean on the other. "The water is so crazy blue. Like a movie."

"Except the Italians overfished it. Now the Tyrrhenian Sea is effectively dead," Sophie said. "Trawlers have to go deep into the

Med just to serve the local restaurants. Though to be fair, our Gulf of Mexico is in worse shape."

"Not a very optimistic worldview coming from a self-proclaimed champion of the environment," Carter said.

Sophie snorted. "We're driving Earth into a coma, and no one gives a shit," Sophie said. "I'm no champion." She gestured at Tommy. "We're cops chasing criminals. Nothing more."

"You do," Tommy said. "You give a shit."

"About people, Agent Jones. I care about people. Mother Earth? Gaia? Terra? We're parasites. There's only saving people." Sophie leaned her head back. "And you can't save everyone."

"You can try," Tommy said.

"Okay, rookie."

Tommy's cheeks flushed. He slunk down in his seat, mute.

"So why do autopsies in Naples? Not in Positano?" Sophie said to Carter in the front seat. Calling Tommy had been a mistake. She was desperate to change the subject.

"Italy." Carter barked out a laugh at his own joke. According to the State Department attaché, the Italian government was so broke Naples handled all the autopsies for most of Campania.

Sophie's head snapped back, and the BMW lurched forward as the corner's van rammed them from behind.

Carter's head whipped around. "Is he drunk?"

The next time the van slammed into the rear bumper of their car, it was with such force that for a moment both rear wheels left the ground. Sophie shot headlong into the front of the car, lodging in between Carter and Tommy, the roar of the van's engine filling her ears. Since Carter's foot was still pressed down on the accelerator, both tires hit the pavement with a squeal, sending the car rocketing forward, and slamming Sophie back into the rear seat. Looking through the windshield, Sophie's vision filled with nothing but blue ocean as they crossed over the oncoming lane, hurtling toward the ribbon-thin barrier lining the Amalfi Highway.

Tommy reached out and grabbed the steering wheel, and yanked it to the right. The car veered back across the road amidst a blizzard of honking horns from oncoming traffic. They passed again through their original lane, crashing to an abrupt stop against a rock wall.

"Godammit!" Carter said, touching his nose and wincing after bouncing his face off the steering wheel. "Is it bleeding?"

"Anyone hurt?" Tommy said.

Despite a few bruises Sophie felt fine. They hadn't hit the wall that hard, just with enough force to buckle the hood and lodge them in the rock.

"I'm okay. Good save, Tommy."

She met his eyes and he smiled. "Sheboygan."

For twenty minutes they waited next to the car, hugging the rock wall as traffic rushed by on the Amalfi Highway. Sophie used the time to call Maria. The little girl answered on the first ring.

"When are you coming home?" There was a sniffle on the other end of the call. Maria was trying not to cry. The small gesture of bravery made Sophie's heart ache.

"I'll be home in two hours, three tops, promise. We'll finish our game."

A pair of police cars and a tow truck appeared. While the police stopped traffic, the truck pulled Carter's BMW out from the rock wall with high pitched squeal of ripping metal. The engine still turned over and the wheels were straight. Carter spoke briefly with the cops. He learned that the coroner's van had been found off an unpaved mountain spur connecting the Amalfi Highway to the higher elevation of the Attalli Mountains. Fattore was already on scene.

When they arrived, two police motorcycles were parked on their kickstands next to the coroner's black van. In front of the van was Fattore's PSC car. The motorcycle cops were bent over someone on the ground next to the vehicle. As they got closer, Sophie recognized the person sitting on the gravel road was Captain Fattore.

The captain was handcuffed to the door handle of her police

car, hat off and blood running down the back of her neck. Crimson trickled from her left nostril. One of the motorcycle cops was using a small saw to cut through the handcuff chain. Carter brought the car to a gravel crunching stop. The three of them leapt out, with Carter reaching Fattore first.

"Adele? Captain, are you okay?"

"He killed Clemeto. The man had two young daughters." She sounded out of it to Sophie, likely from a blow to the head.

Sophie and Tommy peered inside the car and didn't see anyone. They walked around the vehicle each taking one end and met on the other side at the body of Officer Clemento. The man lay on his back, arms outstretched in dark pool of his own blood, two clear stab wounds in his chest. Both deep punctures were of near equal dimension and in the exact same spot on either side of his heart, severing both pulmonary arteries.

"*Mio Dio.*" Fattore dropped her head. "We found the van, but when I got out he must have struck me from behind. When I woke up, Clemento was dead and I was handcuffed to the van."

An excited voice came over the motorcycle cops' radios, speaking too fast in Italian for Sophie to catch.

"They found the van driver," Carter said. "Positano. Two stab wounds to the chest. Did you get a good look at him?" Carter said.

Fattore shook her head. "It doesn't make sense."

"What doesn't?"

With a metallic snap, the saw cut through Fattore's handcuffs. Carter and Tommy helped her to her feet. Sophie pressed a handkerchief against the gash on the back of her head. "I should be dead. Why not kill me?"

"Captain!" With Fattore freed, the motorcycle cops searched the van. One of them came running with something in his hand while the other threw the rear doors open.

"It was on the driver's seat," the cop said and handed the object to Fattore. With a shaking hand she passed it to Carter. "From a friend of yours."

Looking over Carter's shoulder, Sophie saw a red, horn-shaped trinket the size of a crayon in his palm. A *cornicello*. On the charm's side was etched two words.

"*Memento mori?* Remember death?"

"Not quite," Carter said under his breath to her.

"*Merda santa!*" The other cop shouted from the rear of the coroner's van. In the cargo bay of the van lay Chris Nicchi's corpse. The sheet was thrown off the burnt body.

Chris's head was missing.

"Someone killed the driver? To impersonate him, to steal my brother-in-law's head?" Sophie said. "Who would do that?"

Carter Boyd held the *cornicello* aloft.

"I have a guess."

"Tell us," Sophie said.

"Not here."

CHAPTER 11

"First class? First class is for suckers."

An animated Jimmy Nicchi stood in the aisle near the cockpit door. Ray Granttano noticed none of the other passengers were listening to him. The younger, and much more alive other son of the Nicchi family patriarch was wearing a blue short-sleeved polo shirt. Ray speculated Jimmy selected the color solely to draw attention to the carpet of orange freckles running up his arms and out the shirt's neck hole.

Ken Nicchi sat to the left of his remaining son in a soft leather chair, holding a glass of whiskey. Off his elbow and out the window of their charted private jet, the Atlantic Ocean radiated indigo. Ray and his brother were seated across the aisle. The rest their crew were ensconced in a pod of chairs near the tail, noisily playing cards.

"You'll change your tune when you're paying the bill," Ken said.

"Sorry, Dad, just excited I guess."

Jimmy ran a hand through his thinning red curly hair. "Apparently spaghetti *alle vongole* is where it's at in Naples. And there's supposed to be an amazing place by our hotel that serves nothing but *ragu*. The diner reviews? Five stars."

Ray was thankful for Jimmy's adolescent clown act. Better to fixate on the dumb shit flying out of his face than dwell on his beautiful girl, gone forever. Ray also found it amusing that for mobsters so proud of their Italian heritage, not one of the Nicchies had been to Italy before.

Big but strong, like a silverback gorilla, all thick arms and shoulders and a boulder for a stomach, neck rolls like a layer cake, Ken Nicchi pointed a ballpeen finger at his son. "This is a business trip. If you eat nothing but smoked almonds from the minibar when you're in Naples, all I want to hear when get home is 'Great trip, Pop.' Got it?"

"Yes, Dad."

"Don't worry, kid, we'll get to eat plenty," David said, patting him on the knee.

Dressed in a gray coat and pants with a dull yellow shirt, David threw back the rest of the bourbon in his glass, held it up and shook the half-melted ice like a maraca. A flight attendant replaced it with a full drink.

David kept slapping Ray and Ken on their backs, asking them if everything was alright. As if Ken and Ray were the same. Even though Chris Nicchi had acted like he was ready to take over the family business, Ray knew for a fact in the end, his son-in-law wanted a better life for his little girl. *Too little, too fucking late,* he thought.

"What is that? Your third?" Ray said.

"When am I going to fly on a private jet again?"

Ray clutched a full whiskey glass to his chest, the alcohol diluted from melted ice. He was in no mood to drink. Really hadn't been since he met Gwen. He looked around at the leather and polished wood. The private plane must be costing Ken a fortune. David told him they had people working on both sides of the business aviation terminals to ensure the Nicchi crew would arrive in Naples hassle free. Ray kept hearing grumbles about not being able to bring guns. Ken reassured the men he had it covered once they were on the ground in Italy.

"Then you take the romaine from Trader Joe's, costs you maybe a buck, buck-fifty tops, put it in a plain paper bag, write *organic* on the bag with a Sharpie, presto, six bucks."

Jimmy had moved on to explaining his latest minor hustle, involving selling cheap produce at a premium at the downtown Kansas City farmers market.

"Rich idiots. They clean me out every weekend."

Poor Jimmy, thought Ray, *he probably figured now that his brother Chris was dead, James Nicchi was next in line to lead his father's crew.* Chris, seemingly laboratory-designed to succeed his father. The guy had been a lion, born to lead the pride, and he swept Ray's little girl right off her feet.

And now he was flying to Italy to retrieve her corpse.

"Get him a fresh drink," Ken said sticking his chin out at Ray. "All his ice is melted. What's the matter, you don't like bourbon? That's twenty-year Pappy Van Winkle. Top shelf shit."

"Not thirsty," Ray said.

"I know how you feel," Ken said. He leaned over and squeezed Ray's knee. "You lost your girl, and I lost my boy. No parent should outlive their kids."

Ray stood. "I'm going to the commode." He passed the second seating pod where five hard looking men were playing cribbage. Ray only knew one of them. BTO, a big, tightly coiled guy with a ponytail and a dark goatee in charge of Nicchi's security. Came by the dealership from time to time to sweep for bugs. According to David, BTO was former US Special Forces and had survived three deployments to Afghanistan. The rest, David said, were ex-military, too.

After a while, when all the old bosses in Chicago and New York went to jail or died, and their replacements went to jail and or died, and the guys that replaced them faced an all-new world, crawling with ruthless competitors and near unbeatable law enforcement surveillance capabilities, Ken Nicchi felt comfortable enough to emerge from exile. He carefully built his new crew with ex-military types like the ones on the plane, cycling back into society from the endless War on Terror.

By the looks of the stacks of bills on the table, they were playing for serious money. Ray met eyes with BTO. He nodded and then when back to his cards. Once inside the coffin-sized bathroom, Ray splashed water on his face and used a white terrycloth towel to dry off. Gripping the sink with both hands, Ray stared into the mirror.

Keep it together. Your girl needs you.

Exiting the bathroom, Ray walked back past the group at the rear of the plane. As he got near his seat, he heard Ken say to his brother, "You sure he's going to be fine?"

Ray retook the leather chair next to Ken and across from his brother. "My eggplants are burning. You guys talking about me?"

Ken snorted. "Ray Granttano. Always the smart ass. So, your brother tells me he didn't get a chance to walk you through what's going down at the meeting with the Camorra."

"Who's that?"

"C'mon, Ray." David said. "Our partners in Italy?"

"Just messing with you guys. Course I know."

"What else you know?" Ken said.

"Well, not much more. I try not to pry."

"Bullshit. Fucking bullshit. You were a detective." Ken pointed a beefy finger at Ray. "A smart one."

Indeed, Ray had been paying attention to the Nicchi crew's business when he shouldn't have been. The deal he made with Ken years ago included a generous salary in exchange for his name on a lease and an ear for eavesdropping cops. Nothing else. Their success so far hinged on Ray not knowing anything deeper about their businesses. Many times, his old colleagues on the force had tried to get him to talk about one illicit Nicchi front business or another. Ray had been able to lie then, using the veneer of deniability. Now stuck on a plane with the boss, he needed to make a decision. Come clean? Or feign ignorance? One choice had the potential of getting tossed from the Gulfstream over the ocean without a parachute.

"You were?" Jimmy Nicchi said. "A cop? Really?"

"Long time ago, kid," David said.

"Probably knows more about our work than you, Jimmy." Ken continued pressing him. "C'mon, spill your guts."

Ray took a deep breath and decided to let it all hang out. "Best I can tell is you have more than one source inside Fort Leonard Wood.

Now besides it being a huge goddamn Army base, Leonard Wood is also home to an advanced weapons testing facility. Figure you get whatever you can from the base, and since you do a lot of business down in New Orleans, and have an office at the KC grain terminal, you ship it down the Mississippi hidden in barges of corn. Maybe soybeans. Whatever. Same goes for the waste side. I imagine with all the fracking still going on up north. In the Bakken fields there's more than a few companies that would rather pay you to get rid of their shit than risk an EPA audit. Whatever comes through, guns, drugs, toxic waste, it goes from New Orleans to Naples. From there I really don't have a good guess."

Ray looked across the faces of Ken Nicchi, his brother and Jimmy. "Did I get it right?"

Ken laughed and slapped Ray on the leg. "Well done, officer. Well fucking done." He stuck his hands out to Ray. "Slap the cuffs on. You passed."

"Passed?"

"Passed the audition."

"Here you go." David took a hundred-dollar bill from his wallet and handed it to Ken. "You were right, he was playing dumb."

"It's not playing dumb, it's called plausible deniability," Jimmy said. "Right Ray?"

"Right, Jimmy." The younger Nicchi beamed at the compliment. Ray wondered how many times he'd skip on the ocean's surface at this speed.

"Here's something you don't know," Ken said, his voice pivoting from bemusement to stone cold. "Something you won't be able to deny."

"What's that?" Ray said.

"Our Camorra partner. In Italy. His name is Luca Pecora. The waste? He dumps it. What we get out of Leonard Wood? He ships it out again."

"Where does it go?"

"I really can't say." Ken sipped his drink, offering a wry grin. "But it's usually very hot and very sandy."

"And this . . . Pecora? Luca Pecora? He's who invited us to Italy? Does he know who killed my girl?"

"That's what we're about to find out."

Ken stood and motioned for Jimmy to move out of his seat. After his son stood, Ken plopped his bulk down next to Ray. "And when we learn who killed our kids, we can take turns pounding the son of a bitch into hamburger with a claw hammer."

"I'd like that," Ray said with a hundred percent honesty.

"Now I'm telling you this not because I think you need to know. It's the exact opposite. We've all stayed out of jail because we keep our shit internal. Compartmentalized. But you were able to sniff out a lot of what we're doing. I need you in that room when Pecora tells us what happened to our kids. Do the same thing to him."

"Because you think he was involved?"

Ken shrugged. "Maybe. We don't know." Ken explained the reason he sent Chris as an emissary was to probe the possibility of negotiating a new deal with Pecora. A deal that would rachet down selling weapons, but dramatically increase the amount of toxic waste shipped out of the country. There was just too much heat on the stolen arms and zero attention in the States on environmental crime.

"But you don't need to know about that. It was just a trial balloon. I'm telling you because Chris had strict instructions not to push Pecora."

"Should we be worried? About an ambush?"

David jerked his thumb toward the back of the plane and the raucous card game. "Sure. But that's why we brought those guys."

"Unarmed guys."

Ken put an arm around Ray's shoulders and winked. "BTO has it covered. Your worry, mister former detective, is to watch. Listen. Tell us if Pecora's lying. Think you can handle that?"

"Won't this Pecora think it's weird that I'm there?"

"You lost your daughter. He'll respect that," Ken said.

Ray realized that Ken had not thought this through. That he was walking into a trap.

"I'll take that whiskey now."

CHAPTER 12

Despite repeated pleas by both Sophie and Tommy to explain who took Chris Nicchi's head, and why, the State Department attaché remained tight-lipped most of the ninety-minute drive from Positano to Naples.

"My boss really wants to be the one to tell you."

Carter plunged the BMW into the center of Naples. They were engulfed by a rowdy symphony of honking horns, roaring engines and dozens of voices screaming at each other in Italian. Swarming around them were pedestrians, scooters, and cars all jostling for position in a chaotic four-lane traffic circle. Every available artery in the dense city of Naples seemed to converge at this one junction in the Corso Umberto neighborhood, so notoriously busy it had the name *Centro Storico*. Sophie found the massive metropolis to be by far the noisiest city in a country not exactly known for bland, reserved citizens. But the food was dynamite and Naples's unique energy contagious.

Three blocks past the motor-vehicle insanity of Centro Storico, Carter directed his BMW into a dense block of Naples's inner city where the buildings were thin, vertical storefronts like rows of books on a shelf. He steered the sedan to an old, crumbling hotel. Above a stone archway that looked to lead inside the taverna, the faded, chipped words Absolute Love were painted in Italian.

Absoulte Amore.

The building was sea-beaten from proximity to the harbor, though the steel doors closed under the stone archway looked sturdy and new. Carter pulled a card out of his pocket. He held it to a black box sticking out of the ground on a thick pole. The metal gates swung open to reveal a small courtyard and another set of windowless gates. Carter drove into the courtyard and the first set of gates swung shut behind them.

"Curds," Tommy said.

Out of nowhere four men in plainclothes with automatic weapons appeared, one on each corner of the vehicle. Sophie flashed back to the moment on the beach when Captain Fattore asked Carter about missing an embassy party, and the brief horror stricken look on his face. Sophie realized what was so different about Foreign Service Officer Carter Boyd, and why she was growing wary of the man.

"You're CIA. I should've known."

"What?" Tommy said. "Really?"

"State Department? Seriously? Are you just being lazy? Gotta say if my country is relying on you and paper-thin cover identities to keep us safe from terrorists, I'm very worried."

Carter snorted. "Guilty as charged."

Sophie was pissed. She didn't like being lied to. What the hell had her sister and brother-in-law been doing in Italy that would have involved them with the CIA? Whatever it was would explain their death, and Sophie suspected she'd soon find out.

"You're a spy? You don't look like a spy," Tommy said.

"That's the point," Carter said.

The gates swung open to reveal another courtyard, this one with five vehicles parked off to the side. Carter slid the BMW next to a black Land Rover and turned the car off. Sophie noted that where the exterior of the hotel was in a rugged state of disrepair, the interior was relatively new construction. And swarming with armed and obvious American black ops military personal. She remembered that the CIA called their muscle Special Operations Group, or SOGs, and were culled from the cream of retired front-line elite troops.

"What happened to Carter?" Tommy said, his head on a swivel.

While Sophie was examining the inner courtyard turned mini-military base, Carter Boyd had slipped away. If that really was his name. One of their armed four-man SOG escorts motioned Sophie and Tommy out of the car.

"Do what they say," Sophie said to Tommy.

They both got out of the BMW. The same member of the security team that waved them out of the car relieved them of their sidearms. They were whisked to the hotel's front desk, which had been converted into a high-tech security gate, complete with a walkthrough scanner manned by two SOGs armed with M4s with grenade launchers mounted underneath. Satisfied they held no secret weapons or bombs, Sophie and Tommy were escorted up a flight of stairs to the floor above. Sophie figured since it looked to span almost the entire floor and five still intact chandeliers hung from the ceiling, that they were in the former hotel's dining room.

"Sit here and wait," a member of their security escort said pointing at a conference table surrounded by metal folding chairs. The quartet left. Sophie presumed to guard the outer gate or possibly help topple a Third World government.

"Special Agent in Charge Grant, Agent Jones, welcome, to *Assoluta Amore*."

Before them stood a bald, deeply tanned man with a shocking white beard. He was of medium height and missing his left arm, the sleeve of his red navy polo shirt pinned to the shoulder.

The man cleared his throat. "Bill Hodges," he said. "Chief of Station."

At least the spook respected her enough to not beat around the bush. *Don't get reeled in,* she told herself. With these guys it was always an appetizer of filet mignon before they served you a main course of a plate piled high with extra rare shitburgers.

"Except this isn't the CIA station. That's in Rome. And this isn't a safehouse, it's a fortress," Sophie said.

Hodges smiled, his white beard curving upward making him

look impish. "We're in the old, old part of town. Lots of commercial renovations are going on around here. You can scrape a rundown hotel clean and build a state-of-the-art operations center." He shrugged. "No one's the wiser."

"What kind of operation are you running?"

Carter appeared behind Hodges. "The secret kind."

Under Hodges's arm was a tablet computer. He placed it on the table before taking a seat in a folding chair across from Sophie. "You're right. Not our typical safehouse. Back in Roman times, Naples was more of forward operating base." He waved at a dilapidated fresco on the dining room wall. The painting depicted a massive fight between swarms of archers on horseback and divisions of manned elephants. "The Battle of Zama. During the Punic Wars. Naples was the decisive tip of the spear against Hannibal and the armies of Carthage."

"And you named the tip of your spear *Absolute Love*?"

While Carter stifled a laugh, Hodges's eyes narrowed. "A nod to the previous owners." Hodges gestured with his finger at Tommy. "How about you take Agent Jones upstairs? Get him a room on the next floor? Take a shower. Watch TV. We'll have some food sent up."

"Not leaving my partner," Tommy said.

Sophie appreciated Tommy's allegiance. But she needed to get answers, and if it made the CIA happy he had to go. Sophie would fill him in later.

"I won't be long."

Tommy acquiesced and followed Carter out of the room. When they were gone, Hodges smiled. He cleared his throat. Twice. This time much louder. "Tell me about your father."

Sophie's heart started pounding. What did Hodges know? Stifling the desire to caress the locket under her shirt, she instead grabbed her thigh and squeezed. "I don't have a father."

Again, the man cleared his throat, but this time it was several small snorts strung together.

"Do you need a lozenge?"

"Sophie Grant. That's a nice name. Exactly like they did in the old days when they got off the boats at Ellis Island." Hodges patted his chest. "We were Hodemochers, from Jena." Hodges squinted at Sophie. "And you're Sophia Granttano . . . of the Kansas City Granttanos."

Sophie leaned back in her chair, doing her best to look cool even though she knew what was coming. She hadn't lied to anyone about her past. But she knew omitting her father on her federal background check was a technicality that could cost Sophie her badge. She thought of Maria and other kids that lost their parents in Malodini, and how failing them would crush her heart. She'd just have to scrape all her savings together, sell her car, and move back to Italy once she was done processing out of the EPA. Sophie would miss training Tommy, too. Once he got a handle on the lab work the kid would be a first-rate special agent for the EPA. A true believer, impervious to cynicism, when there were so few like him.

"So, what's next? Reprimand? Expulsion?"

"Only if you say no."

"To what?"

"A temp job."

Sophie bayed out a laugh that startled Hodges. "A temp job? With the CIA? I've seen this movie. It doesn't end well."

"That's too bad," Hodges said.

"What is?"

"The letter I send to the CID Director shutting down the entire operation on Vesuvius."

"Threaten their kids. Works every time." Sophie's words on Vesuvius to Tommy had come back to haunt her. "Blackmail. How very old school spook of you."

"If the shoe phone fits," Hodges said.

Sophie slumped back in her chair. "What's the job? Assassinate Archduke Ferdinand the third?"

"Tell me about your father," Hodges repeated.

"Like I said. I don't have a father."

Hodges looked down at his tablet. "Raymond Enrico Granttano, born June 4th, 1952, Kansas City, Missouri. After high school he was drafted into the Navy during Vietnam. Served two years as a boatswain's mate on the USS *Okinawa*." Hodges lifted his shoulder and the stump of his left arm. "We have something in common, your dad and me. I was in the Navy in 'Nam, too."

"Not just that."

"What? What else?"

"You're both colossal dicks."

From the doorway, fresh from squiring Tommy to his room, Carter snickered. Hodges glared at him over his shoulder before turning back to Sophie. "After he gets back, Ray joins the Kansas City police force and, in a few years, makes detective. Marries Anne Carlton, your mother, now deceased."

At the mention of her mother, Sophie stiffened but did everything in her power to not react, to not give Bill Hodges the power over her he so clearly wanted. Hodges squinted. Sophie gave him nothing but a blank slate.

"What does my family history have anything to do with this . . . temp job?"

"Everything." Hodges continued reading from his tablet. "How much do you know about your father? His time with the Kansas City PD?"

Sophie reached into her shirt and rubbed the locket around her neck. "What's there to say? I was only six. Shouting, drinking, horrible fights. He was a bad cop. They fired him. Then we left for Colorado. Never looked back."

Sophie was lying. From the moment she was old enough to access the internet she dug for every scrap of information she could find on her father. The headlines from the *Kansas City Star* were seared into her memory.

KC COP PASSED CONFIDENTIAL INFORMATION TO MAFIA BROTHER

DISGRACED DETECTIVE ESCAPES JAIL TIME

NICCHI MAFIA WAR CLAIMS THREE IN NIGHTCLUB SHOOTOUT

"Indeed. After your mother dies you work your way through a chemistry BS at the University of Colorado. Grab a fat new scholarship for the environmental law program in Berkeley. Graduate with a master's degree in criminal justice. Were you recruited right out of school? Into the EPA?"

"You could say I recruited them. Went to the Denver field office and demanded they hire me." Sophie figured there was little to be gained by lying. It was true; Sophie had refused to leave the building until they gave her a shot.

"After you pass the federal agent training, you're assigned to the EPA's Criminal Investigation Division and work on an impressive string of cases. Successfully prosecuting Halliburton over abandoned uranium mines on Navajo land? Taking on the Pentagon over Camp LeJeune water pollution? That's pro-level."

Sophie would never forget the haggard face of the Army sergeant as he handed her documents showing strontium-90 from a radioactive military dumpsite near the camp's rifle range contaminating the base's water supply. His nine-year old son had died of leukemia the Christmas prior.

"Your testimony led to a fourteen-million-dollar cleanup fine imposed on Gruden Industries for PFOA contamination. You know the CEO is pals with the former president?" Another string of phlegm-laced throat eruptions from the man.

"Yes. The Commander in Chief tweeted about it. He wasn't happy."

Every case Sophie worked, environmental crime was part of a sprawling, larger web of illegal activity that included offenses like tax fraud, money laundering, drug dealing, and even homicide. In the presidential pal's case, it was two out of four.

"But then there's Fort Collins Paint and Solvents LLC. The very same company your mother worked for," Hodges said. "Kinda shocked an EPA CID director would allow an investigation involving a close family member."

Sophie bit her lip at the memory of the two brothers that founded and owned the paint company. In a cost-cutting measure, they decided not to replace industrial air scrubbers from the factory where her mother worked. For years she ran the business office unaware she was inhaling huge volumes of toxic fumes.

"I threatened to walk."

"And then you threw it all away by stealing an EPA jet and flying to Kenya?" Hodges slapped the table. "I bet that's a good story."

Again, more bait. If Hodges knew about her father, then there was nothing about her time at EPA he didn't know. "It's the EPA. There are no good stories."

"So, the whole job, your whole reason for working as a water cop was revenge?"

"No." Sophie imagined punching Hodges, one arm and all, in his sanctimonious, white-bearded face. "I wanted to prove I was a better cop than he was."

Sophie saw her father exactly one time in the past thirty years. Standing in the back of the main auditorium at her UC Berkeley graduation ceremony. They made eye contact from the stage moments after receiving her diploma; Ray nodding and smiling in approval while Sophie froze in place. Then he was gone.

"What does any of this have to do with Ray Granttano?"

Hodges slid his pad across the table to Sophie. There was a closeup of a man's mugshot on the screen. His head was shaped like a cinder block with a joyless mouth framed by jowls.

"Ken Nicchi. KC mob boss. So?"

"Swipe right."

Sophie did as Hodges asked. The next screen over from the mug shot was a flight tracker. A plane was halfway across the Pacific Ocean. "Ken is on his way here to Naples, this minute, to pick up his son's body."

"About that," Sophie said. "Aren't either of you the least bit freaked out someone killed an Italian cop, almost ran us into the sea, all to steal Chris Nicchi's head?"

"Yes," Hodges said. "Very *freaked*. But at the moment I'm more interested in your father."

"Why, exactly?"

"Because he's on that plane, too."

Sophie felt the air leave her body. She couldn't catch her breath. "Of course, he is. He's coming to get Madeline."

"That's not all," Carter said. He twirled a red cornicello in his fingers.

"Is that from the coroner's van?"

"No."

"Ever hear of Fort Leonard Wood?" Hodges said.

Sophie nodded. "Missouri. US Army base, down in the Ozarks."

"Leonard Wood is special. Every three years by US Army code, all active-duty weapons . . . small arms, M4s, SAWs, but also some heavier stuff like mortars and AT 4 anti-tank rockets must go through a rigorous testing protocol. Around a quarter fail. They're slated to be decommissioned and sent to Leonard Wood's industrial smelting facility. I can't tell you the number of times Congress has tried to force the Army to change the policy, but defense contractors are stone cold fucking pros. Anyway, Mr. Nicchi has several well compensated, high-level sources in the base. They tip him off to weapons destined for the slag heap. They steal weapons no one will miss, ship them out of New Orleans to Naples where they're sold to the highest bidder," Hodges said. "Sold by your new friend."

"Friend?"

Hodges swiped the screen on his tablet and slid the device across the table to Sophie. She looked down at the face of a middle-aged man with a closely shorn scalp, hard eyes and a long beard. Sophie recognized the man from her briefing packet. It was the same monster responsible for the death and misery in Malodini.

"Luca Pecora."

Hodges nodded. "Ken Nicchi is coming not just to collect the dead, but for a business meeting."

Carter handed a small plastic case over to Sophie. She examined it for a moment, then snapped the lid open. Inside was a pin stuck in white foam. By squinting, Sophie could see a tiny chip on the pin's head.

"We need to hear what goes on in that meeting," Hodges said.

"You want me to plant a bug on my father?" Sophie leapt to her feet. Holding the pin up between her thumb and forefinger, she said, "And if I tell you to stick this somewhere very private and very painful?"

Hodges's expression darkened. "Then I have to call your boss and tell him about your dad." He cleared his throat, this time with two loud grunts.

Hodges shook something loose in Sophie. Having worked her share of combative interrogations, she realized there was only one reason for the aggressive posture—they were desperate. It dawned on her that Chris Nicchi and her half-sister, Madeline, weren't caught up in some turf squabble or crossfire. They were informants for the CIA. And it got them killed. Sophie wondered if it had been drugs or another crime that tripped Madeline and brother-in-law up? What gave Hodges the leverage he needed to flip them?

"You play hardball with Chris and Madeline, too?"

Carter shook his head. "They came to us."

CHAPTER 13

Il Ramingo was exhausted. Days of little sleep conducting surveillance on the Nicchi yacht, and the aftermath had taken its toll. His knees ached. Many years before, the climb up and down the Attala aqueduct pass was much easier. The signs of aging were unmistakable. Better to acknowledge them, heal, and return to the struggle.

Dropping his center of gravity, he slowly pulling his right leg behind his head until he felt the angry tendons in his knee stretching. Using measured breaths, he switched legs, and stretched the left knee. Holding himself aloft with just the palms of his hands on the ground, Il Ramingo threw his head back with knees bent, legs tucked under his body while arching his back.

The new phone buzzed in his pocket. Stopping his yoga regimen, Il Ramingo looked at the number on the screen before answering.

"When do you leave?"

"Tonight."

"Did you get the map? The Catacombs? And the picture? Will you be able to recognize him?"

DeSalvo's insistent tone was detectable despite the electronic voice distortion.

"I did. Very helpful. The picture too. Good to put a face with the voice."

"You're not very talkative . . . you are at the cemetery?" DeSalvo asked.

"I am."

"This is your last one."

"It is."

"My apologies. I'll leave you to it."

Il Ramingo put the phone back in his pocket, making a mental reminder to destroy it when he was finished with his task.

At his feet was a black backpack. From inside he removed Chris Nicchi's head, wrapped in a thick sky-blue towel. A faint scent of grilled meat wafted from the head. He examined the face for a moment, blackened by fire, the eyes rolled backwards into the skull, just as Il Ramingo left him after stabbing Chris through the left and right atriums.

Before Il Ramingo was a hole in the dirt the size of an office safe. He stretched his arms out and let Chris's head drop, where it bounced once before settling on its right cheek. Il Ramingo picked up a shovel from next to the hole. He filled it in with fresh dirt piled to its rim and tamped the dirt down until it was well packed. From inside the backpack, he took a small white wooden cross and stuck it into the dirt above where Chris Nicchi's head was buried.

Leaning on his shovel, Il Ramingo took in the view. Before him in the small, hidden mountain clearing were dozens of similar mounds marked by identical white crosses. Beyond his secret alpine graveyard, the otherworldly blue of the Tyrrhenian Sea sparkled.

"Memento mori."

CHAPTER 14

"Your mother," Sophie's father had said to his six-year-old daughter, seconds before walking out the front door of their house for good, "is an aw-shucks woman in an oh-shit world."

Sophie Grant had never seen her dad cry, but he did that day. A few brief tears accompanied by a choked, "For your birthday," as he pushed a jewelry box into her hand before disappearing. Inside, a small silver locket with *mi amore* etched on its surface. Over the years that followed, Sophie would alternate between wearing the locket around her neck and stuffing it deep in her sock drawer.

If anything, Sophie later learned, her mother was a strong person, perhaps the strongest she would ever know.

The courage it took to kick Sophie's dad out of the house, and *then* moving Sophie to Colorado? Incalculable. Putting in long days managing the office for a Fort Collins-based paint company while still showing up for every soccer game, every after-school event had to be exhausting, but her mother did it. Never complained. Never got hopelessly drunk. Never cried in the corner for her ex-husband. Sophie's mom was hell bent on not falling into a caricature of the divorced single mother, opting instead to put her daughter on a course of self-sufficiency.

"Your father chose being a criminal over us. A degenerate. We're better without him," her mother would say anytime Sophie asked about him. "We control our future."

When they learned that Sophie's father had remarried and sired a daughter, instead of wallowing in pity Sophie's mom took her on a shopping spree to the Cherry Creek Mall in downtown Denver. Despite money being tight, she bought Sophie anything she wanted. New bejeweled sandals and a Smashing Pumpkins poster did little to fill the ice cream scoop sized hole in her heart, carved out by a sister Sophie never met. She followed her mother's lead that day, stuffing the ugly pain down deep, ignoring the gnawing sense that her father chose one daughter over the other. The locket relegated back to the sock drawer, where it stayed until college. Awake at night, struggling to go to sleep, someday Ray Granttano would know how much he lost by abandoning Sophie, she told herself.

During Sophie's senior year of high school, when the cancer in her mother's bones kept her confined to bed, the woman uttered not one complaint, even when the pain was overwhelming. Like any skilled sorceress, her mother turned the illness's toll into motivation for her daughter's studies, pledging to haunt Sophie as a ghost if she didn't score in the top percentile for her American College Test.

The upshot was that a week after her mother died, Sophie scored a perfect 36 on her ACT. The only Coloradan to do so that year.

Now fifteen years later, after a near sleepless night spent wrestling with the decision to help the CIA plant a listening device on her estranged, Mafia-employed father, Sophie wished more than anything that she had tanked the ACT. It would've forced her mother to follow through on her promise to hound her daughter in the afterlife.

Sophie needed the help.

Sitting on the red and white sofa in their comfortable converted Amore Assouta hotel room, her fingers turning over the silver locket around her neck, Sophie knew one thing for certain. The CIA didn't care about her. Or Maria. Spooks like Bill Hodges gave zero shits about the kids living in Malodini. He and Carter Boyd were only concerned with the Camorra leader Luca Pecora. Sophie wanted to see the man responsible for Malodini's pollution brought to justice, too. But was that enough to put her whole operation, the welfare of Maria and Tommy, in the hands of intelligence operatives who lied for a living?

Sophie had conducted unsavory business before as an EPA agent. Done so in the name of common cause. Like paying bribes to Somali warlords for access to a Kenyan refugee camp. Bribes that would later finance more guns, more bullets, and more death. Sometimes there was no right choice, Sophie learned from chasing criminal polluters. You did what you could to bring lawbreakers to justice.

"I'm a salesman," her first partner had said while riding in an aluminum Lund at midnight up and down the Ohio River. Crusty old Ted Staymitch, one of the original sixteen special agents the EPA hired, took her under his wing. Ted retired the next year, but Sophie learned the nuts and bolts of the job from him. How polluters preferred the dark to do their dumping. How their arrogance manifested in pipes spewing green fluid into the river and were shocked when Sophie and Ted knocked on their door. "I sell jail time."

But every year more regulations got rolled back and more greedy corporations were granted the right to pollute in the name of freedom. Real justice for ordinary people was out of reach. Replaced with congressional fossil fuel puppets with a new target—the EPA's budget. During Sophie's tenure, the number of special agents plummeted by nearly a third. Ted had died of cancer, which was for the best since the man wouldn't recognize the job today.

Sophie's phone vibrated in her pocket. The caller ID showed no name, only the US Environmental Protection Agency.

"SAC Grant."

"Agent Davies. What can I do for you?"

"Your phone tracker. It says you're in Naples? You're supposed to alert me when you're going to travel."

Sophie froze. How could she be so stupid? The phone tracker. It was for her own safety, of course, should the Camorra target her for abduction—or worse. If she told Davies the truth about why she was in Naples, that was it. He'd happily write her up, and with Sophie's record, she'd be out. Hodges was right, he had her in a goddam box.

So, Sophie lied. To her EPA supervisor. Again.

"After Vesuvius the PSC brought me down to Naples for a debrief. Nothing I can't handle. Back on the mountain in a few hours."

"Good. Maybe it's for the best to be in Naples. Until your Marines arrive. Think about spending the night? As much as I'd like you out of my hair, I don't need dead agents on my watch."

"I'll take it under advisement."

"One more thing. There was a military flight from Andrews to the Joint Naples base with extra room. Your replacement SPAGOs will be parked and ready for you when you get back to Malodini."

"That's excellent."

"Whatever." Davies hung up.

Pulse pounding, Sophie texted Tommy to meet her out in the hall. She hustled out the door and into the hallway where Tommy waited. He was wearing boxer shorts and a faded Wisconsin Badgers tee.

"S'up boss? Something wrong?"

"I have to tell you something."

Standing in a hardened CIA facility, she spilled everything about her secret past life to Tommy Jones. That her uncle was a high-ranking member of a Kansas City crime family. Her father? A corrupt ex-cop and Mafia pawn. Then she drowned him in a torrent of apologies for dragging him unwittingly into this mess and offered him a way out.

"You're a federal agent. I just told you about a federal crime I committed."

"Crime? Sin of omission. At best."

"You have your whole career to think about."

"My career? Do you know why I wanted to do this job?"

Sophie felt a rush of shame. Together for a year, and she never once asked why. "Jesus, Tommy, I'm so sorry. Please. Tell me. I'd like to know."

Tommy explained that there was a burn pit at his forward operating base in Kandahar Province while he was in the Army. The site was used to dispose of an array of toxic waste, from human feces to depleted uranium shells. After five of his fellow infantrymen were incapacitated from inhalation of dangerous fumes, an EPA trained cleanup crew was brought in.

"It was never clear over there if you're shooting at the right people," Tommy said. "But the idea of working to make things better, the clarity of the EPA's mission. It may have been just a waste site. But it's what I wanted to do. I'd never been more certain." Tommy cracked a smile and leaned against the hallway wall. "They talked about you. At Glynco. How you could've had your pick of agencies, but to a person they were dumbfounded by EPA." He stopped smiling. "They didn't know what I know now. My career? After a couple of years as an occupying force shooting at villagers four thousand miles from home, all I wanted was a job that I knew for certain was doing good." He let his arm drop to his side. "You gave me that."

"What are you saying?"

"That we stay. We help the CIA. And when we're done, and Pecora's dead or having his nails pulled out somewhere, then you can tell the director about your family history."

Sophie couldn't believe what she was hearing from her rookie partner. "Come with me." She motioned for Tommy to follow her into her room. After grabbing a couple of cold Peronis from the fridge, she sat Tommy down at the dining room table.

"Since we're being honest," Sophie took a sip of beer, "do you know why I lost my command title? Why Davies hates my guts?"

Tommy shrugged. He looked embarrassed. "Word around the campfire is that you stole an Agency plane. Flew it to Africa?"

Sophie nodded. Because it had happened internationally, the case files had been sealed. She was forbidden from talking about what transpired, but figured Tommy had a right to know.

"I was working out of the Boston office, got a case where a two-year-old Sudanese immigrant boy . . . poor kid died of lead-paint poisoning. Real shithole rental in Manchester. Through an interpreter, the mother . . . the grief in her eyes . . . nothing but pain. Pain and agony. She said to me, 'If you don't put the landlord in jail, I'll kill myself.'"

"Jesus Christ."

Sophie nodded. "Kid was just eating the lead paint like potato chips off the wall. No disclosures to the tenants. Which, as you know, is required by law. Instead, the landlord digitally scanned the renter's signatures from their lease, and then used those to backdate and forge the forms making it look like the scumbag told them about the lead. So, I execute a search warrant, stop the guy just as the big dummy is leaving his house with all the phony disclosure forms printed off in his briefcase."

"Nice."

"No. Not nice. His equally morally bankrupt lawyers argued to the judge that since the poor kid and his mom fled genocide in the Sudan, and stayed at two different refugee camps, one in South Sudan and another on the in Kenya, before being granted asylum in America, that there was no concrete evidence that the kid wasn't poisoned there."

"What'd you do?"

"Normally it would take two to three weeks to get all the proper paperwork cleared. But one of the places mother and son stayed was the Dadaab refugee camp in Kenya. Fighting between Somali insurgents and the Kenyan Defense Forces was raging and getting so close to the camp that UNICEF was bugging out. The evidence I needed was in that camp. But it was a day, maybe two from getting overrun in the fighting. So, I fudged the paperwork, lied to the transnational desk, and took the plane."

Sophie didn't mention that her lie to Agent Davies resulted in an official reprimand for the transnational desk officer. A reprimand that would follow Davies throughout his career. She couldn't fault the guy for holding a grudge. But had Sophie wasted time with the EPA's bureaucracy, there would've been no justice for the boy. Another piece of shit slumlord would've gone free. A mother dead by suicide.

During the two years hunting fugitives for her penance, Sophie had plenty of time to reflect on her choice to lie. The one thing she knew for certain was there was no choice involved. There was either justice or there wasn't.

"And?"

"Negative samples from the camp proved the kid was poisoned in Manchester."

"Curds." Tommy took a long swig from his Peroni. "Did a jury convict?"

Sophie nodded. "Jury deliberated in the morning. Found the landlord guilty in the afternoon."

"Sheboygan."

"He got eighteen months."

Tommy's mouth dropped open. "That's it?"

"That's it."

Sophie took a deep drink of her beer. She hadn't thought of Hisanta and her son in years. How hollowed out the woman was. Like her soul had been ripped from her body. And the feeling of absolute despair at the light sentence for the killer. That same day two weed dealers got longer jail times.

"At least the mother didn't kill herself, right?" Tommy's eyes said don't give me more bad news. "Right, Sophie?"

Sophie smiled. "Right. Last I heard she was remarried. Kid on the way. Owns a snack bar concession at the Mayo Clinic in Rochester, Minnesota." She drank again. "You can't save everyone."

"But you can try," Tommy said.

CHAPTER 15

"Two teams. Two teams, plus a drone overhead," Hodges said.

Carter stood in Absloluta Amore's sunny inner courtyard, watching a group of heavily armed SOG operatives in full body armor frozen at attention before three black Mercedes vans parked in a line behind them.

"We couldn't protect the Nicchi kids. Do you really think we can keep Il Ramingo from getting to The Wheel?"

"It's a prisoner transfer. Not a *Mona Lisa* heist." Hodges said. Then he looked off in the distance while tapping his toe to a song Carter couldn't hear. Carter sipped his second coffee of the morning from a paper cup, his perfectly valid question to his boss just hanging there. Maybe a better-crafted broadside might shake something loose from the old man?

"Using the Italian kid, the orphan, and her whole town on Grant? That was some dirty pool."

"Dirty pool means no *dirty bombs*. Be smarter, Boyd."

"Think she'll say yes?"

Hodges grunted. "With her psych profile? And the kid? I bet she begs us to wire up daddy."

"And if she doesn't?"

"Always have a hole card, Boyd."

"Hole card?"

What the hell was going on with Hodges? He was ruthless when American interests were on the line. That was the job. Carter had learned to embrace it. But Sophie Grant was a dedicated federal agent. Despite a couple of missteps, all in service of solving cases, a very effective one by all accounts. It was an inspired move to bring her over to Italy to disrupt Pecora's operations on Vesuvius. They had the man off balance on multiple fronts. Pico in custody. Vesuvius closed for business. Even though the Nicchies were dead, Pecora had to be looking over his shoulder wondering who in his operation would turn on him next.

"Bill, what aren't you telling me?"

Hodges turned to Carter, his demeanor combative. "It's the Agency, kid, which means, plenty. What exactly are you—"

A pudgy man with wild brown hair and horned rimmed glasses burst out of Absolute Amore's front doors.

"Hodges! You can't make me leave!" he yelled in broken English with a thick Italian accent. When he reached Hodges and Carter, he poked the station chief in the chest with his finger. "He will kill me. I won't go. *Rifiutare!*"

"Pico, would you calm down?" Hodges said while swatting away the man's hand.

A SOG sprinted to catch up to the man. "Sorry sir, he took off on me."

Pico dropped to his knees in front of Hodges. Despite smelling of fear and body odor, what Carter found most repellent about Pico "The Wheel" Graffiato was that he used a global cheese export business to clean dirty money for the Pecora System. Money made from selling drugs and weapons.

Lately Pico had graduated from laundering to transporting arms. When SOGs operating on Carter's orders stormed the cheese merchant's warehouse, they found enough military grade Semtex plastic explosives stashed in giant Parmigiano-Reggiano wheels to level Naples. But that's not what got Hodges' interest. It was the discovery of an empty, lead-lined, coffin-sized chest with a fingerprint lock. Pico swore he didn't know what it was for, only that Pecora ordered him to secure it and wait for further instructions.

It didn't take a career in espionage to know the Camorra boss was planning on moving something much more dangerous than a pallet of shoulder rockets.

Clasping his hands in prayer, Pico said to Hodges, "He'll know where you are taking me. He'll find me. You promised to save me."

"And we are. You leave for Rome, nine am tomorrow, sharp." Hodges waved at the three vans and the platoon of trained killers. "And this will be your escort."

"There must be twenty men?"

"See, Pico. We take care of our own." Hodges turned to the vans. "You're with us now." The CIA station chief told the SOG commander his men could get back to their duties after the successful demonstration for his quivering ward.

"Still," Pico said, his voice catching, "how can you be sure? Il Ramingo is everywhere."

Don't I know it, thought Carter, the red cornicello from the assassin still in his pant pocket. Pico was holding on to the account numbers where he stored Pecora's cash. Account numbers directly linked to the System's customers. With them, the CIA could identify dozens of his terrorist contacts. The Wheel's plea deal with the Italian government—brokered by Hodges—was contingent on handing the numbers over. Tomorrow, he was set to appear before a Roman magistrate and receive a full pardon. Until then, Pico kept the account records in his head.

"Hodges." Carter looked past Pico at Sophie Grant and her partner standing in the old hotel's entrance.

Hodges saw them, too. He held his open palm out to the EPA special agent communicating that he needed his prize informant to leave before they could talk. "Pico, you can trust us." Waving the Wheel's SOG escort over, he said "Back to your room."

The SOG, furious at Pico for giving him the slip, put a hand on his shoulder and squeezed. "Walk or be carried."

Pico, his eyes darting back and forth in fear, whimpered once before getting to his feet. The SOG escorted him past Sophie and back into the CIA's converted hotel.

"What can I do for you, SAC Grant?"

Sophie held a closed fist out to Bill Hodges. Opening her hand palm up, Carter could see the pin microphone they'd asked her to plant on her father.

"I'll do it. On one condition."

"Just one?"

"Fix her record," Tommy said, stepping out from behind Sophie. "Her dad never existed. No one's the wiser."

"That can be arranged," Hodges said.

CHAPTER 16

"Twenty euros."

With a gloved hand he handed a crisp bill to the cashier. The woman was seated behind a small pane of glass. She looked to be at least sixty. Thankfully, she was engrossed in an Umberto Eco novel and didn't look up to comment on why his head and hands were covered in such oppressive heat.

"Audio tour is an additional ten euros."

"*No gratzi.*"

Timing his arrival to late morning to coincide with the rush of tourist foot traffic, Il Ramingo entered the exhibit in a stream of bodies. They filed down three flights of dimly lit steps, carved from ancient tuff, a porous stone native to Southern Italy. Once at the bottom of the steps, he entered a large underground space the size of a soccer pitch. A recorded voice intoned to the gathered crowd, repeating the greeting in Italian and English.

"Welcome to the Catacombs of San Gennaro, known as the Valley of the Dead. The gift store is on the main level next to the entrance. Bathrooms are . . ."

The ancient underground tombs, where the early Christians of 4 A.D. Naples started burying their dead, was today crammed with tourists eagerly exploring the various historically important crypts and graves. Over three hundred confirmed burial spots were spread among two levels. A plaque on the wall informed him four saints were interned here, and that the restored frescos adorning the walls had been commissioned by the wealthier dead.

Wearing a long cloak buttoned to his neck, wide brimmed hat

pulled down over his head mask and goggles, Il Ramingo walked through the center of the room. He nodded at every corner mounted security camera that caught his eye without flinching. By the time the police reviewed the footage, Il Ramingo would be gone.

In the far corner was another set of stairs leading from his level, called San Gennaro Superiore, down to San Gennaro Inferiore. After descending to the far less crowded San Gennaro Inferiore, Il Ramingo noticed the crypts were bigger, older and cruder than the resting places above. DeSalvo's briefing packet, sent via digital encryption, explained that during World War II and the infamous "Four Days of Naples," Italian resistance fighters used the Catacombs to stage their attacks against Nazi occupiers. This allowed US Marines time to land and liberate the city. Ironic that today, the Catacombs would be used against the Americans.

Il Ramingo was well-versed in the history of Saint Bessus, patron saint of soldiers and protector of warriors in battle. Bessus, a centurion in the Roman Theban Legion, died along with his entire six thousand, six hundred and sixty-six fellow legion members at the hands of the Roman army. The Theban Legion had converted to Christianity and the enraged emperor was not having it. He ordered the beheading of the entire legion one centurion at a time. Il Ramingo considered his mountain cemetery a tribute of sort to the saint.

Eight crypts down the right side, Il Ramingo found Bessus's tomb right where DeSalvo's information said it would be. Peering at an inscription carved in tuff above the stone sarcophagus holding Bessus, Il Ramingo waited for a chatty young couple to pass by before stepping into the crypt's alcove.

A chi bene crede, Dio provvede.

Have faith and God shall provide.

Following DeSalvo's instructions, Il Ramingo used the first three fingers on his left hand to press on the worn inscription letters, *DIO*. There was a soft thump behind the stone. Checking again to make sure no one was close, Il Ramingo pushed on the stone tablet. Dust puffed from the seams as a meter-wide door swung in, opened for the first time since the end of the Second World War. From underneath his cloak he unclasped a massive duffle bag strapped around his waist and thrust the bag into the hole. Then by first sticking his leg into the dark gap and twisting his hips and falling in with his other leg following last, a contorted Il Ramingo made it inside another chamber.

From his belt, Il Ramingo removed a flashlight. He aimed the beam down the tight passage dug by partisan resistance fighters. Dust clogged the light beam. After picking up the duffel bag and clasping it over his shoulders, Il Ramingo moved for a hundred yards down the tunnel, his feet sloshing through an inch of brackish water. He reached a juncture where the tunnel split into four directions. He turned right. A pair of rats scuttled over his boots. Traveling another five minutes and two more right turns and one left, he found himself at an old steel door. A chain with a padlock was wrapped around the door handle. Producing a pair of bolt cutters from beneath his cloak, Il Ramingo severed the chain. He dropped the bolt cutters into the water at his feet. From inside his coat, he took out a new chain with a padlock attached and looped it around the door handle. Next, Il Ramingo drew a silenced pistol with his right hand. With his left, he opened the door to a loud squeak and stepped inside an old boiler room.

He paused. After waiting a minute, he was satisfied that no alarms had been tripped or that the loud door noise alerted anyone to his presence. Hearing only the faint sound of gunshots from the shooting range adjacent to the boiler room, Il Ramingo took out a small black device with a four-inch screen. A 3-D map of the building appeared with dotted line showing his path out of the boiler room to the second floor via an unused freight elevator shaft. Climbing fast hand over hand on old elevator cables, Il Ramingo arrived on the second floor. After stuffing an earpiece in his left ear, he toggled the device to listening mode.

"Pico, it's your last day in Naples. Just tell us what you want for lunch."

CHAPTER 17

Bang! Bang! Bang! Bang!

Tommy Jones pushed a red button mounted on the shooting range lane's wall. While Sophie ejected the empty magazine from her pistol, her silhouette paper target rushed from the end of the land back to a stop in front of her face. Tommy said something she didn't understand. She removed her noise dampening headphones.

"Say again."

"Sheboygan!" Tommy said, grinning as he held up the target with all ten shots grouped at center mass.

After the gun battle on Mount Vesuvius, Sophie realized she needed to hone her combat skills. The range in the basement of the converted hotel was small, only four shooting lanes, with the other three occupied with SOGs emptying their weapons downrange. She fired over a hundred rounds in a half-hour.

"Again?" Tommy said holding up a fresh box of .45s.

"No, I think I'm good." Sophie said examining the perforated target with pride. "Now it's time to kick your ass."

As part of her training as a federal agent, Sophie had learned basic MCMAP, the Marine Corps Martial Arts Program, a hybrid system of hand-to-hand combat drawn from a constellation of disciplines ranging from Brazilian jujutsu to kickboxing. But that training was years ago. She was rusty. Tommy offered to spar.

After they checked their sidearms back in with the SOG manning the security booth, Tommy and Sophie took an elevator to the fourth floor to Sophie's room. She had the bigger space with enough open room to fight. From the gym the SOGs used for workouts, Tommy secured protective headgear, boxing gloves and a punching bag. For twenty minutes under her partner's close tutelage, Sophie practiced punches and kicks on the bag. The old training started coming back to her. Muscle memory kicked in.

"I'm ready for the real thing," Sophie said.

"Give me your best shot."

The two faced off, circling each other until Sophie, frustrated with Tommy treating her like a rare orchid by refusing to throw any real punches, darted inside his glove and gave him an uppercut that generated an agitated, "Curds, that hurt."

"Stop going easy on me. I'm not made of sugar."

"Is that an order?"

"It is."

The next couple of minutes they spent grunting, huffing, and throwing punches and kicks at each other. Even Tommy was feeling the exertion, his forehead wet with sweat. Sophie tried a lazy haymaker that Tommy easily ducked. He spun and connected with a roundhouse kick to her ribs. The air went out of her lungs and she dropped to her knees.

"Oh shit, I'm sorry boss, I didn't mean to—" Tommy's head snapped toward the door at a faint popping sound. Gunfire.

"Is that?"

Tommy nodded.

Another crackle of shots fired, this time closer. Tommy shucked the boxing gloves and dashed to a drawer in the kitchenette. "Here." He held out a steak knife he found out to her handle first just as Sophie removed her own gloves.

Gripping a butcher knife in his right hand, Tommy went to the door leading out to the hallway.

"There is no way I'm letting you go out there alone and unarmed."

There were more popping sounds, closer, louder, like firecrackers. Then a muted scream. Tommy brandished the knife. "Just a peek."

He pulled the door to the hallway open, darted out, knife at the ready. Sophie heard two metallic clicks and then a wet thump. Tommy staggered backwards into the room his hands clutching at his chest, his face white.

"Tommy?"

He turned to face Sophie, his hands dropping to his sides. Two expanding red spots appeared on his chest, soaking his shirt. He tried to talk but could only make a clucking sound. Staggering toward her, his mouth convulsing in a silent "O," Tommy collapsed face first into the carpet.

A tall, thin man dressed in a cloak buttoned to his neck, his head covered in a dark mesh sock and black goggles over his eyes, stepped into the room. Something large was strapped over his back in a duffle bag. Sophie could see that his gloved hands were covered in blood. Tommy's blood.

With Sophie's chest beating fast but time moving slow, she told herself not let the terror take over, that despite her partner dying on the floor, she needed to stay focused on the threat before her. Dropping into a crouch, she jabbed the knife out in front of her.

Il Ramingo bent at the waist and stretched one arm out. He placed a red cornicello on the table in front of Sophie. On its side, two unmistakable words.

Memento mori.

"For Bill Hodges," he said in a raspy, heavy Italian accent. Then he spun and ran from the room.

Sophie fell to her knees next to Tommy, turned him over in a spreading pool of blood. His eyes were open, staring at the ceiling. She put her fingers to his throat. There was no pulse. She sobbed, her body shaking as the adrenaline left her system. With her hand she closed his eyes.

"Where is he?" Carter burst into the room, M4 assault rifle in his hands. "Oh, no," he said, seeing Tommy dead on the floor.

"You just missed him," she said, her voice a twisted croak.

CHAPTER 18

Il Ramingo expected the three men guarding Pico to be highly trained veterans. They didn't disappoint. After he killed the first, the second was able to draw his sidearm as the life drained from him, reflexively firing into the floor. The third got off a burst from a machine pistol before Il Ramingo's left blade sluiced through his neck. Pico darted for the door but wasn't fast enough to evade a syringe of the tranquilizer Rohypnol.

But for the young man that came at Il Ramingo with a butcher knife, his escape would've been seamless. Instead, the time he wasted killing him and talking with the sister brought his pursuers too close. So close, that as he looked back over his shoulder before entering the elevator shaft, a man rounded a corner with an assault rifle raised to his shoulder. Carter Boyd. The same CIA man who was on the boat with the Nicchies.

Il Ramingo leapt for the cables, a sedated Pico strapped across his back, caught them with both arms, and slid down as bullets zipped above his head. He landed well, but Pico's weight sent fire shooting through his knees. Limping slightly, Il Ramingo made his way to the boiler room. There he pulled the old iron door shut with a loud squeak. As he tied the new chain he'd left around the door handle, he heard footsteps approaching from the boiler room. Clasping the padlock shut, Il Ramingo went as fast as he could down the passage. Muffled shouts and banging on the metal door echoed behind him.

After following the same route he used from the Catacombs, Il Ramingo stood back in the crypt of Saint Bessus. None of the tourists on the sparsely populated San Gennaro Inferiore level noticed his arrival. He took a smoke grenade from his belt, activated it with the flick of his thumb, and tossed it out into the space. As smoke billowed, Il Ramingo strode to the steps and walked to the first level. There he dialed 118 on a new phone.

"Ciao, what is your emergency?"

"There's a fire, San Gennaro Inferiore in the Catacombs of San Gennaro. Please hurry." Then he tossed the phone aside. Il Ramingo waited a moment until screams and shouts erupted from the second level. Tourists scattered, followed by rolling clouds of black smoke. The historical attraction devolved into pandemonium.

Il Ramingo walked out of the Catacombs of San Gennaro amidst a throng of panicked sightseers. Two blocks to the north he'd parked a stolen ambulance. As a torrent of sirens descended on the area, Il Ramingo put the unconscious Pico on a gurney in the back and drove away.

CHAPTER 19

"I thought I'd be happier when I took your badge."

Owen Davies opened their conversation by reminding Sophie that Tommy Jones was only the third EPA special agent to die in the line of duty. The first caught lethal food poisoning while on a protection detail for an EPA administrator's trip to Indonesia. The second was conducting surveillance when he stumbled into a convenience store robbery. Now the third was in a body bag in the old hotel's walk-in freezer, awaiting for transport and burial back in Washington DC.

"Pending a formal investigation, you're suspended. Indefinitely. There's an Air Force passenger flight leaving the joint base in an hour. Be on it."

"No," Sophie said sitting on the sofa in her room while staring at the drying pool of blood Tommy left behind. "I'm staying. Whether I have a job to come back to or not."

"I'll start the paperwork." Davies hung up.

Sophie thought of Maria and the other kids of Malodini. How they would no longer benefit from her help. The US military was deeply worried about the contamination reaching servicemembers and their families, so the odds were high another team would be sent. But for Sophie, her time was over.

A stiff drink was in her immediate future.

Sophie wandered downstairs to the old hotel's converted dining room. There, Sophie found Bill Hodges and Carter Boyd sitting at the conference table. Before them the bank of monitors was glowing with one tech on station. Sophie joined them at the table. There was a bottle of Macallan scotch in the center on a platter. Both Hodges and Carter were imbibing. Hodges poured two-fingers into a tumbler and slid it to Sophie

"Good. You're here." Carter sounded tired. "Was going to send someone to find you."

"Thanks," she said, raising her glass to Hodges and then took a sip. The burn of the alcohol was comforting. "What's up?"

"We have news," Hodges's eyes were bloodshot.

"Me too. You first."

"Security camera footage from the Catacombs of San Gennaro." Hodges pointed at the monitors. They watched, captivated, as the tall thin man who killed Tommy strode through the exhibit, purposefully looking at every security camera. *He wanted to be seen*, Sophie thought. But something was weird. His head looked pixilated like TV news shows did to people's faces that didn't give consent to be on camera.

"What's wrong with his face? It's all blurry."

"Metamaterial cloaking," Hodges said. "Has to be. Bleeding edge headgear. Uses electromagnetic radiation to distort a face. Military and the special ops guys have been toying with it for years. Field prototype went missing a while back. Guess what base?"

"Fort Leonard Wood?"

"Affirmative." Hodges cleared his throat. It sounded like he was pulling snot from the top of his skull.

"You really should see someone about that."

"I'm fine."

Sophie glanced over at Carter. His eyes were trying to communicate something to her. Like he was being held hostage. On the monitor the killer descended to the second level. He gained access to the wider Catacombs and disappeared.

"That's all they sent," the tech said over her shoulder.

"Fucker snatched Pico right out from under us," Hodges said.

"Who?"

Hodges and Carter stared back at her, stoneface.

"I talked with him. He killed Tommy. Who gives a shit right now if it's classified?"

"The System, they call him The Midnight Rambler, aka *Il Mezzanotte Ramingo* in Italian," Hodges said. "*Il Ramingo* for short. Carter'll brief you, soon, every detail we have on the guy. You have my word," Hodges pointed at Sophie. "You had something to report?"

Sophie told them about her call with the EPA transnational desk. How furious her superiors were at Tommy's death, and that instead of getting on the next plane home as ordered, she told them to pound sand.

"I'll still plant that bug on my dad if you need me to."

"Excellent," Hodges said. "Because he lands in two hours."

Sophie felt a tightness in her chest. Anxiety crept up her back.

"We have a thank you gift. To show our gratitude." Hodges bowed his head. "And our condolences. Agent Jones was a true patriot." Hodges cupped his hands and shouted at pair of closed doors. "Bring her out."

Maria appeared escorted by two SOGs. The girl sprinted forward. "Sophie!"

CHAPTER 20

The CIA surveillance van was parked down the block from the Grand Hotel Vesuvio, a luxury property in the heart of Naples's downtown district two kilometers away from Assoluta Amore. Vesuvio, Carter had told Sophie, was a favorite of wealthy Americans. Early morning sunlight filtered through the front windshield as Sophie and Carter sat drinking coffee in the rear compartment of the black Mercedes van. She'd finally had a decent night's sleep. It helped to have Maria. Staved off the visions of Tommy dying.

Two plainclothes SOGs occupied the front seats. Carter used the bank of monitors in the back to brief her on everything the CIA knew about Il Ramingo. Grateful for the distraction, Sophie perpetually replayed the anguish in Tommy's mother's voice when she called to apologize for her son's death.

"It's Latin. Technically, *memento mori* means 'remember, that you die,'" Carter said. "The phrase originated in ancient Rome. Used as an ego check for the Empire's top generals, the story goes that when one returned home after a successful conquest, Rome held a citywide celebratory spectacle called a *Triumph*. The ultimate tribute. But such lavish attention might give a general the idea he was better than his fellow Romans. Make some poor life decisions. So, when a general would enter a Triumph in his chariot, surrounded by cheering and adoring crowds, a slave seated behind him would whisper in his ear."

"Memento mori?"

Carter nodded. "It was a reminder that power and fame are temporary, that from street beggars to kings, we are all mortal."

"Pictures?"

"None exist, except for what we got from the Catacombs. Not even hotel CCTV." Carter typed on a keyboard. The middle of three monitors in the back of the van illuminated. "But plenty of his victims." The monitor showed a succession of gruesome images of men in various states of mortality, from gunshots, to hangings, bombings, several bodies with clear dual knife wounds in the chest like Tommy's, and finally her brother-in-law's burnt body on the beach. In each image there was a zoomed in box showing a horn-shaped trinket like the one found in the coroner's van. Each cornicello one had the same two Italian words etched on the talisman's surface.

Memento mori.

"And his name? The Midnight Rambler? From the Rolling Stones song?"

Carter nodded. He typed again on the keyboard. The images of Il Ramingo's bloody work replaced with a photograph of a young Mick Jagger and Keith Richards sitting on a balcony. Richards was strumming an acoustic guitar while Jagger looked to be singing.

"There is no word in Italian for *rambler*. My working theory is that he bastardized *Il Mezzanotte Ramingo,* which strictly means the Midnight Ranger, *Il Ramingo* for short. Song's off the band's 1969 album *Let it Bleed*. Fun fact. They wrote the song right here, in Southern Italy. On holiday in Positano."

Sophie squinted at the screen. Sure enough, she could see Positano's signature bay where her half-sister had perished in the photo's background behind Mick and Keith.

"And it's about another mass murderer, the Boston Strangler. The only song from the entire album composed outside of their London studio." Carter continued briefing her on what little they knew about the assassin, that he was tasked to eliminate the Pecora System's highest value targets, mostly top cops, judges, and leaders of competing syndicates. Best the CIA could figure, the Naples System used him as a killing tool going on fourteen years.

"No matter who's in charge, they get Il Ramingo as their starting

QB. And the guy is a first ballot, hall of famer. An expert at disguise and infiltration. Lethal with a blade in close quarters—his preferred method of killing. Proficient in hand-to-hand combat, demolitions, long range sniper, shit, you name it."

"Special forces?" Sophie said and handed the chunk of burned wood from her sister's boat back to Carter.

"Maybe. Probably? Bastard never leaves a whiff of DNA at crime scenes. Not a single hair." Carter played with the cornicello between his fingers. "I still can't figure out how he knew what we were doing with Pico."

"Someone on the inside?" Sophie said.

"It is Italy. In many spots the System does government better than the actual bureaucrats. But the information was compartmentalized. We didn't tell Fattore we had Pico. And it's in our agreement that we have to."

"I get the sense she's kind of a badass."

"You don't know the half of it."

More keystrokes from Carter followed by another suite of images on the van's monitors. The first showed a young man in a tight alley sprawled on the ground with his throat slashed. Carter explained that as a rookie cop in Campania, she single-handedly ended the murder spree of the *Mostro of Amalfi*, a serial killer that racked up six deaths before Fattore caught up to him. The screen changed to a photo of a body on a gurney covered by a blue sheet.

"Put two bullets in his head. Made her career. The System hates her. Tried to have the good captain taken out twice now. And she's still standing."

Sophie looked away. Her stomach lurched. She told herself it was the coffee, but that was a lie. Soon she was going to see and talk to and try her best to be strong in front of the man that had left her. Discarded Sophie and her mother. Abandoned her mom to die alone. And then for his next move replaced them both.

Across the street in the front window of a butcher shop, a woman carved some sort of Italian cured meat on a silver meat slicer. She would hold a plate-sized, pink slice to the sunlight coming through the window and examine the white ovals dotting its surface.

"What is that?"

Carter squinted at the woman. "*Mortadella*. Those white bits are chunks of neck fat. Sometimes they add pistachios."

"Oh, like baloney?"

"It's nothing like baloney."

Sophie sipped her coffee. "So, you're one of those. A foodie."

"Air Force brat. Moved around a lot. Base food sucked and I got to try everything."

"Didn't want to be a flyboy like Dad?"

Carter shook his head. "And my uncle. And my brother." He took off his glasses and held them to the light. "Washed out of flight school."

"Sir, we have movement out front."

With more keystrokes, Carter switched the monitor to a video feed from cameras mounted on the van's roof. Using a joystick, he zoomed in a man smoking in front of the hotel.

"One of the older Nicchi lieutenants." Carter looked over at Sophie and raised his eyebrows.

Sophie sighed. "That's my Uncle David." The guy looked awful. Her uncle had doubled in size from when she was a kid, but there was no mistaking his dark plank of a brow and boxer's stance.

"Indeed." Carter read from a dossier on the screen. "David Granttano, long time made man in the Nicchi crew, now second in command to Ken Nicchi. Two stints in jail, racketeering and felony accessory to murder. Felony sentence commuted when a witness recanted their testimony. Witness later turned up dead. Sheet looks clean though for the past ten years. Been keeping his head down."

"Who are those guys?" Sophie leaned forward and tapped the screen. Two men had walked out the front door of the hotel and straight for her uncle. The duo was younger and fit and did not carry themselves like the others. Sophie was pretty sure they were ex-military.

"Yeah, who is that?" Carter's fingers blazed across the keys. "They look like meat eaters. We've known that the Nicchi have used mercenaries for a while, mostly down in New Orleans. When the weapons ship out. The large one is called BTO."

"BTO?"

"Big Trouble Ortega. Brad *Tjeo* Ortega, born Corpus Christie, Texas nineteen seventy-nine, served three years in the Army in Afghanistan as—" Carter sat back in his chair.

"What is it?"

"Says here he was in the 160th Special Operations Aviation Regiment. Elite operators. Trained to fight from helicopters. If there's an ambush of US forces, these guys hop on birds and head right into the action. Missions are usually conducted at night, at high speeds, low altitudes, and on short notice. They call 'em the Night Stalkers. Soldiers from the 160th were part of the raid that got Bin Laden." More keystrokes. "Guy has over a dozen combat decorations, two purple hearts."

"Boyd." Sophie saw a tall figure in a sports coat and pants exit the hotel.

"Yes?"

"He's here."

"Who?'

"My dad."

"He's a handsome guy," Carter said into Sophie's earpiece. The CIA officer was back in the van monitoring a galaxy of SOG buttonhole cameras.

"Not something I was thinking about."

Sophie had to admit, despite being deep into his sixties, Ray Granttano still looked fit and healthy. He moved confidently, as if he belonged on the crowded Naples sidewalk, weaving through clumps of wandering tourists. He stopped occasionally to gaze into a shop window, with Carter warning Sophie in her ear to stay out of the window's reflection. They were in the *Centro Storico* neighborhood and counting on the element of surprise for her to surreptitiously plant the bug. Centro Storico was notable for its thin, stone-lined streets packed with people and scooters. It was a place where ancient churches mingled with gelato counters and cafés on dense city blocks.

Sophie kept a discreet distance from her father. A four-man, plainclothes SOG team was spread out on both sides of the street behind her. When Ray veered off the main thoroughfare and down a tight alley, they were forced to split into two teams. Directing the team over her radio earpiece, Sophie ordered three SOGs to set up surveillance on the other side of the alley while she followed with one protecting her back.

When Sophie exited the alley, she was on the edge of a city park. There were a few people walking among the trees and sculptures, but no sign of her father.

"He's sitting on a bench near the exit. On the north side," an SOG operator said in her ear.

"What's he doing?"

"He . . . he's crying."

Sophie anticipated her father might not be in the best mental state. His other daughter had just been murdered, likely a result of his brother David's association with the Nicchi crime family.

"Good. He's vulnerable. Make your move," Carter said.

She strolled down the park's bush lined path. Pausing at a statue of a robed man wielding a giant sword, Sophie pretended to read the plaque. Her father sat on a bench fifty feet to her right. An elderly couple at the next bench over was talking loudly to a young man.

"What are you waiting for?" Carter said in her ear.

"Just checking out the statue."

"Of Giuseppe Garibaldi? The Father of the Fatherland?"

"Don't rush me, Boyd."

"There's a very good chance the Nicchi crew meets with Luca Pecora later today. He leaves, you miss your chance. We have no one in the meeting and no way to get closer to Il Ramingo. That's the father who abandoned you. You don't owe him anything. Think of getting justice for Tommy, nothing more."

"Easier said than done."

"Then think of Maria. Think of how this gets you closer to Il Ramingo. Closer to Pecora."

With feet made of stone, she forced herself to turn and walk toward her father. Footsteps away, so close she could smell the hotel shampoo on his hair, she opened her mouth, but was cut short by a sudden commotion near the elderly couple. The woman started screaming in German.

"Hilfe! Hilfe! Dieb! Dieb!"

While his wife cried for help, the young man struck the old man in the face, pushing him to the ground. Just as the street thief reached for the old woman's purse, Sophie's father was behind him and grabbed the thug by the shoulder, spinning him around. With two quick jabs to the face, Ray Granttano knocked the young mugger backwards.

But the thief didn't flee. Instead, he pulled out a knife and marched toward Ray, who squared up and raised both fists.

"Fai cadere il cotlello!" Sophie said to the mugger, her pistol drawn and aimed at his head.

He relented and dropped the knife to clatter on the asphalt path.

"Andare," Sophie said.

The young man turned and sprinted for the park exit. Ray spun to face her at the sound of her voice.

"Sofia?"

"Sophie. Please. No one calls me that," she said and holstered her pistol.

"You're fluent? In Italian? That's fantastic."

"Scusa," Sophie said. She walked over to the old woman and helped her to her feet.

"*Polizei! Polizei!*" The woman said to Sophie while tugging on her sleeve.

"*Nein*," Sophie said, and pointed to the park exit. Then she turned to her father and grabbed him by the elbow and whispered in his ear, "Trust me, neither of us want to be here when the cops arrive."

They started walking fast toward where both had entered the park. Her father was smiling, but was he happy? How could she know?

"You're a vigilante now?" Sophie asked.

"Hardly." Ray shook his head. "I probably should find a restroom and check my diaper."

"I know a place."

Café Bene Fagilio was on the main street leading back to Ray's hotel. Being mid-morning after the work rush, father and daughter found a table away from eavesdroppers. A waiter stopped at their high-top table and took their orders. When he left, Ray fixed Sophie with a sober stare.

"What are you doing here?"

Ray looked like he hadn't slept in weeks. His eyes were bloodshot and sunken in their sockets. There were food stains on his shirt. He took a breath.

"What I meant to ask was why the EPA sent you here? Why now?"

"Special assignment. Attached to the Naval base in Naples. All I can say."

"Do special assignments include hazard pay?" Ray pointed at Sophie's bandaged ear from the gunfight.

"I'm fine."

Their waiter appeared with two espressos and left. Ray closed his eyes as he sipped his coffee. "It's true, everything tastes better here." He sat and sipped for a few silent moments.

"So again, what the hell are you doing here? In Naples, in this café? With me?"

"It's about Madeline."

Ray dropped his chin into his chest as tears welled. It was only the second time she'd seen her father in thirty years.

Sophie stretched her hand out and tapped his, twice. "I'm sorry, Ray."

Her father took his napkin from under his coffee and dabbed it at his eyes. "Thanks. You would've really liked her."

"For once, I bet you're right."

The jab made Ray smile. Sophie sipped her coffee. "But yeah, I've been *sent*." Sophie used the dreaded air quotes with her hands. "They figured you might respond to your long-lost daughter, you know, after."

"After I lost another daughter?"

Sophie nodded.

"Let me guess, this *they* is the CIA?"

"They want you to come in. Tell them more about why Madeline was killed."

"You wired?"

Sophie nodded. Ray leaned forward, his face inches from her neck and spoke. Her first instinct was to resist. Pull away. Tell him to get stuffed. But for a moment, with the tenor of his voice and the intimacy, she heard her father singing to her a lullaby. Like he did when she was young.

"You know if I talk to them, it's a death sentence." Ray aimed his head toward the front café window where two of the SOG officers sat drinking coffee. "Those two with you?"

Sophie nodded.

"They are here to bring me in when I say no?"

Sophie shrugged. "Protection."

Ray stiffened. "From me?"

Carter and Hodges fully expected Ray to turn down the offer of protection. The proffer only for show.

"Who knows? You did land in Italy with a planeload of mobsters."

Ray sat back. "You have every right to hate me. Every right. And yeah, I haven't done much to be proud of in my life, but you have to believe I wouldn't hurt you." Ray swiveled his head around the café. "Shit, Sofia, I could get strung up and bled like a chicken just for talking to you."

Sophie knew his story well, having read every news story she could find, even pulling strings through her Agency connections to read Ray's file from his time in the Kansas City PD. Ray stole evidence that helped his brother, David, kill the hitmen stalking him. Cost Ray his detective badge. But never from her own father's lips. In that moment she realized she needed to have him say it. Just once.

"I get why you did it. I can understand that you might not have thought you had a choice. But did you ever once think about me? Mom?"

"Every day since."

"Bullshit."

Ray recoiled as if she's spat in his face. Then he put on sunglasses and tossed back the rest of his coffee.

"I told myself if I ever saw you again, I'd give this back to you." Sophie reached into her shirt, took the locket from around her neck, and pulled it over her head.

With a trembling hand Ray accepted it. He swallowed, but with his sunglasses on Sophie couldn't gauge his reaction. She stood and turned and walked toward the exit.

"Sofia."

Sophie turned back to face her father. "What is it?"

"I'm really proud of you."

Without responding, she walked out of the café and onto the bustling Naples's street. After five minutes in hot foot traffic, she reached the van and entered the vehicle from the rear doors.

"How'd I do?" Sophie asked Carter.

Carter was sitting at computer monitors. He smiled at Sophie. "Sheboygan."

CHAPTER 21

"You don't have to do this."

Pico the Wheel hung suspended from a dead, leafless tree branch. Behind him loomed the silhouette of Mount Vesuvius's summit. His feet were bound by nylon cord, also used to tie his hands above his head in thick coils to a rope that held the cheese merchant's body suspended above a bubbling pool of illegally dumped cadmium sulfide.

"*Dacci oggi il nostro pane quotidiano, rimetti a noi i nostri debiti, come noi li rimettiamo ai nostri debitori. Essi non compresero le sue parole.*"

Pico was repeating an old Italian protection prayer. One Il Ramingo had heard many times before. From men whose desperation had given away to the acceptance of death.

"The heavenly Father cannot spare you. Only Luca can."

Il Ramingo squatted at the edge of the pit, a breathing mask on his face and an air tank strapped to his back. His long limbs and the mask made him appear as a large spider perched above its prey. Using binoculars, Il Ramingo scanned the pumice mounds and barren fields of black and red lava surrounding the pit. There was not a soul in sight aside from the two of them, a good thing because he had one more task to perform after disposing of Pico the Wheel.

Fumes from the lethal stew right under his bound feet were already affecting the cheese merchant. Pico let loose with several body wrenching coughs, hacking up gobs of black phlegm.

"I . . . I . . . have money." Pico's breathing was labored.

"Feel lucky he didn't decide to feed you alive to his pigs," Il Ramingo said. He pulled an iPhone from his pocket and tapped a number DeSalvo gave him. Positioning the phone on the edge of the pit, Il Ramingo aimed it at Pico. The shaved crown of a dark, bearded man appeared.

"Luca... Luca..." Pico labored to speak, the fumes from the pool starting to overwhelm him. "I didn't tell them anything... please... you have to . . ." another massive coughing spasm racked his body. "The accounts . . . I never . . ."

"A chi fa male, mai mancano scuse," Pecora said.

He who does evil, is never short of an excuse.

"Drop him. I want to watch."

Il Ramingo's Szell knife sprang from its sheath on his left wrist. With a great swipe, Il Ramingo cut the rope holding Pico above the pool. Wriggling like a worm on a hook, the cheese merchant dropped into cadmium sulfide up to his waist with a wet *plop.*

Both of Pico's tied hands dunked into the noxious muck. With a massive, grunting effort he pulled them out and held them to his face. Skin sloughed off in a great clump, dropped back into the chemical stew, and exposed the bright white bones of his right hand. Light rivulets of blood streamed from his eyes.

Pico screamed until another coughing fit overtook him, producing a chunk of internal organ that dribbled down his chin. He moaned and said, "Kill me."

"Oblige him," Luca Pecora said over the video call.

With a deep sigh, Il Ramingo cocked his arm back. He paused for a moment to let the fog from his breathing mask clear.

"Memento mori."

With a gloved hand he punched his Szell between the cheese merchant's eyes and deep into his brain. When Il Ramingo withdrew the long blade, Pico's body dropped into and disappeared after a moment with a burp. Il Ramingo picked up the phone and peered at Luca through his goggles and oxygen mask. He had business to discuss with Pecora.

"What happened on the yacht with the Nicchi . . . DeSalvo convinced me it was important to speak to you . . . in person," Il Ramingo said to Pecora, exactly as coached by his sponsor.

"You've worked for us for a long time. You know the price of disobeying me."

"I do. But I have a code."

Pecora's eyes narrowed. "The only code you need is my word. Do you understand?"

Il Ramingo nodded. Luca's eyes widened and he smiled, showing a silver incisor on his lower jaw. "Fine work you did with The Wheel, stealing him out from under the Americans. Their incompetence is breathtaking."

Il Ramingo felt a twinge of anger. What did Luca Pecora know of the CIA's failings? Snatching Pico was meticulously planned, and almost flawlessly executed, something a thuggish bastard like Luca Pecora couldn't comprehend.

Over the phone's screen, the namesake of the Pecora System pushed his face closer to the camera and fixed Il Ramingo with a piercing glare. "So, Il Mezzanotte Ramingo, DeSalvo tells me you have a plan for the sensors the Americans put in my mountain."

"I do. But I must test it first." Il Ramingo looked down at the bag at his feet.

"I want to see the top of Vesuvius." Il Ramingo turned the phone so the camera was pointed at the mountain's summit. "What's up there, you know how important it is to our mutual friend? The Russian?"

Il Ramingo was very aware of what was important to the man who had saved his life. Put him on his current course. He turned the phone back to face Pecora.

"I do."

"Good. Then you know that if the American woman from their EPA is successful it would anger him?"

"I do."

"Then you kill her after you remove the sensors. There is no longer a fucking code."

"I am your humble servant."

"I look forward to seeing you in person." Pecora laughed. "The Americans have no idea what's waiting for them." He disconnected.

They're not the only ones. Il Ramingo tossed the phone into the pool to dissolve next to The Wheel. He pulled another device from a side zipper pocket. The pre-loaded GPS tracker DeSalvo had given him displayed a bright green flashing dot two hundred meters to the west. Shouldering a black gym bag, he sprinted across boulder strewn rock fields, careful to avoid Camorra dump pools and burn pits. Once he was at the spot marked on the GPS, Il Ramingo stopped.

Fifty meters upslope, just as DeSalvo had said, there was the burned-out wreckage of the EPA woman's tracked research vehicle. Next to it, as promised, a newly drilled hole with a perfect ten-centimeter diameter. Il Ramingo dropped a rock down the hole and was rewarded with the faint sound of it landing deep in the Earth. He wondered if the rock strike would show up on the EPA woman's sensor.

From the gym bag he removed a coiled mechanical plumber's snake. Il Ramingo had modified the tool for today's task, removing the oscillating head and replacing it with a three-fingered claw. He affixed a block of formed Semtex plastic explosive to the head. He turned a knob on the machine's base as the flexible metal serpent descended into the hole. A minute later the snake stopped and the base beeped.

Il Ramingo stood and jogged until he was at a safe distance. From his pocket, he produced a small silver box with a red detonator switch, pointed it at the hole, and flipped the switch. There was a dull thump underground followed by a geyser of dirt and smoke erupting from the hole.

"*Memento nori.*"

CHAPTER 22

"I know she's not my wife, anymore, Steve. The fact that Karen married you was a big ole red flag. But Bryan is still my son. And I'd like to talk to him, now." Brad Tejo Ortega took a deep breath. Reminded himself what was at stake. "Please."

Three thousand miles away from Naples, in Fort Worth, Texas, Steve sighed into the phone. BTO sat in a high backed red velvet chair in an opulent suite on the top floor of Grand Hotel Vesuvio. Covering the floor before him were a dozen suitcases. BTO imagined reaching out across the deep blue of Atlantic Ocean, hooking each forefinger in Steve's ridiculously large hole earrings, and jerking down, hard.

"Be quick. We have Benihana reservations."

"Hi Daddy."

"Hey Doctor Funkenstein. You being a good boy?"

"I am. Where are you?"

"Somewhere far away . . . but I'll be home tomorrow."

BTO stopped for a moment. He sure hoped his boss knew what he was doing, flying them all the way to Italy for an audience with the local crime lord. There was a high degree of mission uncertainty. Things could easily go wrong for his employer, and that meant they could go bad for BTO and his men, too. There were plenty of parallels for BTO to dwell on between his time in the military and this Italian fiasco. Foremost, that the guys in charge always thought they knew more than the locals. Thinking of not making it out of Naples alive and that tatted up asshole Steve raising his son ripped BTO's insides out. He breathed in deep through his nose.

"OK daddy. I love you."

"I love you, too."

BTO put the phone on a small table next to his wallet and an Army issued G10 folding knife. He hated having shit in his pockets. Made him feel weighed down. His clothes always felt too tight as it was.

When he was just sixteen and a shadow of the six-and-a-half-foot, two-hundred-and-eighty-pound now chiseled body, Brad Tejo Ortega played varsity football in a small Texas town so rabid about the sport, they moved Halloween one year because it fell on a home game. Playing defensive end, every time he rushed the quarterback in practice, the bigger offensive linemen would slap him on the helmet so hard his vision blurred. They kept it up, slapping and pounding his helmet so hard his teeth hurt, until one day BTO was so frustrated he removed the screws that fastened the small pads inside his helmet and reversed them. The next time a lineman slapped his helmet the poor bastard impaled his hand on the screws covering the headgear's surface.

"You're big trouble, Ortega," the coach said, helping the whimpering player off the field as blood leaked from his hand. Big Trouble Ortega, or BTO; the nickname followed him all the way from the practice field to Afghanistan's blood-drenched Tanghi Valley as a member of the US Army's elite Night Stalkers.

BTO stood from the chair and surveyed his room. There was a shit-ton of work to do before their meeting and not much time to do it. While Ken and the rest of the Nicchi crew were in the hotel bar boosting their courage before the sit-down with Luca Pecora, BTO had all their bags delivered to his room. From the table he opened the G10. Satisfied the knife was sharp enough for the work at hand, he knelt next to a brown suitcase with a dull metal trim and used the blade to pry it open. Underneath was a small pocket holding a pistol slide with Sig Sauer etched on it. Inside were all the parts for the 9mm handgun. With quick, practiced movements hammered into his soul during training, he assembled the weapon. The Night Stalkers had served as the transportation element for the US military's most sensitive and dangerous covert operations. BTO's squad included two Blackhawk helicopter pilots, door gunners, a medic and his two-man fire team to ferry special forces on attack, assault, and reconnaissance missions conducted almost exclusively at night, at high speeds, low altitudes, and on short notice. Many times, the Night Stalkers came thundering in from dark sky, less than a hundred feet off the deck, leaping off their bird's skids into a ferocious melee to give cover for escaping soldiers. Some of his fellow Stalkers didn't make it back.

The private jet and payoffs to customs officials may have been enough to smuggle the guns, but BTO didn't take chances. The Nicchi crew needed to go into the meeting with Pecora armed. The way Ken explained it, he wasn't expecting any trouble, but the Camorra had a reputation for ruthlessness.

"If you're prepared, you never have to get ready," BTO's coach used to say.

Once BTO left military for life in the real world, he tried but failed to make an already shaky marriage, strained by three tours, survive. Despite leaving the Army with an honorable discharge as a staff sergeant, good paying work was scarce back home in Texas. Even for a trained combat veteran. The best he could find was security at a reservation casino, which, with shitty pay and a regular string of robbery attempts by methheads, was a high-risk, low-reward situation.

Luckily, BTO was recruited by a fellow retired soldier to work for the Nicchi crew. They were looking for private, discreet security. They were eager to pay a premium for combat experience. The job was to make sure no one interfered with shipments leaving Kansas City, with a stop for customs in New Orleans and eventually bound for Naples. The friend who recruited him was upfront. What they were doing was illegal, but they kept a low profile. He'd be expected to guard shipments but wasn't hired muscle. At five times what the casino paid, BTO couldn't say no. He wasn't a criminal. Paid his taxes. But Bryan's alimony payments were murder. And he had to eat. Taking the money meant a better life for his son. It helped that the Nicchi ran a covert, calculated operation. BTO assumed what left the New Orleans port was drugs or other contraband and didn't ask. Better for everyone involved the security team didn't know the details.

The first few months were uneventful, but when a biker gang tried to hijack one of their shipments, BTO sent three of them to the hospital. After that his role in the organization grew, along with his paycheck, though he never envisioned running security for a trip to Italy.

BTO had all the suitcases in a pile, and a table full of pistols with loaded magazines. He checked his phone. Still a half-hour to spare before the meeting with Pecora. Enough time for a nap. But though the bed was comfortable, he couldn't sleep. All he could think of was Bryan and how good it would be to see him again. To sit on the couch and play whatever dumb video game his son wanted him to.

CHAPTER 23

"I never told you this, but my mom got sick like your parents, too."

Maria had brought Tommy's cribbage board. She and Sophie were halfway through their second game.

"Really? And she died?" Maria sat on the bed in their room. She stared at Sophie with eyes like two big bowls of milk with a raisin floating in the middle.

"Where she worked."

Sophie nodded. They were seated on a rock-hard, candy cane striped sofa in their new Absoluta Amore room. After Il Ramingo's breach of the facility, Carter moved Sophie one floor up to the penthouse level where there were only two suites, and the security was fierce. Chief of Italy Station Bill Hodges occupied the other room across the hall. The views were far superior to the lower floors. She could actually see the city. The white bleached spires of Santa Maria Assunta loomed to her right, the very same church ensconced above the Catacombs of San Genero used by Il Ramingo to infiltrate Absolute Amore. To her left the mewing of seagulls and the shimmering blue hue of the Naples port beckoned.

After all this time, the agony of that last year with her mother, dealing with the pain both physical and emotional, remained just beneath the surface. Ready to hurt all over again.

"Did she cry?" Maria asked. "My mom cried a lot."

Again, Sophie nodded.

A single drop rolled down Maria's left cheek. "I miss my mom."

Sophie wrapped her arms around the girl's shoulders and ruffled

Maria's hair. Sophie learned a neat trick to avoid collapsing into a body-lurching crying jag every time she talked about her own mother's death. She visualized the faces of her bosses, Dale and Frank Hughes. Specifically, the day when both brothers, their chunky, half-melted marshmallow faces frozen in shock, were found guilty and sentenced to five years of federal time.

She'd sat in the back of the courtroom to watch the verdict. The two dipshits thought they were smarter than the EPA. Retroactively forging their monitoring tests to cover up for years of running defective air scrubbers while their employees, including Sophie's mother, inhaled carcinogens. And away they went to the supermax prison outside Florence, Colorado.

Later in her career, Sophie was reminded by looking into the Sudanese refugee mother's hollow eyes after her son died that there'd always be a steady supply of cold, calculating assholes who valued money over human life. Like the ones who killed her mother. She knew that a solitary EPA agent couldn't protect everyone's water and air.

"You can't save everyone," Sophie had told Tommy on the Strata De Amalfi.

"But you can try."

Now looking at Maria, she realized Tommy Jones, in his own way, was right. You can't save everyone, but you can try. Sophie didn't have a proper handle yet on the how, but helping the CIA stop Pecora seemed like a good start. While she knew she couldn't really trust Hodges, they each needed something from each other. That, she could trust.

A knock on the door was the signal for Sophie to head downstairs. The operation was about to start. Sophie stood from the couch and walked to her closet. She removed her pistol from a small hotel safe, an accommodation from Hodges made post Il Ramingo. After Sophie slid the holstered weapon into her waistband, she put on a suit jacket and returned to the living room.

"I won't be long." Sophie reached down and brushed the girl's cheek. Then she pointed at the cribbage board. "And when I get back I'm going to kick your butt."

"Curds," Maria said.

Sophie locked the door behind her and nodded to a duo of SOG operatives stationed on either side of her door. The elevator was a few steps down the hall. After Il Ramingo, Hodges ordered new locks on all the stairwells, so she rode the elevator four floors down. Sophie walked into the converted conference room bustling with activity.

"They're heading through the upper Naples neighborhoods now. Both vehicles just left Piscinola-Marianella. Entering the Chiaino quarter. We estimate twenty minutes until they hit the Scampia outskirts," Hodges was saying into a cellphone.

"Who's he talking to?" Sophie asked Carter. She took a seat next to the CIA operative at the conference table. Carter's eyes were on the screens, his tie loose. The man looked tired. They all were. Sophie had grabbed a blissful hour nap earlier but felt like she needed a week.

"Fattore."

While Hodges talked to the Campania Special Police Captain, techs and SOG officers rushed around the room. Overheard drone footage of the Nicchi caravan played on a trio of massive flat screens mounted on the wall. Her father was in the first car, and Nicchi family henchmen in the second vehicle.

"Keep your men at a safe distance. I'll tell you when to move," Hodges said to Captain Fattore. He ended the call, putting his phone back in his pocket.

"Does the captain know about the bug I planted?" Sophie asked.

Hodges shook his head. "No. I'd trust her with my life out there, but there's no telling who in her division is System first, Neapolitan pizza second, international law third. After what happened to Pico . . . I'm not taking any chances."

Carter sipped from a paper cup and winced. "Maybe it's me, or maybe it's that this coffee tastes like a human rights violation, but I don't feel good about sending them in there, Bill."

"Why?" asked Hodges gruffly.

"Because they're bait?" Sophie said.

"Either you're at the table or you're on the menu," Hodges said. He turned back to monitors and addressed the room.

"Once the Nicchi reach Pecora's neighborhood, no more aerial surveillance. The drones peel back. Captain Fattore says Camorra snipers using fifty cal rifles have brought down their drones before. That's why Agent Grant's bug is super important. Our only ears."

"I don't hear anything," Carter said.

"Volume!" Hodges shouted at no one in particular.

A dark-haired woman typed on a keyboard. The audio feed from the locket around her father's neck broadcast into the room.

"No matter what happens, no one does anything unless I say so. Keep the guns holstered. We don't want Pecora to know we're carrying unless we have to. No trigger-happy accidents, you got that Jimmy?"

"I'm cool. I just want to find out who killed my brother."

"Then why are you twirling your pistol like you're Wyatt Fucking Earp?"

"Keep the safety on, Jimmy, and you'll be fine."

Sophie recognized her father reassuring the nervous Nicchi scion. There was a flutter in her throat thinking about him heading into one of the most dangerous neighborhoods in Italy. Did she really care that much about the man that abandoned her? Her dry mouth and queasy stomach hinted that she did, with Sophie chalking it up to their shared DNA. A trick of biology, an evolutionary impulse to circle the familial wagons. A reflex, nothing more.

"Ray. You stay in the back. Keep your eyes open. Me and David are going to be busy talking with Pecora. I need your expertise taking everything in. Like we talked. Cool?"

"Cool."

"And BTO?"

"He's our exit strategy."

"No, we are, polenta for brains," Sophie heard Hodges say under his breath.

While everyone was focused on the screens and the Nicchi caravan, with what Sophie told herself was White Bronco intensity, Carter took a seat in a metal folding chair to Sophie's left. He was chewing a piece of gum, his jaws grinding hard like it owed him money.

"They've entered Scampia," a female tech said.

"Switching to overwatch," said the tech piloting the drone.

The cars disappeared into the maze of crumbling apartment complexes at the heart of the rundown neighborhood. They were deep in Pecora System territory now and on their own. After the 1980 earthquake, the police refused to enter the area. With a few keystrokes the female tech switched the screens to thermal imaging with the tracking chip around Ray's neck flashing red.

"Working only off the bug," the tech said.

"I've been meaning to ask how'd you plant it on him, your dad. How'd you get the bug on him? Brush pass?" Hodges asked.

"No, I had this locket he gave me when I was a kid, and I—"

"What'd you say?" Carter bolted to his feet.

"It was a locket—"

"No. Not that." Carter was staring at the red cornicello in his hand. The same one the CIA operative had been carrying with him since the yacht exploded. "Brush pass," Carter said under his breath. Without warning, he slammed the cornicello on the conference room table as hard as he could. The loud sound made the already on edge room jump.

"For Christ's sake, Boyd!" Hodges said.

Carter pawed through red debris until he found what he was looking for. Holding up to the light between trembling fingers the entire room saw the small chip that had been stashed inside the trinket.

CHAPTER 24

Ray Granttano was going to die.

Not like his obese brother David, whose heart walls were long overdue to blow out like the sides of a worn tire. No. Ray's end was destined to be a painful, gruesome, bullet-riddled death at the hands of Camorra clan leader Luca Pecora.

Pecora and his crew were ruthless killers, dealing weapons and drugs across Italy and chunks of Europe. Even though they were the subject of numerous books and TV shows, as Ray understood it, Pecora the man was more of an enigma. He'd avoided recent sweeps by law enforcement that had jailed the heads of other clans, somehow clinging to power for more than ten years. Ray figured guys like that put a bullet in a trusted associate at the slightest whiff of danger. Whoever was responsible for his daughter Madeline's death, as much as it hurt deep in his chest to think about it, her murder was clearly part of something bigger. Which raised serious questions. Questions like was the killing part of a Camorra clan turf war? Was it revenge for some action Pecora took against a rival? Or was it as Ken had hinted, Pecora responded to the Nicchies desire to leave the weapons business in favor of toxic waste with a clear *no grazie*? The biggest unanswered question that hung over the car like the gas from a bloated corpse, was whether the System leader believe the Nicchies were compromised?

Because if he did, then they were driving right to their deaths. And that made Ray nervous. He might have erupted into a full-blown panic if not for his overriding need to find out what happened to his Madeline.

Ray fired two boxes of .45's in his old department issue sidearm every Thursday. There was an indoor gun range in a repurposed Kmart in North KC that was clean and always had available lanes. But the pistol BTO handed him that morning, currently tucked in his waistband, felt foreign. What was he going to do? Ray was no mobster. He was here for one thing and one thing only - his family. Despite enduring her contempt, seeing Sophia that morning cemented his goal.

"Boss."

BTO's giant form was behind the Mercedes's wheel. The man's shoulders filled most of the front seat making Ray, who was not a small guy, feel claustrophobic sitting next to him. This was on top of the unnerving sense of impending doom. The big man had grunted a brief acknowledgement to Ray, greeting him through a full black beard stretching to his neckline. Now navigating Naples's streets, BTO offered a robust two words, pointing out the windshield at the trash strewn, teeming slums of the city's northern Scampia neighborhood.

"Getting closer."

"Good." Ken Nicchi grunted from the back seat. Poor Jimmy was sandwiched between his dad and Ray's brother, David. Both men were swollen, half drunk, and doing decent jobs of hiding their apprehension. They were hard guys. Killers. But in over their heads. Poor Jimmy couldn't cloak his fear, eyes shooting back and forth in their sockets.

"David. You know that long wooden chute at the KC stockyards?" Ray called over his shoulder. "The one they push the squealing cows down? Right before they get a bolt to the brain?"

"Sure, Ray," David croaked from the back seat, lit cigarette dangling from his hand out the window as the car rushed through streets. Both curbs were lined with shirtless kids and grim looking young men, some visibly armed.

Ray jerked his thumb out the car window. "That's exactly what this drive feels like. Calves to the slaughter."

"Slaughter?" Jimmy said.

"Calm down. There's nothing to worry about," Ken said. "After this is over I'll buy you all a nice fat *bistecca al sangue*." Ken mooed like a cow at his son, who recoiled. *Classic projection,* Ray thought. *The boss is nervous.*

"No matter what Pecora does or says when we get there, remember, he's a businessman and you don't butcher your prize bull." Ken said.

"Right. We're his best supplier. No way he gets what we give him on the open market," David said, blowing smoke.

"But you *do* send a message to keep the herd in line," Ray said. "Especially when the prize bull says he wants out of the arms biz."

"Stop being dramatic. You've seen too many mob movies," Ken said, showing his irritation with Ray by grinding his jaw.

Too dramatic? Who lost their job, their family helping Ken and David all those years ago? Ray wanted to grab the fat bastard by the collar and shake those answers loose but decided to leave the pin in that grenade for another time.

"We're here," BTO said.

He steered the Mercedes to the side of the street in front of a pair of big wooden doors under a red brick archway. Three men wielding automatic weapons appeared. A tall, thin, unarmed woman dressed in slacks and short-sleeved black silk shirt stepped up to the driver's window. She peered inside the car.

Ken rolled down his window and stuck his face into the outside air. A wave of heat from the blistering summer filled the car. "Ken Nicchi, here to see Luca Pecora, *por favore.*"

The woman stared hard at Ken's face and then down at her phone. Ray looked over and caught a glance of the phone's screen showing the Kansas City mob boss's jowled visage. Silk shirt brought the phone to her mouth, speaking a few words in Italian. Then she gestured toward the wooden doors that swung open to reveal a cobblestone piazza.

"Welcome to Villa Pecora," she said in decent English. The woman waved the car inside.

BTO drove into the piazza, followed by the other Nicchi car. Once inside, they had a better sense of the massive urban fortress Pecora called home. Bayonet-sized chunks of broken glass crowned a ten-foot-high wall surrounding the property. Armed men were everywhere. Ray figured there were at least two-dozen assault rifle-toting thugs in the piazza alone, a space that was essentially a parking lot with a brace of luxury cars parked in formation. BTO guided the Mercedes to a stop next to a blue vintage corvette.

The Nicchi crew spilled onto the sunbaked pink brick piazza. Keeping his eye on a nervous Jimmy Nicchi, Ray glimpsed Ken's son tucking something into his sock. Before he could pursue it further, one of Pecora's goons stepped in between them. Ken was clear to his troops before they left that no one in his crew was to draw a gun unless confronted with mortal danger. Pecora was notorious for ghoulish tactics, Ken cautioned his men, one time placing the severed head of a rival on the center spot before the start of an SSC Napoli soccer match.

"If Luca Pecora himself shoots me in the face," Ken said to his son Jimmy, "I want you to take a deep breath and count to five before drawing your piece and returning fire."

With Camorra thugs circling, the tall woman gestured for them to follow her inside.

"But just you four, the rest stay outside by the cars."

"Us five," Ken gestured at BTO.

"Fine." Silk shirt said. She waved two massive goons close to BTO's size over. One held a leather bag zipped open. "No guns."

Ken motioned with his hand for them to disarm. Ray went first. He pulled the silver Colt from his belt and put in the bag, happy to see the pistol gone. After the rest disarmed, BTO told his remaining guys not invited inside to stick close to the cars and make no trouble. Silk shirt and three armed men escorted their select group out of the piazza and through a set of double doors. Functioning air conditioning welcomed them, with BTO making the most vocal sigh of pleasure. She led them down a long hallway lined with framed pictures of what Ray assumed were members of Pecora's family. The hallway opened into a smaller courtyard bathed in sunlight, a raised walkway around the circumference of the area. BTO sighed again, this time a sad wheeze as the intense heat returned. In the courtyard was a square table with a black tablecloth.

At the table sat Luca Pecora.

"Welcome to my home," he said in English even better than Silk Shirt's.

When they approached, Pecora stood and made a determined effort to shake all their hands. For a moment, he met each of their eyes with his own intense stare before returning to his chair. Five empty folding chairs were set up opposite from him on the table. BTO picked one up, setting it back down behind the others in what Ray assumed was to keep a broader view of the situation.

Ken, Ray, and David each took a seat across from Pecora, while Jimmy Nicchi sat in the only chair close to the System leader, just off his right elbow. Ray scanned Pecora's face. The man's expression was blank. Blank by design. Murdering without mercy anyone who posed a threat to him took a cold soul, Ray imagined. But maybe he was just being nice. Calm. They were business associates after all. Ray slid back in his chair, trying to relax enough to appear as sedate as Pecora.

"*Mi apologia* . . . for the show of force, all the guns." Pecora said. His accent was pleasant. "The Nigerians. They want everything we have. But do not worry, you are safe here with me."

Pecora explained that the Sicilian Costra Nostra had allowed Nigerian crime lords to set up a human trafficking hub in the abandoned coastal town of Castel Volturno. Beachhead established; the West Africans were now looking to hijack the Camorra's drug trade in all Southern Italy.

"Jesus Christ!" Jimmy jumped up from the table, knocking Pecora's glass of water over. "Something just bit my hand."

David and Ken shot their chairs backward in fear, as a thick snout with yellow stained tusks poked its head out from under the table.

"*Cochi!*" Pecora said. Breaking his cool he kicked at something under the table. "Out from there."

A big fat, black, hairless pig almost took the table with it as the thick animal scampered away with a squeal. The massive hog ran to the raised walkway and plopped down next to a near identical swine save for a pink splash on its brow.

"House pigs?" Ray said.

Pecora smiled. "*Trained* house pigs. Casertana pigs. The *peletalla* or hairless ones." He slapped his chest. "From Campania. Bloodline stretches back millennia. The Romans painted frescos celebrating them." Pecora made a clicking sound with his mouth. "Cochi, Renato." The two pigs, each the size of a steamer trunk, hopped up and trotted to the table. The leader of the Pecora System snapped his fingers. One of his men appeared holding a ceramic bowl that he handed to Pecora.

"Are you hungry, *mi amicos?*" Pecora dipped his hand into the bowl and started tossing little nubs of meat to the pigs.

In horror, but as cool as he could, Ray leaned over and whispered to his brother David. "It's fingers."

"What?"

"Fingers. He's feeding those pigs human fucking fingers."

"And toes," Pecora held up a gray, severed big toe. "Thanks to the Nigerians." He tossed it in the air. The two pigs battled over which one consumed the fat nub. Jimmy stood off to the side, his face white.

"Come, sit down, son," Ken said. Ray could see that the Nicchi boss was as unsettled by the digit-eating swine as the rest of them. Pecora noticed, too. The man lived up to his reputation. In terms of a negotiation position, the Nicchies were now far downrange.

"I'm fine right here, pop." Jimmy's eyes were wide and focused on the two hogs.

"In America we feed our pigs corn, makes 'em fat and tasty fast," Ray said.

"Oh, I would never eat them," Pecora said. "I swear Renato can tell if someone is lying. And Cochi? Cochi is fiercer than any attack dog."

Ken Nicchi leaned forward with his meaty hands clasped together into one massive fist. He squeezed his hands and the veins on their surface popped out. "You said you knew who killed my son."

"And my daughter," Ray said.

"I do," Pecora said.

Pecora picked a pinkie finger from the bowl and flicked it airborne. Cochi put a fat hoof on Renato's head, stretched his massive body out, and snagged the extremity with the snap of yellow-tusked jaws. Renato squealed in hunger and frustration.

"It was me. I killed them."

"You killed my Christopher?" The Kansas City mob boss was on his feet, both hands grasping the table so hard Ray Granttano heard the wood creak and pop.

"Give me one reason. One fucking reason why I shouldn't tear your head off?"

Ray Granttano shared Ken's desire for vengeance. He came to listen, but hearing Pecora admit to killing his sweet Madeline made him want to empty his discarded pistol into Luca Pecora's chest.

"I have many reasons." Pecora snapped his fingers again. This time, dozens of armed men appeared on the raised walkway behind him and aimed their weapons at the Nicchi crew.

"There's no way they get me before I get you," Ken said.

Jimmy and David sat frozen. BTO had shifted in his chair, ready to move if he had to.

"Be a shame to lose both of your sons, wouldn't it, Ken? What kind of father would that make you?"

"The kind that avenges his family."

Pecora waved at Silk Shirt now standing behind him and to the left. She stepped to the Camorra boss's side and handed Pecora a tablet computer.

"What if that son was, how do you say . . . *traditore* . . . *a ratto*?

Would he still be worthy of vengeance?"

"A rat? No way," David said. "Not Christopher."

"See for yourself." Pecora sat at the table and put the tablet in the middle. He beckoned Ken with his hand. "Please sit. I understand your anger. And confusion. Sit down. See for yourself."

"Boss, we should go, this doesn't feel right," David said. Ray's brother once again marshaling his core defining characteristic of self-preservation.

"No. You're staying and watching the video because I'm not yet convinced your Christopher didn't act alone," Pecora said pointing at the tablet.

Ken Nicchi swayed for a moment, his hands still gripping the table. His eyes wandered over to the legion of Camorra poised to open fire. Ken let out a deep sigh, resigned to the situation and took a seat. Pecora waved his hand, and his men lowered their weapons. Ray sensed a significant relaxing of everyone's body language. The bulk of Pecora's men left.

"Chiara," Pecora said to Silk Shirt and pointed at the table. The woman stepped forward, placing a bucket full of ice stuffed with big brown bottles of Peroni Reserve on the table. *"Por favore,"* Pecora said to the Nicchi crew while taking a beer from the bucket.

Ignoring the beer, Ken Nicchi reached forward and picked the tablet up from the center of the table. Ray and David peered over his shoulder. Ray glanced back at Jimmy whose eyes were locked on Pecora's two pigs lounging in a half full, inflatable kiddie pool. Ken had warned them Pecora would pull some macabre intimidation trick. Ray had seen some wild shit in his time but feeding fingers to pigs was insane enough to make him feel sorry for Jimmy.

Ray tuned back as Ken stabbed at the tablet's screen with his hand. On the device appeared a sleek silver yacht floating in bright blue water, the name *Esperanza* stenciled on its hull. Due to how the shot bobbed up and down with the boat in frame, Ray figured whoever filmed the craft was lurking nearby on another boat.

Three people sat at a table on the *Esperanza's* rear deck, one with an unmistakable mane of blonde hair. Ray bit hard on his lip seeing his daughter in her last moments alive. An image of a grinning nine-year-old Madeline, proudly holding a tomato she grew on her own, appeared before his eyes.

"That man. See him there? On your son's yacht? With Christopher and Madeline. He says he's with the US State Department, but that's most certainly a cover. My people tell me he's CIA. Look, he posted to Instagram under his cover from Positano the same day."

Ray's mind careened to his other daughter, Sophie, and that morning's café meeting, the grim operatives sitting at other tables monitoring their conversation. Ray felt the air in his lungs escape.

"Our CIA?" Ken said.

Pecora nodded. "The Americans are here." He dunked his hand into the ice bucket and came out with a dripping bottle. After opening a beer and taking a long drink, Pecora wiped his hand across his mouth. "And they're hunting me."

It was subtle, maybe too subtle for others to notice, but Ray saw something shift in Pecora's confidence. *Could it be he's paranoid? Who can blame him?* With mention of the CIA there was a flicker of fear in Pecora's eyes. Cornered predators never go down easy. Ray recognized his son-in-law's voice on the video playing on the tablet. He was talking with the man while holding hands with Madeline.

"No one saw you? Are you sure? We're taking a big risk just being seen with you. Pecora would feed us to his goddam pigs if he knew."

"We were very careful, it's kind of what we're good at," said the man, now obviously full of shit in Ray's view.

"And we both get new identities, me and Madeline? Witness protection?"

"You deliver Pecora, and you get the whole nine yards. New identities, around the clock security . . . you name it."

The video ended.

"I can't believe it," Ken Nicchi said, slumping in his chair, his face white. With the flick of his wrist, he shoved the pad to the middle of the table in disgust. "Luca, what happened? Didn't you two meet?"

Pecora nodded. "Your son indeed did sit with me, we ate dinner. We talked. But he made me suspicious... kept asking about acquiring things."

"What, things?" Ray said.

Pecora waved his hand over Naples. "The quake. In 1980 the earthquake leveled everything as far as the eye can see. That's the kind of weapon he was seeking," Pecora said. "So, I had my best man watch them." He shrugged. "They were meeting with the Americans." He pointed at Ken. "Have you all been careful since you arrived? No chance meetings with an old acquaintance that just happened to be in Naples? None of you been approached since you have been here?"

Ray fidgeted in his chair. Moving his hand slow so as not to attract attention he pushed the locket hanging around his neck that Sophie gave him back inside his shirt and then ran his hand through his hair. He let his hand drop back down to his side. Was Pecora hinting he'd had them followed as a precaution after landing in Italy?

"No," Ken said in a whisper.

Ray could tell Ken was wrestling with the revelation his son and anointed next leader of the Nicchi crime family was a government informant. Good. Ken should have to reckon with the wreckage his choices created. Just like Ray, who was barely dealing with the huge hole his daughter's death left in his chest.

"I'm not buying it." Out of nowhere, Jimmy Nicchi stood and picked up the tablet from the table and waved the device in his father's face. "It's got to be a fake pop, some type of image manipulation. You know, like Photoshop. What do they call it? A deep fake? Chris would never fucking do that."

"I assure you the man that took the video is a professional of the highest quality," Pecora said.

"They must've had some leverage on him, Boss," David said. He patted Ken on the back. "It's the only explanation."

"Not now, Granttano." The Nicchi family boss put his face in his hands. "It should have been me."

"You thought Chris was ready," David said. "We all did."

Then Ken Nicchi did something unexpected. Turning to face Ray he took his meaty fist and poked him in the chest. "It was her, Madeline. She did it to my Christopher. She made him weak."

"What did you say?"

Ray stood and the two men faced each other nose to nose.

"Fellas, let's cool it down," David said, his eyes all whites. Pecora stood and backed away with a look of delight.

"If your whore daughter hadn't taken Chris's eye off the ball, he'd still be alive," Ken Nicchi snarled.

"Take that back," Ray said.

"Go fuck yourself. And fuck your daughter."

With his right hand, Ray faked a hook, drawing Ken's attention, and hit him with with two hard jabs with his left. The Nicchi boss's cinder block head snapped back. Ken threw a punch at Ray, who leaned into it so that Ken's fist connected with the crown of Ray's skull.

"Shit!" Ken said in pain. He roared in rage like a quilled grizzly bear, lunging at Ray, wrapping his arms around him, taking both men to the ground.

Ken reared back, his fist cocked, a trickle of blood running from his nose. Just as Ken swung down, BTO scooped him off Ray. While BTO corralled an enraged Ken Nicchi off to the side, David pulled his brother to his feet.

"You're dead, Granttano, fucking dead," Ken said.

"You have no idea how in over your head you are," Ray shot back. "A fat minnow in a big ocean full of sharks. You're bait! Nothing else."

"Gentlemen, please," Luca Pecora said. "This is supposed to be a business meeting."

"We don't mean to disrespect you Luca," David said. "We're all still a little raw about what happened is all." David grabbed his brother by the elbow and leaned into him, speaking in a low voice only the two of them could hear.

"What the hell do you think you're doing?"

"Thirty years ago, you and that asshole got me tossed off the force. Now one daughter is dead. And the other hates my guts?" Ray said while swatting at some dirt on his pants. "You ask me what I'm doing? I'm standing the fuck up."

"About your daughter," Pecora said. The patio grew quiet. He had picked up the tablet from the table and was typing on the screen. Then he walked to where the two brothers stood and handed the tablet to Ray. "*Por favore*, press play."

Another video started playing. It showed what looked to be a dark jail cell with a cot and a bucket in the corner. Straw covered the dirt floor. Though partially obscured by shadows, Ray could tell the person sitting on the cot was Madeline.

Alive.

Her wrists and ankles were bound, and a gag dangled around her neck.

CHAPTER 25

"Get them out, now!" Sophie had yelled at the bank of big screen monitors in the CIA safehouse in the seconds after Carter discovered the bug planted by Il Ramingo in the cornicello.

Her eyes were fixed to the blinking red dot on the center display. It represented her father and the tracking beacon in Sophie's locket. Pleading to every god from Zeus to Vishnu for the dot to move, she needed the flickering red orb to travel south, away from Luca Pecora, and away from his clan of killers.

Toward Sophie.

"He knows everything. Pecora knows. He's going to kill everyone." Sophie pointed at the chip in Carter's hand from the smashed cornicello. "Il Ramingo has been listening in. He knows we have a bug on my father. Get him out."

With a thumb and forefinger, Carter held it aloft. "Someone see if you can run a backwards trace." A tech swooped by, took it from his hand, and scurried out of the room. "She's right, Bill."

Hodges looked her up and down as if to say he could have Sophie renditioned to Guantanamo Bay with the snap of his fingers. "So far no calls have gone into the Pecora compound. If Il Ramingo was listening to us, he hasn't tipped them off. Remain calm. If Pecora was going to line them up against the wall he would've done it by now." Hodges cleared his throat long and loud and nodded back at Sophie's chair. "Sit down. I have a plan."

"I looked up your symptoms. Chronic throat clearing? You're either pregnant or have Tourettes," Sophie said.

"Wait, what did he just say? Pecora?" Carter said.

"My sister is alive." Sophie said.

She couldn't believe it. But there it was, from the mouth of Luca Pecora. Everyone froze, with techs and SOG operatives staring at the bank of monitors on the wall. Mouth agape, eyes unblinking, Bill Hodges stood with them.

"She's alive," Carter said, smiling. "Madeline's alive." The man jumped to his feet.

Sophie grabbed Carter by his shoulder and spun him to face her. She felt disconnected from her emotions, unable to control the anger surging inside. Like another person.

"No thanks to you."

Carter's eyes narrowed. "Don't put your guilt on me. Tommy stayed because of you. You made a choice. Grow up and own it." He pointed at the screen. "Same as Madeline. She came to us."

Sophie took a step back. Was she reacting this way because Tommy's death was her fault?

"Would you people shut the fuck up?" Hodges said. He snorted twice. Hodges held his hand over his cellphone. "I'm talking to Fattore." He put the phone back to his ear.

"Arrest everyone."

CHAPTER 26

"She's alive. Did you hear that? Alive."

Ray's head was spinning like he was drunk. He fell backwards into a chair and laughed once, a deep yelp of pure emotion. "My girl's alive."

David walked to Ray and put a hand on his brother's shoulder. Tears streamed down Ray's cheeks. "Incredible. Just incredible."

"That's great news, Ray," Jimmy said. He was standing next to his father wearing a child's grin. "Hey what the fuck?" Jimmy jerked his hand away from Renato's snout. The pig had once again snuck up and started licking his fingers.

"Get it together, Jimmy," Ken Nicchi said. "Remember your brother? The dead rat?" He used a handkerchief to dab at the blood Ray drew from his nostril. Ken turned and faced Luca Pecora. "What happened? I thought this Il Ramingo was supposed to be the ultimate baddass. All I hear from you. An unstoppable killing machine. Why'd he let her live?"

Pecora shrugged. "Truthfully, Il Ramingo was supposed to kill her, too. He's served two bosses before me, and this is the only time he's failed an order." Pecora gestured for Ken to join him back at the table. Both men sat across from each other.

"Until this recent unpleasantness, you and I, we had a good business going. No?"

"Yes," Ken Nicchi said. "Yes we did."

"At first, I felt betrayed. Disrespected. My longtime partner. My old friend Ken Nicchi. Sends his son in his place. And what happens?

Without Il Ramingo maybe we're all in a CIA torture prison?" Luca Pecora picked up his half empty beer from the table and took a sip. "Most days, if I lure you here, I kill you outright. Pig food. I don't have to explain that reputation is very important in our System to you, do I?" Pecora stood and pointed over Ken's head to the east. "See that mountain top? See Vesuvius?"

Ken stood and put his hand above his eyes to shield from the bright sun. Since Pecora's compound was high above Naples city center, the two tips of Mount Vesuvius's saddle poked above the skyline.

"Normally there is smoke. From our burn pits."

Ray craned his neck. The only thing hanging over Vesuvius were a few white fluffly clouds against a blue sky.

"Waste management," Ken said. "Never glamorous but it always pays the bills."

"Well, the same Americans that turned your son, just shut us down on Vesuvius."

Pecora explained how the night before a team of US military personal stormed their illegal dumping grounds, killed five of his men and installed high-tech monitoring sensors deep into the ground. Pecora drank the rest of his beer. Then pointing to the top of Mount Vesuvius peeking out over the Naples skyline, he said to Ken, "Don't think I don't know our friend, that his protégée has been whispering in your ear. Whispering about getting out of the gun business?"

Ken shrugged. "Just talk at this point."

"Just talk. Just talk. Indeed." Pecora stood and walked around to the table and knelt next to Ken. "I understand. The weapons. So much attention. CIA. The War on Terror. One minute you're making some money and the next you're a smoking crater. But the waste? No one's watching the waste."

"What are you saying?"

"You used to ship it out. I'm asking you to take it in. I have more than I can handle."

Ken nodded. Ray could see the big man's shoulders were tensed.

"No more weapons?"

Pecora shook his head. "No more weapons. A whole new business."

"Whole new businesses cost money to start. We're a small crew."

Pecora leaned back in his chair and kicked his feet up on the table. "Three million? US dollars?"

Ken's eye twitched. "That'll work."

"Good. Good." Pecora stood from his chair and walked to Ken. "America is an untapped market for waste. Shit, *mio fratello,* your country allows your companies to dump poison wherever they want. We're going to make so much fucking money."

Ray was still so gob smacked by Madeline's appearance that Pecora's next words didn't immediately register.

"There's just one more thing. Il Ramingo. He will bring Madeline here. To Naples. Tomorrow. In exchange for my investment and to reestablish trust, I will watch you put a bullet in her head." He stuck his hand out. "Deal?"

For a minute, one glorious goddamn minute, Ray was happy. Three hellish days he floated in darkness after learning about Madeline. Now there was light. But just as fast as the joy flooded his body, it was replaced with an aggressive tumor of sheer terror in his stomach. He jumped up from his chair, ready to choke Madeline's location from the System leader.

"Get the fuck away from me!" Jimmy Nicchi shouted.

Ray froze. The younger Nicchi had pulled a snub-nosed revolver from his sock. It was aimed at the foaming snout of Renato.

"Jimmy, what the hell are you doing?" David said.

"Put the gun down, brother," BTO said.

Jimmy looked at them, his eyes bulging. "That thing was chewing on my hand. It's been licking and nibbling my fingers and I can't take—"

The pig darted forward, and faster than Ray had seen any dog move, clamped its tusked jaws down on Jimmy's hand.

"Ahhhhhhhhhh." Blood shot from all sides of the hog's mouth.

Then it shook its head like a rat terrier. The pistol dropped from Jimmy's hand. He hit the pig on the head with his other hand but that made it bite down harder.

"Get it off me . . . it won't let go!"

Bang! A gunshot rang through the courtyard. The pig slumped on its side, dead, a fresh bullet hole in its head. Ken stood over it with a curl of smoke escaping from the barrel of Jimmy's dropped revolver he'd scooped up from the dirt.

"Deal."

CHAPTER 27

He has the same dream every night. Or is it a vision? A waking nightmare? A hallucination? No matter, from the blackness of sleep it arrives. First, sun and sea air wash over his body, the scent of lemons fills his nose, while his mother's voice coos a soft lullaby.

From the aroma of bright, life-affirming citrus, the scent turns. Burning fuel mixes with the stomach-lurching smell of sweet, charred flesh. The sun's warmth on his skin switches from a nurturing, seaside embrace to blast furnace intensity. He now stands on a sand-blown hill of shattered stone and steel. An assault rifle is in his hands. In a 360-degree panorama, rocket trails crisscross followed by rolling explosions. Small arms crackle. Bombers thunder overhead in formation followed by a wall of orange fire. At his feet, men he knows, brothers even, are mutilated and broken, their bodies mangled by the gears of war.

One soldier who fought by his side from Tripoli to Mosul, lies begging to be taken home to his family's cemetery outside Parma. Begging to be buried in a soldier's funeral. Begging while trying to stuff his slippery entrails back into a cavernous, blown-out stomach cavity.

Bending down, he consoles the dying man. Promises him he will personally see that he is buried with honor, back home in Mother Italy. But as he speaks, he along with the rest of their unit melt away into a looming blackness.

All grows dark and quiet.

Then, like he's peering through a widening camera lens, a circle of white light appears in the distance. It grows bigger. Inside the circle is a dented Honda four-door sedan bouncing down a rutted desert road. Its black paint is chipped. Thick maroon rust frames the doors. The driver is gripping the wheel. A woman is in the back seat. He can hear a baby crying, but he can't see evidence of an infant in the car.

"Stop your vehicle! Stop your vehicle or I will shoot!" he says. Why is he yelling? And why is he yelling in English?

But they don't stop. He can see the woman now; she has a wild mane of blonde hair with a white streak that leaps from widow's peak like an eagle feather. Strangely, the man's face is obscured, reminding him of a pixelated head on a television show. And the baby's crying is loud and getting louder, like an air raid siren.

Horrified, he realizes he can't control the rifle in his hands; the barrel keeps rising on its own until the sights are dead on the windshield of the car. No matter how hard he tries to keep his finger away from the trigger, demanding his tendons and muscles to cease their movements, it curls around the rifle's metal tongue and pulls.

Fire leaps from the gun. A stream of bullets pour into the car until the rifle's chamber locks open, the magazine empty. He approaches the bullet-riddled vehicle and looks inside. Red ruin is all that remains of the driver's face. In the back seat the woman with the blonde, white-streaked hair lies still and blood-spattered, her eyes open and staring skyward for eternity. Next to her sits a basinet riddled with bullet holes, leaking crimson.

He drops the rifle in his hands. Runs into the blazing desert, shedding his clothes, caring not that his skin burns and burns and burns. Friend or foe, he kills everything in sight. He becomes a predator of the desert, and does not stop moving, killing, moving and killing. His skin never stops burning.

The nightmare always ends the same, with his mother's hands around his throat. She bends down and whispers in his ear.

"*Memento mori.*"

The same dream, night after night, for years.

Until last night. Last night there was no dream.

Il Ramingo stood from his sleeping bag on the floor feeling well rested, euphoric even. He walked to a metal table pushed against the wall. On the table were two big flat screens and a laptop. With a few keystrokes he watched footage from security cameras mounted around his home at 5X speed. Confident no interlopers had discovered his mountain sanctuary during the night, Il Ramingo toggled to the cameras looking over his captive.

Madeline Granttano paced about in a twelve-by-twelve-foot cell. There was an unmade cot in the corner and straw on the floor. Il Ramingo squinted at her hair. It was wild and unkempt.

From his fatigue pants pocket, he took out a head sock and pulled it over his hairless, pink, scar-crossed scalp. Next, he went into the kitchen to prepare a breakfast of eggs scrambled in olive oil and toast with orange jam. Holding a platter with the steaming plate of food and a tall glass of milk in one hand, Il Ramingo used the other to open a locked door leading down to the basement with a great ring of keys. After locking the door behind him, he carried the platter down a flight of circular stairs and past two empty cells to a stop in front of Madeline's.

Upon his arrival, Madeline froze. Il Ramingo didn't say a word, instead, he unlocked the gate and placed the platter and glass of milk on the ground. Then he stepped out, locked the gate and left, returning upstairs to the video monitors. While he ate his own breakfast identical to what he cooked for Madeline, Il Ramingo studied the terrified woman standing in the cell. After ten minutes of contemplation, she lunged for the plate and devoured the food. Five minutes after that, she staggered to the cot, and fell face down, unconscious. The victim of the narcotic Il Ramingo sprinkled on her eggs.

He went to the kitchen and scraped his plate into the trash.

After cleaning up, Il Ramingo took a plastic bag from a pharmacy in Pompeii and a bucket of hot water back downstairs to Madeline's cell. After unlocking the cell door, he went to the prone form of the girl on the cot. Using products from the bag and the hot water, he carefully washed and conditioned her hair. Once Madeline's blonde locks were clean, Il Ramingo rummaged around in the bag until he found what he was looking for.

A tube of white hair dye.

CHAPTER 28

"Just get in the car, Raymond, we'll figure something out."

A phalanx of armed men escorted the Nicchi crew from the patio area to the courtyard where their cars were parked. On the way out, Ray glanced over his shoulder at Pecora. The System leader's lip was twitching as he knelt next to his dead Campania pig.

"Not today, Davey."

Working fast while they walked, Ray Granttano typed a quick text message with his thumbs to his wife back in Kansas City. The message said nothing more than Ray would call soon with good news. Cathy was a decent woman. Not that he deserved one. They met at a Nicchi-owned bar where she waited tables and Ray emptied bottles of Bombay Sapphire. She didn't care he was mob connected. She just wanted to take care of him. They had Madeline, and Ray tried his ass off not to repeat his past mistakes. Instead, he just made new ones.

Cathy was likely still so zonked on sedatives and anti-depressants she would be unable to read her phone. Ray put the phone in his pocket and sat in the front seat next to BTO. Ken, seated in the back with Davey, didn't seem to notice his presence. He was focused on his whimpering son, and Jimmy's swine-mangled hand wrapped in a bloody towel.

"It hurts like shit, Dad." Jimmy was pale with dark circles around his eyes.

"You're fine, pour some grappa on it. Couple of bandages and you're good to go, right kiddo?" Ken Nicchi was in a celebratory mood.

"Right." Jimmy said, his voice thin and high.

The phone in Ray's pocket buzzed. Cathy must have seen his message. He pulled it from his pocket and looked at the screen. The number for the five-word message was blocked.

Help is on the way.

"Who you texting up there, tough guy?" Ken Nicchi taunted from the back seat.

Ray froze. While there was no way to know for sure who had sent him the message, he had a pretty good idea. If Ken sensed who Ray had been talking to, he would be tortured and killed, and so would Madeline. Out of the corner of his eye he could see BTO stealing a glance at him while he drove them through Naples.

Ray thrust the phone in the air with the screen pointing out the windshield and away from Ken. "Cathy."

"Sharing the good news your kid's got just one more day on planet Earth?" Ken said.

"Fuck you," Ray said.

Ken touched his nose where he'd stuffed toilet paper to stem the blood from Ray's punch. He held up a finger with a red dot of blood on it.

"Does it hurt?" Jimmy said.

"Less than getting hit by grandma's handbag." Ken snorted. "BTO, pull over at the next bodega. Three million? No more guns? Execute a rat? I'm buying a lotto ticket."

"It's Italy, you moron, no lottery," Ray said.

Ken reached out faster than Ray anticipated and plucked his phone from his hand. The Nicchi family boss read the screen, his expression confused. "*Help is on the way?* Who you been talking to, Ray?"

"No one."

"And what's that?" With Ray's phone in his left hand, Ken reached out with his right and pointed at his throat. Ray looked down at the locket dangling around his neck, the one he had given to Sophie. The clasp had sprung open, likely during his fight with Ken. Exposed for all in the car to see was a small chip. A listening device.

"I don't . . . I wasn't—"

Ken handed the phone to David, reached inside his coat pocket, pulled out his pistol and chambered a round.

"Jesus, Ken, what are you doing?" David said.

"He's about to shoot your brother, you goddam idiot," Ray said.

"No, he's not," BTO said.

"Oh yes, I am," Ken said and pointed the gun at Ray's head.

"Dad. Look." Jimmy, his face twisted in pain, pointed with his bloody bandaged hand out the windshield.

Blocking the road was a dozen Polizia Speciale Campania vehicles with their lights flashing. Officers in tactical gear pointed assault rifles at their car. BTO brought the vehicle to a stop fifteen feet before a tall dark woman in a blue police uniform. BTO's eyes flashed to the rearview mirror and saw a cluster of flashing police cars behind them, too. *Trapped!*

The woman walked to the driver's side window and rapped on it with her knuckles. BTO rolled the window down.

"Ciao. I'm Captain Fattore of the Polizia Speciale Campania. You're not from around here, are you?"

CHAPTER 29

Sophie Grant peered through a one-way mirror at Ken Nicchi, his son Jimmy, and her Uncle David Granttano. The space where the Nicchi's sat was one half of a converted Absolute Amore adjoining hotel room, repurposed for questioning and debriefing. Sophie stood in the observation side. Carter Boyd was seated across from the three men on the interrogation side, each man shackled to the table. Though in Jimmy's case, they only cuffed his right hand, leaving his bandaged claw limply at his side. So far there was no sign of Ray or Bill Hodges.

"You want someone to look at that hand?" Carter said.

"My son don't need no doctor. Just get us our lawyer."

Sophie marveled at Ken Nicchi's bravado, though she wasn't surprised. Projecting false confidence in the face of a clear reckoning was a common among criminal polluters she had chased stateside. Often the crooks she dealt with were chemists and engineers. Highly educated. Prestigious schools. Sophie would ring a doorbell to serve a criminal complaint and a perp would lie to her face with barely concealed contempt. Like they were too smart to get caught by a girl. Of course, lying to a federal agent was just another charge, because by the time Sophie knocked on their door, enough evidence had already been gathered to convict.

Carter laughed at Ken's answer. "You're an international arms trafficker who steals from the US military and sells the weapons to terrorists. You also happen to be in a foreign country," Carter said. "A country where you're shipping toxic waste from America to be burned on an active volcano. The best. And I mean the absolute best move you can make today is not getting familiar with the taste of your own breath in a wool hood on the way to a black site. That's a win."

"So?" David said. "What do you want from us?" Sophie's uncle looked worse than he had out in front of the hotel Grand Vesuvio. The way he tapped his thumbs on the table told her he was jonesing for a cigarette. "Easy," Carter said. "Go back tomorrow and meet with Pecora. Once Madeline appears we take him down."

"Not in a million years," Ken said, rolling his head as if loosening up.

"No one's coming to help you or your guys. No lawyer."

"That can't be true," David Granttano said.

"Yeah, I call bullshit. I'm an American. A legitimate businessman," Ken said, the last part at a lower pitch, like he didn't really believe what he was saying, the reality of his situation sinking in.

The door to the observation room where Sophie stood watching opened. "Enjoying the show?" Bill Hodges said stepping inside. He was in full peacock mode, relishing his command of the situation.

"Where's Ray?"

"Your father's arrival is imminent." Hodges tucked his arm behind his back. "I'm going in there to assist Boyd, but first wanted a quick word. You're going to see and hear things of an extremely classified nature. Someone could make the case that allowing you to observe would be a breach of national security."

Hodges and Sophie's agreement was strictly of the handshake variety. No paperwork. Which meant going around the usual CIA security protocols. Hodges knew Sophie could make trouble for him. He wanted assurances.

"I am picking up what you are laying down," Sophie said. "I wasn't here."

"Good. Very good." Hodges said.

"So, you got all the other wiseguys locked up in the basement?"

"Nope. Fattore has them at PSC HQ. Don't want Pecora knowing they got pinched by us. She slipped us these three, real quiet like." Hodges turned and left the observation room. Sophie glimpsed her father waiting outside in the hall.

"Ray, time for us to go in."

"Us?" Sophie said, before the door closed. She turned back to the glass as her father and Hodges joined Carter Boyd opposite her Uncle David and the Nicchies.

"What's he doing here?" Ken Nicchi said, nodding at Ray Granttano as he sat in a metal folding chair. Ken's body language changed from dominant silverback with his chest thrust out in defiance, to sunken resignation, realizing in the moment that Ray had played him. Jimmy sat still, his head bowed with his swine gnawed hand now hugged to his stomach.

Carter pushed a tablet computer across the table to the KC mob boss.

"That's surveillance footage," Carter said. "Drones, assets on the inside, gas station security cameras . . . step by step chain of custody from PFC Haley's hands at Fort Leonard Wood, to the warehouse you own in Westport, Missouri through a shell company that sells used cars, to your crew in New Orleans, to Luca Pecora here in Naples."

Ken didn't look down. "Westport's a KC neighborhood, not a town, you dipshits."

Carter ignored the insult, took the tablet, and expanded one of the video boxes. "That's you inspecting a crate of Javelin rockets about to ship out."

"Wasn't me."

"Can I get some water, and aspirin?" Jimmy asked, his eyes sunken in his skull, his expression pained.

"When we're done," Carter said. He grabbed the pad and tapped the screen and put it in front of the junior Nicchi. "You're in here too, lefty. There you are carrying an armful of M4's into a truck."

"What is this?" David said. "Good cop, bad cop?"

"We're not cops." Hodges smiled.

The next round of surveillance footage showed pallets with white barrels being loaded by forklift onto a truck. Hodges used two fingers to zero in on the yellow and black triangle containing a skull-and-crossbones emblazoned on one of the barrels.

"Wondering who shot the footage?" Carter said.

"So, my son was informing on us before he came over. Small rat, big rat, still a fucking rat."

"Not Chris," Ray said. Sophie's father patted his chest. "Me."

In the adjoining room Sophie's heart was beating fast. She felt drunk, suddenly wanting nothing more than to run into the interrogation room and hug her dad.

"You've been working for the feds? This whole time?" Jimmy said, his voice weak.

"Yes," Ray said. "The whole time."

The whole time? How long was that? Sophie couldn't believe what she was hearing. Couldn't process the revelation that her long-hated absentee father turned out to be working for the good guys. The sudden flip was disorientating. If he was working with Hodges, why had Ray let his daughter plant the bug on him?

Ken shook his head, then let out a low, rumbling laugh. "Of course. You've been holding a grudge like a little bitch against me for thirty years."

Ray turned around and looked straight at the one-way mirror, and even though she was pretty sure he couldn't see her, locked eyes for a moment with Sophie, and winked.

Turning back to Ken Nicchi, Ray said, "I made a dumb choice to save my brother's life. And it cost me everything." Sophie watched her uncle squirm in his seat. "That's on me. This," Ray tapped on the table hard with his forefinger, "this is about my daughter marrying the man she loved. Madeline married Chris despite my every plea to her to not do it, but she joined your toxic family anyway. I already lost one girl, my daughter Sophie. I wasn't going to lose another. I had to get Madeline out."

Ken Nicchi laughed. Then he tilted his bulldog head. He thrust his chin out at Carter Boyd. "Don't think I don't recognize you from the video that psycho shot. What's his name? Il Ramingo? On the boat? I bet you promised them you'd protect them, didn't you? Ray, your new friends here couldn't protect your girl." Ken spit on the ground.

"Speaking of protecting your children," Hodges said. He took his phone out of his pocket and dialed a number.

A second later the door to the interrogation room unlocked. Two CIA SOG operators walked in pushing a cart, the contents of which were covered by a thick blanket.

"Why can't we see their faces?" David said nodding at the SOGs. Both men had thick black hoods with eyeholes pulled over their heads.

"Yeah," Jimmy said. "Why the hoods, man?"

"They don't want to be on camera for a future judge to witness what they're about to do," Ray said.

"Is it true that when your father caught Freddie Chains skimming from the Vegas take that he put a scorpion in his underpants? Then put a bullet in his head?" Carter asked. "That's what Ray told us."

"You don't have the balls," Ken Nicchi said. Sophie could hear the hollow spot in his voice where the bluster had drained out.

"Dad, what's going on." Jimmy's eyes were focused on the cart. Sophie watched Jimmy shiver thinking about what tortuous, hidden horror lay underneath. Ken didn't say anything but clenched his teeth and stared straight ahead at Sophie's dad.

"The next part is my favorite," Hodges said, eyes dancing.

One of the hooded SOGs seized Jimmy's free arm while the other started peeling off his gauze bandage. "Dad . . . Dad . . . Help! What the fuck are you doing. Jesus Christ! No . . . no . . . please . . . no." Jimmy was writhing and flopping about as they took off his dressing. The hand was red and bloated with at least a half-dozen puncture wounds oozing foaming pink fluid.

"Get your hands off my son!" Ken jerked at his cuffs but couldn't break free from the table.

While his partner held Jimmy's arm, the other SOG went to the cart and with a flourish, threw off the blanket exposing a large glass jar. He hefted the jar into his hands and held it up to the light.

Inside the jar were thousands of writhing bugs.

"Crab beetles," Hodges said. "Indigenous to the Amalfi Coast. Get this. The little buggers are so ferocious and hungry they eat through any unlucky crab's shell that strays too far up the beach. Thirty seconds flat. Swarm like piranhas." Hodges leaned down and sniffed at Jimmy's hand. "They *love* fresh meat."

"You can't do this. You can't torture an American. Jimmy is an American citizen," David said.

"Like I told your Chef Boyardee ass, you sell guns to terrorists," Carter said. "There are no rules."

"C'mon Jimmy, whatcha say?" Hodges lifted his left shoulder, making the flap of his shirt draped over the stump of his arm move. "Meet the Beetles? Join the one arm club?"

"Fine. I'll go to the meeting. I'll wear the wire." Ken shook his head.

"Excellent," Hodges said. "Stand down. Clean and dress that wound and give the kid something for the pain."

"Oh, thank God," Jimmy said, his glassy eyes fixed on the teeming jar of beetles.

"What do we get in exchange?" David said.

"Once Pecora and Il Ramingo are in custody, two amazing words. *Your. Freedom.*"

Watching through the glass, Sophie had two different words on her mind.

Memento mori.

CHAPTER 30

"Ravioli."

Maria's eyes glittered as she shoved a coaster-sized, stuffed pasta pocket into her mouth. Sophie was grateful for her presence. The orphaned girl was in a surprisingly good mood after been cooped up in the CIA's Naples facility for hours. When Carter invited Sophie and her father out for dinner, she insisted Maria accompany them. After a tense day watching video monitors and the interrogation of the Nicchies and Ray's brother, sampling some of Naples famous food was a welcome distraction.

Plus, Sophie's dad was a wreck, veering between elation and despair over Madeline. Ever since learning of his role in helping the CIA, she'd felt protective. She thought maybe eating a meal out with a radiant little girl would buoy Ray's spirits. Take his mind off his other daughter being the captive of a mass murderer. Give Sophie some time to evaluate her feelings.

It was just after eight in the evening and Naples was waking up. By eleven the avenue would put Bourbon Street at the height of Mardi Gras to shame, and it was only Wednesday. They were seated in a small private dining room in the back of a trattoria Carter chose. The space was noisy but electric, not annoying. Two blocks from Absolute Amore with a ragu the intelligence officer promised was "so good it would make him spill state secrets," they sat down for a dinner. Once the food arrived, per Carter's request, the doors to the room were shut. Two tables of plainclothes SOG operatives stood guard on the other side.

"Did you always love other languages?" Sophie asked Carter before taking a fatty, salty bite of pork ragu sweetened by slow cooked tomatoes that sent fireworks through her mouth.

"Not really." Carter said, picking at a plate of clams. "More of an environmental response if you will. Growing up on base. We moved a lot. All over the world. It's not something I can easily explain, but I could just hear someone talking in a foreign language and what they said . . . I understood." He swirled a strand of *bucatini* around his fork.

"Speaking of which," Ray said reaching into his collar. He took off the locket and necklace containing the bug. "I'd like for you to take this back, so Carter's people can track you."

"You let me—" Sophie turned to Carter. "You two played me. Why?"

"To protect your father. He gets caught with that tracker in Pecora's compound, you planting it on him, well, it would give him deniability. Maybe give us enough time to get him out."

"So, after you apprehend Pecora? He flips, right? Works for you?" Sophie said.

The CIA officer leaned forward, whispered so only Ray and Sophie could hear. "Once you've infiltrated a global terrorist marketplace with an asset they trust, the possibilities are endless. Hodges likes to make everyone think this is his swan song, but really, it's his legacy. This makes my job much easier when I take over." A look crossed Carter's face liked he'd said too much. He pulled back, dabbed at his mouth with his napkin, and stood. "Remember, not too late tonight. Big day in the morning. We're hunting rabbits."

"I like rabbits," Maria said.

"And I like you." Carter mussed the girl's hair.

Sophie stood and stuck her hand out. Carter shook it, nodded at Sophie, spun on his heels and went out the door. One set of security personnel followed him out of the restaurant. The other remained behind.

Sophie turned back to their table in time to witness her father and Maria, each of them held one end of the same long piece of spaghetti from Ray's plate in their mouths, slurping towards each other until they were nose to nose and Ray bit down on the pasta, severing the noodle. The action blunted the high Sophie felt about her father, conjuring a pang of jealousy toward, of all people, Maria.

"How long?"

"It's complicated."

"Oh, so you and a girl you just met can be best pals, but you can't even come clean with your own daughter?"

Maria stopped eating, her eyes moving between Sophie and her father.

"I know you hate me, and you have every right to. I'm not going to try and—"

"How long?" Sophie pressed.

Ray swallowed hard and looked down at his feet. After a moment he looked up. "When Chris proposed to Madeline." His voice caught, and he delivered the last bit in a strained choke "When she said yes." A tear streamed down his left cheek that Ray quickly wiped away. Maria reached out and placed her hand on Ray's.

"Finish up your dinner, Maria, it's time to go." Sophie signaled the waiter for the check.

"Stay. Please. Let me explain." Ray reached out with his hand and squeezed Sophie's. "From the beginning."

She pulled her hand away and turned to Maria. "Can you find the bathroom and wash up before we leave?"

Maria eyed the request suspiciously, knowing she was being shuttled away from an adult conversion, but obeyed anyway.

"You have five minutes," Sophie said after Maria was gone.

Ray took a deep breath before launching into his story.

"All I was trying to do was protect my family."

Ray spoke in a series of halting sentences, with his words carefully chosen. It all started with his parents' deaths in a house fire when he and his brother, David, were young. A fireman on the scene convinced him on that day that Ray Granttano was destined to help people, too. Sophie was transfixed. She'd never heard this part of her family history, her mother choosing to keep most of their time with Ray locked away. Something about not looking back, but always looking forward.

So, after fighting in Viet Nam, then an impressive five-year run as a Kansas City beat cop, Ray was promoted to the major crimes unit as a detective.

"I didn't know how good I had it. I loved my job. Loved being a cop. And I had a beautiful wife and daughter who adored me."

But the same event that altered the course of Ray's life sent David's hurtling in the opposite direction. According to Ray, without parents to guide him, David fell in with petty crooks making good money boosting cars. By the age of nineteen he was a member of the Nicchi crime family, having befriended Ken Nicchi through the family's car fencing business. Ken's father was boss back then, and through a series of partnerships with the bigger, more powerful Mafia families in New York and Chicago, was put in charge of a major Las Vegas casino skimming operation.

When the Nicchi patriarch was caught bragging about the decade's long crime on an FBI wire, the skim was shut down for good, costing the other Mafia families millions in yearly revenue. Several high-level mobsters ended up in prison.

"Someone had to pay," Ray said to Sophie. "It was obvious who was to blame. The day Ken Sr. made bail they found his body in a dumpster. Stabbed fifty times. All the other families declared war on the Nicchi. It was so bad, four, five killings a day, shootouts in the streets of Kansas City. Not Detroit. Not Chicago. Sleepy Kansas City. All we could do in the department was keep regular folks out of harm's way and let the animals kill each other."

"And David? Didn't you suspect he was part of it?"

Ray shook his head. "Guess I wasn't that good of a cop. I knew he was into some bad stuff, but once I joined the force, we never really saw each other. Or talked. That glorious time before cell phones and the internet, I guess. I never would've dreamed he'd join the Nicchi. That was until he knocked on my door."

As Sophie's father told it, Uncle David Granttano and Ken Nicchi Jr. were in hiding, trying to stay alive as hit squads from New York roamed the streets of KC hunting for them. Fearing for his life, David begged Ray for a favor, to ask around the station and see if anyone knew what the New York mob's next move would be. Ray heard of a wire the KCPD had on one of the Big Apple outfit's safehouses. One night, he broke into the evidence locker and listened to the tape.

"Didn't think twice about it," Ray said, shaking his head. "What turned out to be the biggest mistake of my life, and I just went and did it."

"So, what'd you hear?"

"A bunch of New York hitmen plotting to kill my brother."

"And?"

"I tipped him off." Ray choked up. "But what David didn't tell me was that Ken put him up to it. And instead of running, they used the information to ambush the Manhattan wiseguys. Gunned down three of them. Was pretty clear, pretty quick to the other cops who I worked with what happened. Lucky just to get kicked off the force in disgrace and didn't spend any time inside."

"I had no idea."

"But that wasn't the worst thing that happened. Losing my job. The shame of one day being a good detective and the next day a bad cop. No. It was losing you. Losing your mother."

"You didn't lose us, Dad, you pushed us away."

"I did. Yes I did." He reached into his coat pocket and pulled out an old, chipped Dictaphone. He sat the recorder on the table. "Press play."

Sophie waited a beat, then reached out and pressed the play button. The recording was fuzzy and old but clearly of her father and his brother talking.

"They know about you, worse, they know about your wife. About Sofia. Best to get them out of town . . . for good."

"You piece of shit. What have you done? That's my family."

With a shaking hand, Sophie turned the player off.

"After everything died down, and I was working for Ken Nicchi because no one else would hire me, well your mom, she never got over the fact . . . she believed I picked my brother over you two. I was just trying to keep you safe. She hated me for it. Made me swear I wouldn't ever be part of your life. It was the least I could do for ruining everything."

Ray reached out and grabbed Sophie's hand. This time she let it stay, feeling the warm comfort run up her arm, her brainstem humming with emotion. "But I need you to do one thing for me," he said. "Whatever happens tomorrow, with Pecora, when we meet him again, whatever happens you have to protect Madeline." Ray wiped away tears with the back of his hand. "Those CIA assholes promised to protect her the last time . . ." his voice trailed off.

"I don't know, Ray," She pointed to the table of CIA operatives guarding them. "They're the pros, I'm just a water cop."

Her father pointed at Sophie's ear where she still had a piece of medical tape on the graze from the Camorra bullet. "I'm pretty confident you can handle yourself."

CHAPTER 31

Brad Tejo Ortega was uncharacteristically nervous. He figured their odds of surviving tomorrow's meeting with the ghoulish Camorra boss and making it back to his son were about fifty-fifty. That was if the Italian cops decide not to arrest them again. After he bailed them out, Ken Nicchi told his crew that he had found a good Italian lawyer, and the charges would be dropped. Even better to BTO's ears, the plane was gassed up and ready to go on the tarmac. Right after tomorrow's *meeting*, they were flying home.

And the minute after they landed, BTO was going to quit working for the Nicchies.

BTO had started out regular Army until selected for training with 160th Special Operations Aviation Regiment at Fort Campbell in Kentucky. For eight weeks BTO endured intensive field instruction in land navigation, hand-to-hand combat, and teamwork. But it was the weapons training that was the most grueling, firing thousands upon thousands of rounds through every conceivable weapon in the battlespace. And that was before he started helicopter training. The upshot was there wasn't a weapon he couldn't use.

Now seated on a leather sofa in the Grand Hotel Vesuvio's foyer, scuffed Army boots kicked up on a coffee table, he deployed a different set of skills. Evasion and counter-surveillance. BTO scanned the room. There were only four guests milling about the cavernous, ornate space. A young couple was looking through a glass case in the corner at jewelry, while an old man in a sky-blue suit read a newspaper. A short woman sipped a coffee next to him on an identical leather couch. *Any of them working for the Camorra?* BTO wondered. He had been told, repeatedly, by Nicchi's second in command, David Granttano, a guy who really needed to brush his fucking teeth, that Pecora System people were everywhere. Maybe it was the tall blonde woman working behind the front desk? Or the balding fellow manning the concierge stand?

Ken Nicchi was now obsessed, bordering on paranoid, with the idea that someone was listening in on their conversations. Tonight, as one of his final acts under Ken's employ, BTO aimed to give his boss some peace of mind. He hoped it would have the added benefit of leaving the criminal enterprise with no hard feelings, to build a life for his son that didn't entail looking over his shoulder.

Because two things were true that BTO would have to atone for. He'd made sure stolen US military hardware ended up in the hands of insurgents and terrorists who used them to kill US soldiers. And he had also helped toxic waste generated in America find a home with poor Italian children.

The more BTO thought about his sins, the more the knowledge shook him. Worse, tomorrow he was going to have to witness Ken shoot his dead son's wife, his daughter-in-law, in the head. There was nothing he could do. He'd die too if he tried to stop it.

Sure, he was aware of what the Nicchi were doing in broad strokes. Something illegal and valuable went hidden in those corn and soybean tankers out of New Orleans. Drugs were quasi-defensible. But not weapons. Not hazardous waste.

BTO was a big boy. Someday he would make it right. So, he decided; BTO was going to do his best to honor his agreement with Ken and keep that fat crook alive until they touched down at KCI, and then he was out. Out for good. Dumbass, dead-end casino security job or not.

Satisfied no one was watching, BTO finished his lobby surveillance. He walked out the front door and down the long front set of stairs to a busy Naples street. He turned right. In his peripheral vision BTO noticed a squat blond man with a receding hairline and younger, much taller man walking behind him. Pecora's men. Once they were two blocks down the street from his hotel, a taxi stopped between them. BTO peeled off to the left, running at a dead sprint. He heard shouting behind him but had a good head start. The next block, BTO used a crowd spilling from a theater to reverse direction down an alley. Walking with purpose, but not too fast to attract attention, he found what he was looking for at the intersection of Via Monete Di Dio and Via Solitaria.

Within five minutes of arriving at the Capriana Market, BTO noticed a young vagrant with a telltale skeletal frame and twitchy demeanor loitering by the corner bodega's entrance. BTO approached him. Speaking crude Italian, he asked the young junkie to buy what BTO needed inside. "Pablo," feigned disinterest until BTO waved 300 euros in his face. Pablo bit. In the trash-strewn alley behind the store, BTO flashed the butt of the pistol tucked in his waistband in case Pablo tried to make a run for it.

"Signore." Pablo appeared in the alley holding a plastic bag in each hand. "Like you asked. I bought all they had."

Glancing around to make sure the Camorra tail hadn't found him, BTO took the bags and looked through them. Happy with Pablo's purchases, he handed the dirty street kid a wad of euros, sending him on his way to convert the money into needle drugs. In five minutes, he was back at the hotel and on his way to Ken Nicchi's suite. BTO entered his boss's room, turning sideways so that his shoulders would fit through the door. Jimmy and Ken were seated at a table eating Neapolitan pizza.

"There's no garlic in the sauce? And it's not sliced?"

"Knife and fork, Jimmy, they eat pizza with a knife and fork here," Ken growled at his son.

Jimmy held up his heavily bandaged hand. "I can't."

Ken sighed. "Slide your pie over here, I'll cut it up for you."

BTO sat in an empty chair to Ken's right.

"You get my eye drops?"

BTO nodded. He handed Ken a new burner phone from the plastic bag.

"Good work. Now pass the rest out to everyone else. Big day tomorrow."

CHAPTER 32

The doctor called it Blue Baby Syndrome.

Madeline and Chris Nicchi had never heard of it, or the disorder's clinical name, *infant methemoglobinemia*. For decades, Missouri farmers slathered synthetic nitrogen fertilizers on their corn crops to boost yields. The result was chemical nitrate plagued water wells for the eastern Kansas City suburb where they lived. The water didn't hurt adults. At least not that the doctor knew of. Possible links to liver cancer but there wasn't much research. But it did starve vulnerable fetuses and infants of oxygen in their blood, turning them blue.

It was Madeline's second stillborn. They tried so hard. A battery of fertility treatments. Strict diets. She got in the best shape of her life with a kickboxing instructor and trained to run half marathons. They saw doctor after doctor. But none of it mattered in the end. Modern medicine could do nothing about something so mundane as too much plant food in their water. While she was heartbroken, Chris descended into a deep depression. Madeline assumed it was the pressure his father put on his son for another heir, wanting an additional member of his criminal organization tied by blood.

One night, after making his way through a couple bottles of Cabernet, a sobbing Chris Nicchi pulled Madeline from bed. He sat her down, and after apologizing for waking her up, told his wife about the family business. When they were first married, he communicated to Madeline in no uncertain terms that she could never know the details of the Nicchi operation, for both of their safety.

But that night, he broke his word. Told Madeline about the

weapons they stole. To learn they were sold to America's enemies was like learning she was a direct relation to Hannibal Lector. Or Hitler. But that's not why Chris woke her up.

Companies that didn't want to follow local environmental laws paid the Nicchi crime family to get rid of their pollution. Barrels upon barrels of dangerous industrial byproducts were shipped by the crime family down the Mississippi River to New Orleans and eventually Italy. Once there, the Camorra mob proudly dumped and burned the dangerous materials on the slopes of an actual, honest to God, volcano. After Madeline lost their second baby, Chris kept asking himself what happened to the people living near Mount Vesuvius? Their water? What happened to their kids?

The next day Madeline turned to the one man she needed to give it to her straight, her father. Ray Granttano shocked his daughter when he said he might have a way for her and Chris to get out. To make things right. Eleven months later they were in a boat anchored off Positano meeting with the CIA. The last thing Madeline remembered of Chris the night she was abducted was his peaceful snoring from the deep sleep of moral comfort.

Madeline Nicchi woke to the sound of her captor singing to himself in a choking, rough voice. He spoke to her only a handful of times. Two or three heavily accented words like "Time to eat" or "Get up." And strangely, he kept calling her Giuliana. Though to be honest, she'd been drugged to the point where strange and normal merged into a foggy dream state.

A point underscored when warm sunlight kissed Madeline's face and she realized she wasn't in her cell.

Her hands and feet were bound, but Madeline's mouth was no longer gagged. She thought of screaming, realizing that her kidnapper would never have left her gag out unless they were somewhere no one could hear her. *A test.* The straps her captor wound around her ankles and wrists were loose enough for Madeline to sit up. She swayed for a moment and felt dizzy, like she could throw up. The man stopped singing. His left hand appeared before her face, thick with rivers of pink scars running across the skin, reached behind her and undid the ties around her wrists. With his other, he pointed in front of Madeline.

"Water. Drink."

Madeline looked down at a blurry glass of water next to her bound legs. She shook her head to try and right her vision. Her mouth was dry. The usually rigid internal rod that kept her posture straight felt like cooked spaghetti. Using both hands Madeline was able to grab the glass and sip.

Next, her abductor handed Madeline a fork and knife, and cloth napkin. Winged angels were sown in white linen around the napkin's edge. While pointing at the knife and shaking his head, he said *"Morte,"* and drew his finger across his throat. The threat was clear even in her semi-drugged state, use the knife against him and Madeline would pay the price.

For the first time she got a look at his face. Or, what covered his face. A thin black nylon head scarf was pulled over his skull and he wore a pair of black welding goggles. The man was well over six feet tall and slender with lithe, cat-like body movements. Except for his hands, not an inch of skin was exposed, despite the stifling summer heat of Southern Italy. As far as she could tell there were no weapons on his body. No knife. No gun.

"Eat," he said pointing to a plate on a small wood table to her left. On the plate lay strips of pancetta, slices of white cheese and a hunk of bread.

He turned his back to her, sat at a long workbench, and started sawing with a hacksaw at something obscured by his body.

Madeline didn't remember much of the past few days, just a hazy succession of transfers between vehicles blindfolded and gagged until she woke in the basement cell. This morning was the first time Madeline felt somewhat conscious.

The house they were in was small and clean. Madeline assumed they were in the main room because there was a dining table in the center, a large sink to her right, and in the far corner a wood-burning stove. To her left was the front entrance consisting of two wooden doors framed by a stone archway. Light streamed through a window above the sink. Other windows were darkened by heavy curtains. She looked over her shoulder and there were two more doors, both open, one to a bathroom and another to what she assumed was her kidnapper's bedroom. A third door with an open iron gate led to the basement, presumably where her captor had been keeping Madeline.

"Eat," he said over his shoulder, still sawing at some unidentifiable object in a vise, the sound of the blade cutting metal shrill and grating.

Madeline obeyed, her stomach screaming for her to wolf down the cured pork. Once the savory meat hit her tongue, memories rushed to the surface. Memories of Chris. Drinking a brilliant Revello white that perfectly matched fresh prawns on the deck of their yacht. All she wanted was for her husband to materialize, wrap his arms around her, tell his wife everything was going to be fine. Except everything wasn't fine. Everything was miles from fine.

Madeline brought a piece of the hard white cheese to her nose. It smelled like walnuts. Before she could pop it into her mouth, the sawing from her captor ended with a banging noise as a heavy piece of metal clamored to the floor, so loud it made her jump and drop the cheese to the ground.

The man stood from his workbench. In his hands he held a double-barreled shotgun, the barrels shorn a foot from the breach end. At his feet in pile on the floor lay at least six pairs of barrels from previously sawed-off weapons. He put the stubby gun on the bench and turned to Madeline.

"*Lupara.*"

"Where's my husband? Where's Chris?" Madeline pressed.

"*Presto. Presto, Giuliana.*" He pointed at the plate of food, ignoring her question.

Madeline picked up the plate and took a bite of bread. It tasted fine but her stomach moved.

"I think I'm going to be sick." She set the plate down.

He walked to Madeline and pulled the strap away from her ankles. Grabbing her by the elbow, the man steered Madeline into the bathroom. He left her there on her knees before a five-gallon bucket reeking of urine. Madeline wretched several times throwing up a string of bile into the bucket. She looked up at a cracked mirror above the sink.

Reflected was a gaunt face, her eyes sunken with black rings around the sockets. But that's not what startled her. It was the white streak in her blonde hair running right down the middle of her head like a skunk's stripe. *Did he do it? Why?* Was there a Giuliana out there with a white streak that had spurned Madeline's captor's advances?

A breeze from the open bathroom window brushed Madeline's cheek. In a flash, she was on her feet and out the window, scraping her left forearm against a bent nail head sticking from the frame, but feet firmly on the ground.

She swayed, then steadied herself, surveyed her surroundings, finding them foreign. Jagged peaks and wisps of clouds surrounded Madeline. A falcon swooped by at eye level. She recognized the bird as a peregrine from a week-long, mountain survivalist camp Chris forced her to attend. The air was thinner wherever she was than in Positano. They were at a much higher elevation. Between the peaks were green mountain meadows and thick strands of chestnut and alder trees. Fear gripped Madeline, auguring her in place.

How can I find my way out of here? Where am I?
Run!

Madeline sprinted for a narrow, rocky path between two white cliffs. Once on the other side, she was in a clearing surrounded by high cliff walls. The clearing was small and walled in on all sides by craggy rock. If she hadn't happened upon the tight path by accident there was no way to see it. But what took her breath away was what occupied the clearing—hundreds of identical white crosses, each knee-high. At the base of every cross was a small mound of dirt.

"There's a saying, between *Soldati*... how do you say, soldiers?" her captor said behind her in his thick Italian accent, covered in his throat's rasp. *"Seppelliam I nostri morti"*

Madeline turned to face him. "Are you going to kill me?"

He shook his head. "No. There is a code."

"Who are you? What do I call you?"

"Il Mezzanotte Ramingo."

"Where are we?"

"Sentiero degli Dei," Il Ramingo said, his long, bug-like arms outstretched to encompass the mountain crags ringing the clearing.

Madeline fell to her knees, sobbing, helpless.

"I want to go home."

Il Ramingo bent down. With a long finger he stroked the splash of white hair in the center of Madeline's head. "The trade is set for the morning, Giuliana."

Hope shot through her. *A trade?* Soon Madeline would be free of her captor. Back with her family. Back in America.

"Does that mean I get to see my husband? Chris?"

Standing erect, Il Ramingo shook his head. "No. He will not be at the exchange."

"Why not?"

"Because he is buried over here. Would you like to see?"

CHAPTER 33

The next morning, Bill Hodges stood next to Sophie's father in Absoluta Amore's underground parking garage, barking in Ray's ear, while a tech fitted him with a miniature earpiece and microphone. In his element, so much at stake, orchestrating a complex mission that would ensnare both Pecora and Il Ramingo while saving Madeline, Sophie marveled at the intensity the old man marshalled in the moment.

Techs and SOG operators swirled around them, busy checking weapons and equipment in final preparations for the rescue mission. On the other side of the garage stood her Uncle David, Ken and Jimmy Nicchi. Ken fidgeting and chain smoking while waiting for their marching orders from Hodges.

"We are this close to getting her back, Ray," Hodges said. "Repeat it. The go codeword."

"*Esperanza.*"

"And when do you say it?"

Sophie watched her father steady himself. "When they bring her out. Madeline."

"And not a second later." Hodges said. He put his hand on Ray's shoulder. "All these ex-Delta guys," Hodges gestured to the SOG personal checking their weapons and body armor. "They'll be stationed on every entry point. They'll breach and enter the instant you give the go command. Your only other job is to get Madeline the hell out of there."

The plan was for Ray to beg for his daughter's life. Pecora would naturally refuse. Then he would offer to switch places with her if the System leader could guarantee her safety out of the country. Again, another refusal was expected. Once they brought her out for the public execution, Hodges's team would take everyone down.

"There's a hundred percent chance Luca Pecora kills all of us today," a grinning Jimmy Nicchi said to no one in particular. "And I can't wait." Jimmy sat in a folding chair, resting his bandaged arm on a crate.

"Should I be worried about junior?" Hodges said to Carter.

"It's the oxy talking," Carter said. He stood at a large folding table off to the side, guarding the aluminum briefcase case holding three million euros. "Medics cleaned up the arm and pumped him full of painkillers. He's mostly harmless."

Ken Nicchi, followed by David Granttano, walked to Hodges. "Our guys are going to wonder where we're at."

"Ken. Good." Hodges turned to the tech. "Wire him up, next."

"I'm not my son. I decided I don't wear wires."

"Leavenworth it is. I hear they serve a mean pepper steak on Thursdays," Hodges said.

"Fine." Ken's eyes narrowed. "Let's get this over with."

While the tech taped a transmitter the size of a thumbnail inside Ken's shirt, the KC Mafia boss pointed at Ray. "Your best hope after this is all over is, they give you a furnished igloo up near the North Pole. I'm coming for you." He let his eyes drift to Sophie. "You and your girls."

Sophie tensed, ready to jump in as her father stepped toward Ken.

"I ain't hiding anywhere," Ray said, his nose inches from Ken's face. "I'll be in the back bar at Arthur Byrant's, eating burnt ends any time you want to find me."

"We done?" Ken said to the tech.

She nodded. "You're live."

Ken pointed at Jimmy. "Let's get in the car. Granttano can ride in the trunk."

"One last thing," Carter said to the senior Nicchi. "One of your men, the one you call BTO? He gave our guys watching the hotel the slip. Do you know what he was up to?"

"On his way to fuck your mother?" Ken said.

Carter shook his head. "Talk that way to Pecora and your son's right, hundred percent chance he kills you."

"One sec," David said to Ken. He lumbered over to where Sophie and her father stood. The skin on his face was gray and the bags under his eyes dark and swollen. He held out his hand to Sophie.

"We didn't get to talk yesterday. Last time I saw you were like seven. I just wanted to say—"

"That you're sorry? For ruining our family? Screw your sorry."

Her uncle squinted, his eyes turning cold. David let his hand drop back to his side. "Just remembered. I don't apologize to cops." He turned and shuffled back to Ken and Jimmy.

From behind, Ray put a hand on his daughter's shoulder. She turned to face him. He was breathing heavier than normal. "Dad, you have nothing to worry about. All these guys are ex-Delta, SEALS, there's probably two Avengers and Jackie Chan under all that body armor." Sophie swallowed. She was putting on a brave front, but fear had her by the throat. She couldn't keep the images of Tommy Jones bleeding out on the carpet from her mind.

Her father took a deep breath. "Appreciate the pep talk, kiddo." He started walking toward the Nicchi's parked rental car but stopped after a few steps. Without turning back to face Sophie, he said, "If I were you, I wouldn't believe this either, but I've loved you your whole life."

Ray took a step, but Sophie's voice stopped him.

"Dad."

He turned to face her.

Sophie tossed him the locket he gave her for her sixth birthday. Ray caught the necklace one-handed.

"I'm going to need that back."

CHAPTER 34

"What do they keep in here? Circus elephants?"

"Shut the fuck up, Jimmy, and try not to get us all killed."

"Just saying, Dad, this is the biggest goddam warehouse I've ever seen."

Ray Granttano agreed with Jimmy; the structure in which they stood was vast. After getting wired up by the CIA, the four of them went back to the Grand Hotel Vesuivo. BTO was waiting in their rented Mercedes in valet parking, with the other car full of their security crew idling behind. Ray slid into the front seat next to BTO. If the big man suspected anything fishy, he didn't say.

After a five-minute drive they arrived at the Naples waterfront and Pecora's warehouse. Armed Camorra foot soldiers escorted the Nicchi crew through a massive roll-up door and inside. Settled on the Naples waterfront like a plump watermelon on a plate of much smaller fruit, with its clean concrete floor, the giant structure looked to be brand new.

And ice cold inside.

"Do you know how much it costs to raise a Campania pig like Renato?"

Dressed in black linen pants and a black tee, Pecora stood on a raised platform at the far end of the space. Behind the wide, flat area were dozens of steel doors. His sole remaining Campania pig, Cochi, orbited Pecora's feet.

"No," Ken said. "But if you aren't familiar with the American health care system, I'm going to assume its roughly the same as how much it's going to cost to fix Jimmy's hand."

His eyes shining like dove eggs under a full moon, a drugged Jimmy Nicchi groggily lifted his bandaged appendage. "It's all good."

Ken Nicchi with his men spread out in a loose semi-circle behind him, walked across the football field sized interior, weaving between pallets stacked with various products. Ray followed, careful to not get too close yet, playing the part of desperate father, not that it was an acting stretch, and marched up a flight of concrete steps to Pecora.

"Please. Sit down." Pecora waved to a wooden table with two chairs. On the table was a bottle of red wine and two glasses. With a grunt, Cochi plopped down at Pecora's feet.

"May want to turn the AC off. I can see my breath in here," Ken said taking a seat.

Pecora pointed to the row of doors. "Cold storage. From lemons picked in Amalfi to pineapple from Honduras. Broiler chickens from America, even. Stays cool. Best man in the world built this. Did Amazon's warehouses for their grocery delivery business," Pecora said to Ken as he took a seat at the table opposite the head of the Nicchi family. "He built a cold storage warehouse in Dubai. If you can make one of these work in a hundred-and-twenty-degree heat, you know what you're doing."

Due to the loud humming thrown off by the refrigeration units, Ray struggled to hear Pecora over the mechanical din. While making sure Sophie's locket stayed tucked inside his shirt, Ray scanned the area for any sign of Madeline. He found no visual evidence his daughter was in the cavernous building.

"Sorry about the noise," Pecora said. "But it helps with surveillance. They can't hear us."

"We can totally hear them."

The CIA tech sat in the second row of seats in a black Mercedes CIA van. Parked in an alley two buildings over from Pecora's warehouse, Sophie squatted next to the tech, headphones around her neck, while audio from the bug on Ray Granttano played over the tech's laptop.

"And see them," the tech pointed at the screens in the rear of the van showing infrared images sourced from sensors mounted on the vehicle's roof.

"Hello, dumb dumb," Hodges said from the passenger seat.

Sophie reached into a gym bag at her feet, removing her Kevlar vest and pulling it over her head, cinching the straps. Carter sat across from Sophie, also clad in tactical gear.

"What do you think you're doing?" Hodges said to Sophie.

"Getting ready. You know, to go in."

"The hell you are. Another water cop gets plugged by one of Pecora's goons on my watch, I get hauled before a Senate committee." Hodges fixed her with a piercing stare. "You stay put, Agent Grant. That's an order."

"Let's get the show started," Pecora said. He waved his hand and Chiara, his second in command, appeared with a metal suitcase and sporting a black hoody. He handed the case to Ken. "I believe this is what you call seed money? For our first American franchise."

Ken flicked the latches open and gazed at the bills stacked inside, then closed the lid. Expanding the toxic-dumping business was the deal of a lifetime, but Ray Granttano sensed the senior Nicchi was chaffing at the idea of being a snitch for the US feds. Ray needed to act and called his own cue.

"Please. Mr. Pecora. I'm begging you," Ray willed tears to pour from his eyes. In choked phrases he said, "For my daughter's life. What can I do?"

"You can watch." Pecora put his fingers in his mouth and whistled.

A man appeared from the shadows in the rear of the building

from between two refrigeration units. He was tall and slender, dressed neck to toe in tight black cloth, spiderlike, with a fluid and efficient gait. No wasted movement. With what seemed like only two strides he was standing next to Pecora.

Up close, the man wore a thin black mesh head sock so tight that it was like a pair of pantyhose pulled over his face. Over his eyes were dark goggles, giving him a mantis-like appearance.

"Gentlemen, meet . . . Il Mezzanotte Ramingo."

Il Ramingo nodded toward the Nicchi crew, then walked to Ray. They were the same height, and the assassin stood for a moment, eye to goggle, seemingly taking in Ray's presence. From nowhere, he produced a phone with a big screen and handed it to Ray.

"You have a beautiful girl," Il Ramingo said, the sound of the words from his throat rough and choked, like he was gargling thumb tacks.

"Yes. Yes," Pecora said. "So dramatic." Pecora looked around Il Ramingo who leaned forward and spoke low so only Ray could hear.

"I will keep her safe. Giuliana. Always."

"I don't understand," Ray said.

Pecora looked around Il Ramingo to the back of the warehouse. "Where is she? I don't see her. Where is the girl?"

"É il codice. Niente donne. Niente bambini," Il Ramingo hissed at Pecora.

Faster than any of the Camorra foot soldiers could react, Il Ramingo shot forward, grabbing Pecora by the head, pushing it back, exposing his throat. A long doubled bladed knife appeared from nowhere in Il Ramingo's right hand. With a flick of his wrist, he cut Pecora's throat from ear to ear, sending a geyser of red from the gaping wound, drenching Ken and Jimmy Nicchi in blood.

"Holy fuck!"

Jimmy Nicchi stumbled backwards, face drenched in crimson, while his good hand clawed for the pistol stuck in his waistband.

Il Ramingo darted to the rear of the room. With a roundhouse kick delivered in a circular blur, he struck a surprised Chiara Opizzi in the head. The blow sent her crashing to the floor. One of Pecora's men lunged at him, but with one great swipe of his right arm, he severed the man's head. The body slumped to the ground, steam from spurting hot blood clouding the cold air in the refrigerated building. Ray heard a metallic click and the foot-long blade on Il Ramingo's right arm disappeared, replaced in an instant with a pistol. Sprinting toward a set of stairs leading up to a glass walled office, Il Ramingo fired into two Camorra standing in his way.

Then he was up the stairs and gone.

To a man, the Nicchi crew was too stunned to move. Except Jimmy, who was able to get his heavy silver revolver out, and fire it at an escaping Il Ramingo. But the assassin was gone. Instead, one of Jimmy's bullets caught a Camorra soldier rushing to the scene in the chin. The rest of the Camorra turned, still confused as to how their boss was nearly decapitated by his top assassin, and returned fire at the Americans.

Ray dove behind a pallet of canned San Marzano tomatoes. Dozens of bullets whizzed over his head, others whacking into the cans. The twenty odd Camorra remaining poured gunfire into the Nicchi. Among the chaos, Ray could see at least two of their men sprawled on the floor, blood spreading around their lifeless forms.

Ten feet to Ray's right, BTO crouched behind a cluster of metal drums. Camorra bullets ricocheted off the metal. BTO had acquired a rifle from one of the dead Camorra and was firing back at the Italians. In front of Ray, Luca Pecora was face down in his own blood, his pig ignoring the bullets crisscrossing over it, hungrily lapping at the red pool beneath its owner. Careful not to give anyone a clear shot at his head, Ray peeked above the pallet. No sign of his brother or Ken Nicchi. Another volley of gunfire from the Camorra tore into the pallet. Ray ducked. The bullets made a wet popping sound as they riddled the tomato cans. More red fluid spilled on the floor, mingling with the blood of the dead.

Ray heard footsteps and popped up with his pistol, emptying the clip. Before ducking, he saw a Camorra goon staggering back clutching at his stomach. Ray stared down at the pistol in his hands. The receiver locked open. He was out of bullets.

"Granttano. Heads up." Ray looked to his right just as BTO slid a fully loaded pistol across the floor to him.

"I can't hold them forever!" BTO fired a shotgun blast point blank at a Camorra rushing his position, sending one half of the man to the left, the other half to the right.

Ray placed his mouth on his lapel and shouted, "Hodges! Sophie! What are you waiting for?" Then he remembered. "*Esperanza!*"

BTO froze for a moment and looked hard at Ray. "Who the fuck are you talking to?"

"Il Ramingo's on the run! We need him!"

Sitting in the CIA surveillance van, everyone inside watched the infrared monitors in growing horror as the meeting with Pecora took a deadly turn. A gasp rippled through the van at the gruesome curtain of blood erupting from Pecora's throat, rendered for all to see on the monitors in stark infrared. A panicked Hodges pulled the SOG teams back and reassigned them to pursue Il Ramingo.

Tossing aside her headphones, Sophie grabbed an M4 rifle with one hand, and reached for the van's rear door handle with the other. "Madeline's not there. You stay," Hodges said to her. Sophie stopped and turned to face him. His eyes were wild, pupils darting back and forth across the screens, the total implosion of his operation happening in real time, and the man unable to do anything about it.

Carter brushed past Sophie and pushed open the van's rear doors. He pointed at two SOGs who had been planning to breach. "With me." They leapt into an Audi sedan parked alongside for contingencies, and lay smoking blue rubber in pursuit of Il Ramingo.

"My father is in there. Your informant? Remember? The American citizen?" Sophie locked eyes with Hodges.

"I understand. Believe me." Hodges pointed at a red dot moving fast on the screen. "But Il Ramingo can't leave Naples. With Pecora dead, I need everybody in pursuit. And you aren't going in alone."

"*Sophie! What are they waiting for?*" Her father's voice jumped from the speakers.

Hodges dropped his head. "Son of a bitch." He cleared his throat. Then to a SOG operative loitering at the bumper, "Adams, go with her."

Sophie darted out the rear of the van. Once outside, a cacophony of gunfire could be heard from inside Pecora's warehouse. Hodges's van, now packed with SOG operatives, squealed after Carter's Audi. She arrived at a side entrance to the warehouse. Adams, a squat brown-haired man, got there a second later, his M4 at eye level. He grabbed Sophie by the shoulder and spun her around the face him.

"I enter, you follow me back and to the right. Watch my flanks. Deal?"

"Deal."

"I'm out!"

"For Christ's sake, Granttano, learn how to conserve ammo."

Without looking, his vision instead focused on Camorra attackers advancing on him. BTO tossed a heavy revolver with black grips over his head. Ray caught it with both hands in time to bring the hand cannon to bear on a Camorra thug charging around the corner of his pallet. He pulled the trigger. *Empty!* The Camorra soldier slumped lifeless to the ground.

Ray glanced back at BTO, the big man firing a submachine gun in one hand and a pistol in the other, bodies scattered in front of his position, empty shell casings carpeting the cement floor. A thin blue cloud of cordite-scented gunpowder hung over Ray and BTO.

As far as Ray could tell, they were the only remaining survivors of the Nicchi crew.

"BTO!"

Looking over his shoulder, Ray watched BTO locked in hand-to hand combat with two Camorra thugs. BTO kicked one in the chest, sending the man reeling, but the other slashed him across the chest with a short blade. Before he could plunge the knife into BTO's neck, Ray jumped on his back, wrapping his arms around the man's torso. With a sickening crunch, BTO punched the defenseless man in the face, and spun, delivering a roundhouse kick to the other man who had just regained his feet, snapping his head back at an unnatural angle.

"Granttano, your six," BTO said, firing a pistol he took from the man with the smashed face at a Camorra charging him. That man went down, but two more Camorra jumped on BTO from his right, knocking him to the ground.

Ray turned to face the new threat, a Camorra with a sawed-off shotgun approaching. The sound of gunfire made Ray jump as he expected shotgun pellets ripping into his chest. Instead, he saw the shooter's head snap back from a bullet.

"Drop your weapons! Put 'em down!" Sophie Grant yelled at the two men kicking BTO on the ground while walking forward, a curl of smoke escaping the barrel of her rifle.

One man stopped and drew his gun. Over Sophie's shoulder Adams shot him twice in the chest. The other turned to run, but Adams fired a burst into his back.

Adams and Sophie crouched next to Ray behind his bullet-riddled pallet. "You came." Ray smiled.

She winked at her father. "For the money." Sophie spied the silver case containing the three million euros. It was ten meters in front of her under a table. "Cover me," she said to Adams. Sophie slung the M4 across her back and sprinted for the table. She had the case in her hands and had turned back to her father when she heard BTO yell.

"More coming!"

Another wave of Camorra charged their position firing wildly. Sophie ran for the pallet, and was transported back to that night in college, feeling the warmth of the water from the cadaver pool around her, the speed of her body in motion. Bullets whistled around her, tearing at the air. Adams and BTO returned fire at the attackers. Adams took a bullet in the shoulder, spinning him around, dropping him to his knees just as Sophie dove behind the pallet for cover.

She shoved the case into her father's hands. "Get Adams out the door. I'll cover you," Sophie said to Ray and BTO while gesturing at the wounded SOG. Then she pointed behind him. "There's an access door and a van outside."

Sophie unslung the rifle, put it to her shoulder and fired bursts to suppress the Camorra advance. Using the cover fire, Ray and BTO scooped up Adams and spirited him to the exit. Spraying her entire magazine in an arc, Sophie turned and ran toward the door. She made it outside, closing the door as a bouquet of bullets hit the impervious metal slab.

Ray and BTO were already in the black Mercedes van, sitting on the bumper, as a medic was attending to Adams. BTO held a compress to the knife wound across his chest.

Her father looked up. His face was dark and pained.

"He still has Madeline."

CHAPTER 35

"It's colder than a dead proctologist's hand in here."

David Granttano's arms were wrapped tight around his shivering body in a futile effort to get warmer. When the gunfight erupted between the Nicchi crew and the Camorra, David's well-honed survival instincts kicked in. He knew the CIA's strike team would be swarming the area in seconds, and if they weren't cut down in a crossfire, they would still be under that prick Hodges's thumb. Grabbing Ken Nicchi by the arm, David steered his boss around one side of a ten-foot pyramid of stacked semolina flour bags. The Camorra horde, enraged by the sudden, brutal murder of their leader, rushed by in a pack on the other side. David glanced over his shoulder hoping they hadn't been spotted and saw Jimmy Nicchi following them.

Ken lurched for the first door he saw, choosing a walk-in freezer to hide in instead of a refrigeration unit. When the door closed behind them with a loud click, David realized—too late—that Italy had much different workplace laws. There was no safety release on the inside. They were trapped with at least a hundred sides of beef, pork, and parts of other butchered animals hanging from hooks in the ceiling. It took them a full minute to travel to the rear of the room to find shelter, shoving aside frozen slabs of swinging meat. While the battle raged outside, the trio sat huddled behind a steel table at the rear of the freezer. Though the door was thick and the generator cooling the room ran with a loud, steady hum, they could still hear multiple gunshots and the occasional scream of pain from outside.

"Shouldn't we be out there fighting with our guys?" Jimmy asked.

David saw now that Ken Nicchi's son was comically ghoulish, one arm bandaged, the other waving a pistol over his head, with Pecora's blood frozen to his face in dozens of red icicles, his eyes opioid-fueled pinwheels.

"If we could open the door, screwhead," David said.

"But your brother's out there," Jimmy said.

"My brother," David said. Jimmy's painkiller addled words hit David like a punch to the nose. Everything had fallen apart so fast he'd had no time to think about Ray. There was a painful flutter in his chest. David wondered if this is what a heart attack felt like.

His mind traveled back to those dark days in the mid-90s. Terrifying days when hitmen from New York and Chicago hunted Kansas City for the Nicchi crew. David was sure he was going to die, as did everyone from the original family. It wasn't like they didn't deserve it. Just the opposite, Ken's dad fucked up so monumentally it was impossible for retaliation from the other families to be anything short of Armageddon. Only David and Ken Jr. survived. Because of Ray Granttano. And for that, Ray lost his family, earning a lifetime of hatred from Sophia. And now was probably dead.

At the mention of David's brother, Ken's eyes bulged. Breathing heavy, clouds of vapor forming from his mouth in the cold storage locker, he muttered "Shit!" then reached deep into his shirt, yanked hard on the bug Hodges made him wear, and came out with a fistful of wires. He tossed the CIA listening device on the cement floor and with the heel of his shoe ground it into small pieces.

"Both of you do the same."

David raised his hand. "Don't we need them? The CIA? To get us back stateside . . . alive?"

"We're on our own, again, Davey," Ken said. He pointed out into the warehouse. "And those CIA clowns have no idea what they're up against."

While David removed the radio transmitter and microphone

taped to his chest, Ken helped one-handed Jimmy remove his. Ken dutifully stomped both into unrecognizable debris. David turned to Jimmy, anger filling his limbs despite the cold.

"If you hadn't shit yourself out there our guys would still be alive."

"It wasn't my fault. It was an accident. The gun just went off."

"You spoiled little bitch."

With that insult, Jimmy lunged at David, who took great pleasure in punching the younger Nicchi right in his bandaged hand.

Jimmy fell to his knees. He looked like he was going to throw up.

"Stop it you two," Ken said. "I'm sorry Davey, about your brother. I'm sure it hurts." Ken put a hand on his shoulder. "But get it in your head. We're on our own. We need each other if we want to get out of here alive."

"How do you propose *we* do that?'

"Easy," Ken said, sitting on a pallet of frozen beef. "We sit tight and wait for it to quiet down and—"

Ken was interrupted by a flurry of muted gunfire outside the door. Jimmy yelped and dove for the floor while Ken and David pointed their pistols toward the front of the locker. Then silence. The trio waited there for ten minutes.

"My hand feels funny," Jimmy said, breaking the silence.

"*Shhh!*" Ken said. "Do you hear that?" He whispered, "I think there's someone out in front of the door."

David concentrated on the shuffling noise outside the freezer door. Ken was right. There was someone outside. Checking his pistol to make sure a round was in the chamber, David Granttano crouched and prepared to meet whatever threat came at them through that door.

"Dad, we should move up front, in case they open the door, so we can get the drop on them." Jimmy started shuffling toward the front of the freezer, edging past swinging sides of meat.

"Freeze, Jimmy," David huffed quietly. "They can hear you."

"Fine, I'll be quiet."

Jimmy turned and pushed aside a beef carcass to reveal the frozen body of Cochi, the Campania pig that had bit his hand, hanging by a hook through its head, Ray's bullet hole visible in the animal's temple. Unlike the other livestock in the freezer, the pig was still intact.

Jimmy shrieked, followed by four hard knocks on the door.

"What do we do?" David said.

Ken said. He reached down and helped Jimmy to his feet, his son's eyes fixed on the pig that had feasted on his hand. "Not a word to anyone about anything."

There was a loud click. Someone was opening the door from the outside. The heavy portal swung open. Stepping though a cloud of vapor condensation, Luca Pecora's trusted lieutenant, Chiara Opizzi, appeared. She was holding an ice pack to the side of her head.

"Is now a good time to talk some business, Mr. Nicchi?"

CHAPTER 36

Carter Boyd fidgeted in the passenger seat of his speeding Audi sedan. He turned the air conditioning on. Then off. Carter had just learned from a tech back at Absolute Amore that the door the assassin chose for his escape was the only exit not on the warehouse's plans submitted to the city. Once again like with Pico the Wheel, Il Ramingo had exploited their vulnerability.

With three SOGSs in his car, they were humming down Naples's frenzied main five lane artery, the Corso Umberto, closely trailing Il Ramingo's white Fiat coup. Hodges in his black Mercedes CIA surveillance van trailed by a full city block.

"Careful, we don't want to spook him," Hodges said over the radio to his SOGs. "Fattore has two squads in birds on standby. She requested we take him outside the city to limit civilian exposure. Once we get him isolated, they'll drop in and set up a blockade on his twelve with us on his six."

"He's turning off." Carter saw the Fiat veer to the right and toward an off ramp. "Looks like he's heading for the E45."

"Stay farther back. Easier for him to spy a tail on the E," Hodges said.

Following orders, Boyd's driver dropped five cars behind Il Ramingo's Fiat. The big four-lane highway connected Naples to Pompeii and was a major transportation artery for Southern Italy. For the next ninety minutes, they trailed Il Ramingo.

"He's turning," Carter's driver said. "Getting off the E45. Looks like a two-lane road called the SP1. Goes over the Statell Valle Mountains."

"Perfect," Hodges said. "The genius assassin just drove himself into a box. Fattore says her men will be at the Pierte junction seven miles ahead. It's surrounded by canyon walls . . . nowhere to run. With any luck they'll have Il Ramingo in handcuffs when we arrive."

Carter's driver hugged the tight corners of the Italian mountain road. Cresting a hill, they entered a short valley no more than five miles long, with tall craggy cliffs on either side of their two-lane highway. Stopped in the middle of the valley at a lone intersection was Il Ramingo's white Fiat, with thirty or so PSC officers spread in an arc in front of the vehicle. Behind the wall of Italian police officers idled three empty sky-blue PSC helicopters.

As Carter drew closer, he saw the door to the Fiat was open. Fattore stood tall with her team spread out on either side of her fifty meters from the Fiat. Carter got out into the hot, bright Campania sun and walked next to Fattore. Hodges's van stopped behind Carter's Audi. With his shirt sleeve flapping, Hodges jogged to Carter's side.

"Is he in the car?" the station chief said.

"No. No sign of Il Ramingo," Fattore said. "A bomb squad is on the way. It would be like Il Ramingo to leave us a surprise."

"Goddammit." Hodges pointed at the cliffs above. "So, he had to climb those to escape, and your men saw nothing?"

"Are you suggesting that we didn't do our jobs?" Captain Fattore's eye twitched. "Il Ramingo killed my driver. I don't want him in jail. I want him dead."

"Order your men to start climbing those cliffs."

"You forget, Hodges, I don't work for you." Fattore twirled her finger in the air. "We have more helicopters coming. They'll drop teams with dogs."

For the first time Carter witnessed a speechless Bill Hodges. No words, no throat clearing. The station chief stared at Fattore who defiantly stared back. His boss took a deep breath and let out a deflated sigh. He turned and started walking back to his van.

"Bill?"

CHAPTER 37

"We hightailed it for the first door we could find."

"Lucky," Chiara Opizzi said pointing at the purple welt over her left eye.

She hovered over David Granttano, Ken, and Jimmy Nicchi, the trio seated at the table, pistol at her side. To their right was Luca Pecora, face down, ass up, in his own congealed pool of blood. Clustered around the Nicchi were a handful of Camorra thugs, the few members of Pecora's gang that managed to stay alive during the warehouse shootout. It was clear to David they were now under Chiara's control. Milling about with its snout to the floor looking for food was Pecora's orphaned pig, Cochi.

Ken was spinning a convincing yarn to Chiara about their escape. Not that they had a choice. Coming clean about wearing wires for Hodges would've had their blood mingling with the dead in the warehouse. Even though there was no sign of Ray among the bodies, David was still pissed at his brother for setting them up. Despite that asshole screwing them over, informing on them for years, David wished he could see his brother. Just one more time to ask Ray if the betrayal finally, after all the time and all the guilt, if it made them square. After he knocked a few teeth out, of course.

"Why kill Pecora?" Ken said. "Did I miss something? I thought this Il Ramingo was the best. Loyal to a fault."

"Oh, he is the best. My father told me the story once, of how he ordered Il Ramingo to murder a *Corte d'Assise* magistrate. Judge Terrazzo was about to rule against my uncle. Life sentence. Terrazzo?

Untouchable. He was at a family wedding in Revello. My father said one second Il Ramingo was just another figure on the street dressed as a fireman. The assassin set a fire in a church bathroom, forced a building-wide evacuation and the judge out on the street, the next second the fire axe was swinging and slicing through Judge Terrazzo's bodyguards. After he killed all four of Terrazzo's men, he plucked out the judge's eyes with his fingers as a present for my father, then stabbed the magistrate through the heart."

Chiara rubbed her eye and flinched. "But he's damaged. Some say he had a great love murdered. Made him *Pazzo*."

"Before cutting Luca's throat, what did he say?" David asked.

"*La e codice. No donne. No bambini*," Chiara winced at the pain in her swollen eye as she spoke to Ken Nicchi. "'No women, no children. His code.'" She tucked the pistol into the small of her back. "We knew he was angry . . . angry about your daughter-in-law. She was supposed to die on that boat. Pecora ordered it so. She looked at her late boss's body and shook her head. "And Il Ramingo disobeyed him."

That's an understatement, David thought. He took out a pack of smokes, shook one out and lit it. To his right, Jimmy was slumped in his chair, mewling like a wounded animal.

"Shouldn't we be worried about the cops?" David asked.

"This is our warehouse. We have cleanup crews on the way. The police will call before they come. So polite. They bring coffee. We have time to talk." Chiara sat next to Ken. "I need your help."

"Anything."

"News of Luca's death will travel fast. The other families will take what we have. Naples is a big prize. And the Nigerians? They must be sent a message, too. I need to assert myself." She gestured to the men gathered in the room. "Everyone must know this is a return of the Opizzi System. *Por mi padre*. The need to know a steady hand guides the ship."

"How can we—" Ken began to ask.

Bang! The breath left David's lungs at the sound of a gunshot. Back legs twitching in a death spasm, Pecora's Campania pig Cochi lay in pool of spreading blood. "Everyone hated those fucking pigs. And that's the last time it nibbles my hand." Chiara made a show of putting the safety on her pistol and tucking the weapon back into her waistband. "You can help me by agreeing to the deal you had with Luca. To start taking waste into America."

David was dumbstruck. Chiara's reputation was impeccable. Groomed by Pecora. Instincts comparable to her very shrewd father, Ken told him. But here she was, offering them a deal when she should be suspicious. An hour ago, they were wearing CIA wires! David asked the next, obvious question. "You don't have any doubts about us? What happened with Ken's son, Chris the informant?"

Chiara met his gaze with an unwavering stare. "You weren't working for the CIA were you?"

"No," all three, including Jimmy, responded in unison.

"Your son does not look well, Ken."

"Dad, what did she say?" Jimmy looked up glassy eyed.

"He's fine," Ken said. David didn't think Jimmy looked anything close to fine. The kid had a seeping mangled hand wrapped in soiled gauze. His face was milk white with rivulets of blood, the result of Pecora's arterial spray melting.

Chiara barked orders in Italian to one of her men, who scurried up the stairs.

"We'll see that his hand is taken care of," she said.

"Thank you."

"No. Thank you for agreeing to continue our business arrangement." Chiara tapped the table with her finger. "And in return for your generosity and trust, I have a trawler ready to sail you back to America. Undetected. You cruise under the flag of Taiwan."

"I don't know what to say?" Ken said.

"Say yes."

"What's the catch?" David Granttano asked. There had to be a catch. There was always a catch. They were criminals! David would've been afraid if there wasn't. Not that it appeared they had much choice at this point. There was no way they would make it back to Kansas City with conventional means if the goal was to evade the CIA's net.

"I need you to shepherd something for me, during the trip." Chiara raised her hand. *"Giuseppe, trovalo."* A tall man in a brown leather coat, machine gun strapped across his back, broke from the group of Camorra standing off to the side. He walked to Luca Pecora's body and searched through his pockets until Giuseppe found the object he was looking for. Next, he pulled out a big pocketknife, opened the silver blade, and severed Pecora's right thumb. He came to the table and set a black and red smartphone in front of Chiara. Next to it he placed the former System leader's digit.

"What is it with these people and fucking fingers?" David whispered to Ken.

Chiara picked up the phone and examined the device.

"Quanto tempo ti ci vuole per aprirlo?"

Giuseppe shrugged. *"Due ore, tre massimmo."*

Chiara nodded and handed the phone back to Giuseppe. The man pocketed it. He reached down and took the thumb, put it in the same pocket and headed for the door.

"You were saying, we needed to watch something?" Ken asked.

"I'm hungry." Chiara stood. "I know a place in Positano."

CHAPTER 38

"Can I pour you a drink?"

Bill Hodges beckoned Carter Boyd into his second-floor office. They had just arrived back at Absoluta Amora. Carter was on his way to lock up his tactical gear. He was looking forward to catching a few hours of sleep.

Carter stopped, looking back over his shoulder. There was a half-full bottle of scotch on Hodge's desk next to a glass holding a finger of brown liquor. After every operation, Hodges would make Carter go line by line over the action reports, the old man's breath over his shoulder. And every time, Hodges would find a mistake or offer a way to tailor the report to please the Agency bean counters. Sloppy expense reports could get a CIA officer into more hot water than missing the next 9/11.

"Can it wait? I'm wiped."

"'Fraid not."

Hodges took a swig of whiskey. Carter stepped into his office. The space was modest but well appointed. His gray metal government-issue desk was clean, except for a closed black folder and the booze. Behind the desk a table held pictures of Hodge's grown children from a marriage dissolved a decade earlier. Carter sat in the chair on the other side of his desk. Hodges knocked back his drink, pulled a clean glass from a drawer in his desk and poured two fresh whiskies.

"Time to read you into this." With his fingertips, Hodges slid the black folder across the metal surface to Carter. "What's inside there . . . not even the deputy director knows the whole picture."

Carter took the folder off the table like he was wearing oven mitts. "We're not doing expenses?"

"Go ahead, open it."

Carter peeled open the black plastic cover. The first page was stamped *Top Secret*. At the bottom of the page was a list of signatures of everyone who had read the document in what looked like the past thirty years. The list had just eleven names. Three were former presidents.

"What the hell is this?"

"You ever hear how I got promoted to chief?"

Carter nodded. "Of course. The stuff of legend. Turin. Ninety-eight. During the Soviet collapse. You caught a gang of Russians smuggling a suitcase nuke out of the Chelyabinsk facility. Stopped 'em right at the Italian border with Germany. Made your career. After that you wrote your own ticket and became the youngest station chief in Agency history." Carter drank from his glass of scotch. "Did I get that right?"

"That's the official story."

Carter leaned forward. "And the real story?"

"It left something out."

"Something?"

Hodges took a drink. "The other bomb."

"The other bomb?"

Hodges nodded. "They called it Little Bear. Model RA 115. Six kilotons, enough to take out a city. Not at all practical considering the network of radiation sensors deployed across Europe after 9/11. But before that, a group of Soviet scientists figured out how to make a decent portable tactical device at Chelyabinsk. Developed a model about the size of those huge fucking backpacks you see kids carry across Europe. Even figured out a failsafe chemical trigger. Then the bottom fell out of the Union."

"What the hell are you saying?"

Hodges's eyes drifted to a spot off in space.

"Bill."

Hodges's gaze returned to Carter. His eyes refocused though he was clearly feeling the effects of alcohol. Carter had only seen his boss this intoxicated one other time. Their SOGs had engaged an ISIS cell outside Rome but failed to contain the gun battle. Two of the terrorists slipped out and charged where he and Hodges had staged. They were easy targets. The first and only time Carter had killed a man. Afterward, Hodges took him drinking. Didn't brag. Didn't try to pump him up. Didn't give him some platitude about breaking his cherry, just knew he needed to get drunk to grapple with the event.

"You know, for one moment. One glorious moment, I was an actual goddamn hero." Whatever noise that next came out of Hodges's throat, Carter had never heard it before.

Carter slapped his hand hard on the desk, making Hodges jump in his seat. "Bill, what are you trying to tell me?"

Hodges, broken from his spell, now looked pissed. "We got one Little Bear, but another got away." He pointed at the dossier. "I tracked who I think smuggled it to Campania, but then the trail went cold. Then this happened."

Hodges flipped the pages of the dossier until he found the sheet of paper he was looking for. He slid it to Carter. The memo was from the president's national security advisor dated eleven months prior. It was peppered with phrases like *"rein in wasteful spending,"* and *"the maintenance and upgrades needed for hundreds of radiation monitors is costly to the US taxpayer,"* and ended with, *"the national debt is also a national security issue."*

"They're getting rid of the monitoring stations?" Carter asked, astonished.

Losing a deterrent in the radiation detection system would embolden WMD traffickers. Once the sensors vanished, anyone sitting on fissionable material would rush to sell to the black market, right when Carter would be taking over from Hodges.

"Defunding. Not the same, but close. Apparently, it was a campaign promise."

"Jesus Christ," Carter said.

"You know him? That would be helpful right now." Hodges tapped the rim of his glass with his thumbnail. "With retirement coming, I didn't have much time left to fix my nuclear fuck up." He stood and leaned over the desk, flipped over two pieces of paper in the folder in front of Carter and tapped his finger on the stapled sheet that remained. "And I thought, I had a really good lead."

Carter quickly read the two-page double-spaced document written in Italian. It was a confidential memo from Polizia Speciale Campania Captain Adele Fattore to her superiors in Rome detailing her suspicions that the Camorra toxic chemical dumping activity around Vesuvius could be hiding something much worse. That it was deliberate in its placement. She speculated it could be a buried weapon of mass destruction. Accompanying the memo were maps and seismic measurements of the volcano from the Campania Geological Survey.

"But Rome sat on its hands, didn't they? And you decided to do something about it. And you brought an EPA special agent over to stir the pot. See if they'd try and move the bomb." Carter sat back in his chair. "You crazy, magnificent motherfucker."

Hodges nodded. "Couldn't take the chance. I'd be complaining about my huge colon on a Tallahassee shuffleboard court while a nuke went off at the Superbowl."

It all fell into place. Why Hodges had been so agitated the past few months. Why Hodges gambled on situations he never would have before. Carter had chalked it up to wanting to land one last great operation.

"You should've told me."

"Aye. Maybe. But at the same time, I thought I had to show the new station chief what it takes. Clean up your own mess." Hodges laughed. "You were too busy perfecting your quiche Lorraine recipe, anyway."

"It's going to work, Bill."

Hodges offered a surprisingly genuine smile. "I know, kid. Just messing with you."

"Oh shit, The Wheel." Carter remembered the secure, lead-lined case they discovered when raiding the cheese merchant's export business. Pecora had without question been planning to move the bomb off the mountain. The enormity of what Hodges told him made it hard for Carter to breathe. There was a rogue nuclear weapon hidden in the maze of toxic waste pits on the slopes of Mount Vesuvius.

Hodges rubbed his temples. He was hunched over in defeat. In that moment Carter got scared. Very scared. *Is this what the job comes down to? The least bad of a horrible choice?*

"Suspects? Do you know who they are?"

Hodges pointed at one of the sheets in the dossier Carter had set aside to read the Fattore memo. He lifted the sheet up and examined a grainy black and white picture of a short man with horn rimmed glasses.

"Andre Sokolov?"

"Supervised the weapons team at the Chelyabinsk facility. An engineer, too. Former KGB with close ties to Russian proxies in the Middle East. Was active selling weapons until 9/11. Then like the other smart ones, disappeared. Not coincidentally, around the same time the Naples System got into the arms business." Hodges pulled a sheet of paper from under Sokolov's picture. "Mossad call intercept from 2003. Between Sokolov and Giancarlo Opizzi."

Carter read the document, which looked to have been photocopied a dozen times. It was the dictation of a conversation between two surveillance subjects talking about an Italian Army deserter during the war in Iraq. Sokolov was telling Pecora's predecessor that as the Naples System leader he had a new employee to groom.

An employee he referred to as *Il Mezzanotte Ramingo*.

"Find Il Ramingo, and the nuke isn't far away?" Carter said.

Hodges shrugged. Then drank.

"What do we do now?"

"Pray that thing's been in the ground too long to go boom?" He leaned back in his chair and groaned. "When you get to be my age, everything hurts except for your tongue."

"Got anything stronger?" Carter drank the rest of his whiskey, the alcohol burning his throat. "Like a Hemlock and Coke?"

CHAPTER 39

Once back at the CIA's Absoluta Amore, Sophie needed to take a shower. See Maria. Hug the young girl and feel her hug back. Sophie took the elevator to the top floor and found the SOG assigned to guard Maria playing electronic battleship with the Italian girl on the floor of their room.

Sophie took a shower and dressed in a black sweatsuit. Maria was now entranced by an epic hand of solitaire and didn't want to leave. Sophie went looking for her father, alone. Ray Granttano sat in the command center, his gaunt, sunken eyed face lit by a single monitor, a can of diet soda in his hand. The screen showed a silent feed from an Italian police drone flying over the Attalla Mountains.

"Hodges said I could watch in case . . . in case my eye caught something," Ray said without turning his head to face her.

Sophie sat next to him and put her hand on his. He squeezed her hand back, hard. Ray swallowed. Nodding toward the phone on the table he said, "I called Cathy. My wife Cathy. To tell her the news." His voice caught and he swallowed again. "That I couldn't save our girl."

"We'll find Madeline, Dad. The CIA isn't going to let him get away."

"No."

There was something different in her father's voice. She barely knew the man, but in their short time together in Italy Sophie had witnessed a full range of emotions from Raymond Granttano. He'd gone from joy with Maria to the pain and anguish from knowing his actions had put those he loved in danger. But there was a deeper edge in his sorrow this evening.

"Cathy didn't answer. A doctor did."

Ray explained that a neighbor had been checking in on his wife since he left Kansas City for Italy. She found Cathy on the floor unresponsive and a half empty pill bottle in the kitchen. She was now stable and would survive, the doctor said, but if the friend hadn't checked in, his wife would've been dead by morning.

"What have I done?"

Her father shook his head like he was waking up from a nap. He looked down at his blood-spattered clothes, and touched the dried blood on his face.

"You have to get that little girl out of here."

"But I don't want to go back to Malodini. I want to stay with you. You and *Nonno* Ray."

Sophie and Maria stood in the bright interior courtyard. Late afternoon sunlight blasted the stone from above. Alone save for a SOG operative on a smoke break off to the side. Maria's packed suitcase was at her feet. Her arms cradled a card game, where players battled each other with monsters and spells. Ray bought her it at a toy store down in the city center. The game was not age appropriate.

Sophie blinked. "Nonno?"

"It means grandfather."

"I know what it means."

Ray and Maria may have only known each other for two days, but apparently became so close in the short amount of time that Sophie wouldn't be shocked if they started finishing each other's sentences. Maria's instant attraction to Sophie's father made sense. Kid was an orphan. She craved paternal attention like oxygen. And Ray was charming. Sophie suspected her father's interest was more self-serving, that he saw Maria as a way to curry favor with his daughter. More than once, Sophie caught herself feeling jealous, the memory of lying awake at night in her Colorado bedroom, wishing her father would be there with her, wishing he would buy her games, a dull ache that never seemed to go away.

Of course, learning Ray Granttano had worked much of his life to right the wrongs of his past by informing for the CIA, and that his other daughter was in the clutches of a psycho killer, tempered the sting. The SOG finished his cigarette and went back inside the hotel, stopping first at the security gate to show his badge. Sophie checked her phone for the hundredth time.

"You've already missed two days of classes," Sophie said. "I'd love for you to stay, but the nuns are going to complain. And the sisters will be right. You still can't convert fractions."

At the age of eleven, Maria had already learned some of life's hardest lessons. Sophie had made the fatal choice to let Tommy stay. Now she was making the same mistake with Maria. The lie to protect Maria came easy. Sophie wondered if it had been that easy for her father.

"Pistachio or chocolate?" Ray asked from behind them. He held a cone of gelato in each hand.

"Chocolate!"

"Good. Pistachio is my favorite anyway," Ray said with a smile, handing the chocolate cone to Maria, her face beaming like the sun. Maria licked the ice cream twice.

"If you think that's tasty," Ray said, you should try Kansas City barbeque someday."

Maria's face scrunched up. "What's that?"

"Why the most delicious thing ever to eat in the whole world." Ray turned to Sophie. "You never fed her barbeque?"

"She's Italian, Dad. She may be an orphan, but she eats well." Sophie beckoned her father with her finger. "Can I talk to you for a moment? Over here? Alone?"

Ray nodded. He turned back to Maria "When I get back that gelato better be gone." He stood and walked a few feet out of earshot from Maria with his daughter.

"I see what you're doing."

Ray tried to look innocent "What?"

"*Nonno?* Barbeque? What's next, adoption papers? She's eleven, going on eighteen. She can handle herself. Best not to get her hopes up."

"I'm an old man, Sophie, and because of you and BTO I'm quite lucky to be alive. Madeline and Chris tried, tried like ever-living hell to have kids. Doctors. Injections. Treatments. The works. She couldn't have children." He peered around Sophie and winked at Maria who was busy devouring her ice cream. "Yeah, she's tough. But that kid needs you. Family can be more than blood."

"That's the kind of talk that got you in trouble with the Nicchi."

"Ouch. Fair, but tough."

From the underground garage a silver BMW sedan appeared. A SOG was at the wheel. He stopped the car in the courtyard and hoped out and walked around the front to stand in front of Maria.

"SOG Carlson here will take you to Malodini," Sophie said.

"Who's ready for a road trip?" Carlson said to Maria. He was average height, thick in the chest and arms, like the other workout obsessed SOGs, but flashed a disarming smile at Maria. From behind his back, Carlson produced a plastic shopping bag brimming with candy, chips and assorted snacks.

"I am!"

CHAPTER 40

Memento mori.

Il Ramingo sprinted through a steep field strewn with boulders and rock outcroppings. Scrapes and cuts covered his hands. His left ring fingernail hung by a bloody strand of skin, a victim of a misjudged handhold as he escaped the Polizia Speciale Campania blockade. Seconds before the PSC arrived in helicopters, he had stopped the car at a predetermined set of coordinates. Abandoning the white Fiat, he ran to the north for a sheer cliff wall. At the base of the wall, he had stashed climbing gear under a dead tree. Il Ramingo was halfway up the rock face when the blue helicopters thundered into the valley.

A hundred meters more running uphill and Il Ramingo reached the summit. During his training a lifetime ago, for three grueling months, new recruits climbed similar craggy peaks and canyons twenty kilometers farther north up the Amalfi Coast. Once atop the cliff, he peered down at the faint dots of Polizia Speciale Campania officers, the white Fiat and the black CIA van. Il Ramingo enjoyed a moment of satisfaction, wishing he could see the American's face the moment CIA Chief Bill Hodges realized he'd been playing chess against a grand master.

The mistake would cost the Americans. A bill paid in rivers of blood.

To Il Ramingo's left, Mount Saint Angelo looked down on them—police and killer. To his right and 5,000 feet below was the glittering Tyrrhenian Sea. His phone vibrated from inside a slim zipper pocket on his chest. A message from DeSalvo.

Success?

Si, he typed back one-handed.

Good. Remember, we are only halfway there.

Il Ramingo froze at the faint thumping sounds of helicopters in flight.

The helicopters are coming, I must go.

Check the device.

Il Ramingo stared at the phone for a moment. What once was a liability was now integral to their strategy. Instead of dropping his phone, Il Ramingo stuck it away in a zippered pocket. After the phone was secure, he sprinted for the cover of a grove of chestnut trees across a clearing. Once behind the massive trunk of a tree easily a hundred years old, he peered back into the clearing.

A blue PSC helicopter burst from the valley below into view over the clearing. The pilot brought the craft down too fast for landing and bounced the helicopter once in the air knocking a police officer standing in the doorway out of the aircraft. Il Ramingo used the distracted pilot to dart away through the trees. Another helicopter flew overhead, but the forest canopy was too thick for them to spy him. It wouldn't be long until PSC officers were combing every inch of Southern Italy. With dogs. If Il Ramingo stayed in the forest too long, or tried to keep going overland by foot, they would catch him for sure. He needed a place to catch his breath.

At the end of the giant grove of chestnut trees was an abandoned vineyard. Gnarled, untended grape vines coiled around sun-bleached trestles, spilling down a steeply terraced hillside. At the top of the vineyard were two crumbling structures, a farmhouse and a small barn so old it looked like *Il Duce* supervised the last grape crush. The farmhouse was in no better shape, teetering on the edge of a stone retaining wall. An old, rutted road ran from the farmhouse and disappeared around a knoll.

He waited a beat, listening for helicopters flying overhead. Hearing none and knowing the CIA didn't have the airspace authority to deploy drones, Il Ramingo ran for the farmhouse. Once inside, he paused for a minute, using a meditation technique to calm his breathing. He peeked his head outside the door. No one was around, yet.

Il Ramingo found the restroom. Beneath a pile of old dirty clothes was a black case. Unlocking the case, he removed a spare handgun with three extra magazines and a compact first-aid kit. He ripped the nail off his finger and stuck it in a zippered pocket on his pant leg. Then he cleaned his wounds with alcohol and gauze, stuffing the bloody cotton in another pocket. After he was sure the wound wasn't susceptible to infection, he pulled out from the case a floppy, well-worn farmer's hat and a long brown cloak favored by the local cattle herders to complete his disguise. One more peek outside. No sign of the police.

Il Ramingo jogged down a two-track dirt road for a half a mile when the faint sound of a helicopter grew louder. Running as fast as he could, Il Ramingo arrived at an intersection of the dirt road with Highway E34. He waved down a produce truck and begged for a ride to the next town. The driver, frightened by his appearance, obliged. But only if he rode in the back with the tomatoes.

Twenty minutes later, the nervous driver dropped him off at a small gas station on the outskirts of the small mountain town of Bomerano. Il Ramingo thanked him, and then put a pistol to his head. He forced the man to call the police with a hand that would not stop shaking. Talking on Il Ramingo's phone, he told the police he gave a strange man with blood-stained clothes a ride. After he was done, Il Ramingo stabbed him through the chest with both Szell knives. He could have left the innocent man alive, but it would've seemed strange to the police if he didn't kill him.

The way Il Ramingo saw it, he was doing the man a favor.

CHAPTER 41

"I got you, you bastard."

The PSC sergeant stared at his cellular signal tracker and the flashing red dot on its screen. He was leading a squad of ten officers clad in tactical gear on foot along *the Sentiero degli Dei*, aka the Path of the Gods.

For centuries the ancient footpath connected the remote mountain towns of Bomerano and Nocelle, and all the way down to sea-level Positano. It was still used by shepherds and the occasional townsfolk. Brave tourists with stamina walked the entire eighteen-mile path to enjoy stunning views of the Tyrrhenian Sea below and the Isle of Capri off in the hazy distance. The steep, often treacherous rocky trail also ran through one of the least inhabited and hard to get to areas in Campania, a perfect place to hide for a reclusive, world-class assassin, the sergeant mused. Isolated, but close enough to major throughfares to make moving around the south of Italy relatively easy.

With his tracker outstretched in front of his face, the sergeant and his men continued down the Path of the Gods, weapons at shoulders, fingers on triggers. But after fifteen tense minutes, the red dot moved to the west while the Path of the Gods veered east. Backtracking, the sergeant noticed a wall of woven vines and brush, slightly ajar over what on closer inspection was a tight spur path leading deeper into the mountains.

"Captain Fattore."

"Sergeant?"

Via radio, he relayed the discovery of a hidden path. His captain was not veiled in her orders. Il Ramingo had killed her driver and she was indifferent to the condition he was brought back in, just as long as he was brought in.

"Go easy, sergeant. I can't attend another department funeral. I just can't. Confirm his position. Wait for the Carabinieri. They are fifteen minutes out."

Moving slow, the eleven men proceeded down the narrow trail two abreast, weapons at the ready. A hundred feet of tense walking later, the sergeant held his tracker up so his men could see the screen. The red dot was now stationary, blinking, unmoving, waiting at what looked like a quarter mile down the path.

"At the end of this trail is Il Ramingo. Remember, his back is against the wall. And he has a hostage."

The squad advanced to where the path opened to a clearing harboring an old stone house. The sergeant looked at his tracker, the red dot blinking in the center of the house. It was quiet; no lights on. He told his men to spread out and form a perimeter around the house, but not to enter until the helicopters carrying PSC strike teams arrived.

A woman's scream from inside the house shattered the stillness in the clearing.

"What should we do?" said one of his men.

The hostage was clearly in distress. Seconds mattered. "We go in."

He ordered two of his men to watch the back of the house, the rest massed at the front door in a pointed phalanx. On the count of three, the sergeant kicked the latch on the heavy wooden door, sending the metal to the ground and the door swinging open. The nine men burst into the big main room on the ground floor.

Standing in the middle of the room was a blonde woman with a stripe of white hair. A rope was tied around her waist. The curtains were drawn and only a single bulb hanging from the ceiling illuminated her. She was holding a phone above her head.

"He told me to tell you . . . *memento mori*." An unseen force yanked hard enough on the rope around her midsection to pull the woman into the kitchen.

The light turned off, plunging the room into darkness. There was an immense wall of fire from a wooden rail with a row of sawed-off shotguns mounted to its frame all firing at once. The dense cloud of shotgun pellets cut down his men into the room like a scythe through wheat. Il Ramingo emerged from the kitchen, emptying a suppressed pistol from each hand, killing his two remaining men. The sergeant raised his rifle just as Il Ramingo sliced his head clean off with a backhanded swing of his right arm. Il Ramingo walked across the room, turning on the light switch, illuminating the slaughter that had just occurred.

"Excellent, Giuliana, it gave me just enough time to—"

The window over the kitchen sink was open, its shade fluttering in the wind.

Madeline Granttano was gone.

"Goodbye, my love."

Madeline said the words aloud, moving fast by Chris's grave, blowing a mental kiss at the white cross over her beloved's head, surrounded by hundreds of other crosses, the terror in her throat demanding she not linger, even though all she wanted was to be back in his arms.

After they became government informants, Chris had become paranoid. Feared his father or someone in the Camorra would find out. Started obsessing over the proper configuration of *go bags* he had stashed in the trunk of their Range Rover. Wanting to buttress his anxiety with action, Chris and Madeline enrolled in a seven-day military style survival bootcamp in Canada's Banff National Park. He told his dad it was a remote getaway to Minnesota's Boundary

Waters Canoe Area.

Madeline hated it. They had to sleep on the ground, hunt their own food, build fires, purify water. It was hell. They were always wet. Rashes and bug bites. And just when she would coax herself to sleep on the damp ground, instructors would hurl flash bangs and smoke grenades into their camp, and pepper them with paintballs as part of faux assaults.

But today she was grateful for that misery. The moment Il Ramingo triggered his mounted sawed-off shotgun ambush, what he lovingly called his *Lupara*, a calm, determined Madeline Granttano slipped out of the rope around her waist, dashed into the kitchen, and dove through the open window without thought to what lie below. Lucky for her, the landing was stubby grass on a slight grade. Tucking and rolling, Madeline was on her feet in a flash, sprinting past Il Ramingo's makeshift graveyard.

"Fermati là!" A blue-suited Italian policeman shouted at her right before a cluster of bullets struck him.

Without thinking, Madeline scooped his dropped pistol from the ground. As gunshots and the screams of dying men echoed from behind, she ran for the secret trail connecting Il Ramingo's home to the Path of the Gods. Madeline was a hundred feet down the narrow rocky path when realizing she was still holding Il Ramingo's cell phone, clenched tight enough to crack the case in her right fist. She paused to check signal strength, but the phone was locked. Madeline dropped it, moving as fast as the tight trail would allow.

Jumping from boulder to boulder, she quickly progressed down the path, worried that because she had no idea where she was going, Il Ramingo would easily track her down. This was his home. After ten minutes of moderately difficult descent, Madeline reached a spot where the trail widened.

"Giuliana!"

Il Ramingo's scream echoed through the canyon. She whipped her head around trying to spot him. By the sound of his voice, he was above. Madeline still had a decent head start and didn't intend to waste it. A few feet more down the trail from the massacre spot, she discovered an elaborate surreptitious wall woven of brush and branches leaning against a large rock. It must have been constructed by Il Ramingo to hide the trail to his home from travelers on the Path of the Gods. Madeline had a decision to make. To her right the path climbed up, down to her left.

"Giuliana!" He was closer, much closer, and angrier.

Choosing left and down, Madeleine could still feel the lingering effects of the narcotics. Eluding a man by running uphill was not the best choice. After fifty feet of descending the Path of the Gods, she found a rock crevice next to the trail, the perfect ambush point.

Settling behind the crevice, she had a clear view up the path. Her father had taught her how to shoot. And the survival course had classes on combat firearms. But it took her an excruciating minute to figure out how to turn off the safety and chamber a round in the dead policeman's pistol. She aimed it up the trail. Another minute later Il Ramingo appeared, his bug-like head and arms perfectly silhouetted against the late afternoon sun.

Like she was taught in her survival training, Madeline let out all her breath and squeezed the trigger five times. The shots reverberated against the canyon walls, hurting her ears. Despite the loud noise, she heard Il Ramingo cry out from a bullet finding its mark. He disappeared.

Madeline ran.

The trail took a sharp right. She wasn't prepared for the radical change in direction, almost pitching over a flimsy wooden railing and into a steep gorge. She stood there for a moment, trembling from fear and adrenalin, staring down into the black depths of the chasm she almost fell into. She needed to be smarter.

"Giuliana!" This time the scream was laced with pain and betrayal.

Now running down with great speed because her life literally depended on it, Madeline felt like she was levitating over the rock and tree-root studded trail. Switch back after switch back down the steep cliff she charged. She heard Il Ramingo yell her name again, but this time sound was faint.

Madeline's toe caught an exposed root, and she was airborne off the trail. The fall happened so fast she couldn't tuck into a ball to soften the impact of her landing. Instead, Madeline tumbled like a doll down the steep hillside, slamming to a stop against a large boulder. The impact snapped her head against the rock.

She blacked out.

When Madeline regained consciousness, the sun had dipped noticeably in the horizon. She staggered to her feet. Touching a throbbing gash in her head, her hand came away covered in blood. With blurred vision she examined the trail leading up and down. There was no sign of Il Ramingo. In her fall she dropped the gun. Gripped with fear, her vision cloudy, Madeline took tentative steps down the trail. Soon she gained more strength and confidence, increasing her pace, but rife with dread when rounding every corner, expecting Il Ramingo standing there.

She traveled another half-mile down before hearing Il Ramingo's voice again.

"Giuliana," echoed through the canyon. This time it was barely audible he was so far above her. *Is he going the wrong way?*

She staggered down the trail another mile, arriving at a junction with a paved road, genuinely shocked to still be alive. Following the road around a wide bend she entered a small town marked by a sign that read *Bomerano*. She burst inside the first café she saw, an empty restaurant. It was dusk out and would be much later when Italians filtered in for their evening meal.

Startling the elderly bartender with her bloodied head, Madeline gestured at the wall behind him.

"May I use your phone?"

CHAPTER 42

"Good God. Drowning in a sea of molten lava?"

"Pumice and ash, to be specific. Says here it was twenty-five feet deep and rained down on Pompeii for six hours," Sophie Grant said. "For six hours."

Sophie and her father stood before a massive scale model of ancient Pompeii the size of a tennis court. Housed in the east wing of the *Museo Archeologvico Nazionale di Napoli*, the model was surrounded by hundreds of artifacts excavated from ancient Pompeii.

Waiting in Absoluta Amore for any scrap of news to come in on her half-sister's whereabouts was driving Sophie and her dad crazy. Sophie was able to pry him away from the drone feed, but after watching him smash a plate in the sink of her room, Sophie decided a change of scenery would be good. So, they walked for a coffee.

After a pleasant couple of espressos at a café a few blocks away, they stumbled upon the National Italian Archeological Museum. For an hour Sophie and Ray forgot about Il Ramingo and Madeline, walking through a museum as father and daughter, looking at ancient art.

Sophie didn't want it to ever end.

The museum was stuffed to the rafters with Greek, Roman and Egyptian artifacts, but it was the wing dedicated to the volcanic tragedy at nearby Pompeii that intrigued them the most.

"Can it happen again? Are they prepared?" Ray questioned. "Could it reach Naples?"

Her father looked legitimately worried at the prospect of Mount

Vesuvius once again covering Campania in deadly ash and lava.

"Why are you asking me?"

"You *do* work on the mountain."

Sophie thought back to one of her first briefings after arriving in Italy. The Italian seismologist from the university she'd spoken to explained in no uncertain terms that ten thousand US service members and their families would be in the blast radius if the volcano ever erupted again. Scientists were split, however, between whether an eruption was imminent or if Neapolitans were safe from harm.

"Apparently, the bigger risk is the active fissures on the south side. Partly why dumping is so dangerous. A highly flammable compound dumped in enough volume, in theory, could spur a mini eruption, but nothing like what wiped out Pompeii."

Ray nodded and smiled, looking off into space.

"What? What is it Dad?"

"What is it?" He put his hand on her shoulder. "Pride. You're a smart lady. Like to think I had something . . . something small to do with it."

Sophie almost choked. "Something to do with it? Listen, Ray, I'm not unsympathetic to what you had to go through, how you left us. I'm coming around. You're a good man. But it wasn't ever easy for us. For me. Everything I achieved I did on my goddamn own."

"Whatever you say, kid."

That piqued Sophie's curiosity. What was he getting at? "Okay old man, spit it out."

"That scholarship, the one for grad school. That degree got you into the EPA, correct?"

Sophie nodded. "The Carol Beeks Memorial Scholarship for Excellence in Environmental Justice. Beeks was a DA or something down south in the late 80s. Successfully sued Dupont for Teflon from non-stick pans getting into the drinking water of a poor Black town. Cancer rates had spiked."

"3M."

"Huh?"

"It was 3M. Not Dupont." Ray had the weirdest look on his face. Pulling out his wallet, he removed a worn and wrinkled business card. He handed the card to Sophie. "Beeks sued 3M."

Sophie stared at the faded card. The letterhead said the Carol Beeks Memorial Foundation and listed Ray Granttano as executive director.

"What the hell is this?"

Her father swallowed, hard, and the smile left his face. His eyes filled with tears. "Cashed out my police pension. I couldn't just give you the money. What if someone was watching?"

"Dad?" The card trembled in her hand. She half fell half leapt into his arms and hugged him as tight as she could. In her ear he whispered. "I'm so sorry, champion, it's all I could do."

For a long time, the two of them stood next to the model of ancient Pompeii, quietly sobbing, clutching each other, years and years falling away into oblivion in favor of the moment. They stood that way until Sophie's phone would not stop buzzing.

"Sorry," Sophie said, wiping tears away. There were two missed calls from Carter Boyd. He was calling again. "Yeah?" She listened intently for a few moments then let the phone drop to her side.

"What is it?"

Sophie smiled. "Madeline."

CHAPTER 43

"Can you walk?"

"I can walk."

Il Ramingo was perched on a rock outcropping overlooking the small mountain clearing where his house stood. Next to him were several discarded pieces of blood-soaked gauze. Madeline's bullet caught him in the side, ricocheting off a rib before it could damage any vital organs. The cracked bone was painful. But after a proper cleaning, field surgeon precision suturing and a well-placed narcotic injection, he was functional again.

"Can you fight?"

Much worse than the ache in his side was the searing pain of losing Madeline. How had she escaped? He was still in shock at the woman just disappearing after ambushing him. Vanished. Like God's hand plucked her from the sky. The only thing that made sense was Madeline double-backed on Il Ramingo, somehow hid from him on the Path of the Gods, and that he had been too distracted by the bullet hole in his side to see her.

"Did you hear me? Can you fight?"

DeSalvo was unrelenting. The intensity for good reason, the plan, *their plan*, was reaching its critical stage. Up to this point DeSalvo and Il Ramingo had been both good and lucky. They needed the same to be true for today, except that Il Ramingo's wound muted his enthusiasm. DeSalvo could sense it through an unpackaged burner phone, set to speaker on a flat rock at Il Ramingo's knee.

"I can fight."

"Are you sure? You don't sound sure."

Il Ramingo stared for a moment over the Path of the Gods. "She's gone. What's the point?"

DeSalvo took in a sharp breath of air. "The point? The point? The point is *memento mori.*"

"I needed Giuliana to witness it. To see what we did to them, for what they did to her."

"Her name is Madeline Nicchi. You do remember the boat?"

"I remember." Il Ramingo couldn't explain it, even to DeSalvo who he trusted with his life. DeSalvo wouldn't understand. When he witnessed her sleeping in the yacht, all he saw was Giuliana. Before the bullets. Before the blood.

"It doesn't matter. She's gone."

"Are you sure?"

Il Ramingo picked up the phone and put it to his ear. "Don't toy with me."

"Oh, now I have your attention?"

"Spit it out."

"The PSC has her."

"Excellent." It would be easy for Il Ramingo to pluck Giuliana from the Polizia Speciale Campania once he was done with his work here.

"I should be there in an hour," Il Ramingo said, hanging up on DeSalvo.

Five minutes later the heavy thump of rotor blades from a helicopter reverberated through the Path of the Gods. A blue PSC helicopter appeared overhead, stopping at a hover over his home. Another helicopter followed behind the first. Both were loaded with PSC strike force officers, legs dangling from open side doors. Il Ramingo took a small detonator from a backpack to his left. With the push of the button the old stone house, his home for the past fourteen years, erupted in an orange fireball that rose high above the valley walls and engulfed the first aircraft. It plummeted into the fiery remains of his house and exploded.

Lying behind him on the rock was a Javelin surface to air rocket launcher. While the pilot of the second helicopter moved the nose of the aircraft closer to the fire to better examine the scene, Il Ramingo hefted the rocket launcher on his shoulder and powered up the sighting mechanism. A friendly electronic tone sounded as the sights locked on the helicopter. Il Ramingo squeezed the trigger and a missile leapt from the Javelin. There was no time for the pilot to react as the missile detonated, shearing off the aircraft's tail, sending it spinning to crash into a grove of trees. The PSC's resources and attention would be consumed by his massacre of so many officers. All part of the duo's plan.

For a short time, Il Ramingo sat on the rock, watching his home burn. Through the clouds of black, oily smoke from burning aircraft fuel, he could see the graveyard where his victims' heads were buried. Moving quickly, he entered the ancient Amalfi aqueduct system through a hidden entrance on the other side of his home. Designed by the Romans and improved upon by Italian engineers over the centuries, the stone-lined canals crisscrossing the cliffs of the region were built before modern plumbing and sewage, they brought fresh water to villages and shipped waste to valley lagoons. Now they were in various states of disrepair from overgrown with weeds to gaping sinkholes. Il Ramingo's current route was a long-discarded sewer line that just a century before had shot waste from the town of Revello down to the ocean by Positano, the very same path he used to bring Giuliana to his home.

While he moved fast down toward Positano, he wondered if when the police arrived if they would even comprehend the honor bestowed upon his victims interned in his graveyard. What they couldn't possibly understand is that number was astronomically small compared to what he and DeSalvo were planning.

Memento mori.

CHAPTER 44

"When do I get a gun?"

"I read your file, Night Stalker. You may be more qualified than some of our SOGs," Bill Hodges said to BTO while adjusting the straps on his Kevlar vest one-handed. "But I can't give a government weapon to a trigger man for the Mafia."

"Only killed for my country," BTO said.

"Gun or not, after what happened in Pecora's warehouse, I ain't going anywhere again without the big guy," Ray said.

Sophie smiled at her father. Along with Carter, the five of them rode in the rear of a CIA unmarked helicopter. There was something different about the CIA duo. They were agitated. Anxious. Sophie figured they'd be buoyed by Madeline's reappearance. Il Ramingo had escaped after killing Pecora. Maybe the sour moods came from the spectacular failure of their intricate plan to infiltrate the Camorra's gunrunning operation all the way to the ISIS Caliphate.

Out her window was Positano's fast approaching main beach, the very same beach she'd come to days ago to view the body of her brother-in-law. The only difference was the sun was now setting, casting a dark auburn shadow across the sand.

"There's Captain Fattore," Carter said.

Standing tall near the beach, unbent by the vicious wind splash from the spinning rotors, Fattore, stood fifty feet from the landing pad, waiting for them to land with her hands thrust into her light jacket pockets. Seated in the rear facing the cockpit, Sophie grabbed a leather loop bolted above the door to her right to brace for touchdown.

Sitting across from her, Ray wore black tactical khakis and a long-sleeved black shirt pilfered from the SOG supply locker. The prospect of reuniting with his second daughter made him all smiles. There was little information about Madeline's condition, just that she was in the PSC's custody, and by the rapid tapping of her father's foot on the helicopter's floor, Sophie could tell Ray was about to jump out of his skin in anticipation.

There was a jolt as the helicopter bounced once on the landing pad before settling on its skids. Hodges was first out the door. In quick secession Carter, Sophie, Ray and BTO followed him on the cement landing pad. Sophie took a moment to stare at the town of Positano shooting up high cliffs from the beach to a thousand feet above them. Waves crashed against the shore. Lights from hundreds of tiny villas flashed. Sophie understood the allure. It was a magical place. *Sheboygan.*

"Who are they?" Fattore said, agitated. She drew one long arm from her pocket and pointed at Ray and BTO. "They're not CIA or EPA!"

"Madeline's father, *my* father, and his friend," Sophie said.

Fattore's expression changed from icy boredom to a terse smile. "Madeline is in my custody." Fattore explained Polizia Speciale Campania swarmed the Bormero café Madeline staggered into minutes after her emergency call to the authorities. A medic treated her sister's minor wounds, mostly scrapes and bruises and one nasty cut in the palm of her right hand, another on her scalp, but she was otherwise fine.

"She has been through much. Strong girl." Fattore gestured to a PSC van parked at the street. "Please. Let me take you to her."

Once they were inside the van, Fattore's driver maneuvered them through the narrow hairpin turns of Positano. The streets were just coming alive as the sun set. Shopkeepers and waiters scurried back and forth across the road, trusting the cars whizzing by would avoid them while tourists strolled the sidewalks eyeing menus for a nighttime meal.

"Are we meeting them at the Positano police station?" Carter asked.

"No, too dangerous. It's the first place Il Ramingo will look." Fattore turned around from the front seat to address her passengers. She told them about the police officers murdered on the Path of the Gods and helicopters he shot down. "His home is compromised. He's on the run. He knows it's a matter of time."

"Where then? Where are you taking us?" Sophie said.

Fattore pointed out the van's windshield. "To Casa Fattore, my family's casa. It's where I grew up."

"Does your family still live there?" Carter asked. "If I remember right, you have a son? It's in your file?"

Fattore's shoulders slumped. "I did. He was a soldier. A good one. But he died in your war in Iraq."

"I'm sorry. I had no idea," Carter said.

"It was a long time ago. Neri is in a better place now."

CHAPTER 45

"Daddy?"

Upon seeing her father, Madeline Granttano rushed across the open-air courtyard in the rear of Villa Fattore to Ray. Falling into her father's arms, they sobbed together in joy. The courtyard was large, paved in red brick and surrounded by a waist-high stone wall. Intricate iron weaving graced the top of the wall, the sea air giving the metal a weathered, ancient look. A small gate in the rear flanked by tomato plants opened to a path that wound up into the cliffs above.

Fattore's ancestral home's beauty stunned Sophie. Sure, it was Positano; every house and building were old and cool and beautiful in the way Italian culture seemed to exude as easy as pouring a glass of Brunello. Fattore explained that her great, great grandfather and his brother built the villa in 1889. At the time, the well-kept, five-bedroom, three-story villa was the highest structure ever built on the Positano cliff. Perched four hundred feet above the ocean, there were no homes behind or above it in Positano's notoriously dense environs. Instead, a craggy rock jutted from the cliffs right above the home. Higher up the peaks that lined the Path of the Gods poked from the clouds.

"Until the Russians and their money no one built as high as us," Fattore said, gesturing at the dozens of opulent mansions now dotting the landscape at the same latitude.

"The family reunion needs to wait," Hodges said, and cleared his throat with three phlegmy hacks.

Carter put his hand on Hodges' arm and said in a softer voice, "Apologies, Madeline, but can we have a quick minute?"

"Why don't you two come inside for some coffee, instead, give them some time to reconnect," Fattore said.

"I don't take orders from you," Hodges gurgled.

"You do when you're in my home."

"Five minutes."

Hodges and Carter followed Fattore, her driver, and bodyguard into the villa through a double wooden door.

Sophie stood off to the side, awkwardly fidgeting with her phone, trying to figure out if she should join in or bail. BTO kept himself ten feet off Ray's hip, embracing his new role as her father's muscle.

"We should probably leave these two alone," Sophie said to BTO, figuring she should check in on Maria in Malodini anyway.

"Nonsense!" Ray waved Sophie over. He smiled. "Come be with your family."

"Sofia, please?" Madeline said.

Her half-sister's face was tear streaked with sunken eyes from exhaustion and narcotics, four stitches on her temple but the offer sounded sincere. Sophie shuffled toward them. When she got closer, she lurched forward like an invisible hand gave her a shove and hugged them both. The three of them stayed that way so long that BTO edged through the towering tomato plants toward the garden's opening and disappeared into the steep broken and rock-strewn area behind the villa.

Sophie looked down and realized she had her sister's hand tightly gripped in hers. Madeline squeezed her hand back.

"Did he? Did he—" Ray's voice caught in his throat. Sophie knew exactly where her dad was going with his question. The terror every parent grappled with in a world awash with sexual predators.

"No," Madeline said. "He was actually quite kind. Gentle. Kept calling me his sweet *Giuliana*. I had no idea he'd killed Chris—" Madeline regained her composure. "Until he showed me his grave."

"Your hair," Ray said, pointing at the bleach white streak in her hair. "Il Ramingo?"

Madeline nodded. "That's when I knew it was not going to end well for me if I stayed."

She went on to describe Il Ramingo's lair high above Positano on the remote Path of the Gods, his pitched battle with the PSC and his employ of the *Lupara,* his sawed-off shotgun blunderbuss defense system to kill the police officers.

"That was the opening I needed," she said, smiling for the first time while recanting her story. "If I hadn't tripped . . . he . . . I don't know." Madeline shivered. "He killed all those men. You should know, he has knives that shoot out on each arm." She blinked. Madeline shook her head to exorcise the image.

"Like a speargun?" Sophie said.

"No." Il Ramingo materialized in the courtyard out of the darkness. The assassin held both arms out, pressed a middle finger to the centers of his palms. Twelve inches of bright steel leapt from each forearm.

"Like this."

CHAPTER 46

"These ceiling beams are gorgeous. Is that wood original?"

Carter Boyd sipped a cup of espresso while Captain Fattore described the provenance of her family home's kitchen in more detail.

"My grandfather told me that wood was from Poseidon's fleet." She sipped her coffee. "But it's really local alder he used when he rebuilt the original home. Back when Positano was just a fishing village." She shook her head. "Before Julia Roberts."

The kitchen had a soaring clay ceiling crisscrossed by huge dark wood beams. A blue, hand-painted tiled counter split the room in half. Carter stood on one side of the counter near a massive brick-arched, wood-fired hearth, and Fattore on the other. Hodges paced between them; arm tucked behind his back. Every few seconds his hand would swing back to his face where he would check his watch, clear his throat, and eyeball Carter.

In the dining room adjacent to the kitchen, Fattore's bodyguard and driver were loudly arguing about soccer. Out of the corner of his eye, Carter watched Fattore's man, a fan of Turin's team, wave a scarf emblazoned with its logo, a skull with a blood spurting knife jutting into its eye socket, in the driver's face.

"It must be worth millions now? The villa?"

"Si, but I will never sell. Too many memories." Fattore's eyes wandered to a series of framed photographs on the wall over the kitchen sink.

Carter followed her eyes to the wall and a myriad of photographs. "Is that your son?" Carter asked, pointing to a picture of a young man in an Italian Army uniform. Fattore nodded. "Neri. The day he finished his training." Fattore drank more coffee. "Do you have children Mister Boyd?"

"Nope. Married to the job."

"It changes you. Forever." Fattore locked eyes with Carter. "You would do anything for your child." Fattore's phone buzzed. She answered and spoke briefly.

"How bad is it?" Hodges asked. "Two downed birds?"

"Bad." Fattore shook her head. "Very bad. At least ten of my men are dead. Most likely many more."

Fattore's phone buzzed again. The Polizia Speciale Campania captain held a hand up to Carter signaling she needed a minute of privacy and walked a few steps away. "Yes. Yes. I am here, with our guests. Come in through the garden." Fattore hung up. "Relief officers. Can't be too careful." Cupping her hand over her mouth, she shouted at her two guardians in the living room, *"Marino, Sabbatinni. Vienni qui."*

Her driver and bodyguard walked into the kitchen. Fattore spoke to them a few short sentences in Italian. They both nodded after she was done, gathered their belongings and left. Carter heard them start a car outside and drive away.

"They've both been on duty for twenty-four hours," Fattore said.

Carter peered out the small kitchen window that looked over the courtyard where Madeline Granttano was reuniting with her family. Hodges had taken to examining the artwork and framed pictures adorning the walls.

What's this?" Hodges said, pointing to a framed napkin on the wall with faded, scribbled handwriting on it. "Does that really say … at the bottom? The signatures. Is that who I think it is?"

Fattore smiled and nodded. "Si. They rented the house next door. I was just out of the police-training academy. Neri must have been only four or five years old. It was fantastic. They played all day. Every day. The same song. Over and over. Until the early morning for a month, and I didn't care. Mama would cook for them around three in the afternoon. They played that song until Neri could recite every word. He loved it. That's why they gave him the first handwritten lyrics for the song."

Carter leaned over to see what Hodges was looking at. "The goddamn Rolling Stones wrote a song next door? That blows my mind," Carter said. What song was it? He read the title and a bolt of ice shot up his spine. Both he and Hodges's eyes met. "*Il Ramingo Mendozzata*, 'The Midnight Rambler.'" They turned around to face Fattore.

The police captain had drawn her sidearm and was pointing the gun at them.

"You sneaky bitch," Hodges said.

"Holy shit," Carter said. "He's not dead. Is he?"

Fattore took a step forward, her face red and contorted. To Carter, the anger made her a different person. A snake that had shed its skin.

"Believe me, the Neri I knew died over there. In the desert. For nothing."

"How is that possible? You're a cop. You caught that serial killer . . . the . . . *Mostro of Amalfi*," Carter said.

"Except you didn't catch him, did you?" Hodges said. "Sounds more like you were covering your son's tracks. Yeah. That's it. And with the added gravy of goosing your career. Getting you bumped to PSC." Hodges snorted two RPGs. "Should've known. All *mosotro's* victims died the same way. Two knife wounds, one on either side of the heart. Everyone thought it was two stab wounds from the same weapon. But it was your son, Enrico Knife Hands, wasn't it?"

"Clever," Fattore said, her pistol aimed in his direction. "But not clever enough, Hodges. And unfortunately, much too late. Just like the American CIA. So blinded by the myth of your own intelligence. Like when you tortured those Basra militiamen without getting our authority. It led to this very moment. I wouldn't have had the access to your system to get the information we needed had you not made such a blunder. You couldn't see the towers falling, couldn't see the trap the jihadist set for you in Iraq, couldn't conceive of a foreign asset running for your president, and now you've handed us an unimaginable gift."

Hodges glanced at Carter and then back at Fattore.

"You mean the Little Bear buried up on Vesuvius, don't you?"

Fattore nodded.

"*Memento mori.*"

CHAPTER 47

Treating them like obedient livestock, Fattore prodded a disarmed Hodges and Carter out of the kitchen and into the warm night air. They joined Ray, Sophie and Madeline in the courtyard at the rear of the cliffside home.

Spying Il Ramingo in the flesh, Sophie realized the physical similarities between he and his mother were comically alike. Both were tall and thin with long limbs. A black head sock and a pair of black tactical goggles obscured Il Ramingo's face. He was holding the Granttanos at gunpoint as Fattore escorted Hodges and Carter into the courtyard. Sophie restrained her father. Ray's face was bright red with veins bulging from his neck.

"DeSalvo," Il Ramingo said with a rasp upon seeing his mother.

Fattore threw Hodges's and Carter's guns to the ground with the weapons Il Ramingo confiscated from their compatriots.

Hodges stepped forward with his hand out far from his body, signaling that he did not want to escalate the situation. "There's a deal to be made. Right now, everyone is looking for you. We can work something out."

"No one is looking for us. All of my officers are on the Path of the Gods because of my boy." Fattore said.

"Hey," Carter said, waving his hand. "We're the CIA. Always on the lookout for good talent."

"We know about Sokolov. That he recruited and groomed Neri for what he was to become. And what you're planning on helping him do," Hodges said. "Boyd's right. We can help you."

"*Cazzate.* The number of police officers my son has killed makes that impossible. And you know it. What did you say to me when I asked for your drone? 'Request denied.'"

Fattore raised her pistol and shot Hodges twice in the chest. He staggered backwards and collapsed to the ground.

"Bill!" Carter dropped to his knees next to his boss, blood spreading across Hodges's shirt.

"*Memento mori,*" Il Ramingo said in his guttural rasp. Then he beckoned Sophie's sister with his finger. "Giuliana. Come."

"Daddy?" Madeline gripped her father. Ray stepped in front of his daughter.

"Her name's, Madeline. And she stays."

Il Ramingo removed his circular sun goggles. Tugging at the hem of his head sock, he pulled the garment off with a hand flourish. Sophie stifled a gasp. His head was hairless and a mass of pink and brown scar tissue. Il Ramingo's eyes blazed, immediately watering.

"Giuliana. You must see."

"Stop calling me that," Madeline said.

Fattore shook her head and patted her son on the back. "After they murdered *mi nipote*, they just left him out there. In that terrible place. He was a good soldier. He followed orders."

Kneeling next to his boss, Carter grabbed his hand. Hodges's eyelids fluttered. He let out one last throat clearing, an unmistakable SCUD, and whispered, "Boyd, Little Bear." His chest stopped moving.

Carter dove for his weapon on the ground. Arms outstretched, he found the grip of his pistol, but Fattore was faster, firing multiple rounds at the CIA operative while he rolled on the courtyard's brick surface. Carter cried out in pain as a bullet found its mark, and he tumbled to a stop.

Fattore pivoted back to Ray. He stood in front of both daughters, arms outstretched to make his body as wide as possible. With his own gun pointed at Ray, Il Ramingo said, "Giuliana, I will kill your father."

"You're not taking her," Ray said.

Il Ramingo raised his pistol, but just as he squeezed the trigger, BTO leapt from the brush leading up the mountainside, knocking the gun out of his hand. Il Ramingo's shot ricocheted with a loud whine off a rock.

Fattore swung her gun to BTO, but before she could fire, he kicked her in the chest, sending the police captain tumbling backwards. BTO turned back to Il Ramingo, using his left arm just in time to block an uppercut from the assassin's extended knife aimed at BTO's throat. Instead, the blade went right through BTO's forearm.

"Motherfucker!" BTO said.

Il Ramingo tried pulling the dagger out, but it was wedged in place. With a loud click he deployed the other spring-loaded blade and swung it at BTO's face. Using his free hand, BTO caught Il Ramingo by the wrist before the knife could penetrate his eye socket. Raising both arms, BTO yanked Il Ramingo off his feet and head butted him in the face. The blow sent the assassin to his knees, pulling the knife out of BTO's arm. He ignored the great gush of blood spurting from the wound, opting to retrieve Il Ramingo's gun. He put the barrel against the assassin's forehead right between his eyes. Sophie noticed a red stain above Il Ramingo's hip. He was wounded.

"Time to die, bug man."

Sophie scrambled over Carter for her pistol. There was blood pooling underneath the CIA operative, and he was groaning. Just as Sophie's hand found the butt of the weapon, Fattore kicked the gun away. Sophie looked up. Madeline stood in front of Fattore with the police captain's hand on her shoulder and Fattore's pistol to Madeline's head.

"Madeline," Ray said, rising from behind the chair. "It's going to be okay."

"Tell this man to take his gun off my son's head or I'll shoot your daughter."

"BTO . . . please," Ray said.

"This asshole stabbed me. Took your daughter. I should blow

his brains out." BTO pulled the gun away and waved the barrel at Il Ramingo. "Go ahead, run to mommy."

Il Ramingo staggered to his feet. Red poured from his nostrils as he stumbled to Fattore.

"Now let my sister go," Sophie said. She was on her feet and standing next to her father. BTO had his pistol pointed at Fattore who still held Madeline at gunpoint.

"Tell the big man to drop his weapon."

"Not a chance. They'll shoot all of us," BTO said.

"I guess we need her now, eh mother?" Il Ramingo said.

CHAPTER 48

"Go." Carter had said through a jaw clenched in pain, urging Sophie and her father to pursue Il Ramingo and his mother. He sat in a defeated heap, a towel from the kitchen pressed to the bullet wound in his leg. His vest stopped one of Fattore's shots, but another found a brief home tearing through his thigh. "Get your sister."

Ray found the keys to the Fiat hanging next to the garage door and they gave chase. Il Ramingo and Fattore had a five-minute head start. But the winding, crowded roads of Positano made a fast escape impossible. Sophie followed a trail of angry motorists, broken glass and freshly sheared side view mirrors until catching sight of Fattore's Mercedes convertible making a sharp turn upward at the far end of the La Costa pavilion, a collection of fruit and art vendors crammed into a small park. Fattore was driving, Il Ramingo and Madeline's heads visible in the back seat.

Watch the scooter!" Ray hollered.

Darkness falling on the Amalfi Coast compounded the difficulty Sophie was having navigating the twisting narrow turns that climbed the steep cliffs of Positano.

"To think, all this time I wished my dad had taught me how to drive," Sophie said through a clenched jaw. Jerking the steering wheel of their two-seat Fiat left then right, the small car darted in between a group of startled tourists huddled in front of a café and an old man on a single gear bicycle.

"I can't imagine your mother teaching you how to do that," Ray said, his face ashen from the whiplash.

"Taught myself."

Fattore must have spotted Sophie approaching from behind in her rearview mirror, because Il Ramingo's mother accelerated out of the piazza and on the Strada Statale Amalfitana like a rocket. The main paved road along the Amalfi Coast cut through Positano, widely regarded as one of the most dangerous roads in the world, due to its daredevil-inspiring serpentine path, that wound through towering cliffs on one side, and a three-hundred-foot plunge to sparkling blue sea on the other.

Sophie ignored the screams and horns blaring from oncoming traffic, weaving in and out of their tight lane, leapfrogging closer to Fattore's Mercedes. One car, one barely averted head on collision after another, until Sophie gained on Fattore, and they were on her bumper.

"Ram them into the guardrail!"

"Dad. Madeline's in there."

"Okay, don't do that," Ray said. He drew his pistol and checked to ensure there was a round in the chamber. "Next chance you get, pull up next to them. I'll take her out."

Sophie gunned the engine and pulled into the oncoming lane. A tour bus appeared from around the corner forcing Sophie to yank them back into the right lane in a squeal of tires to avoid splattering like a bug on the bus's windshield. She gripped the wheel tight for another try, but as they drove past a sign announcing their departure from Positano's city limits, the left rear door swung open, Il Ramingo leaned his head and torso out of the Mercedes, and one-handed pointed a submachine gun at their windshield.

Before he could pull the trigger, Madeline's arm snaked around his neck. She jerked backwards causing Il Ramingo to fire a burst of bullets into the air. The assassin ducked back into the vehicle, and there was a commotion in the back seat they couldn't quite tell what was going on. The Mercedes careened against the guardrail and into the center of the road and then back into its lane. Sophie accelerated, hoping to catch a distracted Fattore unaware, but once more, Il Ramingo popped out of the left rear door and opened fire on them.

Yanking the wheel to the right, Sophie ran the car into a concrete embankment. Bullets meant for them went wide, splattering against the road. Il Ramingo fired another burst. Sophie leapt on her father and pushed him down into his seat as rounds tore into the windshield. Poking her head above the shattered glass, Sophie watched the Mercedes round a corner and disappear.

"Thanks," Ray said brushing shards of glass from his trousers.

"Need every hand on deck," Sophie said.

She threw the car's transmission in reverse and with a squeal of metal pulled back away from the embankment. Then she gunned the engine and rounded the corner. There was no sign of the Mercedes. Sophie put the pedal to the floor, hitting the tight curves of the *Strada Statale Amalfitana* so fast that at one point she had the car on two wheels, coaxing a concerned squeak from her father's throat. After the next curve the Mercedes was parked in front of them. Sophie skidded to a stop at the convertible's bumper.

Sophie and Ray jumped out of the Fiat, pistols out and aimed at the Mercedes, but it was empty. The driver's side door hung open. Standing at the side of the road was an old portly Italian man. He looked shaken and gestured wildly behind them.

"What's he saying?" Ray asked.

"A man with a bad sunburn put a gun to his head. Took his van. Il Ramingo doubled back on us."

"What do we do now?" Ray said. Sophie looked hard at her father. His shirt was drenched in sweat, eyes bloodshot and wild.

She put a hand on his shoulder. "We're going to find her Dad, I promise. The Captain of the Polizia Speciale Campania shot a CIA agent. Her son has killed more Italians than George S. Patton."

With her other hand Sophie took out her phone. "The old man said it was a white ninety-four Atori van. I'm going to put Carter on it."

"*Polizia! Getta le tue armi!*"

To Sophie's right, a trio of white Italian police cars stopped. Several blue clothed officers left their vehicles, taking cover behind their open car doors while aiming their guns at Sophie and Ray.

"Il Ramingo! Getta le tue armi o ti uccideremo!"

"What the hell are they saying?" Ray asked.

"Drop your gun, Dad. Now."

"Why?"

"They think you're Il Ramingo."

CHAPTER 49

Captain Adele Fattore tossed the phone used to call the Positano police on Ray and Sophie out the passenger window of their recently commandeered white panel van. It sailed for a moment before dropping out of sight down a steep cliff toward the ocean.

"The garage is just ahead," she said.

With his black head sock back on, hands gripping the wheel, Neri stared forward as they entered the tourist-choked streets of Positano.

"Did you hear me?" Fattore could tell something was bothering her son. "What is it?"

"Giuliana," he rasped. "You hurt Giuliana."

Fattore glanced back into the van's rear compartment. Madeline was still unconscious, sprawled out with a trickle of blood on her temple, her chest lightly rising and falling. With the Americans in pursuit, she had the nerve to grab her son's arm as he tried to fire. Using the butt of her pistol, Fattore was able to stretch from the front seat and knock the woman unconscious.

"She attacked you."

"It was her father."

Fattore felt a chill despite the summer heat. She'd underestimated how far the girl dominated her son's thinking. Did he really expect to bring her along? She wasn't just dead weight, she was going to sabotage their plans. Though she had been useful as a hostage, enabling their escape from Villa Fattore.

"Neri, are you sure she needs to see?"

Her son didn't respond. Instead, he turned a sharp corner, as the engine struggled, they broached a high hill. "There it is."

The row of old brick homes, smashed together like slices of bread, were not on posh streets lined with million-dollar villas, but a rundown poor section of Positano, a grungy neighborhood that had persisted despite the pressure of gentrification. From her pocket, Fattore retrieved a garage door opener and pointed it at three-story building with chipped white paint. The garage door on the ground floor rolled up. Neri pulled the van into the garage next to a dark green Volvo sedan.

While Neri transferred Madeline into the back seat of the Volvo, Fattore punched in a five-digit code on a pad next to the door leading into the home to disarm the security system.

"Zip tie her arms and legs. Tape a gag to her mouth."

"Mother."

"Can't have her waking up going through a roadblock now, can we?"

Neri muttered something unintelligible but obeyed. While he trussed Madeline, Fattore opened the door into the house to reveal a thin, red brick lined wooden staircase. Once on the second floor she turned on a police band scanner set on a folding table. Calls crackled over the speaker. Most of the attention remained on the Path of the Gods. But there were squads of police now scouring Northern Positano as well. Using a pair of binoculars, Fattore scanned the surrounding streets.

"Trovate Capitan Fattore, lei é una complice di Il Ramingo."

There it was. Clear as a bell over the police radio. She was an accomplice to Il Ramingo. Accomplice. Wanted. *Fools.*

Satisfied the area around the house was clear of police, she took a radio from its charger and clipped it to her belt. Fattore picked up two duffle bags and a locked metal briefcase that were sitting on a worn velvet sofa and walked back down the stairs and into the garage.

Neri had Madeline bound and gagged and ensconced in the trunk of the Volvo. Taking a duffle bag from his mother, her son replaced his head sock with a black hoody, hood up and drawn tight with a pair of aviator shades to cover his face. From the same duffle bag, Fattore put on a long red dress and fitted a blonde wig. Opening the silver case, she handed her son two holstered Berettas with extra magazines, slipping a third in her purse.

A half-hour after arriving at the garage, Neri drove the Volvo out. Within minutes they were on the northern stretch of the Amalfi Strata. The sun was almost gone and the wind low. In her lap was the second duffle bag. It contained more guns and over two million euros, bounty from Il Ramingo's decade of contract killing. Most important, two full identities including credit cards, driver's licenses and passports identifying them as the Calambo's from Rome. There were also two ferry tickets to the Italian capital city.

After thirty minutes of driving the tight coastal highway, they arrived at a faded red marker indicating a left turn down a winding road to the sea.

"Stop, here," Fattore said to Neri, pointing at a tiny scenic overlook with just enough space for their car to park.

There was one more bit of misdirection to commit for the authorities. Looking through a pair of binoculars, she spied at the water's edge an old marina that for over a hundred years served the wealthy of Amalfi. Today, the marina held a twenty-two-foot motorboat fully gassed in a slip for Fattore. On board, a briefcase with money, guns, and Egyptian passports for she and Neri under assumed identities. The boat was rented under her name, and she watched as blue-suited PSC officers swarmed the vessel.

"*Scemos*," Neri said.

When they were finished, and the desperate Americans were frantically searching for who was responsible, they would start in Africa. Meanwhile, they would be gone.

"To Sokolov," Fattore said, pointing out the windshield.

CHAPTER 50

"I always feared the Polizia Speciale Campania would knock on my door one day."

Flanked by armed guards, Andre Sokolov opened the wrought iron gate that led into his four-story villa. His home was perched high above Positano's main square on a private drive. Fattore could make out the tiny roof of her villa below.

"Just not today," he said to Fattore. "I must say Captain Fattore, it's been what, fifteen years since we last met? You haven't aged a day."

"Captain no longer."

Fattore stuck her hand out to the diminutive, spectacled Russian. He shook it with his left hand. Fattore towered over Sokolov, who though short, was broad shouldered with a bald dome and a short black-and-gray beard.

"A life of crime never truly pays," Sokolov said with a grin. "Is that who I think it is standing behind you?"

Neri Fattore, hood pulled tight on his head, sunglasses over his eyes, stepped out from behind his mother, ready to activate his Zell knives should the armed men standing by Sokolov as much as sneeze in his mother's direction.

"Neri Fattore, *Il Mezzanotte Ramingo* . . . the fucking Midnight Rambler!" Sokolov said with a hoot. "You don't remember me?"

Neri nodded. "I do. You flew me home."

"I did indeed." Sokolov stepped forward and patted Neri on the shoulder. "You're lucky my friends found you in the desert and not the Americans, or you'd still be in prison."

"And we returned the favor," Fattore said. "How many did he kill to protect your business?"

"Too many to count. Best I've ever seen." Sokolov's eyes sparkled.

"Better to talk inside," Fattore said. "No need for a CIA drone to see us."

"I concur," Sokolov said, waving Adele and Neri Fattore into a courtyard surrounded by ten-foot-tall brick walls. Just as they entered, a helicopter thundered overhead, stopping for a moment to hover above the top floor of Sokolov's mansion. Neri and Adele both drew their weapons and aimed them at the helicopter.

"Please, please, no, no," Sokolov said, shouting over the humming rotors and holding his hands up. "My daughter. Her wedding is in seven days. I am hosting." He pointed at the helicopter. "This is the decorator arriving from Brussels."

As the helicopter set down on the pad on the villa's roof, heart beating through her chest, Adele holstered her gun, motioning her son to do the same. She noticed mounted cameras and near invisible strands of razor-sharp filament wire stretched across the tops of the walls. One of Sokolov's men closed and locked the gate behind them.

Sokolov ushered the Fattores into his home. The ground floor was a huge open space with a gleaming marble kitchen. Massive picture windows delivered a panoramic view of Positano and the Tyrrhenian Sea below. They followed Sokolov up a curved marble staircase to a small salon on the second floor. Once inside, he offered them a seat at a clear glass table. A grim looking man with a shock of red hair stood off to the side with his arms crossed.

"This is Gregor." Sokolov said.

"So?"

Sokolov tapped his fingers on the table. "Your son killed Luca Pecora." Sokolov held up his phone. "My new partner, Chiara Opizzi, she's going to want a word with him about that."

"You don't need her, Andre."

"But I do. Thanks to your son, the Naples System is looking for a new leader. My business needs stability in that port."

Fattore shook her head. "No. What you need, Andre, is to get the nuclear device off the mountain and out of Italy. The Americans are closing in. It's only a matter of time, within days, hours maybe. What will become of your daughter's wedding when you've been whisked off to a CIA black site?"

Fattore refrained from bragging about killing Bill Hodges. Best Sokolov thinks the whole pack was still nipping at his heels.

Sokolov frowned. Fattore had expected him to not enjoy hearing his closely guarded secret being spoken about in the open.

"Go on."

"Show him, Neri," Fattore ordered her son.

Neri stood and removed a phone from his pocket. On the screen was a picture of a strange box-like vehicle on four sets of tank treads.

"What exactly are you proposing?" Sokolov said.

"My Neri can drive you to the site." Fattore pointed at the ceiling toward Mount Vesuvius. "We help you get what's on the volcano. Tonight. Then tomorrow morning it goes with us. All of us on your yacht. We have one more passenger waiting out in the car, and the three of us will accompany you to Tripoli. From there, do what you want. Sell it to who you want. Throw the bomb in the fucking ocean for all we care."

Sokolov removed his glasses and used his shirttail to wipe the lenses clean. "And the price for this service?"

"Three new passports, credit cards, Italian and German national health cards, bank cards linking to accounts in Bermuda totaling two million euros."

"That's not much time to get all that together," Sokolov said.

"Time? The Americans could be up there tonight. You are a well-connected man. Surely this is a small problem considering the very big problem we are solving for you?"

Sokolov pinched his nose and contemplated the former police captain's pitch. He had to know the CIA was closing in. The desperate

Russian would have few better options. Losing the bomb meant losing leverage.

"We're here tonight not just for the payment. We also need to repay a debt. You saved my son. Gave him a purpose all these years after the Americans left him for dead. He was a hero." She put her hand on her son's knee. "Let us help one last time. Help you to beat the Americans."

Sokolov nodded and smiled.

"*Il Mezzanotte Ramingo.*"

CHAPTER 51

Established in 1965, the Three Sisters restaurant was staple of Positano's beachside dining, with tourists lining up to eat steaming platters of seafood stew and lemon poached *branzino*. But tonight, the acting leader of the Naples System took over the whole place. Menacing looking thugs flanked the entrance, thrown open so the warm sea breeze blowing off the Tyrrhenian Sea could flood the space.

Inside the restaurant Chiara Opizzi's crew milled about. It had been three hours since they left the death scene at the Naples warehouse. Chiara paced. In a corner booth and across from an untouched pile of *frito misto*, Jimmy Nicchi's chin rested on his chest. The kid snored lightly while his father and David Granttano sipped brandy next to him. David kept his eyes on Chiara because, at this point, she was their only lifeline out of Italy.

David was exhausted. He felt the full weight of the Earth's gravitational pull. Like Jimmy, David attempted a catnap, but every time he closed his eyes he saw a vision of his niece, Madeline, bound and gagged with a knife at her throat, her eyes full of terror.

There was a commotion at the front door of the restaurant. Giuseppe from the warehouse had burst in. Walking fast and straight to Chiara, he put the strange phone taken from Luca Pecora in her hand.

"*Scusa per l'ora,*" he said.

"*Grazie, Guiseppe.*"

Chiara pushed one button on the phone and then put it to her ear. "*Buenosara.*" She said to a voice on the other line. Chiara waited for twenty seconds, then spoke for just under a minute in Italian. When she was done, Chiara Opizzi smiled, and put the phone in her pocket.

Sliding into their booth, she took a piece of fried squid from the plate in front of Jimmy. Washing the shellfish down with a glass of white wine from the table, she tapped Ken Nicchi on the arm.

"How would you feel about taking a nuclear weapon back with you to Kansas City?"

"Come again?" David said.

"Duke Nuke'em," Jimmy said. The young Nicchi was awake, using his good hand to pop red pills into his mouth, crunching down on several tabs.

"You don't need anymore of that shit," David said.

"Live a little, Granttano," Jimmy said, chewing the pills with a red speckled smile. "I got these from one of her guys. Take enough and it gives you sonar like a bat."

Chiara explained to Ken and David that the System had a dangerous partner in an ex-Russian intelligence officer named Andre Sokolov. The man was responsible for finding customers for the weapons the Nicchi stole from the US Army. He was also a world-class stake who had brokered the major deals for dumping on Vesuvius.

"Luca already had a lead-lined container ready for transport. And a trawler we own flying a Singapore flag is docked at our warehouse."

"The same one you offered us a ride home in, how convenient," David said.

"Easy Granttano, you're starting to sound like your brother," Ken said.

Like that's a bad thing.

"We ship it back across the Atlantic, undetected. Imagine how much China, or Russia would pay to have the key to a bomb parked at the Washington Monument. Or Mount Rushmore? A billion dollars? More?"

"They never have to actually detonate it," Ken said. "Be a helluva negotiating tactic."

David Granttano may have been a lifelong criminal, wiling to steal guns, deal drugs, intimidate or even disappear the occasional witness, whatever it took to make a living. But profiting off a nuclear bomb going off in the US of A was unthinkable. He believed Ken shared the same sentiment. Until now.

"You're okay with this boss?"

Ken fixed David with a bloodshot eye. "It's just a bigger gun, Davey. And that's what we do. We sell guns."

"Good. It is settled." Chiara jumped to her feet. "We leave immediately for a town called Malodini at the base of Mount Vesuvius. That's where Sokolov is headed. You three ride with me."

David tapped his boss's arm. "Be right back. Gotta take a piss."

"Hurry," Ken said. "Or you'll get left behind."

David walked to the restroom into an empty stall. He tapped one word into the message window on his burner phone and hit send.

CHAPTER 52

"Do everything I say, and you live to see sunrise."

Sandwiched between the Fattores, Madeline Granttano sat still in the back seat of a Sokolov's tan Land Rover, calmly contemplating her escape. She had slipped away from Neri once before. She would try again. All Madeline needed was an opening. And for her head to stop pounding. She doubted, as dizzy as she still was from the blow to her skull from Fattore's pistol, that she could make it more than twenty feet before running into a tree.

"Mother be kind," Neri said.

Sokolov rode in the passenger seat while his bodyguard and driver, Gregor, handled the vehicle like an angry bull as it lurched and bounced traversing the rough mountain road. Another Land Rover full of more Sokolov men followed.

"How much farther?" Adele Fattore said after the Land Rover hit a massive hole that sent them a foot in the air. She had changed from a red dress into a long-sleeved black shirt and pants. Neri was back in his usual garb that included a head sock and goggles.

"Not far. Fifteen, twenty minutes at the most."

Sokolov's phone buzzed. He ignored it. The phone buzzed again. He took it from his coat to answer the call. "Hello?"

"Who is it?" Fattore said. Madeline was more scared of Neri's mother than the assassin. Her son might have some deranged fascination with Madeline, but his mother would slit her throat on the spot should Madeline endanger them. She'd made that clear with the butt of her pistol.

"*Un momento,*" Sokolov said into the phone. Then he put his hand over the receiver and said to Adele, "My daughter. Another crisis. The cake maker's mother had a stroke. *Pardoneme.* The things we do for our children."

"Indeed," Fattore said.

Sokolov stepped out of the vehicle. Gregor exited the Land Rover, too. Leaning on the hood of the vehicle, lighting a cigarette while his boss talked to his daughter on the phone.

"I want to go home." Madeline said. "Please let me go home."

"*Shhhh,* it's okay," Neri said. "Soon. Very soon, you'll get to see what we've been planning for you."

"I want to go home."

"You are."

CHAPTER 53

"I've got five minutes."

Sophie stood in Fattore's kitchen amidst a swarm of busy techs and SOGs ferried to Positano on CIA helicopters. Pressed against the far wall was the kitchen table crammed with portable computers connected by satellite uplink. Carter sat behind techs working on the machines, tracking every piece of information coming out of the Il Ramingo manhunt.

His voice was weak, sucked of energy. Fattore's bullet went clean through Carter's left thigh without severing his femoral artery. While Sophie and her father pursued the Fattores home, BTO had used a tube of military grade topical-narcotic, wound-suturing gel from a cargo pocket to stop Carter's bleeding.

Carter was grappling with three simultaneous events: his new role as the interim station chief; hunting down Il Ramingo; and the death of his friend and mentor. Bill Hodges still lay in the Fattore's courtyard, zipped up in a body bag. Carter asked Sophie to analyze a trove of documents on Adele and Neri Fattore. If Sophie had to guess, Carter had leaned on the NSA to hack into the *Agenzia Informazioni e Scicurezza Interna's* servers to find the detailed dossiers on the mother and son killers.

Starting with Neri Fattore's Positano birth in 1963 to Adele and Christian Fattore, Sophie recanted to Carter that Christian Fattore was a young beat cop and only on the job two years when a bomb planted in his superior's car killed him. The PSC never found the murderer but surmised it was collateral damage from a turf war between the System and Cosa Nostra. In her entrance essay to the police academy in Pompeii, Adele Fattore wanted to show her son, Neri, what it meant to serve. Following his mother's example, Neri became a decorated and highly skilled member of the elite Italian 9th Paratrooper Assault division, called Col Moschin. Eventually he attained the rank of major and the command of a paratrooper platoon.

"Evidently Col Mushin soldiers are total badasses. Developed their own fighting style pulling from Ninjutsu, kickboxing, and Krav Maga," she said as Carter nodded along.

During Operation Iraqi Freedom, Neri was deployed to Bagdad as part of the coalition's counter-insurgency operation. Reading from a tablet, Sophie detailed his combat service. Fattore had been decorated on several occasions for displaying courage under fire. One time he single-handedly repelled an attack on an oil refinery by calling in an airstrike. "Did it while surrounded by Al Qaeda fighters. But he's wounded in the shoulder. Let's see here . . . taken off active duty while it heals. Reassigned as a liaison slash bodyguard for an Italian journalist and . . . oh shit."

"What? Who?"

"Giuliana Uliano."

"Giuliana?" Carter's eyes grew wide. "But that's—"

"What he called my sister?"

Sophie flipped her tablet around so he could see Giuliana's picture. In the photograph she was wearing a tan trench coat while interviewing a bald man in a suit. The resemblance was passing between the two women, both had round, fish-like eyes and manes of blonde curls, but it was the streaks of white down the center of their scalps that brought them closer in appearance.

Sophie turned the tablet back around and continued reading to Carter about how Giuliana reported for *Il Matina*, the leading Naples newspaper. She was notorious for breaking stories about the Italian government. The documents included a letter from Neri's commanding officer, General De Andre, warning him to keep a close eye on her when she arrived.

"He totally boned her," Carter said.

Sophie read aloud to Carter the emails Neri sent home to his mother. After a few weeks of a secret affair, they were deep in love and told Adele that Giuliana reminded him of his mother.

"Italians and their mothers," Sophie said.

Sophie had also learned that a few months later General De Andre suspected that Giuliana was writing a negative story about Col Moschin units. The rendition scandal that engulfed the CIA used the Italian paratroopers to ferry Al Qaeda soldiers from the battlefield. He orders her out of the country and tasks Major Neri Fattore to escort Giuliana to the airport.

"Then it gets real bad," Sophie said.

According to the incident report written by a US Army lieutenant on duty that day, Neri didn't follow proper identification rules when he approached the checkpoint to enter the airport. The soldiers opened fire. Giuliana was killed.

"It gets worse," Sophie said. "According to this email to his mother, she was pregnant."

Carter pointed to the door leading to the patio. "She said it. Right there. *Mi nipote*. Her granddaughter."

"Neri sends one last email to his mother. The subject line reads *Il Mezzanotte Ramingo*. In the body of the email only one sentence. *Memento mori*."

Grimacing in pain, Carter hobbled to the kitchen sink. "That day the *Esperanza* exploded? It always bothered me how quick Fattore got to the scene. How could we not see it? The goddamn song. It was right there, in the title," he said, pulling the handwritten lyric sheet for "Midnight Rambler" off the wall. "*Il Mezzanotte Ramingo*. I mean, it's about a serial killer!" Carter threw the framed lyrics in the sink so hard the glass shattered.

Sophie scanned the rest of the document. After the shooting, Neri abandons his post. Left everything in his quarters and walked out into the desert. Reports trickle in over the following weeks of a man, so sunburned skin was peeling off his body, walking the desert, killing indiscriminately. From Iraqis to coalition forces, he shot them all. "My question is how does Neri get from a desert war zone back here to sunny Positano?" Sophie pondered.

"Sokolov." Carter muttered.

"Who?"

BTO and her father, who had been waiting out on the patio, marched into the kitchen.

"*Malodini*," Ray said.

Sophie's head whipped around. "What did you say?"

"*Malodini*." Ray held up his phone. "Someone with an Italian number just texted me this one word. *Mal-oh no*. Isn't that—?"

"Maria." Sophie felt a pang of fear in stomach. "Maria. That's where Maria lives. At the base of Vesuvius."

"Remember, Carlson's top notch. Marine. Four deployments. Give it to me," Carter said. Ray handed him the phone. Carter passed the device to a tech sitting in front of a computer.

"Scrape everything."

The trio huddled over the tech. Sophie pushed away her darkest thoughts. *If something happens to little Maria* . . . For a moment, Sophie understood the rage behind Il Ramingo's actions. Something Neri loved so much, ripped from his hands. Then her mind drifted to her father. Twice now the man's choices had put his family in danger. Sophie had made bad choices, too. She let Hodges manipulate her into staying, and Tommy died for it. Now her choice to send Maria away put the young girl in danger. Sophie was all Maria had. Sophie searched for a word to describe how she felt, the slow-motion plummet into a deep pit, realizing the word was *helpless*. Sophie hadn't felt this unmoored since her mother died.

Then Ray's hand found its way into hers. Whispering in her ear, her father said, "Say the word, and I'll jump into Mount Vesuvius for that little girl."

"It's a burner. Bought in Naples with three others at a corner shop called Giovann's," the tech said.

"Holy shit. That's me," BTO said. "I bought those. Bought 'em for Ken Nicchi."

"David," Ray said. "It's David."

"You think it's your brother? Your brother is tipping us off?" Carter said.

Ray nodded. "Madeline is his niece. Has to be him."

The tech typed on her keyboard. "Looks like the text was sent from right here in Positano, at an address pretty high above us."

Carter stiffened. "Are they still there?"

"No. It's on the move with the other numbers," the tech said. She pointed at a cluster of red dots on a map traveling along a road. "They've just entered the Amalfi Parkway."

"Let me guess, they're heading to Malodini," Carter said. He flinched at the pain in his leg.

"They have a big head start," the tech said. "Twenty minutes at least. No way you can get there in time."

"We can if we fly," Sophie said.

"You want to take a CIA helicopter," Carter asked. "To an area heavily contaminated with toxic chemicals?"

"Not just chemical. Biological. Some radiation, too," Sophie said.

"Radiation? I don't remember you mentioning anything about radiation."

"Because it's been dumped in a very tight area. And away from the water table, so it's a low priority. It's the industrial solvents and toxic byproducts that have been causing cancers, getting into the bases's taps."

"The base . . . the Joint Operations Base?"

Sophie nodded. "Ten thousand service members."

"Show me." Carter hopped from the kitchen to Sophie while pointing at a map on a tech's computer screen.

Sophie took her phone out and tapped the screen. "Mirror me."

The map on Sophie's phone appeared on the tech's screen. She pointed at a collection of nine orange squares that were arranged in a circle.

"That's the area."

Carter shook his head. "That has to be where Sokolov buried it."

"Buried what?" Sophie asked.

"The bomb." Carter turned to the room. "Rotors up! Five minutes and we're airborne."

"A bomb? What kind of bomb?" Sophie said.

"The bad kind."

To Sophie's growing horror, Carter described Bill Hodges's thirty-year search for Sokolov's suitcase nuke. "It has to be there. In the dumping grounds you identified. The perfect place to hide something with a radioactive signature."

"It's a long time for that bomb to be buried in the ground," Sophie said. "What are the chances it still works?"

"Hodges told me it had a chemical trigger. Azidoazide azide, rare but reliable."

"The Camorra poisoned entire towns just to hide a nuclear weapon on a volcano?" BTO said.

Carter nodded. "*Memento mori.*"

CHAPTER 54

For the first time since Glenn Carlson accepted his current CIA SOG posting, he found a part of Italy relatable. Born in the arid scrubland of eastern Kansas, the beat-down hamlet of Malodini reminded him of the wind-swept farm towns of his youth. Tucked inside a massive grove of giant ash trees centered in an ocean of volcanic scrubland on Mount Vesuvius's southern flank, Malodini's isolation was reminiscent of his hometown of Hayes, a handful of buildings surrounded by oceans of wheat and corn. But it wasn't just the geography that he found familiar.

It was the silence.

Aside from a few Italian tree crickets, there was nothing. The town felt deserted.

"*Signore?* When is Sofia coming?" Maria said, her voice breaking the quiet.

Glenn stood next to his car in front of the ramshackle three-bedroom house EPA Special Agent Grant rented near Malodini's town center. Just one road ran from the highway through Malodini and passed in front of the villa. The sweet little Italian girl he delivered was not fond of waiting inside alone.

"Soon."

"My stomach hurts."

After he took the wrong exit in a snarl of traffic near Pompeii, the mistake added an hour to their trip. Carlson was still in awe at the amount of candy the kid put down on the drive.

"I'm not surprised. Now go inside, and drink some water. It'll help." Glenn's phone buzzed in his pocket. He squinted at the screen.

"Boyd?"

"Il Ramingo. We have good intel that says he and an unknown number of Russians are heading to Malodini. To you."

The hair stood on Glenn's arms. After four combat deployments in Iraq as a US Marine, he caught the eye of a CIA recruiter and didn't look back. Traveling the world as the tactical arm of any given CIA field operation was thrilling, the work testing his skills daily. Glenn had some tense exchanges since joining the Agency, but nothing near the level of violence of the past week in Campania. Glenn lost a good friend to Il Ramingo the day the assassin took out Pico the Wheel.

"Should we make a run for it?"

"No time. Hunker down. We're airborne and coming to you. Stay quiet. Don't engage. Do you hear me Carlson? Don't engage."

"Roger that." Glenn walked around to the trunk of his car.

"Was that Sophie? Is she coming to get me?" Maria was now standing at the top step with the front door of the house a foot away.

"It wasn't Agent Grant. But yes. Yes, she is coming to get you."

"What are you doing?"

The dark eyed Italian girl's English was pretty good. Glenn popped the trunk, reached inside and removed a tactical vest festooned with extra ammunition. "I'm going to stick around until Agent Grant comes just make sure you're safe," he said pulling the vest over his head. "Is that okay?"

"*Si,*" she said.

"Good. Now hurry inside, I'm right behind you." The girl ran into the house. He pulled a compact M4 rifle from the trunk, inserted a magazine and racked the action to chamber a round. He locked the front door with the deadbolt. Then using a code the EPA agent gave him, he accessed the external camera mounted over the front door with his phone. Glenn was rewarded with a panoramic view of the villa's front step and street.

For twenty minutes he sat, rifle at the ready, eyes locked on his phone's screen. Maria came out of her bedroom with a worried look. Glenn, who had a boy and a girl back home in the States, told her everything was fine. Sophie was on her way. Satisfied, Maria returned to her room.

Several cars appeared, their headlights cutting through the dust kicked up by the road in front of the villa. The gravel audibly crunching under their tires. But they didn't stop, and instead drove out of the view of the camera. A few minutes after the caravan sped past and disappeared, another vehicle approached. A white Land Rover stopped in front of the villa. A tall bug-like man stepped out wearing dark goggles.

Il Ramingo.

Glenn considered for a moment easing the front door open. While Il Ramingo stood and surveyed the town, Glenn could put a dozen bullets in a man that had killed his fellow SOGs. But he had orders—keep Maria safe above all else. So, Glenn did as Carter Boyd told him and hunkered down. He slowed his breathing to keep quiet. Any noise would alert the assassin to their presence. Il Ramingo didn't move, instead kept his head stuck in the air like a wolf trying to catch a scent.

Eyes fixed on his phone, Glenn watched Il Ramingo, satisfied no one was around, wave at his compatriots from the Land Rover. Two women and three men appeared and with Il Ramingo walked past the villa's front door. Once they passed out of sight, Glenn allowed himself to breathe again.

Then Maria tapped his shoulder.

"Signore?"

CHAPTER 55

Neri cast his eyes skyward. Striations of pink wove through the night sky above Malodini. The dark volcano with a halo of faint orange loomed over the town. Outside the tight ring of homes and shops around the square was a dense strand of ash that gave way to scrub higher up the ancient volcano's flanks.

They had parked in front of the EPA woman's rundown villa. Neri paused next to an older Audi sedan with rental plates. He placed his hand on the hood. It was cold. For a moment he stared at the dark house. Nothing moved inside. With his hand he waved at the two idling Land Rovers behind him. Adele Fattore emerged with Madeline in tow. Sokolov and his two men followed.

"Show him, Neri," Fattore said.

Neri walked to three massive, tarp-covered forms next to the villa. He threw the tarp off the first one, exposing a strange, multi-tracked vehicle.

"They are here, just like you said, mother."

"Bravo." Sokolov smiled "These should make it easy."

Neri whipped his head around at a sound from inside the villa.

"What is it?" Fattore asked.

"A voice." He pointed at the house.

White light bathed them from the headlights of three vehicles parked in Malodini's square. Chiara Opizzi stood in silhouette before the lights backed by a group of armed Camorra thugs. Ken and Jimmy Nicchi stood off to the side with David Granttano.

"Il Mezzanotte Ramingo!"

"*Minchia!*"

While Sokolov and his men took shelter behind the tracked machine Neri had uncovered, his mother darted to the Land Rover and crouched behind its open passenger door, pistol out and in her hand. "Is that Chiara Opizzi?"

"It is," Sokolov said.

"What do think she wants?" Neri asked while standing behind his mother's vehicle with a hand firmly gripping Madeline Granttano's elbow. Madeline was feeling better, her eyes darting from side to side, but her feet were augured to the ground.

"You."

"Why?" Neri said.

"You killed Luca Pecora, dear. It's only right she takes your head. If Chiara wants to run her own System, she has to earn respect from the other clans." Adele Fattore said over her shoulder. "Are you ready to fight?"

"I am."

"Wait. She wants to talk to you." Sokolov held his phone over his head. "Chiara wants to make a deal."

"Cake maker *milo culo*." Fattore said.

Fattore realized that Sokolov and Chiara had been talking. She poked her head above the open door frame. Satisfied that she wasn't going to get picked off, the former PSC captain moved back to Sokolov and took the phone from his hand. She gave him a look designed to communicate she knew of his treachery. Sokolov shrugged.

"I'm listening."

"I'm walking to the center of the square. Unarmed," Chiara said. "Meet me there if you're interested in making a deal where everyone lives and everyone wins."

She ended the call and handed the phone back to Sokolov. Fattore walked to her son and laid her pistol on the ground at Neri's feet.

"Wait for me here."

Fattore turned and strode fifty yards to the center of the Malodini town square. As she approached the midpoint, Chiara appeared, lit from behind by the headlights of two cars. She looked to be unarmed.

"You cannot have my son's head," Fattore said.

"Oh, I don't want the great Il Ramingo dead," Chiara said. "I want to hire him for a job."

Fattore squinted. Twenty-eight years on the planet and this girl Chiara thought she could lead the Camorra. Usually, it was some ruthless brute like Pecora, or an old bird next in line like Chiara's father who took the mantle. Fattore admired her ambition, herself having risen through the ranks of a testosterone-fueled organization. But there was no way she could trust this woman.

"His help for what?"

"Getting what Sokolov has hidden up on Vesuvius to America." Chiara smiled. "I assume that's why you are here. To take the bomb?"

"Something like that."

Chiara explained her plan to send the device in a Singapore-based trawler Pecora owned. He had planned to use it to sail the weapon to Tripoli, but now Chiara had desperate partners in the Nicchi. Partners so eager to escape Italy that they had agreed to shepherd dangerous cargo. The transport ship was docked at a System slip in the Naples port. *Good plan,* thought Fattore, *but how could anyone even be certain the device still works? It's been buried in a volcano for forty years.*

"Can you imagine what someone, some government, would pay to have a nuclear weapon hidden in America?" There wasn't a flicker behind Chiara's eyes. *Youthful confidence has no bounds,* Fattore mused.

"But I have a problem." Chiara stuck her chin out at the Camorra cars parked behind her. "These fat fucking American buffoons. I can't trust them. Who better than *Il Mezzanotte Ramingo* himself to provide security on the voyage?"

Fattore met Chiara's eyes. "And after we land?"

"You and your son can vanish."

CHAPTER 56

Moments after they lifted off from the helipad at Positano's beach, Sophie called Glenn Carlson, the SOG guarding Maria in Malodini. She wanted to alert him to their arrival. But he didn't answer. Instead, he replied with a text.

Il Ramingo here. Safe. For now.

On our way, Sophie responded.

"Don't worry, she's fine," BTO said, his booming voice filled Sophie's headphones. He put a hand on Sophie's knee, squeezed and left the hand there. Sophie gently lifted his hand from her knee, dropping it back on his leg.

"Chasing a nuke is no time to make a pass, dude."

"Counterpoint. It seems like the perfect time."

Sophie didn't know what to say. BTO was attractive in a Viking warrior sort of way, but she needed to focus on Maria.

They were flying through the night sky over the Lattari Mountains in one of the CIA's black helicopters. Before them Mount Vesuvius loomed. Pockets of red lava pools dotted the massive volcano's flanks. Its glowing caldera bathed the sooty sky in a hellish orange. The helicopter wove in between plumes of smoke rising from Vesuvius, their pilot careful to not fly them through a venting incident.

"Trade seats with me," Sophie's father said to BTO with narrowed eyes. Ortega obliged.

"That little girl's tough," Ray said plopping down next to Sophie in the passenger bay. A single CIA SOG sat across from them next to BTO. "Probably have the whole Camorra at gunpoint when we arrive."

Sophie dropped her head and shook it from side to side.

"What is it?" Ray said.

"I owe you an apology."

"For what?"

"For judging you. I left her. Abandoned a girl that has no one else. Because of what I wanted, not what Maria wanted."

"Take it from the master of bad choices. You don't owe anyone an apology, kiddo."

"Agent Grant, Station Chief Boyd for you," the pilot said.

"Patch him in."

Carter Boyd was aboard a separate helo flying above them. He aimed to land close enough to the radioactive cluster Sophie found high up on the volcano's side before Il Ramingo acquired the nuclear bomb. The plan called for Sophie and company to secure Maria in Malodini.

"Il Ramingo is in Malodini," she said. "Positive ID from Carlson."

"Good. We have time," Carter said. "There's only one place to put down up on the volcano that's safe. Fire and brimstone up here. Looks like we got lucky, though. Landing site's only two, maybe three hundred meters from the cluster you identified," Carter said. "There's plenty of space for both birds."

The pilot of Sophie's helicopter pointed the nose down. Dropping through a layer of brown smoke a small collection of lights illuminating Malodini became visible. Sophie typed a quick note to SOG Carlson.

Approaching.

I hear you. Il Ramingo stole two of those tracked machines and started up the mountain.

The SPAGOs! Sophie flashed back to the day on the beach with Fattore. The PSC captain had expressed dismay about the firebombing of Sophie's vehicle. Disappointment Sophie interpreted as concern. Alarm that turned to relief when Fattore learned two new SPAGO's were being shipped out. They'd planned on using the tank-like EPA machines all along. What better way to transport the bomb off the volcano?

"I'm going to land right in the square," the pilot said, while descending.

We're going to land in the square Sophie typed to Carlson.

Be careful they may have left a rearguard.

"Fifty feet off the deck," the pilot said.

"Looks quiet," Ray said.

Muzzle flashes from a trio of weapons erupted from the square. Multiple bullets slammed into the helicopter. Head rocking back from an errant round to the eye, the SOG slumped dead in his shoulder harness next to Sophie.

"Bugging out!" the pilot said.

"Not without Maria!" Sophie said.

"I got this." BTO unhooked his harness using his thumb. With one fluid motion he scooped up the SOG's rifle from the floor, pulled the chopper door open and stepped onto the skid. Bullets from below whistled around him. Weapon to his shoulder, he pulled the trigger until the shooting from the square stopped.

"All dead." He grinned from the open door, the rotor wash whipping his hair around his head.

"Night Stalker, indeed," Ray said.

A grinding noise erupted the rear of the helo as the tail rotor tore itself from the aircraft. It must have been damaged by the gunfire Sophie thought as the helicopter spun out of control.

"Buckle your chin straps!" the pilot said.

Sophie and her father grabbed hands and locked eyes. The pilot was trying to set the chopper down as gently as possible in a small clearing. He cut the engine right before impact so the rotors wouldn't disintegrate into hundreds of flying daggers. BTO leapt from the skid as they hit with a loud bang followed by the tearing of metal as the tail broke off and the aircraft rolled on its side.

"Everyone all right?" the pilot called over the radio.

"We're good except for Givens," Sophie said. "KIA. You?" Sophie felt another pang in her gut looking at the SOG's lifeless body hanging inside the chopper's cabin. A bullet from groundfire had struck him in the temple. Someone would have to make another devastating call to another family.

The pilot grunted in pain. "I think my leg is broken. It's pinned between the door and my seat." Ray and Sophie exited the helicopter, scurrying around the wreckage to the cockpit amid gunfire. Blood from a small gash above Ray's left eye trickled down his cheek.

"Here," Sophie said, taking a thumbnail sized quick sealing suture from a pack on her hip and sticking it on the cut.

"That's my girl."

While Sophie kept watch with an M4 rifle to her shoulder, Ray used a wrench the pilot handed him through a jagged hole in the windshield to pry open the cockpit door. "Just one more, one more," Ray grunted as he pulled on the wrench he wedged next to the pilot. "There!" With an audible crunch the door and seat came apart. The pilot yelped in pain as the pressure on his leg released, falling into Ray's arms.

"Let's get him to safety," Sophie said. She stepped forward into the trees. A stick cracked to her left. BTO appeared before her unscathed. He smiled at Sophie.

"S'up?"

"Really?"

"Where's your dad? The pilot?"

"Right here," Ray said. He appeared in the gulf between the helicopter's body and the tail section. The pilot had an arm draped around Ray's shoulders and was hopping on one foot.

"Let's get Maria," Sophie said.

With Ray helping the pilot limp along, a submachine gun liberated from a dead Camorra strapped across his chest, they crept through quiet Malodini, guns out, ready for anything, stepping over the occasional dead body. After a few more careful steps, Sophie's rented villa appeared. The house was dark. In front were two empty Land Rovers.

Parked around the corner and next to the house was the only remaining SPAGO - Tommy's. The night on Vesuvius when Pecora's men destroyed her research vehicle seemed a lifetime away. Once again, her partner's lifeless eyes staring at the ceiling for eternity flashed across her mind. The tarp had been thrown off Tommy's vehicle. There were clusters of different footprints in the dirt where it looked like the new SPAGOs had been temporarily parked, and caterpillar belt marks from two vehicles leading away from the villa.

With BTO and her father standing watch, Sophie walked up the steps to her villa. She waved at the camera mounted above the door, and after the deadbolt was thrown open, Carlson stuck his head out. Maria peeked around his leg. When she saw Sophie she leapt out the door. Sophie swung the rifle across her back and hugged the overjoyed eleven-year-old.

"I was so scared," Maria said into Sophie's neck. "There were gunshots."

"You are very brave," Sophie said.

"Nonno!" Maria said spying Ray on the steps. Sophie let her down and she ran to Ray and gave him a hug.

Ray swung her around and kissed Maria's cheek before setting her back to the ground. "Who are you?" Maria said, noticing BTO towering next to her.

"I'm the big bad wolf."

"You don't scare me."

BTO snorted. "What does?"

Maria pointed out into the dark. "Vesuvius."

The radio velcroed to the injured pilot's shoulder crackled to life. "Agent Grant? Do you read me?"

Sophie pulled the radio off the pilot with a loud rip. "Copy."

"Where the hell are you?" Carter asked.

Sophie explained as fast as she could about the downed chopper.

Most pressing, however, was how Il Ramingo and an unknown number of others had commandeered two of the EPA's SPAGOs. "Have you seen them yet?"

"No, but we're on foot approaching the site."

Sophie looked over at her father who had acquired a discarded assault rifle, swapping out a spent magazine for a full one. "What are you doing?"

"Going to get my daughter."

BTO pointed up the slope of Mount Vesuvius. "How fast can you get us up there?"

Neri had a good head start, but SPAGOs were near impossible to handle for first time drivers.

"We can catch them." Sophie took a deep breath and let it out. Turning to Maria, she stooped face level with the little girl. "I'm going to need you to go back inside, lock the door, and wait for me to come back."

"We got her," Carlson said pointing to himself and the injured pilot.

Minutes later the pilot sat in a chair just inside the front door, his leg up on a chair and lashed with duct tape to a broom handle liberated from the villa's kitchen pantry. A submachine gun lay across his lap. Carlson took a firing position opposite the pilot.

Sophie had grabbed three breathing masks and oxygen tanks.

"We need to make a decision about PPE's. Last time we were up there, the air quality wasn't that bad. I'm not saying we have a sleepover, but if you're careful to avoid venting or fumes from a dump pool you should be fine. The other option is limited visibility through the masks."

"Hard pass," BTO said. Her father nodded in agreement. Sophie let the PPE equipment drop to the ground.

"I'm going to make you a promise, this is the last night you're going to spend here," Sophie said to Maria who stood on the other side of the pilot inside the door. BTO and Ray were already walking toward the SPAGO.

"Promise?"

"Promise."

"Ciao Nonno," Maria called after Ray.

CHAPTER 57

"Wait, I have to ride in a boat across the ocean with a nuclear bomb *and* that fucking psycho?"

David Granttano bounced around in the rear compartment of the strange, caterpillar tracked vehicle they'd pilfered from his niece's basecamp. Over boulders and rocks the machine crawled. Often it tossed in the air the occupants riding in the rear cabin. If that wasn't bad enough, it was hot and getting hotter as they ascended toward Mount Vesuvius's caldera.

One of Chiara's men drove their vehicle while she sat in the front passenger seat. They followed behind Sokolov's tank-treaded contraption as it churned upward through pumice and volcanic rock. The driver cursed and spat trying to maneuver the tracked machine upslope. As part of their truce, Sokolov stayed with Neri and his mother in the lead vehicle, while Chiara kept Madeline. The woman bumped around in the rear with Ken and Jimmy, but hewed close to her uncle David.

"It's our only way out, Davey," Ken said. "Be grateful."

What a turn for his old friend, David thought. *The guy's only concerned with his own skin.* David wondered if in the end Ken Nicchi would cut him loose if it meant only one of them could survive.

Chiara turned around in her seat. "And you will be rich, too." In that moment, with his niece squeezing his arm for more than just physical stability, the old Kansas City crook realized events were about to go from bad to thermonuclear.

Sokolov brought his machine to a stop next to a burned-out

tree stump. Ken Nicchi and the Russian had hugged upon sight. They'd met once, years ago. Sokolov had brokered the deal for waste and guns sent to Naples. David hadn't met him yet, but one of Sokolov's protégées had been in contact with Ken about expanding the American side of environmental crime. Everyone piled out and stood around the stump. David noticed a flat spot of dirt a lighter shade of gray than the surrounding soil.

"There," Sokolov said and pointed at the dirt. He and his man each took a shovel. While Ken Nicchi smoked and Chiara Opizzi paced, they used the tools to clear an inch of the dirt from a flat rectangle of cement on the ground. Neri and Adele stood watch across from them. Once the dirt was away, David could see a set of double-cellar doors, set in a concrete frame, locked with a thick chain and heavy padlock. Sokolov produced a key. He unlocked the chain and pulled the two doors open. A set of cement steps led down into a chamber below ground. Sokolov plunged down the steps. Minutes later he emerged with a large olive drab military style backpack, but to David Granttano it looked more like a canvas covered barrel with shoulder straps then a college kid's backpack.

"That's a nuclear bomb?"

"Shouldn't there be a bunch of dials? Trigger keys? A countdown clock? It's just a fucking backpack." Jimmy Nicchi said. He cradled his bandaged arm to his stomach.

"*Medvezhonok*," Sokolov said. "The Little Bear. Model RA 115. Inside are a chemical trigger, two linked neutron generators, a lithium battery and enough fissionable material to create a six-kiloton blast, roughly equivalent of two million tons of TNT. Sufficient to wipe out Manhattan. We designed the battery and trigger system to last for a long, long, time. The only downfall is the trigger needs a few minutes to formulate before detonation."

"What are you doing now?" Chiara asked.

Sokolov had opened a flat black panel on the side of the Little Bear. "Before we move it, we need to make sure it works. I don't want to go through all the hassle of getting it down the mountain and out of the country and find out we have a dud. This Little Bear has been asleep in the ground for thirty years."

"You can do that?" Ken asked.

"Of course," Sokolov said. "I designed and built it. And one more like it when I was with the GRU. But unlike the propaganda our operatives spread with the West, we never got them to the production stage. Only working prototypes. Problem was the chemical trigger. *Azidoazide azide.* Perfect application. Lasts forever. Failsafe. But we couldn't find enough of the rare mineral to ramp up production. Then the Soviet Union collapsed. One of mine was seized coming across the border in ninety-four. This is the other."

David watched as Sokolov connected his phone with a cable adapter to a cluster of wires he pulled from the panel. After a few minutes of nodding at what he saw on his phone, he said to Jimmy "Here, young American," and pointed to the curved side of the device. Then he pushed a button and a panel slid out. On the panel were a keyboard and a keyhole. Sokolov reached into his shirt and pulled a silver chain with a key on the end. "Just like in the movies." He inserted the key into the slot next to the keyboard and turned it to the right. A screen above the keyboard illuminated. After a flurry of keystrokes, Sokolov turned the key back to the left. The screen went dark.

"All systems go," he said and removed the key.

"I'm thirsty, Uncle David. Do you have any water?" Madeline said.

"All I got." David took a plastic water bottle from his back pocket that held two inches of warm water and handed it to his niece.

She drank it in one gulp and grimaced. "Why are you helping these people? I'm so tired. I just want to go home."

Ken Nicchi, his black polo shirt soaked with sweat, stepped close enough to Madeline for David to smell him. "The only way you're getting home is if we get that bomb off this mountain. And even then, I may decide to leave you behind."

"He hated you," she said to the senior Nicchi.

"Oh shit," Jimmy said.

Ken's voice disappeared. Only a squeak came out. "Who?"

"Chris," Madeline said, her bottom lip quivering. "Your son. My husband. He hated you."

Ken drew his hand back to strike Madeline, but she didn't budge. As his open fist descended, David caught Ken's forearm in mid-air, stopping the strike.

"What in the hell are you doing?" Ken said.

"That's my niece. She's been through a lot."

Ken yanked his arm from David's grasp. "I'm going to put your fat fucking face through *a lot.*"

David squared his shoulders, ready to fight his longtime friend and boss. "Take your best shot." Granttano made sure he was in between Ken and Madeline, cracked his knuckles and settled into a pugilist's stance.

"Fermare!" Chiara Opizzi shouted. David and Ken dropped their hands and turned to her. She was aiming her pistol at Neri who had his right hand Szell knife extended and held under Sokolov's chin. Neri plucked the key and its silver chain from Sokolov with his left hand.

"What do you think you're doing?" Chiara said.

Adele Fattore gestured at the bomb with her chin. Her assault rifle was at her shoulder and pointed at Chiara's men.

"As much as we'd like to see the New World, we have other plans for the Little Bear," she said.

"I'll kill you first," Chiara said.

"No. No, you won't," Fattore said.

Fattore and Neri met eyes, communicating something unspoken David couldn't decipher. But then Neri smiled, exposing a row of jagged yellow teeth. In a flash, he stabbed his foot-long Szell through

Sokolov's chin and out the top of the Russian's head.

"*Memento mori.*"

Adele Fattore let loose with a long burst from her rifle that cut down two of Chiara's men.

While Ken and Jimmy scurried out of the way, David grabbed Madeline, pulled her to the ground and covered his niece with his body. He lifted his head to see Chiara, her remaining foot soldier and Sokolov's lone man return fire.

Lurching toward the tracked vehicle they used to ascend Vesuvius, his knife lodged in Sokolov's skull, Neri held the dead Russian upright. Bullets thumped into the body, shielding himself and his mother. Adele Fattore was dragging the Little Bear nuclear device one-handed while firing back with the other. When his mother was almost to the tracked machine, Neri whipped his arm to shuck the dead Russian to the ground, but instead the Szell knife broke off at its base. He raised and fired a machine pistol with his other hand into Sokolov's man, who collapsed to the ground like a punctured balloon. Chiara and her goon dove for cover.

With two long strides Neri was back at Madeline's side. He pulled her to her feet and drug her toward the tracked vehicle where his mother had brought the Little Bear.

"Let go of me!"

A mass landed on Neri's back, knocking him to his knees. He jerked his elbow into David Granttano's face. As David staggered back, hand on his bloodied nose, Neri slashed him diagonally across the chest.

"Uncle David!" Madeline cried.

David pitched over on his side, his right leg pawing the air like it was trying to push him down the street on a skateboard.

Frozen by shock, Madeline hardly noticed when Il Neri grabbed her around the waist and shoved her into the tracked vehicle. He then helped his mother lift the Little Bear into the rear compartment. While Neri started the research vehicle's diesel engine, Adele Fattore swung the upper half of her body out the passenger side of the treaded conveyance, assault rifle aimed downrange, and started firing. A return salvo from Chiara and her man thwacked into the metal cabin, a trio of bullets zipping all the way through and out the windshield.

"Go, Neri!"

Adele Fattore dropped an empty magazine, slammed in a full clip, racked the action, and kept returning fire. More bullets punctured the cabin. One ricocheted off the dash and whizzed under Neri's chin. He heard his mother grunt and saw her slump in the passenger seat out of the corner of his eye.

Neri pushed both tread accelerators forward. Four sets of tracks tore into the rock and shot the machine downslope. They bounced twice, the last time high enough, Neri thought, that they might land askew and tumbled, but he throttled back. The machine settled down. He looked over at his mother. Her face was white. She held both her hands to a bullet wound in her stomach oozing blood.

"Get us to the hole, Neri."

CHAPTER 58

Everywhere Sophie looked she saw ghosts.

Camorra assailants with guns out, charging toward her, engaging US Marines in armed combat, Tommy Jones, off her right shoulder, driving his own Self Propelled All Terrain Geoprobe. Though it felt like a century had passed, it'd been only three days since they drilled holes deep in the rock and put those first sensors in the ground on Vesuvius.

Once again, Sophie was piloting her Model 84 tracked vehicle up the side of the semi-active volcano, dodging jagged fissures venting gas and pools of dumped toxic chemicals, BTO and her father crouched behind her. She followed in the tracks of the two SPAGOs that had come before them, SPAGOs stolen from her base camp by Il Ramingo to spirit a nuclear weapon off the mountain.

Save Madeline. Get the bomb. Stop Il Ramingo.

They were moving at a good, twenty-five mile per hour clip, with Sophie weaving between the menagerie of Vesuvius's perils. BTO pointed out the windshield. "What's that?" Fifty feet upslope sat a pile of black melted plastic and twisted metal. A chuck of track jutting from the wreckage was the only identifiable piece.

"Did one of them explode?"

"No." Sophie recognized where they were. She spied the pond of cadmium sulfide identified on her first trip up the mountain with Tommy. "That's mine." She brought the SPAGO to a stop. She quickly recounted the night with the Camorra and the Molotov cocktail attack that destroyed her vehicle. She opened her door and pointed at a hole in the ground. "See, right there is where I put the first sensor . . . what the hell?"

What had been a tight excavated hole ten centimeters in diameter was now a huge gaping maw descending deep into Vesuvius. It looked like a ragged mineshaft. She wondered if her seismic calculations had been off or if somehow her drilling that night caused a fissure to crack. It was possible an underground chamber formed by cooling lava had collapsed because of her drilling. But there were rocks sprayed around the hole as if it had exploded outward with great force.

"Look!" Ray said.

Like an apparition, another tank-like SPAGO crested the hill upslope through a smokey haze. It was just under a hundred meters above.

"They stopped. Can you see who it is?" Ray said.

"No." BTO said. "But I highly doubt they're friendly."

"Oh God," Sophie said. "They're not stealing the bomb."

"They're not?" Ray said.

"No," Sophie said. She pointed out the windshield at the SPAGO. "They're going to use it to blow the whole damn volcano."

CHAPTER 59

"I suppose I'm now a CIA asset," Chiara Opizzi said.

After setting their chopper down on the only flat piece of land they could find—a rock-strewn strip saddled between two knolls—Carter and his two-man SOG detail moved as fast as he could on his injured leg. The trek was longer than he hoped. Most of the pain from the gunshot wound was dulled by pills, but every rock he stepped on wrong could still feel like a fresh bullet.

"Depends on where the bomb is." Carter said. "And Il Ramingo."

When they approached the spot marked on his map, Carter spied the lone SPAGO parked next to a stump. Chiara and her remaining man didn't see them coming. The two SOGS snuck up on the acting Camorra leader just as she was trying to start the tracked vehicle. After disarming them, Carter had the SOGs zip tie Chiara and her man's hands behind their backs. Ken and Jimmy Nicchi, upon seeing Carter, tossed both their pistols in the dirt without being prompted, and put their hands above their heads.

Carter tapped his wrist. "Time's a wasting."

"He took it," Chiara said. She nodded at Sokolov's body. "After he killed the Russian. "He and his *cagna* mother drove down the mountain no more than a minute ago."

"Boyd? Boyd? Do you copy?" The radio on Carter's hip cackled with Sophie Grant's voice.

"I copy," Carter said.

Sophie talked fast, words jumbling together. "We see him. He's right in front of us. Carter, I think I know what they want to do with the bomb. My God! The base. Ten thousand American troops and families. They seek vengeance. For Giuliana and Il Ramingo's unborn daughter."

"Sophie, I'm not following. Slow down."

He heard her take a deep breath over the radio. "The seismic reports from the Campania Geological Society. Requested by Fattore. There's a fault line. A big one, running right under Vesuvius. Someone used explosives to make the hole I drilled big enough to drop the Little Bear right on top of that fault line."

Carter envisioned the bomb detonating deep inside the volcano. A towering, nuclear powered wall of lava, rock, white heat and deadly radioactive isotopes that would wipe the massive US base and the nearby metropolis of Naples clean off the Earth.

Memento mori. Remember that you die.

CHAPTER 60

"It's going to be goddamn Cobra Island, all over again."

It was May of 2009. Sophie and Ted Staymitch were wrapping up his final case as an EPA special agent before retirement. In Baltimore, a man had fleeced the federal government's nascent renewable fuels program for eight million dollars. He spent it on luxury cars, Lamborghinis, Ferraris, and parked them in front of his house. It was not a hard collar. The problem was, after 9/11, Congress was desperate to wean Americans off Middle East oil. To jumpstart homegrown biofuels, they wrote a law so sloppy anyone could claim government credits. In the ten years that followed, over a billion dollars of Uncle Sam's coin was stolen from the program.

Though a rookie at the time, Sophie got the reference. *The law of unintended consequences* was one the first concepts taught in her environmental justice class. One famous example was Cobra Island. While under British rule, India's Sentinel Island became infested with venomous cobra snakes. The Brits offered a bounty for every dead cobra. Entrepreneurs started breeding cobras for extra money. When government officials learned of the scam, they stopped the bounty program and fraudsters released their snakes into the wild. The result was more deadly cobras on Sentinel Island than before. Ted recognized the biofuel program for what it was—an honest attempt to make the environment better that was backfiring.

But nothing would compare in the universe of unintended consequences to Sophie drilling a hole in a volcano to help the children of Malodini, only to have a deranged killer and his mother repurpose it for nuclear genocide.

Sophie squinted through the windshield up at the SPAGO she was pretty sure held the Little Bear bomb. She, BTO and Ray were the only thing standing between Il Ramingo and oblivion.

"If only there was some way to plug the damn hole," Ray said.

"That's it," Sophie said. She pushed the ignition to start the diesel engine. "There is."

"Cover us, Ortega?" She asked over her shoulder.

"Aye." BTO exited out the rear doors. He jogged around to the SPAGO's front to position himself between them and Il Ramingo, knelt on one knee and put his rifle to his shoulder. Sophie asked her father to go to the rear of the vehicle and direct her, the back camera aperture was too small for her to see where she needed to go.

"Here goes nothing." With her right hand, Sophie pulled all four treads in reverse.

CHAPTER 61

Pain rippled through Adelle Fattore's torso. The bullet had struck her in the back, exiting just to the right of her belly button. Fattore had already lost a good amount of blood. Her feet were cold. She knew the odds of her getting off Vesuvius were small and getting smaller. She would never make their appointment in Rome. Plotting a new life, a fresh start, considering the crimes committed, it was pure hubris to think they could escape, especially after what they were about to do.

But she could ensure their plan saw fruition.

The former PSC captain was seated in the SPAGO's passenger seat. Her son had kicked out the bullet-riddled windshield. She laid the assault rifle's barrel on the dash with it pointing out the front of the vehicle. From a first-aid kit in the rear, Neri put several large adhesive bandages on the entry and exit wounds and wrapped a whole roll of gauze around her midsection. But the blood was already seeping through. She was getting weaker. And drowsy.

"Who is it?" Neri said from the driver's seat.

A hundred meters below them, an identical vehicle stood guard over the spot where the Fattores would exact their vengeance, not just on the Americans, but those complicit Italians as well. The ones who whored out their soldiers for a corrupt cause. But the distance was too great, with the smoke from volcanic fissures complicating their vision, to make out who exactly was in the tracked vehicle.

One thing was clear, they needed to be removed from the equation. Fast. But Neri had discarded his empty machine pistol.

Aside from her assault rifle, they were outgunned.

"Giuliana!" Neri said. The assassin's head whipped from side to side. The rear doors to the SPAGO had swung open. The woman was gone. While they'd concentrated on the threat down below, Madeline Granttano had escaped out the back. "Giuliana!" Neri jumped from the driver's seat to the ground below. He ran in a circle around the vehicle but found no sign of Madeline. "Giuliana!"

"Neri, she gone."

Il Ramingo climbed back into the driver's seat. "But mother, she needs to see."

"No, she doesn't!" Fattore coughed. She put her hand to her mouth, and it came away red. "It's not her my love. You have to get that through your . . .what are they doing?"

Mother and son watched as the SPAGO downslope backed up until it was directly over the hole Neri had made. With the machine parked where it was, there was no way the Little Bear could do its work.

"So simple and effective," she said to her son. "It will require a simple and effective response." Fattore coughed again. She felt her strength ebbing away. "You need to decide, right now, if you're going to finish this with me or not."

Neri Fattore, decorated former special forces soldier, forged by war in the Iraqi dessert into the vicious killer Il Ramingo, picked up his mother's hand and brought it to his lips.

"I am."

"Excellent." Her vision occasionally blurring, speech interrupted by bloody coughs, Fattore outlined how she intended to finish what they had started.

"A good plan, worthy of DeSalvo."

CHAPTER 62

"Pretty smart, kiddo," Ray Granttano said to his daughter from the passenger seat. Sophie shut down her SPAGO's engine. BTO stood guard in front of them. His weapon was aimed at the treaded machine holding Il Ramingo parked in the distance above them. With the flip of the hydraulic stabilizer switch, four outriggers mounted on each of her SPAGO's corners extended and augured themselves to the ground.

Her father pointed out the windshield at Il Ramingo's SPAGO. "Checkmate, mister Midnight Rambler."

The SPAGO above them launched from its parked position. Engine roaring, rock and pumice shooting into the air in its wake from four churning treads, the machine burst downslope directly at them, moving fast.

"It's a bluff," Ray said. "Don't budge. No way they ram us with a nuclear bomb."

"Wouldn't have the time even if I wanted to," Sophie said. With her SPAGO anchored to Mount Vesuvius, and the speed with which Il Ramingo was closing in on them, it was impossible to avoid a collision. No. They were trying to make them move. Il Ramingo's plan didn't work with Sophie parked over the hole. She gripped the wheel, tight.

"*Giocco Pollo*," she said.

From inside the descending vehicle erupted a long, wild burst of automatic gun fire. Sophie's father pulled her to the SPAGO floor by the neck just as the bullets struck. Their windshield shattered. Glass rained down on father and daughter. Bullets perforated the seat where she had just been.

Sophie heard BTO return fire, his rifle spitting out controlled clusters of shots. She poked her head up to spy Il Ramingo's SPAGO close, no more than twenty meters away, the whirring of its treads filled her ears. A bloody Adele Fattore was slumped forward over the controls.

"I can't reach my gun," Ray said, fumbling for the assault rifle he'd dropped to the floor.

"There's no time!" Sophie said.

Using both hands, Sophie reached up, grabbed the front roll bar, and with her legs kicked her dad in the chest as hard as she could. The blow propelled Ray out the passenger door. She turned, Fattore's SPAGO filling her vision, and lurched backward out the driver's side door. Sophie fell toward the rocky ground just as Fattore's SPAGO rammed into theirs.

A split second before impact, her body inverted mid-air, Sophie glimpsed a dark shape with a long spidery arm holding on the rear of Fattore's SPAGO. Then there was an ear-splitting crash of rending metal and breaking glass. She tumbled over rocks. A clanging severed metal tank tread whizzed inches over her rolling body. Sophie came to a stop and staggered to her feet; pain shot from her hip as she surveyed the scene.

Sparks crackled among a twisted nest of metal tank treads. The pneumatic auger arms from her SPAGO hung like severed spider legs. When Fattore's SPAGO struck, it accordioned both cabins. The combined mass had tumbled in a destructive embrace ten meters downslope. There was no sign of her father, or Fattore, or Il Ramingo.

But the Little Bear nuclear device stood unscathed right next to the hole.

There was a shuffle of dirt from behind. Sophie drew her pistol and spun to face BTO.

"I almost shot you," Sophie said.

"I've had worst first dates," the big man replied. He reached with his hand out near her face and Sophie pushed it aside.

"What are you doing?"

BTO turned his hand palm up to reveal her locket. It must have come off when Fattore rammed them. The locket her father gave her. "Thanks." Sophie took it, then with her pistol out in front, hurried around the pile of treads. Next to the Little Bear, her father's leg stuck out from under a heavy section of metal caterpillar belt.

"Ray. Shit!" Sophie reached her father, holstered her gun, grabbed the belt with both hands and pulled, but hardly budged the chunk of wreckage. Her father groaned at her feet. "Jesus. BTO help me. What are you doing?"

BTO's head was moving side to side as he limped to her. "Keeping an eye out."

"You hurt?"

"Twisted my knee getting out of the way." Like he was picking up a pile of dirty laundry, BTO hefted the severed tread from Ray and tossed it aside, but he winced doing it. "It's fine."

She crouched next to her father. Blood streamed from a cut on the back of his head down his neck. There was also a nasty gash on his thigh that didn't look to be life-threatening.

"Dad. Dad. Are you hurt?"

Ray moaned again. His eyes fluttered open. "I'll live."

"On your feet, Granttano," BTO said, extending his right hand. Just as Ray grabbed it, Il Ramingo emerged from the hole next to the Little Bear. He stabbed BTO through the armpit from behind. The upward thrust stuck the blade out the top of his right shoulder. BTO dropped to the ground and rolled on his side clutching the joint to stem blood gushing from the wound.

Sophie drew her pistol and pulled the trigger just as Il Ramingo slashed down with his knife. The blade connected with the gun's barrel, slid down the weapon's frame and cut into her hand all the way to the bone between her middle and ring fingers. The bullet went into the dirt while the white-hot pain shooting up her hand caused Sophie to drop her gun. Her weapon clattered away into the darkness.

Everything slowed down. She stared at the blood pouring from her hand. She looked up, expecting Il Ramingo to kill her with his next move, but instead her father was on his feet. Ray punched the assassin square in the jaw. His blow stunned the Italian killer, leaving an opening for Ray to pummel him repeatedly in the face. With wet smacks, the punches kept sending Il Ramingo backward, until for a moment the assassin teetered on the edge of a nearby volcanic vent. Sophie noticed he had a coil of climbing rope wrapped around his torso.

But Il Ramingo caught himself, executed a near perfect pirouette on the fissure's rim, spun in the air, positioned his right leg across Ray's chest, dropped to the ground, and closed his left leg behind her father's knees in scissor motion that sent him sprawling flat on his back. Il Ramingo jumped forward and thrust his knife into Ray's chest. Ray yelped in pain; his hands extended out from his body in temporary crucifixion.

"Dad!" Sophie stumbled to his side, the pain from her hand making her dizzy. She put her good hand on the wound in his chest. The blood coming from it frothed; his lung was punctured. "Press down, Dad. Hard. I'm going to be right back. Do you hear me?" He nodded slightly.

Sophie stood and almost fell over. She took a deep breath and steadied herself. For her father. There had to be a first-aid kit somewhere in the destroyed SPAGOs. She walked three steps toward the wreckage and glimpsed her pistol lying next to a chunk of wall insulation.

"Stop." Il Ramingo knelt next to the Little Bear. His remaining Szell knife, covered in her father's blood, pointed at Sophie.

"Or what?" she said. "You'll kill a woman? I thought you had a code."

With his other hand Il Ramingo took a silver cord with a key on the end from around his neck. Sophie watched in horror, unable to stop him, as Il Ramingo inserted the key, turned it to the right, then all the way back to the left. The bomb chirped three times. A keyboard slid out. Il Ramingo typed into the counter. He turned the key back to the right. The keyboard disappeared. A panel with an illuminated green button appeared in its place.

"Code?" Il Ramingo mocked.

He stabbed the green button with his finger. The bomb chirped and the counter started. With a downward swing of his knife, Il Ramingo severed the silver key's bow from its shank, leaving the shaft stuck in the lock. Il Ramingo then looked at Sophie and smiled.

"Memento mori."

Il Ramingo removed the rope from around his body. He fed a length through two canvas loops on the Little Bear's exterior, then hefted the nuclear device off the ground. He walked it a meter to his left and set it next to the hole. He wavered for a moment, exhaustion taking hold. Sophie glanced over at her pistol. She felt nauseas. Cold from shock. Could she get to her gun in time to shoot Il Ramingo with her bad hand before he cut her down? He was only a few steps away and operating at a fraction of his powers. Sophie knew she had to try. She just needed the right moment.

Il Ramingo took a deep breath and grabbed the rope, prepared to lower the Little Bear into the Earth and its final destination—the seismic fault line running below Mount Vesuvius. From behind, her sister, Madeline, rose above Il Ramingo, and with both hands brought a football sized rock down on his head. The assassin dropped to his knees and released the rope. She swung it again, this time like a pendulum into the side of his head knocking him on his side.

Sophie gripped her gun with her left hand and stumbled to her feet. It was still slick with her blood and the gun almost slipped out of her fingers. Il Ramingo was on his feet as well but swayed like he was drunk. He staggered toward Madeline and swung his knife in a lazy arc at her. She easily stepped away from the strike, careful to avoid a red-hot vent hissing steam.

Sophie aimed at Il Ramingo, her left hand unsteady, and thought of the Camorra thug, knee deep in a tardum pit, a stone's throw from where she stood, scared out of her mind. She remembered blindly firing at the man and hitting him in the shoulder, and how Tommy stepped in and finished him for her.

Tommy.

Sophie squeezed the trigger and fired the last three shots in her pistol at the assassin with clinical precision. Il Ramingo jerked from each of the bullets' impact, all in a tight group in his chest. He fell backwards into a glowing volcanic fissure without making a sound.

"Sheboygan."

Sophie and Madeline darted to their father's side. His shirt was soaked in blood. He blinked and smiled when he saw them. Then his eyes widened.

"The bomb," he said raising his arm and pointing at the nuclear device sitting at the hole's edge.

Sophie looked down at her useless right hand. Madeline locked eyes with her. "We can do this." They rushed to the Little Bear.

"Three minutes and counting," Madeline said. Sophie was out of breath. Pain ran from her hand all the way to her neck. Her sister looked at her with pleading eyes. "What do we do now?"

Sophie ran her hand over the keyhole with the severed shaft of the key lodged inside. "We're not going to turn it off."

"Is there any other way to dismantle the bomb?"

"I don't have the faintest idea," Sophie said. *Call Carter.* She reached down at her hip for her radio to discover it had been ripped from its pocket during her escape from the SPAGO collision.

So, this was how she was going to die. At least the Little Bear wouldn't be detonating inside Vesuvius. Keeping it out of the volcano saved thousands, maybe millions of lives. Just not theirs. Sophie took in a great lungful of air to calm herself. There was a burning sensation in her chest. Breathing in the combination of microscopic volatile air compounds due to volcanic activity and aerated chemicals from the Camorra dump pits was going to take a day or two off her life. The pool of cadmium sulfide identified on their initial ascent was only thirty or so meters upslope. Not that she had to worry about that now.

"He broke the key off and it supposedly has a failsafe chemical trigger."

"Yeah, the Russian guy said it was... *azi*...something. Then he got stabbed through the head," Madeline said.

"Azidoazide azide." Sophie bolted to her feet. "That's it." She grabbed one end of the rope looped through the Little Bear and coiled it around her shoulder. "C'mon!"

"What are you doing?"

"No time. Just help me pull it up there." Sophie nodded with her head upslope as Madeline wound the other end of the rope around her shoulder. *2:24... 2:23...2.22...*

The two sisters started dragging the Little Bear up the rocky side of Vesuvius. The going was rough, steep, and rocky. "Cadmium sulfide neutralizes the whole azide family." Sophie said in between heavy breaths. "And there's a pool of it just ahead."

"So, we just plop it in and hope for the best?" Madeline asked.

Sophie nodded, grabbed the rope and started pulling in unison with Madeline.

"How much time?"

"A minute fifty-five," Madeline said.

"Keep pulling." Sophie looked upslope. They'd only traveled half the distance to the pool, maybe less. They were running out of time.

"There's no way we're going to make it," Madeline said.

The roar of an engine above stopped them. A SPAGO launched itself off a small hill. It landed and bounced once. For a moment Sophie thought it was going to tumble, but somehow the SPAGO remained upright and headed right for them.

"Over here!" Sophie and Madeline both jumped up and down, Sophie waving her one good arm.

The treaded machine made it to them in seconds. She could see Carter Boyd behind the controls. A wave of relief washed over her.

With his SPAGO they could now move the bomb with ease. The vehicle came to a rock showering stop. A huge cloud of ash blew over as Sophie watched, her heart pumping, as the counter dropped below one minute. It would be close.

If it worked.

A SOG with a thick mustache accompanied Carter out of the SPAGO.

"Help us! There's less than a minute before it blows. If we throw it into that pool of cadmium sulfide it should kill the trigger!"

With Carter wincing from the bullet wound to his leg, he Madeline and the SOG carried the Little Bear to the rear of the SPAGO.

0:45 . . . 0:44 . . . 0:43 . . .

Carter then put all four tread throttles down, and they rocketed to the cadmium sulfide pool in seconds, jumped out and took the Little Bear from the back. The counter was at *0:18.* Gathering the bulky olive drab backpack, their knees nearly buckling under the weight, Sophie directed Carter and the SOG to the edge of the chemical dump.

"Thank God," she said. They were mercifully upwind of any toxic fumes from the cadmium sulfide pool.

"Easy peasy, nice and easy," Carter said.

With one back-wrenching twist of their entire bodies, hurled the bomb into the dark green morass of dumped chemicals. The device disappeared with a slight gurgle. Standing at the edge, Sophie counted down. "Four . . . three . . . two . . ."

Nothing happened. No flash of light or wall of cell disintegrating nuclear energy.

"Amazing," Carter said.

Sophie reached out and wrapped her arms around Madeline, and then almost collapsed in her grasp. "You did it." A beaming Madeline said. Then her face went dark. "Oh no, Dad."

They rushed back to the hole and SPAGO wreckage in time for

the sisters to each hold one of their father's hands, while a rivulet of blood ran out the corner of his mouth.

"It worked." Ray said. He lifted his hand and brushed away the tears streaming down Sophie's cheek. "You, Madeline, Maria... we made it."

Ray dropped his arm and died.

CHAPTER 63

Special Agent in Charge. That never got old.

Sophie read the email on her phone for the twentieth time. In conjunction with the Department of Justice, the EPA's Criminal Investigation Division was putting together an elite task force targeting organized crime and illegal toxic waste dumping in America. Because of her experience with stakes in Italy, the memo read, Sophie had been reinstated and tapped by the CID Director as the team's SAC.

"Do I have you to thank for this?" she said to Carter Boyd, holding her phone's screen up to his face.

Carter was dressed in a short-sleeved polo shirt and jeans. He shifted his aluminum crutches so the hot wind blowing across the US Joint Command airfield didn't knock him on his ass. Then smiled. "It's classified."

Located on the outskirts of Naples, Sophie watched as Air Force personnel attended to the various airplanes parked on the tarmac. None knew, and could ever know, how close they came to facing a tsunami of deadly lava and nuclear devastation released by Il Ramingo. Or the ultimate price her father and Bill Hodges paid to keep it from happening.

In front of Sophie was a flight of roll-up stairs leading to the door of the main cabin of a sleek CIA passenger jet. At the bottom of the stairs, Madeline and Maria stood to her left, Carter at her right.

"Where's my husband?" Madeline said.

"They already loaded him on board," Carter said. The Italian government had balked at letting them take Chris Nicchi's corpse home. But Carter reminded them that one of their top intelligence officers had been the assassin's caretaker for decades and they relented. Carter pointed at a window above the wing. "Along with BTO."

With a pained expression, his right arm ensconced in a massive cast up to his neck, the big man blew a kiss with his left hand out the window at Sophie.

"That mustache looks like it tickles," Carter said.

Sophie blushed. "A little."

"Don't forget, full debrief next week at Langley. Get there early."

"Noted. Will you be there?" Sophie said.

Carter shook his head. "Stuck here. First order of business as the new chief of station. Clean up the mess we made." Carter pointed at C-47 cargo plane parked the next runway over. Someone was backing a SPAGO out of the aircraft's massive hold.

"Another EPA team?" Sophie said.

Carter nodded. "And DOE. Our Italian friends are anxious for us to get that uranium core out of the mountain."

A hydraulic lift hummed at the baggage compartment at the rear of the plane. It was lifting a silver coffin. Carter raised an eyebrow and nodded at the casket as two men inside the plane pulled it into the cargo hold.

"Tommy," Sophie said. She clenched her fist, promising herself that she wouldn't cry today, despite how awful it felt to watch her loved ones being loaded on a government jet. Her other hand was bandaged tight. She was scheduled to have surgery on the severed tendons when she got stateside.

"You can't save everyone," Carter said.

"Yeah," Sophie said. "But you can try."

For a moment Sophie watched pain on the CIA station chief's face, like Carter had stubbed his toe. Then he bent and mussed Maria's hair. "Oh. Almost forgot. You're going to need these when you land." Carter pulled an envelope from inside his jacket pocket and handed it to Sophie. "All the wheels are properly greased."

Sophie took the envelope and peered inside. As promised, it held Maria's US adoption papers certifying Sophie as her legal guardian.

"There's also a one-year visa in there. Don't see any reason why permanent citizen status won't be granted once her application is processed stateside. CIA takes care of its own."

"Thank you."

"No, thank you."

The hydraulic lift hummed again, lifting another silver coffin.

"Is that . . . Ray?" Maria asked.

"No." Sophie took Maria's hand in hers.

"That's Grandpa."